JEFFERSON BASS

BONES OF BETRAYAL

A BODY FARM NOVEL

HARPER

An Imprint of HarperCollins*Publishers*

This book was originally published in hardcover February 2009 by William Morrow, an Imprint of HarperCollins Publishers.

This is a work of fiction. Names, characters, places, and incidents are products of the author's imagination or are used fictitiously and are not to be construed as real. Any resemblance to actual events, locales, organizations, or persons, living or dead, is entirely coincidental.

HARPER
An Imprint of HarperCollins*Publishers*
10 East 53rd Street
New York, New York 10022-5299

Copyright © 2009 by Jefferson Bass, LLC
Excerpt from *The Bone Thief* copyright © 2010 by Jefferson Bass, LLC
ISBN 978-0-06-128475-5

All rights reserved. No part of this book may be used or reproduced in any manner whatsoever without written permission, except in the case of brief quotations embodied in critical articles and reviews. For information address Harper paperbacks, an Imprint of HarperCollins Publishers.

First Harper paperback printing: January 2010
First William Morrow hardcover printing: February 2009

HarperCollins® and Harper® are registered trademarks of Harper-Collins Publishers.

Printed in the United States of America

Visit Harper paperbacks on the World Wide Web at
www.harpercollins.com

10 9 8 7 6 5 4 3 2 1

If you purchased this book without a cover, you should be aware that this book is stolen property. It was reported as "unsold and destroyed" to the publisher, and neither the author nor the publisher has received any payment for this "stripped book."

Resounding praise for JEFFERSON BASS and BONES OF BETRAYAL

"Mystery buffs who like their forensic details of the rock-solid authentic variety may want to try the books of Jefferson Bass."

Oklahoma City Journal Record

"If you're pining for the understated humor and genial patriarchy of *CSI*'s Gil Grissom, this book's main character, Bill Brockton, may hold your melancholy at bay. . . . The forensic details build a solid backbone for the story's suspense. . . . Beatrice, a funny, feisty old woman . . . adds flesh to the '*bones of betrayal*' and life to the novel."

Minneapolis Star Tribune

"This series . . . just keeps getting better. [*Bones of Betrayal*] features both the most compelling story and the best portrayal yet of Brockton, who has completed the transition from fictional representation of co-author Bass to fully realized protagonist."

Booklist

"*Bones of Betrayal* has more than its share of twists, turns, and red herrings. . . . Wartime Oak Ridge proves nearly as atmospheric a crime scene as Sam Spade's San Francisco or Philip Marlowe's L.A."

Wilmington Star News

"The story moves with a satisfying pace and the clues appear with gratifying regularity. . . .The history and local color . . . are spot-on. The writing is lively. . . . . The science and forensics are perfect. . . . Fans of forensic TV shows like the *CSI* franchise will love these books."

Baton Rouge Advocate

By Jefferson Bass

BONES OF BETRAYAL
THE DEVIL'S BONES
FLESH AND BONE
CARVED IN BONE

Nonfiction
BEYOND THE BODY FARM
DEATH'S ACRE

Coming Soon in Hardcover
THE BONE THIEF

ATTENTION: ORGANIZATIONS AND CORPORATIONS
Most Harper paperbacks are available at special quantity discounts for bulk purchases for sales promotions, premiums, or fund-raising. For information, please call or write:

Special Markets Department, HarperCollins Publishers, 10 East 53rd Street, New York, New York 10022-5299. Telephone: (212) 207-7528. Fax: (212) 207-7222.

To Oak Ridge,
and to the men and women
of the Manhattan Project,
humanity's most daring and desperate endeavor

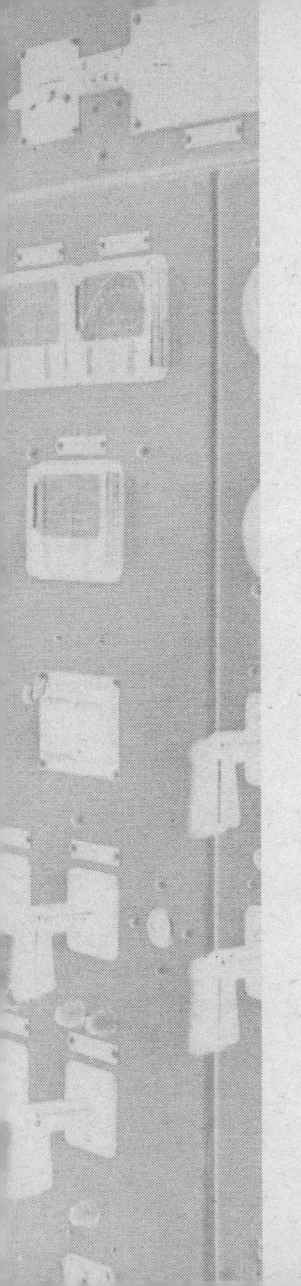

PART ONE

There will be a city on Black Oak Ridge. . . . Big engines will dig big ditches, and thousands of people will be running to and fro. They will be building things, and there will be great noise and confusion, and the earth will shake. Bear Creek Valley someday will be filled with great buildings and factories, and they will help toward winning the greatest war that ever will be. I've seen it. It's coming.

—Tennessee backwoods preacher
John Hendrix, circa 1900

1

THE COLORFUL TENTS CROWDING the clearing where I stood wouldn't have looked out of place at a carnival or Renaissance fair. It would be an interesting irony: a Renaissance fair—a "rebirth" fair—here at the University of Tennessee's Body Farm, the one place in the world that revolves around the study of the dead and how they decay.

The tents—white, red, green, yellow, blue—jostled for space at the Anthropology Research Facility. Decades earlier, an FBI agent had dubbed the UT facility "the Body Farm" after seeing the corpses scattered throughout the three wooded acres. The nickname had stuck, and now it was even inspiring a spin-off nickname: a former UT graduate student was now setting up a similar research facility in San Marcos, Texas. Even before her first research cadaver hit the ground, the Texas facility was being called "the Body Ranch."

Several of the tents huddled together were supported by inflatable frames, the rest by spidery arcs of geometric tubing—Quonset huts, twenty-first-century style. Normally there were no tents here; normally the brightest splash of color, apart from the grass and the leaves on the trees, was a large blue tarp draped over our corrugated-metal equipment shed and its small, fenced-in concrete pad. The tents—whose festive colors belied the barren winter landscape and bitter cold of the day—had been erected just twenty-four hours earlier, and twenty-four hours from now they would be gone again. Despite the carnival look, the tents were a stage for the acting out of a nightmare scenario, one of the darkest events imaginable: an act of nuclear terrorism.

A nude male body lay faceup on a gurney within the largest of the tents, his puckered skin gone gray and moldy from three weeks in the cooler at the morgue at the University of Tennessee Medical Center, visible just above the Body Farm's wooden fence and barren treeline. Fourteen other bodies—selected and stored over the preceding month—were locked in a semi-tractor-trailer parked just outside the fence. The fifteen bodies were stand-ins for what could be hundreds or thousands or even—God forbid—tens of thousands of victims if nuclear terrorists managed to inflict wholesale death in a U.S. city somewhere, someday.

Five people surrounded the gurney. Their faces and even their genders were masked by goggles, respirators, and baggy biohazard suits whose white Tyvek sleeves and legs were sealed with duct tape to black rubber gloves and boots. One of the white-garbed figures held a boxy beige instrument in one hand, and in the other, a metal wand that was connected to the box. As the wand swept a few inches above the head, then the chest and abdomen, and then each arm, the box emitted occasional clicks. As the wand neared the left knee, though, the clicks became rapid, then merged into a continuous buzz. Having spent my childhood shivering through the Cold War—practicing "duck and cover" during civil defense drills, as if my wooden school desk could shield me from a Soviet hydrogen bomb—I was well acquainted with the urgent clicking of a Geiger counter.

As the wand hovered, the other four people leaned in to inspect the knee. One took photographs; two others began spraying the body with a soapy-looking liquid and scrubbing the skin, paying particular attention to the knee. As they scrubbed, one of them removed a small orange disk, about the size of a quarter, and handed it to the team leader. A tiny, safely encapsulated speck of radioactive strontium—enough to trigger the Geiger counter, but not enough to pose any hazard—simulated contamination on the corpse. Once the scrubbing was complete, the technician with the Geiger counter checked the knee once more. This time the instrument ticked lazily, signaling normal background radiation. At a sign from the team leader, the body was wheeled out of the tent and returned to the trailer that held the other fourteen corpses, which had already undergone similar screening and decontamination procedures.

One by one, the Tyvek-suited figures rinsed off beneath what had to be the world's coldest shower: a spray of soapy water mixed with alcohol, a last-minute addition necessitated by the day's subfreezing temperatures. The team's contamination, like that of the bodies, was simulated, but the goal was to make the training as realistic as possible, despite the added challenges provided by the bitter cold. Only after the shower did the goggles and respirators come off. My red-tressed, freckled graduate assistant, Miranda Lovelady, emerged from one of the white suits, followed shortly by Art Bohanan, the resident fingerprint expert at the Knoxville Police Department. The team leader was Hank Strickland, a health physicist, one who specialized in radiation and radiation safety. Hank worked at a facility in Oak Ridge called REAC/TS—the Radiation Emergency Assistance Center and Training Site—that sent medical response teams to help treat victims of radiation accidents anywhere in the world.

But Hank, like Miranda and Art, was here today as a volunteer team member of DMORT, the Disaster Mortuary Operational Response Team. Formed in the early 1990s to identify victims of mass disasters such as airliner crashes and hurricanes, DMORT was part of the U.S. Public Health Service, but the teams were staffed by volunteers with specialized, and even macabre, skills: their ranks included funeral directors, morticians, forensic dentists, physicians, forensic anthropologists, police officers, and fire fighters—people accustomed to working with bodies and bones. DMORT volunteers, including some of my students, had performed heroic service at Ground Zero after the World Trade Center bombings. They'd also spent two months recovering and identifying bodies after Hurricane Katrina devastated New Orleans and the Gulf Coast in 2005.

Art himself had spent six weeks in Louisiana after Katrina, lifting fingerprints and palm prints from bloated, rotting corpses. One body was that of a man who'd been trapped in an attic by rising waters. More than a hundred days after the man drowned in the attic—how ironic was that?—Art and a colleague managed to lift a print and ID the man.

DMORT teams were acquainted with death and decay. But this training exercise represented a grim new twist to DMORT's mission, a response to the nightmare of September 11, 2001. DMORT's Weapons of Mass Destruction team had been formed shortly after 9/11, in grim recognition of the fact that terrorists who would turn civilian airliners into flying bombs might also attempt acts of wholesale chemical, biological, or nuclear terrorism. Because of the contamination such attacks would create, they would pose unique problems for workers recovering and identifying bodies. The WMD team's exercise here at the Body Farm was a first step in developing and testing DMORT procedures for handling radiation-contaminated bodies—the sorts of contaminants that would be unleashed, for example, if a radioactive "dirty bomb" were exploded in New York Harbor.

Although it grieved me that nuclear-disaster procedures had to be developed, it made me proud that my research facility could help in the process. The Body Farm was the only place in the world where an emergency-response team like DMORT could simulate a mass disaster realistically, using numerous bodies. Although fifteen bodies was a tiny fraction of the number of victims who would die in an actual dirty-bomb explosion in New York—some estimates put the worst-case number of fatalities from that scenario at fifty thousand or more—fifteen was a place to start, and that was far more bodies than DMORT would be likely to use anyplace else.

Miranda and Art emerged from the decontamination shower stomping their boots and rubbing their arms, their breath steaming in the bitter air. "Sweet Jesus, I am *so cold*," said Miranda. I wasn't getting sprayed with cold water, but I was cold, too; I'd gotten an artificial hip about six months before, when a bullet shattered the top of my left femur, and the cold titanium implant ached deep within my hip. Miranda's teeth began to chatter. "Whose bright idea was it," she said, "to do this on the coldest day of the worst cold snap on record?"

"It's not as fun as reading by the fireplace," Art said, "but unless you can get the terrorists to attack only when the weather's nice, it helps to practice in the worst conditions you can."

"I know, I know," grumbled Miranda. "It's just that I'm *so cold*. After that shower, I might not have an impure thought ever again."

"I didn't realize you'd had them before," said Art. "I didn't think graduate students had time for such things."

"Only during spring break," I said.

"Spring break? What's spring break?" said Miranda, feigning puzzlement and indignation. "I just want to spend the next six months in a hot bath."

Just then my cell phone rang. Tugging off a thick glove, I fished the phone from my pocket and flipped it open, the cold biting at my fingertips. According to the display, the caller was Peggy, the Anthropology Department secretary. "Hi, Peggy," I said. "I hope you're calling to tell me a heat wave is bearing down on us in the next five minutes."

"I'm not," she said. "I'm calling to tell you I have an agitated police lieutenant from Oak Ridge on the line."

A small city about twenty-five miles west of Knoxville, Oak Ridge was home to a wide range of high-tech research and manufacturing industries, but the city's main claim to fame was its pivotal role in the Manhattan Project, the race to develop the atomic bomb during World War II. "Did the lieutenant say what he's agitated about?"

"They've just found a body they want you to take a look at," she said. "Apparently they don't find a lot of bodies in Oak Ridge."

"No, the radioactivity helps protect them," I said. "Killers are afraid of folks who glow in the dark." It was an old, tired joke Knoxvillians tended to make about Oak Ridgers—one that Oak Ridgers sometimes made about themselves, in a sort of preemptive first strike of defiant civic pride.

"Well, you be careful," she said. "All those fences and guard towers and nuclear reactors and bomb factories scare me."

She patched through the Oak Ridge officer, Lieutenant Dewar. When I hung up, I said to Miranda, "You didn't really want that hot bath, did you?"

"No, of course not," she said, having heard my end of the conversation. "What I really want to do is complete my transformation into the Human Icicle."

"That's good," I said. "I've got just the job for you."

2

FIVE MINUTES AFTER THE phone call from Oak Ridge, Miranda and I pulled away from the Body Farm, navigated the asphalt maze surrounding UT Medical Center, and crossed the Tennessee River. Far below the highway bridge, a ribbon of frigid green swirled between banks sheathed in ice.

A thought occurred to me, and instead of staying on Alcoa Highway to Interstate 40, I angled the truck onto Kingston Pike and threaded the winding streets into my neighborhood, Sequoyah Hills.

"I thought we were racing to a death scene in Oak Ridge," said Miranda.

"We are," I said. "But I just thought of something we might need, so we're racing to my house first."

"I hope what you're thinking we might need is called 'lunch,'" Miranda said, "because I'm getting hungry enough to chew my arm off."

"The cupboard's bare," I said, "so you might as well start chewing. Don't eat both arms—I'll need you to take notes at the scene."

"Your concern is deeply touching."

"I know," I said. "Sometimes I move myself to tears. Oh, if you'd prefer something vegetarian, I think there's a Snickers bar in the glove box." Evidently she did, because she opened the latch and rummaged around beneath a sheaf of registration papers and maintenance records.

"There better not be a mousetrap hidden in this—YOUCH!" She jumped, and that made me flinch. She laughed as she fished out the candy bar. "You are *so* gullible," she said. "It's like shooting fish in a barrel."

"I knew you were faking," I said. "But I also knew you'd sulk if I didn't play along." As I pulled into the driveway, I tapped the remote to open the garage.

Miranda unwrapped one end of the Snickers bar—the giant size—and bit down. "Youch!" she said again, this time in earnest. "This thing is hard as a rock." She studied the faint impressions her teeth had made in the frozen chocolate. "Lucky I didn't break my teeth—I'd be suing UT for workers' comp."

"You'd file a claim for missing teeth? In Tennessee? You'd be laughed out of the state," I said.

She flashed me a big, sarcastic smile—Miranda had one of the best smiles I'd ever seen—and then began gnawing at one corner of the Snickers with her right molars, the immense bar clenched in her fist. "You stay here and work on that," I said. "I'll be right back."

I found what I was looking for in the garage—an oblong case made of bright orange plastic—and stowed it in the rear of the pickup. As I got back in the cab, Miranda's eyebrows shot up quizzically. I smiled, backed out of the driveway, and headed for Oak Ridge. Miranda's jaws were working hard—evidently she had sheared off a huge hunk of the candy bar. Finally she mumbled, "Ih at wuh I ink ih ih?"

"What? I can't understand a word you're saying when you mumble like that."

"Ih AT wuh I INK ih ih?!"

"The problem here," I said, "is not that I'm deaf. The problem here is that you're talking with your mouth full."

She rolled her eyes but swallowed hard, and I could see her running her tongue along the front and sides of her teeth to swab off the chocolate and caramel and peanuts. She swallowed again. "Is that what I think it is?"

"Is *what* what you think it is?" She popped me one on the shoulder, hard. "Youch," I said. "Oh, you mean that thing I put in the back? It is if you think it's a Stihl 'Farm Boss' chainsaw, model 290." I liked the name, Stihl—German, originally, I guessed—and the fact that it was pronounced "steel." A manly name for a manly power tool.

"Why on earth are you bringing a chainsaw to a death scene? You planning to dismember the body, just to make the case more interesting?"

"I used to be a Boy Scout," I said. "It's always a good idea to be prepared."

"Yeah, well, it's always a good idea to be sane, too," she said, "but I don't see you taking giant steps in *that* direction at the moment."

"Watch and learn, grasshopper," I said. "Watch and learn."

We drove the twenty-five miles to Oak Ridge in silence. Near-silence, actually, broken only by the grinding, smacking sounds of Miranda's molars steadily dismantling the rest of the Snickers bar.

As we topped the last rise before dropping down the four-lane into Oak Ridge, Miranda pointed at the Cumberlands, ten miles to the north. High atop Buffalo Mountain, a serpentine line of white wind turbines reared against the azure sky. The three-bladed rotors—they looked like the world's largest airplane propellers—flashed as their tips caught the sun's rays and whirled them back again. Judging by how far the turbines towered above nearby trees, they must have stretched nearly four hundred feet into the sky.

"Man, this place is like Energy USA," Miranda said. "Talk about your microcosm of kilowatt production."

She was right. The ridges around the wind farm had been carved into the sharp, right-angle benches and shelves of mountaintop strip mines. To the east, the smokestack of Bull Run Steam Plant soared eight hundred feet into the sky. Alongside the power plant, the Clinch River—still twitching from its spin through the hydroelectric turbines of Norris Dam—traced the boundaries of the city in swirls of emerald green. And then there was Oak Ridge itself, the Atomic City: birthplace of the bomb, cradle of nuclear power.

"I wonder if these Oak Ridge brainiacs will ever figure out how to harness nuclear fusion," Miranda said. "The power of the stars. Run your car for a year on a teaspoon of water, right?"

"Right," I said. "I think that's next on the list, as soon as they invent the transporter beam and figure out how to turn lead into gold."

"It's been done," she said.

"Done? The transporter beam?"

"No-o-o-o," she groaned. "Lead to gold."

"Lead to gold? Done?"

"Done," she said. "Tiny amounts, mind you—nanograms or angiograms or some such. They can probably do it right here in Oak Ridge, with one of their particle accelerators or research reactors. All you do is smash a jillion protons or neutrons or quarks or what-have-you against an atom of lead, and presto-chango: you've got an atom of gold. Oh, and a boatload of deadly radioactive contamination."

"Damn," I said, "there's just no such thing as a free lunch, is there? By the way, you owe me a Snickers."

We crossed a set of railroad tracks and threaded through a series of shopping centers, then turned east on Oak Ridge Turnpike—the city's main thoroughfare—and passed still more shopping centers and strip malls. Oak Ridge was a town without a downtown—many towns these days were, including some of Knoxville's bedroom communities. But Oak Ridge had a better excuse for its lack of center. The city had been flung up practically overnight by the U.S. Army during World War II, and even though six decades had brought changes, the place still had a provisional, makeshift feel. Strung along the floor of a wide valley that angled from southwest to northeast, Oak Ridge's main business district was one block wide and five miles long.

Sprinkled amid the modern banks and medical buildings and engineering firms, a few sagging clapboard buildings still showed their origins as army barracks and offices. Their quiet dilapidation seemed at odds with the urgent role they had once played in a desperate wartime gamble. Here, in a top-secret military installation—so secret the town was not shown on maps until after 1945—eighty thousand production workers and scientists had raced night and day for two years to produce the material for the first atomic bombs. Those awesome, awful clouds that roiled up from Hiroshima and Nagasaki were created, in great measure, here in this sleepy town in East Tennessee.

Following the map on the truck's GPS screen, we made a left off the main street and meandered partway up a hillside, through a handful more buildings that dated back to the wartime years. A steepled white chapel, which could have been transported from New England, perched atop a grassy hill. Beneath it, a sprawling, white-columned hotel—the same vintage as the church, but not in the same pristine condition—lurked behind boarded-up windows, sloughing scales of chalky paint. Fading letters above the wide veranda told us the hotel was THE ALEXANDER INN; four Oak Ridge police cars—engines idling and exhausts steaming—told us this was the right place.

I parked beside the cars and we got out. The sun was brilliant but the day was still bitterly cold: barely twenty degrees, and windy enough to feel like minus five. Worse, this was the warmest day we'd had in a week, and the nighttime temperatures had hovered down in the single digits. As the wind bit my cheeks, I winced and wondered, *Where's global warming when you actually want it?*

One uniformed officer huddled miserably inside the waist-high fence that surrounded the hotel's swimming pool. As Miranda and I approached the gate, the doors on the police cars opened and two more uniformed officers emerged reluctantly, followed by two plainclothes officers. One was Lieutenant Dewar, the head of Major Crimes; the other, Detective Emert, would be the lead officer on the case.

We shook gloved hands all around, then Dewar and Emert led us through the gate and up to the edge of the pool. Although the hotel dated from the 1940s, the pool itself—modest in size, a kidney in shape—looked more like an afterthought from the sixties. Moreover, it appeared not to have been drained or cleaned since the sixties; it was nearly full, and the cold snap had turned the greenish black water into greenish black ice.

Entombed in the filthy ice near the deep end of the pool was a human corpse, frozen facedown, its arms and legs splayed wide. Although the shape of the body was masked by layers of winter clothing, the head was bare and the scalp was bald, so I assumed the corpse was male.

"Whoa," said Miranda. "I've seen plenty of bodies *on* ice, but never one *in* ice. How we gonna . . ." She paused, and I could see a smile twitching at the corners of her mouth. "Ah, master," she said, "grasshopper is beginning to learn." She excused herself and went back to the truck, then returned bearing the orange case.

The policemen looked as puzzled at the sight of the chainsaw as Miranda had at first, but gradually I saw the light dawn in their eyes as well. "They call me the Man of Stihl," I said, grinning at the pun. I fired up the chainsaw—cold as it was, it took a few pulls on the starter rope—and stepped carefully onto the ice. Glancing back, I saw the six cops nervously eyeing me, the chainsaw, and the ice. Miranda's face, in contrast, expressed pure amusement.

I squeezed the throttle a bit and eased the tip of the saw down onto the ice near one of the body's outstretched hands. In an instant my face and glasses were covered with a layer of shaved ice. Sputtering, I let off the gas, set the saw down, and wiped my cheeks and lenses. For my second attempt, I cocked my head to one side as I lowered the snarling teeth into the ice. This time, the shower of ice crystals streamed onto my arm and shoulder, but my face remained clear. The chain bit into the ice easily, and before long I felt the saw break through the underside. Now the saw sprayed both ice and water onto me, and I could feel my coat beginning to get soaked and cold. I squeezed the throttle trigger all the way, which churned more water but also sped the saw's progress through the ice. It took less than a minute to cut an arc stretching from just beyond one of the corpse's outstretched hands, up and over the head, and down to the other hand. I stopped, knelt near the waist, and began cutting through the ice along the right side of the body. My plan was to work my way down to the feet, which would put me safely back on the pool's deck when I made the final cuts to free the slab from the surrounding ice.

Once I'd cut through the ice on the right side down to the knee, I switched sides and began cutting down the left side, not stopping until I was alongside the left foot. Then I shifted back to the right side. By this point, the slab containing the body was barely connected to the main sheet of ice; only a few inches of ice beside either foot held the slab in place. With one foot, I gave an exploratory tap on the slab. It did not move. I tapped harder. Nothing. I stomped, and suddenly, with a sound like a rifle shot, the ice cracked—not just the small tabs of ice holding the slab in place, but the larger sheet on which I stood. The surface buckled beneath my feet, and I felt myself begin to fall. Instinctively I flung up my arms to regain my balance, and the chainsaw flew from my grasp. My arms were seized by two pairs of strong hands, and two of the uniformed officers hauled me up onto the deck of the pool. As they did, my prize chainsaw thudded onto the slab of ice, which had now been set free. As the slab bobbed, the saw slid back and forth a time or two, and then slithered past the corpse's head and plunged into the pool. The deep end of the pool.

There was a moment of collective silence, broken by a soft "oops" from one of the officers. Then I heard a snort that I recognized as Miranda's, followed by a giggle—also Miranda's—and then rising gales of laughter, not just from Miranda but from the six cops, too.

AN HOUR LATER, back at UT, I eased the truck into the garage bay of the Regional Forensic Center. Miranda fetched a gurney and we carefully slid the icebound corpse onto the gurney, faceup, and wheeled it toward the autopsy suite. Detective Emert, who was also authorized to serve as a coroner, had gravely pronounced the iceman to be dead, once he'd stopped laughing about my chainsaw.

Miranda and I stopped in the hallway outside the autopsy suite long enough to weigh the corpse on the scales that were built into the floor. The scales, which automatically subtracted the weight of the gurney, gave the weight as 162 pounds. I knew that fifteen or twenty pounds of that total was ice, though, and I made a mental note to weigh the body again once the ice had thawed and dripped off.

As we wheeled the gurney into the suite, the medical examiner, Dr. Edelberto Garcia—an elegant Hispanic man in his late thirties—looked up from the corpse he was autopsying, a young black male. One of Garcia's purple-gloved hands cradled the top of the man's skull; the other hand held a Stryker autopsy saw, with which he had just opened the cranium. Sixty seconds from now, he'd be removing and weighing the brain. Garcia nodded at us, glanced at the body we'd just wheeled in, and looked a question at me. I nodded back at him and said, "Okay if we park this guy by the sink for a couple days, Eddie?"

Garcia's eyes looked mildly surprised through the blood-spattered shield he wore. "Don't leave him in here," he said. "He'll smell to high heaven. Put him in the cooler. I'll try to get to him tomorrow."

"He's frozen solid," I said. "If I put him in the cooler, it'll take him a week to thaw out. Even in here, at room temperature, it'll take a day or two."

"Ah," he said. "Sure, right there is fine." He looked more closely at the body, noticing the ice that formed a rectangular frame around it. "You fish this guy out of a frozen pond?"

"Frozen swimming pool," Miranda said. "Dirtier than any pond I ever saw. Ask Dr. B. how he got the guy out of the ice." She snorted, just as she had in the momentary silence that had followed the splash at the pool. "Ask him about being prepared."

"Watch it, smarty-pants," I warned. "You are skating—" I stopped, one word too late.

"On thin ice?" She finished my sentence gleefully, then proceeded to recount my chainsaw misadventure to Garcia. As she pantomimed my whirling arms, the chainsaw's slow-motion arc through the air, its slithering to-and-fro across the bobbing ice, and its plunge into the murky depths, they laughed until tears streamed from their eyes.

"Very funny," I said. "Except to the guy whose chainsaw is rusting at the bottom of the pool."

"Fear not, master," she said. "All will be well. Because you are the Man of Stihl."

3

TWENTY-FOUR HOURS AFTER I parked the gurney in the autopsy suite, the body was still half frozen, but the clothing had thawed. Water dripped slowly through the drain at the foot of the gurney and into the sink, to which I had latched the lower end of the gurney. I had taken the precaution of fitting a fine wire screen over the gurney's drain to catch any hairs or fibers or other debris that came off the clothing as it thawed. Glancing at the screen, I saw only a few small, rotting bits of leaves, which I assumed had been floating in the pool before it froze.

Detective Emert had asked if Miranda and I would be willing to take the clothing off the corpse and hang it up in the morgue. "I need it to be dry so I can go over it with evidence tape," he said, though I already knew that was the reason.

"Sure," I said. "No point your making a trip just for that." It wasn't easy to undress the frozen body, but we managed it. As we removed the pants, I noticed that the underpants were soiled. The man appeared to have had diarrhea, and it looked reddish brown, possibly bloody. I made a note to point it out to Garcia the next day, when he did the autopsy.

As Miranda and I were driving back to the Anthropology Department, I called Emert. "Hello, Detective, it's Dr. Brockton."

"Hi, Doc," he said. "Call me Jim, if you don't mind."

"I don't mind. The clothing's off and should be dry by tomorrow. Your man's still half frozen, though. Reminds me of Thanksgiving dinner."

Emert laughed. "How so?"

"Well, my wife—my late wife; she died several years ago—she always bought frozen turkeys, and she never seemed to remember that it takes a couple of days in the fridge to thaw one of those. So every Thanksgiving morning, she'd panic when she realized the turkey was still frozen solid. Every year I'd end up putting the damn thing in the bathtub in warm water to thaw it."

"Hmm," said Emert. "And you never remembered to put it in the fridge ahead of time, either?"

"Truth is," I laughed, "I kinda got a kick out of it. After the first couple of times, it seemed like part of the tradition. For all I know, Kathleen might have been pretending to forget, just to amuse me. Or just to make me feel useful."

"Some women are smart that way," he said. "My wife has me cooking the turkeys at Thanksgiving and Christmas now. I deep-fry 'em. You ever done that?"

"No, but I've heard it's good. True?"

"Once you've done it, you'll never go back to baked turkey."

"But it's not like fried chicken, is it? You're not dipping it in batter?"

"No, no," he said. "You inject it with a marinade—my favorite's a Cajun marinade, which has some kick to it—and when you put it down in the oil, the oil browns the skin really fast, seals in all the juices. Makes an oven-roasted turkey seem dry as shoe leather."

"Sounds tasty," I said. "Wish it weren't ten months till Thanksgiving."

"Tell you what," he offered. "When we close this case, I'll do a turkey-fry to celebrate."

"Deal," I said. "Dr. Garcia scheduled the autopsy for one o'clock tomorrow. Is that okay with you?"

"This is the only homicide I'm working," he said. "Of course it's okay. How about if I show up at twelve-thirty, so I can go over the clothing?"

"I'll meet you at the loading dock behind the hospital," I said.

"HEY," I CALLED as he opened the trunk of the white Crown Victoria the next day. "You got my chainsaw in there?"

"Sorry," he said, removing an evidence kit and closing the lid. "We haven't been able to empty the pool yet. Drain-pipe's frozen solid; so is the valve mechanism. We'll need a few days above freezing to thaw it out enough to drain."

"Can't you just put in a sump pump and pump it out from the top?"

"We could, but then there's that thick layer of frozen ice hanging up near the top of the pool. If we pump all the water out from underneath, a ton of ice could come crashing down on your chainsaw and bust it up. You don't want that, do you?"

"Busted or rusted," I sighed. "Not sure which is the greater of two evils."

"I don't think it's actually rusting while it's submerged," he said. "I think the rust starts to form only after it comes out of the water—takes moisture plus air to oxidize the steel."

Now that he said it, it made sense. I'd seen a gruesome version of that phenomenon affect decomposing bodies. Soft tissue that decayed in moist environments, such as basements and caves, was transformed into a waxy or soapy substance called adipocere. A few years before, in fact, I'd had a case in the mountains of Cooke County in which a young woman's body—hidden in a cave for decades—turned into a remarkable adipocere mummy. In the absence of oxygen, though, completely submerged bodies did not turn to adipocere.

"So when we do get the saw out," Emert continued, "we'll put it in a trash can filled with water, so it stays submerged till you can take it to a shop and get it taken apart and dried out."

In one corner of the loading dock I noticed an empty plastic trash can lying on its side. I picked it up and handed it to Emert. "Take good care of my baby," I said. He laughed as he put it in the trunk.

Emert patted down the clothing thoroughly with evidence tape. The tape's sticky side would pick up hair and fibers, much like the lint roller I had at home. I'd seen evidence tape used many times, but Emert's variety had a plastic backing I hadn't seen before. "This is a fairly new kind," he said. "The plastic's water-soluble. Once I'm through, I put it in warm water to dissolve the backing. That leaves the hair and fibers in the water. Pour the water through a coffee filter, and voilà—everything's together in one nice, neat place."

Once Emert was satisfied that he'd gone over the clothing thoroughly, he began checking the pockets of the pants. Easing a gloved hand into each of the front pockets, he extracted a set of keys and a few coins. Then he felt the seat of the pants—left, then right—to check the rear pockets. The left hip pocket was empty, but I saw him smile when he felt the right pocket. Unbuttoning the closure carefully, he slipped a hand into the pocket and fished out a worn leather wallet. He laid it on an absorbent pad and unfolded it gently.

His eyes widened. Looking down to see what he'd seen, I made out the familiar markings of a Tennessee driver's license through a clear plastic window in one side of the wallet. "Wow," Emert said. "No wonder he looked familiar."

"Who is it?" Instead of answering, Emert held the wallet up so I could take a close look. LEONARD M. NOVAK, the small print on the license read. "Novak," I said. "Rings a bell, but only vaguely."

"Dr. Leonard Novak is a living legend in Oak Ridge," he

said. "Or was, anyhow. He was one of the top scientists back during the Manhattan Project. He played a big part in making the atomic bomb possible. Last picture I saw of him was probably taken twenty years ago. Back when he was a fresh-faced kid of seventy-something."

"A big fish," I said, "in that small, frozen pond."

"Very big," he said.

"But nobody'd reported him missing?"

"No," he said. "The only missing-person report we've had in the last six months is a runaway teenager."

"Be hard to mistake this guy for a teenager. Was he married?"

"I don't know," Emert said. We both glanced at the dead man's left hand, which had no wedding ring. "Maybe not. Maybe a widower. Must not have had anybody checking on him regularly." With a gloved finger, he poked the corpse gently, in the thigh and in the abdomen. "You sure our bird's thawed out enough to autopsy?"

"If he were a Butterball turkey," I said, "I'd be preheating the oven right now."

He gathered up the evidence bags containing the coins, the keys, the wallet, and the evidence tape, and ran them out to his car at the loading dock.

4

"SHALL WE BEGIN?" IT was a rhetorical question—even as he said the words, Dr. Garcia was already pressing the scalpel to Leonard Novak's scalp—but it served to focus everyone's attention on the tip of the blade. Garcia was suited up in a blue surgical gown with a mask, a plastic face shield, and two pairs of purple gloves. So was Miranda, who was serving as his assistant, or *Diener*: a German word that literally translates as "servant" or "slave"—not the sort of job description that would normally sit well with Miranda, who sometimes chafed beneath her title of "graduate assistant." I was wearing scrubs, as was Emert, although as far back as the detective was hovering, he would probably have been safe in a white linen suit. "Call me if there's something I need to see," he said. "Meanwhile, I'll be over here hanging on to my lunch."

Normally Garcia would have begun the autopsy by making a Y-shaped incision to open the chest cavity and abdomen. But Novak had a gash on the left side of his scalp, high on the left side of the forehead. The wound didn't look serious—an oval contusion a couple of inches long by an inch wide, and more like an abrasion than a cut—but it was the only visible trauma to the corpse, so it was a place to start. The old man's body, naked and thin and ashen, looked sadder and more vulnerable, somehow, than most bodies I saw.

With one swift sweep of the blade Garcia laid open the scalp, cutting from behind the left ear, up over the crown of the head, and down to the back of the right ear. Laying aside the scalpel, Garcia worked his fingers under the front flap of scalp, then gave a strong tug. With a wet, ripping sound, the scalp peeled free of the crown and forehead, and Garcia folded the flap down over the face. Behind me, I heard Emert gasp and whisper, "Christ." I could scarcely imagine his reaction to some of the sights and smells he would encounter later in the autopsy. Garcia peeled the other half of the scalp backward, folding it down to the nape of the neck into a sort of gruesome collar, so that the entire top of the skull was now exposed.

Garcia studied the bone in the region beneath the contusion, then stepped back and motioned to Miranda and me, inviting us to look. The bone—the frontal bone, near where it joined the parietal—showed no sign of damage, not even a hint of compression. "Well, I don't think he died of blunt-force trauma," I said.

"No, I don't think so," said Garcia. "Maybe just scraped his head when he fell. There's no scabbing, so it's perimortem—around the time of death. Hard to tell, though, since he was in the water, whether it's antemortem or post."

"How could you tell?" asked Emert. "I mean, if he hadn't been in the water?" He leaned closer, but only a few inches closer.

"If he were still alive, the wound would have bled," said Garcia. "But not if his heart had already quit pumping when he fell."

"Or got dumped," said Miranda.

"Or dumped," echoed Emert. "But if there's water in the lungs, that'll mean he drowned in the pool?"

"Or somewhere," Miranda pointed out.

"Not necessarily," said Garcia. "Water can seep into the lungs after death. Or be absorbed from the lungs after drowning. Don't believe everything you see on television."

Emert sighed, though I couldn't tell whether it was because people kept complicating the scenarios or because he was having trouble with the sight of the scalped skull. His gaze, I noticed, kept straying toward the peeled bone, then flinching away.

Next Garcia took a Stryker autopsy saw from the shelf along the wall. The saw's motor was about twice the size of a hand blender—a kitchen gadget whose name had always struck me as a marketing department's worst nightmare. When he switched on the motor, a fan-shaped blade on the end of a shaft began to oscillate back and forth, its strokes so rapid and tiny as to be almost invisible. I never ceased to marvel at the ingenuity of the Stryker saw: if Garcia accidentally grazed his hand with the blade, his skin would simply vibrate in time with the blade: it might tickle, but it wouldn't cut. If he pressed down hard, though—on his own finger, or on one of the corpse's—the blade would chew through flesh and bone in seconds.

Starting at the center of the forehead, Garcia eased the blade into the skull, going slowly to make sure he didn't cut into the brain. When the pitch of the motor rose, telling him the blade had penetrated all three layers of the bone, he began cutting horizontally, just above the left brow ridge, across the left temple, and around toward the back of the skull. Once he was nearly there, he shifted back to the forehead again and made a mirror-image cut around the right side of the skull, so that the top of the skull—the calvarium—was attached to the lower part of the skull by a one-inch bridge of bone at the back. Then, with two deft dips of the saw, he cut that bridge into a V-shaped tab.

I heard Emert whisper to Miranda, "Why'd he do that?"

"Because it's so stylish," said Miranda. "And because it keeps the top of the skull from sliding around when the pieces are put back together. Helps hold things together, which is particularly good if there's an open-casket funeral."

"Ah," said Emert. "Good idea." His words sounded casual, but his tone sounded strained.

With one hand Garcia gripped the corpse's face, clamping his fingers hard around the zygomatic arches of the cheekbones; with the other, he gripped the calvarium and tugged. As the top of the skull pulled free, I heard a wet sucking sound from the vicinity of the brain, and a horrified gasp from the direction of Detective Emert.

Garcia made a few cuts with the scalpel to sever the spinal cord and a few membranes, then gently removed the brain from the skull. It always surprised me to see how much more easily the brain could be disconnected than, say, a femur or a rib, which took some determined cutting and tugging. After weighing it in the meat scales used to weigh organs—it tipped the scales at 1,773 grams, or a bit shy of three pounds—he laid it on a tray and nodded at Miranda. Miranda tied a loop of string around the bit of spinal cord dangling down, then suspended the brain upside down in a large jar of formalin, a weak solution of formaldehyde. Marinating for a couple weeks in the formalin would "fix" the brain: not as in "repair," but as in "preserve and harden." Garcia pronounced the appearance of Novak's brain as normal, though from what little I'd heard about the scientist's work, his brain sounded better than normal, at least during his working life.

As Garcia gripped the scalpel and prepared to make the Y-shaped incision that would open the chest and abdominal cavities, I turned to Emert. "You okay? You ready for this?"

"Ready," he said, but he didn't say it like he meant it. When Garcia used the chest spreader to cut the ribs from the sternum, I heard the detective grunt slightly as each rib gave way with a crunch. It was when Garcia cut open the abdominal cavity and prepared to "run the gut," as pathologists call it, that things took an interesting turn. Two of them, actually.

Running the gut involves removing and dissecting the

stomach and intestines—slicing them open to examine the contents and the linings. I had mentioned the diarrhea to Garcia, he had merely nodded, but I knew he'd be paying particular attention to the gastrointestinal tract. As anyone who's ever thrown up or had a bowel movement knows, the contents of the digestive tract are not the most appetizing features of the human species. In fact, although the decomposing bodies at the Body Farm tended to smell bad, especially in the heat of summer, they were practically fragrant compared to the odor released when a pathologist was running the gut.

But Novak's gut was different. It began to leak in Garcia's hands as soon as he began lifting it from the abdominal cavity. The first smell to hit was the stench of vomit and gastric juice, which began oozing from the stomach. I don't have a keen sense of smell, which is fortunate, given my line of work, but the smell of stomach contents is tough even for me to take. Then the intestines began to tear in his hands, overlaying the smell of vomit with the stench of feces. There was another layer of odor, too, which I recognized as the smell of decomposition. Leonard Novak, I realized, had died from the inside out. "Jesús, María, José," breathed Garcia in Spanish, with more of an accent than I'd ever heard from him. "Miranda, help me with this." Miranda rushed to his side, and together, their four hands cupped beneath the organs, they eased the dead man's entrails into the sink.

The sight and the smell were enough to challenge even the most stoic of people.

And Detective Emert was not the most stoic of people. Just over my shoulder I heard a groaning, retching sound. That was followed, with unfortunate and unavoidable swiftness, by a gurgling noise, and then the splash of vomit cascading over my right shoulder and arm.

"Thank you so much," Miranda said. "It was seeming a little too pleasant in here to suit me."

I helped Emert out of the room, mopped up his mess, and found a clean pair of scrubs for me. When I got back into the suite, Garcia was puzzling over the gut, going through it with scissors and forceps. "Hmm," he said, at regular intervals. After a half dozen or so "hmm's," it seemed worth asking what he meant.

So I asked. "What do you mean, *'hmm'*?"

"I'm seeing a lot of blood and necrosis in the gut," he said. I nodded. Necrosis—dead tissue—fit with the smell of decomp I had noticed. "There's some in the stomach, but a lot more in the intestines. Almost like the GI tract has been burned."

"How? Poison? Acid?"

Garcia shook his head and studied the inside of a loop of intestine. "That's the thing," he said. "While you were out of the room, I checked the mouth and esophagus. Both of those are normal. If the guy had drunk enough acid to do this, they'd be damaged, too."

Then he said one more "hmm," this one deeper in pitch—more in the vein of an "aha" than a "what the hell?"

"Find something?" It was Miranda who asked the question I had been on the verge of asking, too.

"Maybe," he said. "Not sure." He plucked a bit of something from the sink with the forceps and set it in the gloved palm of his left hand. He laid the forceps aside and rolled the object around with his right index finger, then picked it up and studied it. It was small and cylindrical—maybe a quarter-inch long and an eighth-inch in diameter, rounded on one end, roughly flat on the other. It was about the size of a dried black bean, or—a more familiar comparison to me—a maggot that had hatched from a blowfly egg four or five days before. I thought I saw the dull glint of metal where Garcia had rubbed the surface clean.

"Miranda, did you X-ray the body before you took the clothes off?"

"I did," she said, "but either the machine's on the fritz or we got a bad batch of film. All of them came out fogged."

My mind was racing. "Eddie, put it down and step away," I said. "Everybody step away."

Garcia looked up at me, puzzled, frozen, the small pellet still pinched between his thumb and forefinger. His hand was twelve inches, at most, from his face, and not a lot farther than that from Miranda's face. I saw comprehension dawn in Miranda's eyes, and behind the surgical mask, I saw the oval outline of her open mouth as she sucked in a breath. Before I could stop her, Miranda reached out, plucked the pellet from Garcia's fingers with her own, and dropped it into the stainless-steel sink. Then she backed away from the counter, pulling Garcia with her. She continued pulling until he, and she, and I, had backed out of the autopsy suite and into the hallway, where an ashen-faced Jim Emert sat in a folding metal chair. Emert got to his feet and glanced at our faces. What he saw there made him turn and look into the autopsy suite. As the steel door closed, all four of us continued to stare at the sink, as if something sinister lurked within it. A monster. A bomb. A shroud of radioactivity intense enough to have ruined our X-ray film. Radioactivity deadly enough to have seared Leonard Novak's internal organs in the hours or days it took that tiny pellet to travel through his stomach and along his intestine, killing him along the way.

5

AS SOON AS MIRANDA had plucked the small metal pellet from Eddie Garcia's hand and dropped it into the sink, she and Garcia and I had hurried out of the autopsy suite and held a brief, urgent conference in the hallway. Detective Emert, still ashen-faced from his nausea, turned a whiter shade of pale when he heard us discussing radioactivity and hospital evacuation.

On the one hand, we weren't certain that the pellet was radioactive, so we didn't want to create needless alarm. On the other hand, we didn't want to put people in danger, and that seemed to be a risk, if Novak had indeed died of some sort of radiation poisoning.

I hadn't touched the pellet or even the body, at least not once the autopsy began, so my risk of contamination seemed lower than Miranda's or Garcia's. I picked up the receiver from a wall-mounted phone in the hallway and buzzed Lynette Wilkins, the receptionist at the front desk of the morgue. "Lynette," I said, as evenly as I could manage, "this is Dr. Brockton. I'm in the hallway outside the autopsy suite with Dr. Garcia and Miranda Lovelady and an Oak Ridge police detective. We have a problem back here. Could you please round up everybody else in the Forensic Center and take them out the front door, into the hospital basement?"

"Oh God," she said. "Is there some nutcase back there

with a gun? All you have to say is 'yes' and I'll call for a SWAT team."

"No, no," I said, "it's nothing like that. The only crazy people back here are us. We have what might be a contaminated body, and we want to make sure we don't expose anybody else to contamination."

"Do you want me to call the hospital hazmat team?"

"I'm not sure hazmat's what we're dealing with," I said. "Miranda's making a call right now that should help us figure it out. Just get everybody out calmly, would you?"

"Of course, Dr. B."

"And Lynette?"

"Yes?"

"Lock the door behind you. And put up a DO NOT ENTER sign."

"God almighty. Y'all be careful."

MIRANDA HAD CALLED Hank, the health physicist who was part of the DMORT team. Hank was on his way from Oak Ridge, but it would take him at least thirty or forty minutes to arrive. In the meantime, he suggested she call Duane Johnson. "Of course," said Garcia when she relayed the suggestion. "If I weren't so rattled, I'd have thought of Duane right away."

"Who's Duane?" I asked.

"He's the hospital's radiological protection officer," said Garcia. "A medical physicist, I think he's called, on the School of Medicine faculty. He trains interns and residents in the Nuclear Medicine Department. He keeps track of all the hospital's medical radioisotopes, and he trains ER teams how to respond if there's a nuclear accident or terrorist act. His office is up on the ground floor, practically right over our heads, and he's got all sorts of instruments and safety gear."

Thirty seconds later Garcia was on the phone with

Johnson, describing the tiny metallic pellet he'd found and the trail of shredded GI tissue leading up to it. Three minutes after the phone call, we heard a clatter at the far end of the hallway and Johnson appeared, wheeling a cart. The cart measured two or three feet square by six feet tall; one side was fitted with a corrugated blue door that resembled the flexible shutter on a big-city storefront or an antique roll-top desk. "Your receptionist didn't want to let me in," he said to Garcia. "I had to explain pretty bluntly that it was in her best interests and yours to unlock the door so I could figure out what's going on in here." He slid the plastic door up, revealing shelves laden with disposable clothing, cleaning solutions, plastic bags, and electronic instruments.

Rummaging around in a bin at the bottom of the cart, Johnson removed a tan Geiger counter, identical to the one Hank had used at the DMORT training, and switched it on. I heard the slow, buzzing clicks I had come to recognize as the baseline sound of normal, background radiation, like a clock ticking or a diesel engine idling. He extended the wand toward Garcia. "Hold out your hands," he said, and when Garcia did, Hank passed the wand over them, front and back. The instrument continued to buzz at the same slow, reassuring rate. Next he waved the wand over Garcia's body from head to foot, with the same quiet results, and then over Miranda, and then over me and Emert. I felt myself starting to relax, and I relaxed a lot more when Duane said, "Well, there's no contamination on any of you."

Then he stepped around a corner and opened the door of the autopsy suite, and suddenly all hell broke loose. The Geiger counter ratcheted up to a harsh, continuous buzz, and a small, pager-looking gadget at Duane's waist began shrieking. "Son of a *bitch*," said Duane, backpedaling fast. Both instruments quieted down once he was away from the door, but my heart and my nerves—which had zoomed up in sync with the gadgets—continued to rev. "Something in there is hot as a pistol," he said. He looked shaken, and that didn't do a lot to calm me back down.

I was feeling some fear for my own safety, but more concern for Garcia's and Emert's, and—especially—for Miranda's. She was a young woman of childbearing age, and if there was risk from radiation, she was potentially the most vulnerable. She was also my student, and I felt responsible for her safety. "Duane," I said, "do we need to get out of here? And do we need to evacuate the hospital, or part of it?"

"We're okay here," said Duane, glancing at the meter as he said it. "These walls are concrete, and they're pretty stout down here in the basement, so they're good shielding. I'd like to figure out what kind of radiation this is, and how hot it is, before we do something as drastic as evacuating patients. If you start moving sick people, you can make them a lot sicker. But let me make sure the folks just above us aren't at risk. Where's the nearest phone?" Garcia pointed to the wall behind Johnson, and Johnson dialed a five-digit extension. "Hi, it's Duane," he said. "Listen, I've got an odd request. I'm one floor below you guys right now. Could you run a survey meter around the offices and labs up there, make sure nothing's coming up through the floor?" I heard the faint sound of questions bleeding out of the receiver. "The morgue," Duane said. "I'm down in the morgue." I heard more faint questions. "Look, just do it, would you? Like, right now? And if your active dosimeter isn't already on, turn it on before you do anything else." I saw a look of impatience flash across his face; he paused long enough for me to hear urgency in the voice at the other end of the line. "We may have an incident down here," said the physicist, "but I don't have time to talk right now. Check the whole lab area, get people out if you need to, and page me if you see anything worth worrying about. I'll call you back in a few minutes, but right now I gotta go." He hung up the phone and turned to the four of us. "We're right underneath the cyclotron lab," he said, "where we make radiopharmaceuticals for PET scans. The floor's really thick, there are no patients in that area, and the staff knows how to make sure it's safe up there." He eyed the corner of the hallway. Around it lay the door of the morgue and the danger lurking within. He drew a deep breath. "Okay, let's see what we've got here."

He went back to the cart and pulled out a bagged garment; as he unwrapped and unfolded it, I recognized it as a biohazard suit like the ones the DMORT team had worn. The DMORT team called the garments moon suits, but Duane called it a "bunny suit," because its built-in booties and gloves and hood make it look like an Easter-rabbit costume, minus the ears. "Bunny suit" seemed an oddly innocent nickname, though, considering how concerned Johnson now seemed. Once he was zipped in, he took a red and yellow instrument out of the cart's bin and switched it on. This gadget was similar to the Geiger counter—boxy and about half the size of a car battery, with a wand attached to a flexible cord—but instead of a dial with a needle, this one had a digital display. "So what is that," asked Miranda, "the all-new, fully equipped 2009 Geiger Counter Deluxe?"

"Sort of," he said. "It's an ionization chamber. A Geiger-Mueller counter gives you a yes-or-no answer—it tells you whether or not there's elevated radioactivity—but it doesn't tell much more than that. This one tells whether the activity is alpha, beta, or gamma radiation, and it measures the wavelength and energy accurately."

"Sounds like a better gizmo," she said. "Why doesn't everybody use these?"

"These cost about four times as much," he said. "And usually the Geiger-Mueller counter is good enough, because usually it tells you there's nothing above background radiation."

"But not always," said Emert, who'd had a deer-in-the-headlights look ever since he'd vomited in the morgue.

"Not always," conceded Johnson. He checked the ionization chamber's display and seemed satisfied with what he saw there, then handed the instrument to Emert briefly while he rummaged around in the cart. First he dug out a pair of toy-looking plastic rings, which he put on his two index fingers. "Ring dosimeters," he explained, showing us a small square of metallic foil in the broadest part of the band, where a gemstone would be if the rings were jewelry. He rotated the rings toward the inside of each finger. "To measure how much exposure my hands get." Then he fished out a lead smock, the sort patients wear while having an arm or leg X-rayed, and put it on. "The body's core is more vulnerable to radiation than the arms and legs," he said. "The GI tract and the bone marrow, especially."

Taking the ionization chamber back from Emert, he stepped around the corner. I saw him reach for the morgue's door and open it, then extend the wand through the opening. He let out a low whistle just as the monitor clipped to his belt began to shriek again, then scurried back around the corner and rejoined us. He scanned our worried faces. "There's good news and bad news," he said. "The good news is, from the reading I'm getting and from what you've told me you found in the body, this isn't something that's spreading contamination."

Nobody else seemed to want to ask the logical next question, so I did. "What's the bad news?"

"The bad news is, the source, whatever it is, is putting out some intense radiation. I'll need to notify TEMA—the Tennessee Emergency Management Agency—and call the medical folks over in Oak Ridge. They're some of the world's best experts in treating radiation exposure."

"Actually," said Miranda, "just before you got here, I spoke with Hank Strickland, a health physicist I know at REAC/TS. He's on his way over now."

Johnson looked startled, but he quickly recovered. "While I call TEMA, call Hank back. Tell him we're looking at an intense gamma radiation source. Ask him if one of their emergency physicians could meet you guys up in the ER." I saw alarm in the faces of Miranda, Garcia, and Emert, and if they were looking, they saw it in mine, too. "It's a precaution," Johnson said. "Triage. We need to see how much exposure you've gotten, and we'll need to start taking blood and urine samples for that."

Just then Eddie Garcia grunted in pain, doubled over, and threw up. From my recent DMORT training, I knew that vomiting was one symptom of radiation sickness. I also knew that the sooner victims began to vomit after being exposed, the worse their condition.

Miranda knew it, too. The cell phone shook in her hands as she struggled to hit the redial button.

AFTER SOME QUICK, back-of-the-envelope calculations, Duane Johnson estimated that the radioactive pellet from Novak's gut was packing somewhere in the neighborhood of a hundred curies of radioactivity, and it was spewing pure gamma, the most penetrating form of radiation. "Like armor-piercing X-rays," Miranda said, and Johnson nodded grimly. The image was vivid, but it was far from reassuring.

Hank arrived just as Miranda, Garcia, Emert, and I were heading upstairs to the ER. He offered to help Johnson retrieve the source and get it shielded. Dr. Chris Sorensen, an emergency physician specializing in radiation accidents, was on his way from Oak Ridge as well, Hank said, and would meet us in the ER. Meanwhile, Dr. Sorensen was on the phone with Dr. Al Davies, a UT emergency physician Johnson had paged, briefed, and asked to meet us in the ER.

Never in the history of UT Hospital's ER had four people been processed so swiftly. Dr. Davies whisked us back to a triage suite, where he assigned a nurse to each of us. In no time, all four of us had tourniquets around our biceps as nurses prepared to draw blood.

Three of us were stuck almost in unison, the blood

spurting thick and dark into a series of five vials. Garcia's arm remained untouched. Garcia was holding his right arm across his belly; his face was tense with pain. His nurse, a thickset and graying woman who appeared to be in her fifties, took a step back. Dr. Davies hurried to her side. "Nurse, is there a problem?"

"I . . ." she faltered. "I heard it's something radioactive. Is that true?"

"We're not certain, but we think so, yes," said Davies. "That's why we need the blood samples, so we can tell how severe the exposure is."

"I'm not comfortable doing this," she said. "I'm afraid. I don't want to be contaminated."

"Oh, for God's sake," snapped the doctor. Then, seeing the near-panic in her eyes, his tone softened. "This isn't something he can spread to you," he said. "It's not like a virus or a chemical. It's more like a sunburn, even though it isn't showing up yet. You can't catch this from him, any more than you could catch a sunburn." He laid a hand on Garcia's shoulder and left it there, showing her there was nothing to fear. "I'd draw his blood myself, but it's been twenty years since I've done it, and it'd be cruel and inhuman treatment if I stuck Dr. Garcia with my rusty skills." Still she held back, motionless except for her head, which began shaking "no."

Just as Davies was drawing himself up to his most authoritative physician posture, my nurse—a young woman who had filled my two blood vials with cool efficiency—stepped in, taking the syringe from the hand of the reluctant nurse. "It's okay," she said. "I've got it." She tapped her index finger on the inside of Garcia's elbow to bring the vein up, then eased in the needle.

Garcia raised his head and studied her face. "What's your name?" His voice sounded reedy and forced.

"Darcy," she said. "Darcy Bonnett."

"Thank you, Darcy."

"You're welcome," she said. When she was finished, she gave Garcia's hand a quick squeeze.

After drawing our blood, they sent us to bathrooms with plastic specimen cups. When I emerged, the cup warm in my hand, I saw a tall, tanned, silver-haired man in civilian clothes—khaki pants, a blue shirt, a red tie—conferring with Dr. Davies. He introduced himself as Chris Sorensen, a radiation-medicine physician from REAC/TS. As Miranda, Garcia, and Emert emerged from other bathrooms and handed off their pee, we all instinctively gathered around Davies and Sorensen. "I just got an update from Hank," Sorensen said. "He and Duane Johnson think they can retrieve the source and get it into a shielded vessel. So the good news is, this should be contained quickly."

"I can tell you're about to drop a bad-news shoe," I said.

"It's not great," he said. "It's a gamma source, for sure; luckily, it appears to be a sealed, single-point source—that little pellet that came from Dr. Novak's intestine. Gamma sources don't spread contamination, they just emit radiation. Like light, from a lightbulb, rather than water from a garden hose." This sounded like something from a high school science-class talk he'd given a lot of times. "But this source is iridium-192, which is very intense."

"You mean dangerous," said Miranda.

He hesitated, but only briefly. "Yes," he said, "dangerous. Those of you who touched it"—he looked directly at Garcia and Miranda, so I knew Hank had briefed him—"will probably have burns on your hands. My other concern is how much whole-body dose all of you got. We need to know whether it's enough to damage your bone marrow or the lining of your GI tract. We'll need to do whole-blood counts again at twelve hours and twenty-four hours to see if your lymphocyte counts are dropping."

"Excuse me, Doc," said Emert. "Our what counts?"

"Lymphocytes," he said. "They're a type of white blood cells. If they drop significantly, it means the stem cells in your bone marrow have been hit hard. Also means you're vulnerable to infection."

"Sort of like radiation-induced AIDS," added Miranda. I was starting to wish she didn't have such a gift for grim analogies.

"Sort of," Sorensen agreed. "Tracking changes in your lymphocytes is one way we estimate the dose you've received. Another is to reconstruct the incident timeline. So I'll need each of you to think back and give me your best estimate of how much time you spent near Dr. Novak's body, particularly how close you were to the abdominal region, where the source was—three feet away for thirty minutes, for instance, and ten feet away for an hour. Between the incident timeline and the bloodwork, we'll get a fairly precise idea of what sort of exposure you each got."

"You mentioned burns," I said, "but their hands look fine." As if on cue, Miranda and Garcia held out their palms.

Sorensen and Davies both shook their heads. "Too soon to tell," Davies said. "Normally the redness doesn't show up till the next day. We see it occasionally in patients undergoing radiation therapy. Redness. You may have itching or swelling or numbness in your hands, too. The redness generally peaks about twenty-four hours after exposure, then it fades. Same with the symptoms of whole-body exposure—nausea, diarrhea, fatigue: they show up, then disappear, and everything seems fine. Even if it's not."

"The 'prodromal stage' is the term for that period of initial symptoms," added Sorensen. "When they disappear, that marks the beginning of what we call the 'latency stage' of ARS, acute radiation syndrome. If it is ARS, the symptoms can come roaring back, anywhere from days to weeks after exposure. 'Manifest illness,' that stage is called. Radiation does strange things to the body. It damages the DNA in cells, and cells that get replaced more often—like the bone marrow and the lining of the gut—are affected first, and the worst."

"So the bloodwork helps you estimate the dose and diagnose damage," I said. "But what about treatment? What can you do for us? What can you do to reverse or minimize the effects of the radiation?"

"Not a lot, unfortunately," said Sorensen. "If your lymphocytes drop significantly, we'll start you on growth factors to stimulate the bone marrow. We can treat localized burns to ease pain and fight infection. If your immune system is compromised, we can isolate you." He hesitated. "We can recommend psychological and psychiatric care, to help deal with anxiety or anger. Beyond that, it's up to the body to repair and heal itself."

"Shit," said Emert. "This sucks."

"I know," said Sorensen. "I wish I had a magic pill I could give you."

The detective puffed out a deep breath of frustration. "So tell me this," he said. "Novak was a physicist in Oak Ridge, from the moment there *was* an Oak Ridge. He worked with nuclear reactors and radioactive materials for forty, fifty years. Could this be a bizarre side effect of all those years of radiation exposure?"

Sorensen shook his head. "Not a chance," he said. "That gamma radiation is coming from that tiny pellet that was in his gut. Iridium-192 is a very unstable isotope, with a very short half-life. You have to work hard to make it radioactive, and once you do, it decays fast. As it emits all that gamma radiation, it's changing steadily from radioactive iridium into ordinary platinum. A year or two from now, it'll be relatively safe to handle."

"So that hot little pellet," I said, "isn't some dangerous bit of flotsam or jetsam left over from the Manhattan Project?"

"It was probably created within the past six months," he said, "and Dr. Novak couldn't have survived more than a day or two after ingesting it. Within minutes he was doomed. Within hours he was what we call a 'walking ghost.' "

6

ARMED WITH PENS AND notepads, Miranda, Garcia, Emert, and I huddled in plastic chairs in a triage room in the Emergency Department, comparing notes like classmates before a test. We were reconstructing what Sorensen called the "incident timeline"—which Miranda, in classic form, had nicknamed the "path to peril." How long had I spent chainsawing Novak's body out of the frozen swimming pool—ten minutes? fifteen? Had Miranda and I spent a full hour driving back to UT with the corpse in the pickup truck? Another fifteen minutes getting it onto the gurney and into the morgue? The next day, when Emert searched the clothing and identified Novak, were the detective and I beside the gurney for thirty minutes, or was it more like forty? How many lifetimes elapsed between the moment the autopsy began and the instant we fled the morgue?

As the four of us debated matters of minutes, Garcia winced and hastily excused himself. Miranda watched him hurry to a restroom, then looked at me. "I'm worried about Eddie," she said. "This doesn't look good. But I don't understand why his symptoms would be so much worse than anyone else's. The rest of us were around the body the day it was recovered, and he wasn't."

"Maybe it's just the stress," I said, but it rang false in my ears even as I said it. Suddenly it hit me. "Dammit," I said. "The autopsy."

"But we were there, too," she said. "Sure, he was closer to Novak, but not that much closer."

"Not Novak's autopsy," I said. "The one Eddie was doing the day we brought Novak in to thaw. Remember? We parked the gurney at the other sink, right behind Eddie. He was two feet away for hours."

Miranda clapped a hand over her mouth. "Oh God," she said, "I didn't even think about that. He did two that day. And another one the next morning, before Novak's. Oh, this is bad, Dr. B. Very, very bad." Her chin began to quiver, and her eyes brimmed with tears.

I glanced at the two doctors and saw them huddled with the nurse named Darcy. She nodded, then disappeared behind a curtain. A moment later she reappeared, wheeling a stand with an IV bag attached. Behind the door of the restroom, a toilet flushed with a roar. Miranda wiped her eyes with the backs of her hands and sniffed quickly. She picked up her pen and notepad again just as Garcia opened the restroom door and walked weakly toward us.

I looked at Garcia with sympathy. "Hurling again?"

He shook his head. "Other end," he grimaced.

Miranda's eyes darted from Garcia to me at the news of this additional symptom. Sorensen and Davies walked toward us. "Dr. Garcia, we'd like to go ahead and put you on an IV," Davies said, "since you're losing fluids." Garcia nodded; as a physician, he had probably known they'd want to do this. "We'd also like to go ahead and admit you for observation." If Garcia had seen this one coming, it didn't show: the look on his face when Sorensen said this was somewhere between shock and despair, but he simply nodded again. We moved back into the ER's triage area; Eddie disappeared behind a curtain long enough to change into a gown, climb into a bed, and get hooked to the IV. Then the nurse pulled back the curtain and we clustered around his bed to finish reconstructing the incident timeline.

"Eddie," I said, "don't forget to estimate how long you

spent near Novak's body while you were doing other autopsies."

"I know," he said. "I was thinking about that on the toilet a minute ago. I spent ten or twelve hours in there, two or three feet away, soaking up gamma radiation." He stared at his notepad, but his pen didn't move. Finally, he picked up his pen and began to write.

Once we'd tallied up our exposure times and distances, I gathered up the notepads and handed them across to Sorensen. He glanced quickly at all of them; Eddie's was on the bottom of the stack, and Sorensen frowned when he saw the number of hours. "Excuse me just a moment," he said. He unzipped a soft-sided computer case and took out a laptop; after a moment, he began punching in numbers. I didn't want to hover, so I went back to the group at Garcia's bedside.

After what might have been five minutes or five hours, Sorensen came over and pulled a chair away from the wall so he could sit facing us. "Okay, this is just ballpark," he said, "based on the timelines you gave me. We'll have a much clearer picture once we get another blood sample or two and graph the changes in your lymphocytes. We're also going to use a technique developed in Oak Ridge called cytodosimetry—estimating your dose by analyzing DNA damage within your cells. So by this time tomorrow afternoon"—he checked his watch, then corrected himself—"by six-thirty tomorrow evening, we'll be able to estimate your dose by three different methods."

"But for now," prompted Garcia, "what are the ballpark numbers, and what do they mean?"

Sorensen drew a breath. "Detective Emert." Emert's forehead creased, and he leaned forward. "It looks like you might have gotten exposed to something like twenty rads."

"What the hell's a rad, and how bad are twenty of 'em?"

"Well, in the course of a year, you get about one-tenth of a rad from background radiation—cosmic rays, radon gas seeping out of rocks in the ground, that sort of thing."

"So I've gotten, what, two hundred years' worth of radiation in the last four days?"

"Something like that," said Sorensen.

"So that's why I barfed during the autopsy? Do I need an IV, too?"

"I don't think so," he said. "Twenty rads isn't something I'd recommend you get again, but it helps that your exposure came at intervals, rather than continuously. I've seen a lot of cases, and I've never seen anyone with symptoms of ARS at this low a dose. I suspect you vomited during the autopsy because it was an autopsy."

Emert took a long breath and blew it out. It was the sound of deep relief.

"Dr. Brockton," Sorensen said, "you and Ms. Lovelady may have gotten somewhere around 40 rads. More than we'd like, but also no symptoms, probably." He looked at Miranda. "But I'm somewhat concerned about local injury to your fingertips." He glanced down at Miranda's notes. "You say you touched the source for only a few seconds?" She nodded. "That's good, but at the surface, a hundred-curie source of iridium-192 is putting out over a hundred thousand rads a minute. If you got a couple thousand rads of exposure to your fingers, you're likely to have some blistering, maybe even some necrosis."

"You mean I might lose my fingers?"

"I doubt it, but it's possible," he said. "We'll hope it's just a bit of blistering at the fingertips, and hope it heals." Miranda looked shaken, but she nodded with remarkable composure.

"Dr. Garcia," said Sorensen, "I'm most concerned about you. You say the pellet was resting in your left palm for about thirty seconds, and between your right thumb and forefinger for fifteen to twenty seconds?"

"That's just a guess," said Garcia, "but I had no reason to think I needed to hurry as I was looking at it."

"Of course not," said Sorensen. "But I'm afraid you're likely to have some localized damage to your hands."

"Sounds like it," said Garcia. "If I followed what you said to Miranda, and my math's right, we're talking, what, tens or even hundreds of thousands of rads to my hands?"

"Could be," conceded Sorensen. "There's some risk to your eyes as well. The lens of the eye is very sensitive to ionizing radiation, and if you were looking at the pellet at close range, you could develop cataracts within the next several years."

"Maimed and blind," said Garcia. "It just keeps getting better. What's next? Things come in threes, right?"

"I'm afraid so. You've also got a higher whole-body dose, because of those additional hours in the morgue."

"How much higher?"

Sorensen hesitated. Not a good sign. "Your exposure could be somewhere in the range of four to five hundred rads."

"And what's the prognosis for someone who's been exposed to five hundred rads?"

Sorensen hesitated again. Another bad sign. "That's getting up around the LD-50," he said.

I heard Miranda draw a sharp breath.

"Excuse me," said Emert. "What's LD-50?"

Garcia answered before Sorensen could. "The 50 means fifty percent," he said softly. "The LD means 'lethal dose.' What Dr. Sorensen is saying, very tactfully, is that first I probably lose my hands, and then God tosses a coin to see whether I live or die."

Then he looked up at Miranda and me. "Would you two do me a favor? Would you please go to my house and tell Carmen what's happened? I'll call and tell her I've gotten delayed, but I don't want her to hear the details over the phone. I want someone to be with her."

Miranda reached out and took his hand. Her face was wet with tears again, but this time there was no hiding them.

SORENSEN AND DAVIES sent Garcia straight upstairs to an inpatient room. Emert, who lived in Oak Ridge, arranged to have his blood drawn at the hospital there so he didn't have to come back to Knoxville in the middle of the night. Miranda and I were free to go, though we had strict orders to return at 6 A.M. for our twelve-hour blood sample. It was shaping up as a long, worrisome night. Before heading to Garcia's house to talk with Carmen, we took a side trip downstairs to the Forensic Center. The DO NOT ENTER sign had been supplemented by yellow-and-black tape that read CAUTION—DO NOT ENTER, as well as a sign containing magenta wedges on a yellow background, with the words RADIATION HAZARD—KEEP OUT.

"Sounds like they mean it," I said to Miranda.

"Probably fends off the door-to-door salesmen and the Jehovah's Witnesses, too," she said, but I could tell her heart wasn't in the jest.

Just then Duane Johnson and a moon-suited technician I didn't know emerged from the elevator, wheeling two rectangular metal slabs about two feet high by four feet wide. The metal slabs appeared to be heavy, judging by the way the two men leaned forward to roll them. "Lead shields," Duane panted as they passed us and headed toward the locked door of the morgue. "Want to watch?"

"I think we've had enough radiation fun for one day," I said.

"No pressure," he said. "But as long as you stay behind the corner, where you were before, you won't get any additional exposure." I looked at Miranda, and she shrugged. Curiosity trumped caution, and we followed as Duane and the technician wheeled the shields toward the morgue.

Duane rapped on the door of the morgue a number of

times—three quick knocks, then three slow ones, then three more fast ones—and I realized that the knocks were the Morse code distress signal, SOS. The door swung inward and Hank peered around the edge. He looked closely at Miranda and me and said, "Everybody okay?"

"We'll see," I said. "Detective Emert's gone back to Oak Ridge. They'll be taking blood samples from all of us every few hours to calculate our dose. They've admitted Dr. Garcia, because he got the highest exposure—four to five hundred rads."

The dismayed look on Hank's face made it clear that he realized how perilous Garcia's situation was. He shook his head grimly, then turned to Johnson. "Okay," he said, "let's get that shit out of there." Johnson and the tech wrangled the shields through the door, and once we were all inside, Hank locked it behind us.

Together, they reached for one of the shields, tipped it to the floor, then flipped it upside down beside the other. The shields were designed to protect the torso of a nuclear-medicine technician or nurse from the activity of radioisotopes being administered to nuclear-medicine patients. That meant the rectangular panel was raised a couple of feet off the floor, to the level of a hospital bed or operating-room table. In this case, though, partial coverage wasn't enough. After flipping the shields upside down, they clamped one to the other, to create an unbroken layer of shielding from toe height to neck height. Next they clamped a smaller shield, fitted with a thick window of leaded glass, atop the upper shield. They had assembled a variety of tools as well, including long tongs—wrapped at the ends with what appeared to be duct tape, the sticky side facing out—and a small round mirror on the end of a telescoping metal shaft. I gathered they planned to use it as a periscope, so they could keep their heads behind the shielding at all times while peering into the sink. They also had a square metal case, about a foot on either side by maybe eighteen inches high. The case appeared to be made of steel, but from the way the two men grunted and strained as they moved it, I suspected the inside was lined with a thick layer of lead.

Just as they were about to wheel the makeshift shielding toward the autopsy suite, Hank's cell phone rang with an urgent warbling tone. He looked startled as he glanced at the display. "REAC/TS, Hank Strickland." After a moment, he said, "You guys don't waste any time, do you?" He listened a bit more. "That's right. . . . About a hundred curies." He glanced at Miranda and me, then looked away. "Too soon to tell; one of the four took quite a hit." A longer interval of listening. "I understand. . . . I will; thanks. Have a safe flight."

He hung up the phone. "Well, that was interesting. That was—"

His words were interrupted by a loud knocking at the locked door. "This is Captain Sievers, UT Medical Center Police. Open the door, please." It didn't really sound like a request; more like a command.

"I'll get it," I said.

Sievers, whom I'd known for years, looked surprised to see me; mostly, though, he looked upset. "We got a report," he began, but then he stopped speaking as his eyes swept the room and took in the tableau of people and equipment: Miranda and me, still in our scrubs, and three moon-suited figures, clustered around a collection of lead shields, radiation meters, and other worrisome paraphernalia. "What the hell is going on in here?"

"We had an autopsy take an unexpected turn—" I started to explain.

"What Dr. Brockton means," cut in Hank, "is that we're simulating a radiological contamination event. It's a cooperative exercise between the Forensic Center and our emergency-response team in Oak Ridge."

Sievers stared at Hank, then at me, then at Johnson.

"Bull. *Shit,*" he said. He pushed past me and the others, heading toward the autopsy suite.

"I wouldn't do that," said Hank.

"You said it's a drill," shot back Sievers.

"Stop *now,*" said Hank.

"You've got about five seconds to tell me why I should," said Sievers.

Hank sighed, then pulled out his cell phone and hit the LAST CALL button. "It's Strickland, with REAC/TS," he said. "We have a slight complication here. Would you mind talking with Captain Sievers, of the medical center police? . . . Yes, the hospital has its own police. . . . No, he's not a rent-a-cop. . . . Sievers. *Captain* Sievers."

Hank held out the phone to Sievers. The officer glared at him suspiciously, then snatched the phone. "This is Captain Sievers. Who the hell is this?" His eyes widened. "Yes sir," he said. "Of course I've heard of your office." He listened intently, his eyes darting around the room all the while. "I understand," he said. "You'll have our full cooperation. Yes sir. Thank *you,* sir." He hung up the phone and stared at it a moment. "Well," he said, but that's as far as he got.

"Hell-*o*?!" A stylishly coiffed and suited woman appeared in the doorway. It was Liz Chambers, the hospital's public-relations officer. A former local news anchor, Liz always looked ready to go on camera at a moment's notice. "Y'all aren't throwing a party without me, are you?" She said it teasingly, but I saw her survey the room the same swift way Sievers had, and I braced for trouble.

"I sent you a memo about this last week, Liz," said Sievers. "The radiation drill?"

It took everything I had to keep my jaw from dropping in disbelief. Out of the corner of my eye, I could see Miranda. She was standing perfectly still, but tension coiled in her body. Despite the stresses of the past few hours, I could tell by her gleaming eyes that she was intrigued by this latest scene in the drama unfolding around us.

"What radiation drill? I didn't get any memo about this," said Liz. "I would have put out a press release. We could have gotten great media coverage."

"I didn't send you the memo? *Crap,*" said Sievers convincingly. "I am *so sorry,* Liz."

"It's actually my fault," I said. I had no idea what I was doing, but something in the phone calls had changed things, and I didn't want to leave Sievers hanging out there all alone. "I pulled this together on short notice." Liz stared at me. "You remember that DMORT training we had a couple of days ago at the Body Farm?" She nodded suspiciously. "Well, Captain Sievers swung by to take a look." Sievers nodded, not very convincingly. "So I asked if it'd be okay if we did a smaller drill in the morgue, just to take the training through the final step." I raised both hands in a gesture of submission and apology. "I should have followed up with an email, so he could have brought you into the loop."

"I told him to follow up," chimed in Miranda. "Didn't I tell you to follow up?"

"You did tell me to follow up," I said. "And I forgot. I'm sorry. I accept full responsibility."

Liz frowned at me. A small muscle beside her left eye was twitching, and the tendons in her neck were taut as bowstrings. "Guys, it's hard for me to do my job if nobody tells me what's going on. There are all kinds of rumors flying around about some kind of radiation accident, and it'll take me days to put out the brush fires. Sure would have been easier to have put out a press release about a safety exercise." She took one last look around, lingering on the moon suits, and shook her head sadly—lamenting not just the hassle of quashing rumors, I suspected, but also the lost opportunity to show high-tech training on the local news—and spun on her stilettos.

"*That* was interesting," said Johnson, once the clicking of her steps had faded. "Last time I heard that many lies back-to-back was when Bill Clinton was describing the platonic nature of his relationship with Monica Lewinsky."

I turned to Hank and Sievers to ask about the phone conversations that had set the series of lies in motion. "FBI," said Sievers. "Special Agent Thornton will be here in a few hours."

Given how intense the phone calls had seemed, I was surprised at the delay. "A few hours? What, he's watching the UT basketball game on television first?"

"No," said Hank. "He's with the Weapons of Mass Destruction Directorate. He's flying down from D.C." Hank looked at Johnson. "So, what was it we were about to do before we were interrupted?"

HUNKERED BEHIND THE massive shield they'd assembled, Hank and Johnson edged toward the door of the autopsy suite, towing the tongs and the metal shipping case behind them on a low cart. As the door opened, I heard one of the dosimeters begin to shriek, then Hank crouched lower and the shrieking stopped. The door closed behind them, and Miranda and I watched and listened anxiously. Suddenly both dosimeters began shrieking. Miranda, Sievers, and I looked at one another, worried but unable to do anything. After a few agonizing seconds, the alarms fell silent and I recognized Hank's voice shouting "Gotcha!" He and Johnson emerged from the autopsy suite, sweating and panting but looking relieved. Hank was wheeling the cart with the metal shipping case on it; Johnson held the wand of the ionization chamber over the box, and I was relieved to hear the instrument clicking lazily.

"Okay," said Hank, "I think we're okay now. We did a survey, and there's nothing in there to be concerned about. Well, nothing except for that really disgusting corpse. Yuck. There's nothing radiological to be concerned about. That one little pellet was it."

"Let's get this upstairs to the radiopharmaceuticals lab," said Duane. "It would probably be fine in this box—we ship medical isotopes in these all the time, and the lead canister inside is about an inch thick—but I'd feel better if we had it locked in a hot cell."

"Sounds like a good idea," I said.

"First, though," he said, "I should call TEMA again, tell them it's under control." He unzipped his suit and fished a cell phone out of a pocket. He hit a speed-dial button, then put the cell on speakerphone.

"TEMA, this is Wilhoit," said a voice from the speaker.

"Hi, it's Duane Johnson, at UT Medical Center again," said Duane. "I'm calling to let you know we've retrieved the gamma source that was in the morgue. We've got it in a lead shipping container now, and we're taking it up to one of the hot cells in Nuclear Medicine now."

"Excuse me," said Wilhoit. "TEMA has jurisdiction over this, not UT. We'll decide what to do with it when we get there."

"Be my guest," said Johnson. "You should've spoken up sooner. I'd've been happy to let you go in there and fish it out of the sink for us."

The speaker fell silent for a few seconds. "Look, I'm glad you guys have secured it. I would have taken it a little slower, called in some more people and equipment—"

"—and generated two or three days of paralysis and panic doing it that way," said Johnson. "We safed an extremely hot source in about an hour. We have years of experience here dealing with radioisotopes. If something like this had to happen, it's hard to imagine a better-equipped place for it to happen than UT Medical Center. So: now that we've safed it for you, what does TEMA propose to do with a hundred curies of iridium-192?"

"We'll have a staff meeting in the morning to discuss the options," said Wilhoit. "Whoever owns the source is the culpable party, and they have a responsibility to collect and dispose of it."

"And you think the 'culpable party' is going to be eager to step forward," said Johnson, "eager to own up to one man's death and four people's exposure in the morgue? Meanwhile—as we wait for this 'culpable party' to step forward to say 'Arrest me, and please sue me for millions of dollars, too'—do you plan on stashing this in your attic?"

The TEMA official fell silent again. "The Department of Energy," he finally said. "DOE has a Radiological Assistance team based over in Oak Ridge. I'll ask the governor to ask the feds to take it off our hands."

"Sounds great," said Johnson. "But at the risk of sounding like a broken record: Until DOE gets here, would you mind if we lock it up in a hot cell? That seems a little more secure than the frickin' hallway it's sitting in right now."

Two minutes and a little fence-mending later, Johnson trundled the box to the elevator and up to a hot cell—a massive box of lead and leaded glass, equipped with robotic manipulator arms—built to handle powerful radiopharmaceuticals without risk to the hands and bone marrow of technicians and pharmacists.

It was a shame Garcia hadn't known to conduct Leonard Novak's autopsy inside a hot cell. Garcia might have looked like a mad scientist, wielding robotic arms to dissect a corpse. But better a mad scientist than a maimed or dying doctor.

7

THE KNOCK ON MY office door made me jump, and I realized that I must have nodded off. Miranda and I had spent several hours with Carmen Garcia. Around midnight we'd returned to her husband's hospital room, where we'd stayed until it was time for our 7 A.M. blood sample. Carmen had been terrified to learn that her husband—who had left home that morning as usual, kissing her and their baby goodbye in the kitchen after breakfast—was now a hospital patient, his hands and possibly even his life jeopardized by one of the bodies he had autopsied.

Garcia had served as the medical examiner for less than a year now; he'd been hired from Dallas to take Jess Carter's place when Jess was killed. At first I'd disliked Garcia—he'd struck me as stuffy and condescending—but I soon realized that what I'd mistaken for stuffiness was actually just a veneer of formality, maybe even shyness. A slight, handsome man, he'd grown up in a well-to-do Mexico City family before being sent to the United States for college and medical school. His wife Carmen was a Colombian beauty; their Latino genes had combined to produce a gorgeous toddler, Tomas, who had a thick shock of curly black hair and enormous brown eyes. Miranda had taken to babysitting for Tomas one evening a week. She claimed it was so the boy's harried parents could relax over dinner and a movie, but I suspected it was because she was so smitten with the child.

Another knock; another awakening. I had fallen back asleep after the first knock. "Sorry," I said, rubbing my eyes. "Come in."

"How's Dr. Garcia?"

"Too soon to know," I said, fully awake now. "But it doesn't look good. Are you Special Agent Thornton?"

"Yes sir. Charles Thornton."

He stepped into my office and gave me a solid handshake. Thornton was tall and lanky—six foot two, maybe, and tipping the scales at around 190; possibly 200, since he seemed to be carrying some lean muscle on his frame. His sandy hair was cut short, but it appeared to contain some styling gel and some color highlights and some attitude. Then there was the tie: he wore one, but he wore it loosely, like it was an afterthought or an ironic commentary; like he might take it the rest of the way off any minute. The tie was printed with an abstract design that was either the work of an artistic genius or a second grader. The guy was almost a cop, but not quite. Too metrosexual, if I understood the term right. I suspected some of his more buttoned-down FBI colleagues regarded his wardrobe with mistrust.

Thornton glanced around my office, taking in the grimy windows, the fretwork of crisscrossing steel girders outside, and the skulls resting on the wide windowsill. "I'm pleased to meet you, sir. I've heard a lot about the Body Farm from the Forensic Recovery Teams who've trained there. It's a great opportunity for them."

"We're always glad to help," I said. "And you don't have to 'sir' me. Hell, you're the high-wattage guy from FBI headquarters."

He grinned, a lopsided, aw-shucks kind of grin. "Weapons of Mass Destruction Directorate—sounds impressive, doesn't it? I'm actually pretty low on the food chain, though."

"Well, Captain Sievers practically saluted Hank's cell phone when you started talking yesterday," I said. "What'd you say to make such an impression?"

"Not much," he said. "Usually the more I say, the less impressive I get." That drew a laugh from me, weary though I was. "The WMD Directorate is part of the National Security Branch. I just told Captain Sievers this incident could involve terrorism and national security, and that we'd appreciate it if he could help us keep it low-profile till we figured out if there was a bigger threat."

"Were you just blowing smoke to keep Sievers in line? Or might there really be a bigger threat?"

"In the post-9/11 world," he said, "we consider any suspicious incident involving radiation to be terrorism, and we assume the threat could be big until we find out otherwise."

Thornton pulled a small, glossy pamphlet out of a jacket pocket and handed it to me. *Weapons of Mass Destruction (WMD),* the title panel read. *A Pocket Guide.* Inside, one panel described various weapons—explosive, chemical, biological, and radiological—while a second panel listed the federal laws terrorists would be breaking if they used weapons of mass destruction. The pamphlet's innermost spread outlined how the FBI would assess the danger from an actual or threatened WMD attack.

"Yikes," I said. "Good to know you guys are prepared, but scary that there's the need to print this sort of thing in mass quantity. Also scary that you have to assume the worst."

"We'll be happy to be proven wrong," he said. "We've sent the source to Savannah River National Laboratory, where we have a forensic rad lab. The lab should be able to tell us where it came from, and when."

"It's already there? That was quick."

He shrugged. "We figured that since we were sending a plane to Knoxville anyhow, we might as well get some more mileage out of it. A couple of my cohorts landed in South Carolina with it about thirty minutes ago. That's not for public consumption, by the way, but I wanted you to know we'll be bringing a lot of resources to bear on this."

"That's good to know," I said. "Listen, I was just about to go look in on Dr. Garcia. You want to come with me?"

"Thanks, but I guess I should pass," he said. "I probably should start seeing what we can dig up in Oak Ridge."

"I understand," I said. "Good luck."

Just then I heard Miranda's voice in the hallway. "Hey, boss, you ready to go back across the river?"

"Can't wait," I said as she reached the doorway. "Miranda, this is Special Agent Charles Thornton. Agent Thornton, this is my graduate assistant, Miranda Lovelady."

Thornton held out a hand—more eagerly than he'd extended it to me, I thought—and said, "Chip. Call me Chip."

"Miranda runs the bone lab and works forensic cases with me," I said. "She was in the autopsy suite yesterday."

"I'm sorry to meet you under these circumstances," he said. "Dr. Brockton invited me to head over to the hospital with you guys to meet Dr. Garcia. We can talk on the way." Miranda looked a question at me; I answered with a slight shrug of the shoulders. Thornton had apparently decided he could wait a bit to start his spadework in Oak Ridge.

DESPITE THE TANGLE of tubes and wires attached to him, Eddie Garcia looked better than he had in the ER fourteen hours before. His nausea and diarrhea had subsided, and ordinary fatigue had replaced panic as the predominant look on his face.

"You look pretty good," I said. "You sure it wasn't just something you ate?" Miranda elbowed me by way of a reprimand, then reached out and gave Garcia's arm a squeeze. I felt a flash of panic when she did that—could that increase her exposure?—then I remembered the scene with the fearful ER nurse, and I felt ashamed. Garcia wasn't contaminated or dangerous, I reminded myself; just exposed and endangered. *Amazing,* I thought, *how easily fear trumps logic.* I introduced Thornton, who shook hands with Garcia and then whipped out copies of the handy pocket guide for him and Miranda.

"Swell," said Miranda. "*Now* I feel better." Thornton glanced at me, but I just smiled. Apparently most people didn't react to the pamphlet with the same pessimism Miranda and I had shown. She fluttered her fingers in the general direction of Garcia's attachments. "What are all these things they've fastened to you since we were here a few hours ago?"

"The wires are EKG leads so they can monitor my heart," he said. "One of the drips is saline and electrolytes, to replace what I've been losing from both ends. I have a line they can tap for blood without sticking me every time. So far, I've managed to fend off the nurse with the urinary catheter."

"Pick your battles," I said. "As good as you look, Eddie, I bet you'll be out of here by this time tomorrow."

He shook his head. "Appearances are deceiving with radiation sickness," he said. "And you heard Dr. Sorensen; once the symptoms disappear, it's just a matter of time before they come back with a vengeance. Sorensen's seen a lot of cases of radiation sickness; if he's worried about me, I'm in trouble." I winced at his unsparing realism, though I admired the courage it took to face his situation squarely.

Miranda wheeled to face Thornton. "Who would have done this, and for God's sake, why? It makes no sense. Why not just shoot the old guy, or strangle him? Why not just let him die of old age?" Her voice shook with anger and sorrow.

"Our people in Behavioral Sciences—the profilers—are asking exactly those questions now." He looked as if he were about to add something, then changed his mind and kept quiet.

Miranda saw the hesitation, and she pounced. "What?"

"Nothing, really," he said. "It's just . . . you know the riddle of the albatross?"

She looked perplexed. "Uh, something to do with a sailor who shoots a bird and brings bad luck down on a whole ship?"

"No, that's a poem," said Thornton. "This is a riddle. A man who has returned from a voyage walks into a restaurant, sits down, and orders the albatross. The waiter brings it, the guy takes one bite, then rushes out of the restaurant and goes home and kills himself. Why?"

"Seems a bit of an overreaction," I said. "It must have been really, really bad albatross."

"It's a guessing game," said Thornton. "You have to guess what happened earlier, before he walked into the restaurant. You can ask me yes-or-no questions."

"Was it really, really bad albatross?"

"No," laughed the agent.

Miranda: "But his reaction had something to do with the albatross?"

"Yes."

Me: "Was it fairly bad albatross?"

"Irrelevant."

"That's not yes or no," I pointed out.

"But it's helpful," said Miranda, "and we need all the help we can get. Had he ever had albatross before?"

"No."

Garcia: "Was there special significance to the fact that it was albatross?" Yes. "Did the man feel guilty about eating an albatross?" No.

A series of questions from me: "Was the man already depressed before he tasted the soup?" Yes. I thought of Jess. "Had the man lost someone he loved?" Yes. "And was an albatross somehow connected to that loss?" Yes. "Was it his wife he'd lost?" Yes. "Did she die on the voyage?" Yes.

Miranda: "Was there a shipwreck?" Yes. "Did she perish in the shipwreck?" Yes. "Was the man marooned on a desert island?" Yes. "All alone?" No. "Were other survivors with him?" Yes. "Did any of the others die?" No. "Were they marooned for a long time?"

"Depends on how you define it," he said. "Ask more specifically."

Me: "More than a month?" No. "More than a week?" Yes.

Garcia: "Did they have food from the ship?" No. "Did they catch fish?"

"No. Not enough, anyway." Thornton was cheating slightly, maybe because we were slow.

Miranda: "Did they eat other food on the island?" Yes. "Albatross?" No. "Did the man *think* it was albatross?"

Thornton began to smile. "Yes, he did."

"Bless his heart," she said. "No wonder he killed himself."

I was utterly bewildered. "What?" I stared from one of them to the other. "So are you two actually twins, separated at birth, with a secret language and some weird twin-logic all your own?"

"The survivors resorted to cannibalism," she said. "They cooked his dead wife, but they told him it was albatross."

"Huh?"

"Ah," said Garcia. "So when he tasted the albatross in the restaurant, he realized that he'd never tasted albatross before—and he realized that it was his wife they'd eaten on the island."

"Hmm," I said. "I still think the guy overreacted."

"Looks like overreaction to us," said Thornton, "but to him, it seemed the only acceptable response. Same thing with the iridium murder or suicide. Once we know the backstory, we'll understand the reason for the bizarre method." He looked at Garcia. "Don't worry," he said. "We'll get the guy who did this to you."

Garcia gave Thornton an odd, sad smile. "Thank you, Agent Thornton," he said. "But I have already eviscerated the guy who did this to me."

Thornton turned bright red. "Wow," Miranda said to Garcia, "you don't even need a scalpel to eviscerate a guy."

The FBI agent blinked as he processed Garcia's joke and Miranda's response. "Man, I'm out of my league here," he said. "I better call headquarters and tell 'em to send the A-Team down to Tennessee."

"Damn skippy," said Miranda. "But don't worry. We'll go easy on you till they get here." She flashed him a smile, and Thornton blushed again. He looked considerably more cheerful about it this time around.

8

BY THE TIME MIRANDA, Thornton, and I left the hospital, the lid was blowing off the story. Rightly or wrongly, I blamed the skittish ER nurse for leaking word of the incident—I could imagine her calling WBIR-TV or the *Knoxville News Sentinel* to complain that she and other ER staff had been exposed to radioactive contamination. The truth, though, was that any number of people besides the nurse could have tipped off the media, including morgue employees (all of whom were being checked for exposure now), hospital police officers, even ORPD colleagues of Emert.

By midmorning, reporters from WBIR, the *Knoxville News Sentinel,* and the *Oak Ridger* were besieging UT Medical Center and the Oak Ridge Police Department for information about what had happened in the morgue. The hospital's PR officer, Liz Chambers, was furious that she'd been lied to. It took a personal visit from Special Agent Thornton to calm her down, though I wasn't sure whether it was the national-security angle or Thornton's personal charm that eased the facial tick and relaxed the neck tendons.

Liz initially issued a terse statement indicating that during a routine autopsy at the medical center, elevated levels of radioactivity were detected in the remains of Dr. Leonard Novak, a former Oak Ridge physicist. The radioactivity had been contained, the morgue was safe, the source of the elevated activity was being investigated, and everyone who had been exposed was being carefully monitored, the statement concluded.

That sanitized version survived only through the noon news. By the five o'clock newscast, the story had attained critical mass in the media. A squadron of news helicopters spent the afternoon circling the hospital for aerial shots. In the Anthropology Department, Peggy was swamped with calls from reporters who'd heard that I was in the morgue at the time of the incident. Luckily, I'd talked with Peggy several times since the incident; otherwise she might have believed the journalist who called to ask how Peggy felt about my untimely death in the morgue. I thought of Mark Twain's famous quip. "Tell the guy I said, 'Reports of my death are greatly exaggerated.' Then tell him those were my dying words."

As the story took on a life of its own, reporters and news anchors began to speculate about whether Dr. Novak had absorbed enough radiation during his decades of work in Oak Ridge to become a hazardous source himself. It was a medical version of the glow-in-the-dark cliché, and it was the same question Emert had asked. Then they began to speculate that he might have been poisoned with polonium-210, as former KGB spy Alexander Litvinenko had been in the fall of 2006. After a parade of experts had refuted the glow-in-the-dark theory, polonium seemed to become the media's prime suspect. REAC/TS took blood samples from everyone who'd been in the morgue during the time the body was there—eleven additional people—and from the five other police officers who'd been at the pool.

Like some insidious form of contamination, the polonium theory spread from one news outlet to another. Polonium-210 was a potent source of alpha radiation, the stories pointed out, and although alpha particles could not penetrate skin—they would, in fact, bounce off clothing or a sheet of paper—the particles were dangerous if inhaled or ingested. Soon the stories were focusing on possible sources of "the polonium." Early on, most stories hinted that the polonium must have come from Russia, where nearly all of the world's polonium-210 was produced. Soon, though, enterprising journalists were pointing out that polonium-210 was found in antistatic brushes widely used by photographers and darkrooms to remove dust from camera lenses and enlargers. The media spotlight swiftly swiveled toward the Staticmaster brush—available from Amazon.com for $34.95—which contained five hundred microcuries of polonium-210, or about one-sixth of a potentially lethal dose. Within hours every camera shop in Knoxville had sold out of Staticmaster brushes, as journalists raced to prove their resourcefulness and bravery by acquiring and brandishing an actual source of polonium. My favorite story was the one that showed the Staticmaster brush approaching the lens of the television camera itself, looming ever closer and blurrier, until finally the brush blotted out the lens entirely, just as the reporter hinted at dark deeds investigators hoped to bring to light.

By the late-night newscast on WBIR, Special Agent Charles Thornton himself—wearing a navy blue suit and sporting a businesslike gold tie cinched tight at his collar—was addressing a crowded press conference. Although he could not, Thornton said, comment specifically on any current investigation, he assured the cameras that the FBI took very seriously any actual or threatened crimes involving radioactive or nuclear materials, and was committed to investigating and preventing any such crimes. Thornton regretfully declined to take questions, including a shouted question about whether the FBI had removed radioactive material from UT Medical Center. Immediately after he ducked that question, though, the station aired a brief, fuzzy video clip—I gathered it had been shot by a hospital employee with a cell phone video camera—showing Thornton and two dark-suited agents wheeling a cart onto the loading dock at the back of UT Hospital and lifting a dark, square container into the trunk of a black sedan. Fuzzy though the video was, I recognized the box. It was the lead-lined shipping case where Duane Johnson and Hank Strickland had secured the tiny pellet of iridium-192 that had killed Dr. Leonard Novak. The pellet that might yet kill Dr. Eddie Garcia.

9

FOR SIXTY-FIVE YEARS, LEONARD Novak lived atop Black Oak Ridge—the ridge John Hendrix had prophesied about and the ridge that later inspired the city's name. Like thousands of other workers who descended on the wartime city-in-the-making, Novak had moved into a mass-produced house that had been knocked together in a matter of days. The walls were made of "cemesto," structural panels formed from cement and asbestos sandwiched around a fiberboard core. Such carcinogen-laden building materials would never pass environmental muster these days—in fact, renovating or demolishing a cemesto house these days was considered riskier than living in one. But Oak Ridge was born of wartime urgency, and cemesto houses—trucked to Tennessee in modules that could be quickly connected—allowed the Manhattan Engineer District to build the city in record time. Local lore held that children walking home from school during the war years often got lost, because whole new neighborhoods would have sprung up during the hours between the Pledge of Allegiance and the end-of-the-day bell.

The people in cemestos were the lucky few. Shared dormitory rooms, small trailers, camplike "hutments," and flimsy "Victory cottages" were far more common. The cemestos were reserved for the people higher in the scientific or managerial or military food chain, and the higher your rung on the ladder, the higher your house on the hill. "Snob Hill," those who lived down in the valley called it.

As I followed the curves of Georgia Avenue up the ridge, I noticed that a few of the houses still showed their original cemesto exteriors. Most, though, had been modernized with siding and thermal-pane windows; many sported carports or garages or additions, small or large. Novak's house was sided in gray clapboards, with white shutters and a bright red door. The house was on the north side of the ridge, and as I parked in front and walked down the steps, I caught a glimpse of daylight and the distant mountains behind the house.

Emert, Thornton, and two forensic techs were already inside; so was Art Bohanan. Emert had taken the ten-week training offered by the National Forensic Academy— a cooperative program of UT and the Knoxville Police Department—and when Art had come in to teach the academy's two-day session on fingerprinting, Emert had impressed him with his conscientious attitude and meticulous work. It had taken a bit of administrative diplomacy—including an informal request from the FBI, which also knew and respected Art's work—but Emert had managed to persuade KPD to allow Art to assist with fingerprinting at Novak's house.

As I walked into the living room, Emert handed me a pair of gloves to wear, so I couldn't inadvertently muddy the waters. I didn't plan to touch anything, but just to be on the safe side, I donned the gloves. They'd been at it for over two hours by the time I got there; they'd begun right about the time my nine o'clock Human Identification class was getting started, the students shedding their coats and fortifying themselves with long swigs of mocha-hazelnut-latte-cappuccinos, or Irish coffees, or whatever it was they had in those quart-size Starbucks cups.

The first thing that struck me about Novak's house was how spectacular the view out the back was. The interior of the house had been opened up by knocking out several walls, and while a brick fireplace remained to hint at the original boundary between living room, dining room, and kitchen, the rest of the space flowed around that fireplace like water around a small island, and the flow seemed to empty out a large bank of windows across the back. Twenty miles north, the Cumberland Mountains—still dusted with a snowfall from the prior week—sparkled in the midday sun. The view was framed by a pair of blue spruce trees, sixty or eighty feet tall, which must have been planted shortly after Novak had moved into the house. A long, low built-in desk ran along most of the back wall, with glass-doored bookcases tucked beneath most of its length. An elegant black spindleback chair was pushed back slightly from a yellow notepad that lay at the center of the neat desk; the lettering on the notepad read "Opp," "GK," "Frank," "JJ," and "Alex."

On either side of the notepad were several books. I bent down to check the titles. Two by Richard Rhodes: *The Making of the Atomic Bomb* and *Dark Sun: The Making of the Hydrogen Bomb.* A gray-and-tan textbookish tome titled *The New World: A History of the United States Atomic Energy Agency, Volume 1.* Three books whose titles contained a word I mistook for Verona, the city in Italy, but then realized was actually "Venona" instead. Their subtitles promised shocking revelations about Soviet espionage and atomic spies.

I wandered back around the fireplace, where Emert and Art were studying a glass display case on the mantel. Thornton had migrated to the kitchen with one of the techs. The display case, roughly a foot square and several inches deep, contained two beautiful knives. One had a handle of horn or ivory, intricately carved with Moorish-looking patterns; the other's handle was laminated, layered with many exotic woods, their colors ranging through all the hues of the spectrum. The most remarkable thing about the knives, though, was their blades: the steel had swirls and patterns as rich as red oak, as complex as burled maple. "Fancy knives," I said. "What's that swirly, grainy kind of steel called? Da Vinci?"

"Close," said Art. "Damascus steel. Actually, if you want to split hairs, it's called 'pattern welded.' It's like the baklava of steel—the way you make it is by folding the steel over on itself lots of times, and forging all the layers together, like pastry with zillions of thin layers."

"The baklava of steel? You never cease to amaze me. How do you know this weird stuff?"

Art shrugged. "I've got a cousin in Nashville who's a blacksmith. He makes stuff like this, when he's not shoeing horses for rich country singers who never actually ride."

"So despite the aesthetic beauty of these two knives," said Emert—he emphasized the words "aesthetic beauty," either to make sure we didn't miss his highbrow vocabulary or to let us know he was making fun of the pretentious phrase—"what I find more intriguing is the third knife."

"What third knife? I only see two," I said.

"My point exactly," he said.

I looked at the case again. The knives were each supported by a pair of wooden pegs, one peg under the handle, the other under the edge of the blade. A third set of pegs stood in the center of the case, empty.

"Lots of dust on the case," said Art, "but see there, and there?" He pointed to two smudges on the glass. "Looks like it's been opened fairly recently. How's about I dust that? See if it was Novak or somebody else who did the opening?"

"I knew there was a reason I asked for your help," Emert deadpanned.

"There's some interesting reading material on the desk," I said. "Soviet spies and such. Did you see that?"

"I did," he said. "We took pictures of the notepad and the book titles. Novak checked the books out of the library pretty recently. Thornton was very interested in those. I'm guessing his cohorts up at Bureau headquarters will be, too, since they're already spun up about terrorists and the gamma source."

"Hey, guys?" It was Thornton, calling from the kitchen.

"Yeah," yelled Emert. "Whatcha got?"

"Spoiled milk and rotten vegetables in the fridge," said the agent. "Healthy Choice entrées in the freezer. And Prince Albert in a can, hiding behind the Healthy Choice."

Emert and I looked at each other. "Shit," he said softly, then—louder, to Thornton and whoever was with him in the kitchen—"don't touch it. Let me come check it out with my chirper." The detective reached down to his belt and removed a small, pager-like device. "Personal radiation monitor," he said, checking a small display to be sure the gadget was on. "An active dosimeter, like Duane and Hank wear. That day in the morgue spooked me bad. I don't even let my wife near me without switching this on."

"I bet she really likes it," said Art, "when you tell her she's not hot."

"I might oughta choose my words carefully," he conceded, disappearing around the chimney. A moment later, he said, "It's okay. Let's see if there's anything besides pipe tobacco inside."

Art and I wandered in to see. With five of us in there, the kitchen was getting crowded. The forensic tech was holding a painted tin can bearing the scuffed image of Queen Victoria's bewhiskered, pipe-smoking husband. A small metal key was affixed to the can's rim—a built-in lever to pry the lid off. The tech set the can on the counter and raised the key. The lid seemed stuck. The technician pressed harder and the key began to bend. Finally, just as it seemed that the key would break, the lid popped from the can, cartwheeled through the air, and clattered to the floor. "Smooth," said Emert. "That's good for the evidence."

"Sorry," said the tech.

Emert peered into the can, then picked it up and tilted it toward Art and me. Tucked into the can was what appeared to be a roll of photographic film. "Looks like 35-millimeter, right?"

"Almost, but not quite," I said. "Look at the ends of the canister."

He looked. "What about them?"

"There's no spindle," I said. "I use a 35-millimeter camera to shoot slides at death scenes, so I've loaded lots of film. If you look at the top or the bottom of the film canister, there's this spindle—like an axle—that the film is wound around. When you've finished shooting the roll, a little crank turns the spindle to rewind the film."

He looked puzzled. "So it's not film?"

"Actually, I'm pretty sure it is," I said. "See that slit, in the edge of the canister? It's lined with black felt. That's the opening for the film. The black felt keeps light from leaking in. I think maybe it's just really old film—like, forty or fifty years old."

"So if it is film," Emert said, "is it exposed film or unexposed film? Are there pictures on here, or was he just trying to keep the film from going bad till he got around to using it?"

"It must've been shot," said Art. "If it weren't, there'd be a little tab of film sticking out—the leader, it's called, right?" I nodded.

"So what the hell's he doing keeping it in his freezer all these years," Emert said, "if he's got pictures on there?"

"Dunno," I said. "Maybe if we develop the pictures, we'll have a better idea. You guys got a darkroom?"

He shook his head. "We send things to the TBI lab. But with everything going to digital, they've cut back their photography unit. It might take weeks to get this processed. And if it's some weird old film, I'm not sure they could even do it."

"The Bureau has a pretty good photo lab," said Thornton.

"You know who's great with old photos and film," I said, "is Thompson Photo Products, in Knoxville. Those guys practically eat, sleep, and breathe in black-and-white. If you want me to, I'll drop it by Thompson's on my way back to UT."

"He's right," said Art, "they're the best. Anytime we get in over our heads at KPD on photography stuff, we go to them."

Thornton shrugged. "Fine with me," he said. "It's probably just pictures of the Physics Department picnic back in 1955, but who knows—we might get lucky." Emert sealed the film canister in an evidence bag and handed it to me, then went to the living room and pulled an evidence receipt from the depths of a battered leather briefcase.

I checked my watch. "I should probably head on over there," I said. "I think they close at five, and it's nearly four now."

"Go," he said. "Thanks for playing courier. Let me know what develops." Art and I groaned in unison.

As I walked out the front door, my eye was caught by a small flash of white in the bushes beside the porch. Bending down for a closer look, I saw that it was a wadded-up scrap of paper. I stuck my head back in the door. "Guys? This is probably nothing, but you might want to check it out." Emert came out, inspected the crumpled paper, and asked the tech to bring tweezers. The detective plucked the paper from the shrubbery, took it back inside, and laid it on a small table just inside the door, beside a handful of unopened mail. Wielding the tweezers gently, he teased open the wadded paper. Thornton, Art, and I gathered around and leaned in to look. As the paper unfolded, the inked squiggles became letters, and the letters became words.

The words read, "I know your secret."

10

IT WASN'T OFTEN THAT I attended the funerals of people whose remains I had examined. For one thing, I usually had no sense of connection with them, despite my strange intimacy with their bodies and bones—despite the fact that in most cases, I had handled the very framework of their physical lives. In Novak's case, I had not actually handled his bones; only Garcia had been unfortunate enough to have close, prolonged contact with Novak's remains. Yet at the moment when I realized that Novak had exposed Garcia—and, to a lesser degree, Miranda (and even me) to gamma radiation—the flash of knowledge and concern and fear had seared me with something as emotionally powerful as the radiation, involving me in this case in a unique and powerful way. I wanted to help catch whoever had murdered Novak—assuming it really was a bizarre murder, rather than an even more bizarre suicide. More to the point, I wanted to help catch whoever had put my friends Eddie and Miranda at risk, even though that was surely not intentional. What was the military euphemism for unintended casualties? Collateral damage. Eddie Garcia's bone marrow and hands, and Miranda's fingertips—if Sorensen's worst-case medical scenario unfolded—might be considered minor collateral damage by a killer. But by my heart's reckoning, those would be grievous losses.

The other factor that had drawn me to Oak Ridge for

Novak's funeral was anthropological fascination. As a physical anthropologist, I'd spent years handling the most basic and tangible remnants of human beings: their bones. Human culture, though—the structures built not of calcium or muscle or bricks and boards—had taken a backseat in my mind, except for the dark corners of culture where murder lurked. I knew, for instance, that men were partial to guns as their murder weapons, whereas women seemed to prefer knives or poison (although those traditional gender preferences appeared, in recent years, to be blurring). I knew that homosexuals often engaged in "overkill"—excessive and shocking violence, far beyond what was needed to end a life—if murdering a partner. I had learned that if a child was abducted by a sexual predator, the odds of finding the child alive plummeted after twenty-four hours. The rich drama of healthier human culture, though, had largely played out beyond my field of view, since my field of view was generally filled by images such as the mark left by a knife as it sliced through a rib, or the pattern of fractures radiating through a skull that had been hit repeatedly with a baseball bat.

Years before, I had taken graduate school courses in cultural anthropology. I had journeyed with Franz Boas—figuratively speaking—as he explored the fluid boundaries and social units of Native American tribes in the Pacific Northwest in the 1890s and early 1900s. I had peered over Margaret Mead's shoulder as she had researched the casual sexual couplings of teenagers on the South Pacific island of Samoa in the 1920s. But the unique cultural creation that was Oak Ridge—a small, secret, authority-dominated enclave where tens of thousands of young men and women were treated almost like worker ants in an anthill, except for a handful of military and scientific leaders who possessed the social status and secret knowledge traditionally reserved for an elite caste of high priests: I had never peered at Oak Ridge through the inquiring lens of an anthropologist.

Now, the odd case study that was Oak Ridge all but consumed me. In the handful of days since I had cut a physicist's body from the ice of a murky frozen swimming pool, Oak Ridge had come to occupy most of my waking thoughts and more than a few of my dreams, and one of the things I found amazing was that it had taken so many years—and such a dramatic turn of personal events—to trigger my fascination. It was impossible to live in East Tennessee without knowing that Oak Ridge had played a pivotal role in the Manhattan Project and the creation of the atomic bomb. It was almost as widely understood that in the decades that followed Hiroshima and Nagasaki, Oak Ridge had helped harness atoms for peace, in the form of nuclear power and radioisotopes for medical research and treatment. Beyond those superficial bullet points, though, I had never bothered to read much or *think* much about the opening chapter in the history of Oak Ridge. As I considered it now, I marveled, again and again, how profoundly this tiny city had changed not just the nation but the entire world. Talk about a lever and a place to stand: nuclear energy was about as long and strong as a lever could get—I suppose a poet might argue that love or hatred could be stronger, but as a scientist, I would find that argument somewhat abstract and unconvincing—and Oak Ridge had been the fulcrum, the fixed point around which the lever of the atom had swiveled to move the earth.

Oak Ridge wasn't the only Manhattan Project installation, of course. There was also Los Alamos, New Mexico, where hundreds of physicists and other scientists devoted themselves to turning theoretical physics into deliverable bombs. And there was Hanford, Washington, where mammoth reactors—scaled-up versions of Novak's reactor in Oak Ridge—cranked out the bomb-sized quantities of plutonium. But Oak Ridge was the biggest of the sites, and everything Los Alamos and Hanford did was built on the foundation of Oak Ridge. That alone made the city a fascinating specimen.

But there was more. There was the whole heroic and heartbreaking backdrop to Oak Ridge's creation behind the veil of secrecy: there was World War II. I wasn't born until a decade after Germany and Japan surrendered, so I knew only what I'd read and heard and seen, and that was only a small smattering of the historical record and archival images and firsthand stories. But from what I knew, it truly embodied the best of times and the worst of times; the best of mankind, and the cruelest and most depraved.

The scale of the cruelty and suffering and loss was beyond my comprehension. The most famous number, of course, was six million: the number of Jews killed by the Nazis as they implemented the madness of Hitler's "Final Solution." But tens of millions more had died, too—another forty million civilians, by some reckonings, and twenty-five million soldiers. Although some four hundred thousand U.S. soldiers were killed in three and a half years of fighting—a dreadful toll, to be sure—American losses represented only a tiny fraction of the war's total. In China, the war dead totaled nearly four million soldiers and *sixteen million* civilians as Japan's armies cut a deadly swath through China. The Soviet Union lost twenty million people as well, almost equally divided between soldiers and civilians, as the German army ground itself down in a prolonged and bloody eastern campaign. Seventy-two million deaths, by bombings, firestorms, massacres, diseases, starvation. How was it possible, I wondered, for so many people to die in such a short time without the very fabric of civilization collapsing? And how did the hundreds of millions of grieving survivors carry on in the face of such sorrow?

As my truck topped the rise and dropped once more into the valley where Oak Ridge sprawled, I looked at the place with new eyes. Against a global backdrop of unrelenting, apocalyptic death, this small place, which to modern eyes might look haphazard and provisional and ordinary, had been the focal point of the biggest, most complex, and most urgent endeavor the world had ever known. That endeavor was all the more amazing considering that it was accomplished without the world's knowledge. Until that knowledge had burst, brighter than a hundred suns, above two cities in Japan.

LEONARD NOVAK'S FINAL resting place was barely a stone's throw from his death scene. The funeral was held in the United Church—called the Chapel on the Hill by every Oak Ridger I heard refer to it—the small, historic church perched on the hillside just above the Alexander Inn. It seemed a fitting place to memorialize one of the pivotal scientists of the Manhattan Project. Although Novak had long since retired, and although Emert had said the scientist wasn't a churchgoer, the parking lot beside the church was packed, and even the faded asphalt down beside the derelict hotel was filling fast, with more than a few spots occupied by television news vehicles. Novak's retirement had been a quiet, almost obscure one, according to Emert, but his bizarre death had thrust him squarely into the posthumous spotlight.

I parked in front of the old hotel and made my way up a sidewalk and a long flight of steps to the front door of the chapel.

One of the first public buildings erected during the city's wartime construction boom, the Chapel on the Hill had done its part for the war effort by hosting services of multiple faiths and denominations. Methodists, Baptists, Catholics, Jews—they'd all held weekly services here during the war, each group distributing their prayer books or hymnals just before their appointed hour in the building, then gathering them up again at the end of the service. Church buildings often sit empty and idle most of the time, but not this one. During the war, it would have been hard to find an hour of the day when someone wasn't preaching or praying or practicing on the church's pump organ. I would like to have seen a time-lapse video—one compressing a week's worth of comings and goings into, say, sixty seconds—just to watch the church's doors open and close, the building rhythmically inhaling and exhaling streams of worshipers.

The chapel's interior was packed; three television cameras rested on tripods at the back, and every seat seemed taken. I scanned the pews, seeking any open space, but I didn't see one. In a moment, though, an usher came up the center aisle from near the front of the church and motioned me forward. There were no rows reserved for family—Novak had been married, briefly, as a young man, the newspaper obituary had said, but he had no children—and I found myself shoehorned into the front row, in a slot better suited to someone half my size. The elderly man on my left—I guessed his age at seventy—pretended not to notice me, even as he drew himself in tightly and scooted, fussily but with no noticeable increase in room for me, away from me. To my right, an even older woman—she must have been eighty or more—nodded slightly as I sat down, then surprised me by turning to speak to me. In a stage whisper that could probably have been heard three rows back, she said, "Well, thank God *somebody* here is under sixty. We'll be lucky if three or four of us don't kick the bucket during the service." I wanted to laugh—she might be old, but she seemed sharp and funny—but I managed to limit myself to a smile, since laughter didn't seem to suit the setting or the occasion.

There was no coffin; instead an unadorned brass urn rested on a simple wooden altar. Within hours after the FBI had whisked the iridium source out of Knoxville, Garcia had phoned the state medical examiner's office and they had sent a pathologist from Nashville to complete the autopsy so that Novak's body—which was not getting any fresher—could be removed from the morgue and cremated.

It had taken three people—Garcia, Duane Johnson, and Dr. Sorensen—to convince the Nashville pathologist that Novak's radiation-ravaged body was no more hazardous than any other corpse. I had heard Johnson explaining the physics of it over the phone. "Think of the gamma source like a really strong magnet sitting on your desk," he had said. "There's a powerful energy field emanating from it—a magnetic field surrounding the magnet, gamma radiation around the iridium-192. If the magnet's too close to your computer, your hard drive is gonna be toast. If the gamma source is too close to your body, well . . ." He'd trailed off then, probably regretting his use of the word "toast," given our concerns about Garcia's hands. "Anyhow," he went on, "once you get rid of the source, it's gone. There's no smear of magnetism lingering on your desk, waiting to trash your new hard drive; there's no radioactivity in the sink or the cadaver."

In the end, though, it was probably not the magnet analogy that reassured the nervous Nashville pathologist, but Sorensen's offer to assist in the morgue. It was one thing to say, "It's perfectly safe"; it was another to say, "I'll stand with you while you do this." And for Sorensen, I realized, participating in the remainder of the autopsy was probably an interesting opportunity to learn more about the specific effects of a lethal dose of gamma radiation.

The body had been cremated by my friend Helen Taylor, in one of the gleaming furnaces at East Tennessee Cremation Services. Helen, too, had seemed nervous about handling the body. Taking a cue from Sorensen, I offered to bring the remains out personally; she thanked me for the offer, but said it wasn't necessary. In my head, I knew the remains—and now the cremated remains, or cremains—were perfectly safe. Still, something spooked me about that brass urn on the altar. It was not what was in the urn that spooked me, I gradually realized, but what was in me—some kernel of superstition in my heart, some fear germinating in a dark corner of my psyche. Fear for Garcia and Miranda, perhaps. A sense of bad karma in the air, or spiritual fallout drifting down from the past.

I shook off my thoughts and focused on the lectern, where an ancient man was telling a story about Novak's absentmindedness, which apparently was legendary. "And so we put this lead brick in his briefcase, to see how long it would take him to notice it. He never did. Carried the damn thing around for months." He laughed, and the congregation laughed with him—enjoying his enjoyment, including the naughtiness of saying "damn" in a church. One of the few consolations of old age, I thought: you can say pretty much anything you want, even outrageous things, and people let them slide, or even find them charming. Beside me I felt a slight shift, then noticed my seatmate jotting a note on her program. She finished writing, then nudged me and held the note toward me with a twinkle in her eye. "Not true," the spidery script read. "It was Richard Feynman who lugged that lead brick around, and it was in Los Alamos."

I smiled. I liked her. She seemed both witty and slightly subversive. Her face said eighty, and so did her handwriting, but the note-passing spoke of a mischievous schoolgirl.

After the ancient colleague told a few more anecdotes—some lighthearted, some more serious—a minister took the podium to put Novak's life and work in a philosophical and theological context. He talked about science and discovery—about Galileo and Leonardo da Vinci—whose given name Novak had shared—and Copernicus and Darwin. He reminded us that curiosity was what had called our primordial ancestors out of the sea and onto dry land. I suspected the aforementioned Darwin might have debated him on that; I didn't remember reading much about curiosity in *The Origin of Species*. But this was a sermon, not a lecture, so I took it with a grain of scientific salt. The minister went on awhile about the quest for knowledge being a hallmark of humans. "The divine spark," he called knowledge. "There is no brighter spark than atomic energy," he went on—the transition to Oak Ridge, and to Novak, at last. He told how Novak had guided the construction and operation of the Graphite Reactor; how he'd created plutonium within the crucible of the reactor; how he'd mastered the steps needed to separate and purify this new element. "Unlocking the power of the atom," he said dramatically. "The fire at the core of the universe. Like a twentieth-century Prometheus, Leonard Novak stole fire from the gods." I heard a small, sharp exhalation from the woman beside me; it sounded surprisingly like exasperation. "Stealing fire from the gods," the minister repeated, his voice rising as he got swept up in the mythology. "A bold theft. A world-changing theft. A perilous theft. The gift of fire; the curse of fire." He surveyed the congregation, and stretched forth his arms as if to encompass us. "May we—those of us who dwell in the light and warmth of that Promethean fire"—he now raised his hands toward the ceiling, and the chandeliers glowing there, presumably powered by nuclear energy—"may we acquire the wisdom to harness that fire for good. Always, only for good." He stood silent, his arms still aloft.

"Oh please." It was the stage whisper again, surprisingly loud in the silence that had followed the minister's big finish. I saw a few heads turn in the direction of my elderly seatmate; one of them was the minister's. A look of confusion and anger flashed across his face, then he regained his composure and directed us to a closing hymn. The words were printed in the program, which everyone but me seemed to have received. We stood to sing, feet scraping and throats clearing, as the organist played a stanza to acquaint us with the melody.

The music sounded quaint and prim, like something from another century. I'd never considered myself much of a singer, so I didn't much mind that I couldn't sing along. I did feel slightly self-conscious, though, to be standing amid the singing throng with my mouth closed and my hands empty.

I felt a gentle nudge at my right elbow. My neighbor extended her program slightly toward me. She gripped the lower right corner of the page between a bony thumb and knuckle, her skin papery and blue-veined. She gave the program a slight twitch to indicate that I should take hold of the lower left corner. The paper certainly didn't require both of us to hold it up; rather, the paper was a sort of bridge, a bond, between two strangers jammed together on a wooden pew. It was an oddly intimate gesture. Two strangers bound, by a link and a story, to a brass urn and the ashes within, which had once been Leonard Novak. Together we sang.

Let there be light, Lord God of hosts,
Let there be wisdom on the earth;
Let broad humanity have birth,
Let there be deeds, instead of boasts.

Within our passioned hearts instill
The calm that endeth strain and strife;
Make us thy ministers of life;
Purge us from lusts that curse and kill.

Give us the peace of vision clear
To see our brothers' good our own,
To joy and suffer not alone,
The love that casteth out all fear.

Let woe and waste of warfare cease,
That useful labor yet may build
Its homes with love and laughter filled;
God give thy wayward children peace.

As the words of the hymn sank in, I decided to cut the minister some slack for his overheated delivery. The beginning of the song fit with his "divine spark" image, and the ending—well, I decided it took some guts to close an A-bomb scientist's funeral with an antiwar plea.

I halfway expected to hear a snort or feel a cynical elbow in my ribs at the song's earnest goodheartedness, but I never did. And as the final notes died away, I glanced to my right and saw that the woman beside me—the same woman who had said "Oh, please" just moments before—had tears on her cheeks.

As the service ended, I turned to her. "Thank you for sharing your pew and your program with me."

"You're welcome," she said. "You're Brockton, aren't you?" I nodded, surprised. "You're the guy that watches the bodies rot?"

I laughed. "You do have a way with words. How'd you know? Do I smell that bad?"

"I saw your picture in the *Oak Ridger* a couple of days ago. Here, let's go out the back door. I don't want to have to shake the preacher's hand—it would just embarrass us both." She steered me through a door that led through a cluttered vestry and out into the thin sunshine. Suddenly I stopped in my tracks. Fifty yards ahead of us, walking down the steps and away from the chapel, I saw Jess Carter, my dead lover. I thought I saw her, at any rate: I saw a striking woman wearing Jess's black hair and Jess's lithe body, walking Jess's walk. Then she turned her head enough for me to see that it was not Jess. Of course not: it had been nearly a year since Jess was murdered; I had attended her memorial service in Chattanooga, had seen her ashes buried in a churchyard, had nestled a granite plaque to honor Jess in the ground at the Body Farm, where her corpse had been taken by her killer. How could it possibly be Jess walking ahead of me down a hillside in Oak Ridge?

I felt a tug at my sleeve. My elderly companion was studying my face shrewdly. "You look like you just saw a ghost," she said.

"I thought I did," I said. "Or hoped I did. Sorry. You were saying something about the newspaper."

"Oh, nothing important. Just that I saw your picture in the story about Novak. By the way, I gather that when you came to fetch the body, you left a souvenir behind, in about eight feet of water." Her eyes were dancing as she pointed a crooked finger at the swimming pool, a hundred yards downslope from where we stood.

"They wrote about my chainsaw?" I meant to sigh but it came out as a laugh. "I wish they'd hurry up and drain that pool."

"Don't hold your breath," she said.

"Oh, it's starting to warm up," I said, although I noticed that the rectangular opening I had cut in the surface had refrozen. "It'll probably thaw out enough to drain in another couple of days."

"It's not just the ice," she said. "It'll be a miracle if the drain still works. That whole place is falling apart."

Even from this distance, the inn's peeling paint and sagging roof were easy to see. So was the murky ice. "It has seen better days."

"Haven't we all," she said, "haven't we all. That crumbling hotel pretty much sums up Oak Ridge, and all of us who've been here since the creation. We used to be young and smart and important—crossroads of the world, at least the world of atomic physics. Look at us now. The glory days are long gone. In a few more years, that hotel will be dust. And so will all the famous people who sat on the porch and figured out how to build the bomb fifty years ago. No, sixty years ago. No, sixty-five, dammit. Oppenheimer, Fermi, Lawrence—they've been gone a long time. Novak was one of the last. They don't seem to make them like that anymore."

"So you knew him?"

"It was a long, long time ago," she said, "but yes, I did. There's a story in it. Would you like to hear it sometime?"

"I believe I would," I said. "I'm guessing you spin a pretty good story."

"Come see me," she said, "and we'll find out."

She dug around in a small pocketbook and fished out a pen. Folding the photocopied program from the memorial service in half to make it stiffer, she wrote her name, address, and phone number and handed the paper to me.

"Beatrice Novak," the name read.

My eyes widened. She smiled slightly. "I was married to him," she said. "Once upon a time."

11

I WASN'T READY TO leave Oak Ridge yet—I wanted to steep myself a little longer in the sepia-toned sense of history Novak's funeral had stirred up—so I drove past the strip malls lining Oak Ridge Turnpike and turned in at the American Museum of Science and Energy, a blocky, mud-colored brick building beside the police station. The sidewalk outside the building was edged with spiky components from coal-mining machines and oil-drilling rigs. Inside—through a doorway bordered by barbed wire and a replica of a World War II sentry post—a series of photos and videos and documents told the story of the Manhattan Project. One display panel featured scratchy footage of Albert Einstein, instantly recognizable from the wild mop of fuzzy white hair, captured on film writing a letter. Alongside the video monitor was an enlarged copy of the letter Einstein had sent to President Franklin D. Roosevelt in August 1939, voicing concern about Germany's atomic-energy research and recommending that the United States embark on a quest to build an atomic bomb. Although it would be two years before much would happen, Einstein's letter had planted a seed, and—at least in historical hindsight—was part of the bomb's scientific pedigree.

What interested me most in the darkened room, though, were the wartime photos documenting the creation and wartime years of the town that came to be known as Oak

Ridge. In three short years, a handful of rural settlements—family farms, country stores, rustic schoolhouses—was transformed into the biggest scientific and military endeavor in the history of the world.

An elderly museum docent wandered through, possibly because I looked like an unsavory character, but more likely because I was the only visitor and the docent was bored. "These photos are amazing," I said.

"They have copies of all of these, plus a lot more down at the library," he said. "In the Oak Ridge Room, which is the local history collection. If you're interested, it's worth a look. It's in the Civic Center, just down the hill." He pointed toward the back wall of the room, and I remembered seeing a pair of buildings, linked by an outdoor plaza and a fountain, set in a park below the police station. I thanked him and resumed wandering through the displays, which culminated in a short black-and-white film on the flight of the *Enola Gay,* the B-29 Superfortress bomber that lumbered aloft from an airfield on the island of Tinian in the predawn hours of August 6, 1945. Many hours later and ten thousand pounds lighter, the *Enola Gay* returned to Tinian, having dropped a single bomb on Hiroshima, Japan. Almost as an afterthought, the film included a brief segment on the decimation, three days later, of Nagasaki by a second atomic bomb. Two entire cities had been reduced to rubble, and many thousands of people vaporized, in the blink of an eye. And although the bombs that destroyed Hiroshima and Nagasaki were small—scarcely firecrackers, compared to the massive hydrogen bombs developed during the 1950s and 1960s—the images of unprecedented devastation weighed on my heart.

Wandering out of the darkened history room and into the brighter light of the lobby, I lifted a hand in goodbye to the docent. "We have other exhibits," he called after me. "Nuclear power, petroleum, renewable energy, neutron research."

"Another time," I said. "Today, I'm in history mode." I pushed through the glass doors, passed the mining and drilling machinery, and ambled down the long, gentle hill toward the Civic Center and the library. In the foreground was an outdoor stage topped by a gleaming white tent of some high-tech architectural fabric. Far off to one side was another, smaller pavilion of some sort, this one a rustic structure framed of wood timber. Curious, I decided to take a closer look. The structure's gabled roof and heavy beams reminded me of a Japanese temple, and as I drew near, I saw an immense bell—long and cylindrical, rather than wide at the base—suspended from the trusswork. Beside the bell was a plaque. FRIENDSHIP BELL, the words read. It had been cast in Japan in 1993, the fiftieth anniversary of the birth of Oak Ridge. A SYMBOL OF THE FRIENDSHIP AND MUTUAL REGARD THAT HAVE DEVELOPED BETWEEN OAK RIDGE AND JAPAN OVER THE PAST FIFTY YEARS, it went on. FRIENDSHIP MADE SO MUCH MORE MEANINGFUL BECAUSE OF THE TERRIBLE CONFLICT OF WORLD WAR II WHICH OAK RIDGE PLAYED SUCH A SIGNIFICANT ROLE IN ENDING. I was particularly struck by the plaque's final words: THIS BELL FURTHER SERVES AS A SYMBOL OF OUR MUTUAL LONGING AND PLEDGE TO WORK FOR FREEDOM, WELL-BEING, JUSTICE, AND PEACE FOR ALL THE PEOPLE OF THE WORLD IN THE YEARS TO COME. Oak Ridge had come a long way, I reflected, turning my steps toward the library.

The library, like its companion building, was a contemporary structure—1970s, I guessed—made of poured, putty-colored concrete topped by bands of clerestory windows. The forms for the concrete had been lined with rough-sawn vertical boards, and the grain of the wood was etched into the concrete. Maybe it was just the reflective mood I was in, but I liked the notion that the wood's contribution—brief but important—had been captured for posterity in the structure's very bones.

Inside, I stopped at the circulation desk to ask about the

local history room. "Yes, the Oak Ridge Room," said the young woman at the counter. "It's right back there." She pointed toward a back corner of the building. I thanked her and headed that way.

The room had been partitioned off from the main area by glass walls and glass doors. Inside, I saw brimming bookshelves, tall filing cabinets, flat map drawers, and a shelving unit crammed with fat, black binders. If it was local history I was hungry for, the Oak Ridge Room appeared to offer an all-you-can-eat buffet. I took hold of the handle of one of the glass doors and tugged. It rattled but did not open. I tugged on the other door's handle. Nothing doing.

"Try pushing," said a female voice behind me. I pushed. Still nothing. "Oh. I guess the lock works after all," said the voice. I turned and saw a woman with black hair and laughing eyes. "Sorry," she said. "I couldn't resist. You looked so serious." I stared at her, and her amusement turned to concern. "Really, I'm sorry," she said. "I didn't mean to offend you. I just thought—"

"No, no," I said quickly. "It's not about the door. The door . . . the door thing was funny. It's just that for a second there, you reminded me of someone." The librarian—Isabella Morgan, according to a plastic nameplate pinned to her sweater—was the woman I'd glimpsed earlier in the day; the woman who made me think I'd seen a ghost. "Weren't you at Dr. Novak's funeral?"

She looked startled. "Yes," she said. There was a pause, and then she added—awkwardly, I thought—"speaking of local history." I introduced myself, and told her about cutting Novak's body from the ice of the swimming pool. "Oh right," she said. "Your picture was in the *Oak Ridger.* You're the one with the chainsaw."

I laughed. "Actually, I'm the one *without* the chainsaw, as everyone keeps reminding me. Anyhow, I've gotten interested in the city's history. I was hoping to browse around in the Oak Ridge Room for a bit."

She reached into a pocket of her sweater and pulled out a key. "Browse away," she said. "Anything in particular I can help you find?"

"Hmm. Well, a guy up at the museum said you've got a whole bunch of World War II photographs. Might be fun to look through those, if they're easy to get to."

She pointed to the shelves of fat three-ring binders. "Easiest thing in the room to find," she said. "It's a remarkable collection."

"From the ones I saw in the museum," I said, "it looks like the photographer started snapping pictures before the Army even set foot here."

"Just about," she said. "It's almost like he wanted to show how the prophecy came true."

"The prophecy? What prophecy?"

"You don't know about the prophecy?"

"I guess not," I said. "What prophecy?"

"Around 1900," she said, "a local mystic predicted the creation of Oak Ridge and the role the city would play in World War II."

"Some hillbilly a century ago knew about uranium enrichment and plutonium production? So *that's* where Fermi and Oppenheimer and Einstein got the idea?"

She smiled. "Well, he didn't go into details about the physics and chemistry," she said. "John Hendrix was his name; he was a preacher who was considered a bit of a crackpot. He also drank a bit, they say."

"Helps the sermons flow more trippingly off the tongue," I said. "Or gives you more knowledge of sin, maybe."

"The story goes," she went on, "that John Hendrix heard a voice telling him to sleep in the woods and pray for forty days and forty nights."

"That's a lot of praying," I said.

She nodded. "On the forty-first day, he emerged and told some people at a little country store that he'd had a vision." She took down a well-worn book—*Back of Oak Ridge*—

and opened it to a page near the front. "Here's what he said: 'There will be a city on Black Oak Ridge'—that's the ridge where all the World War II housing was built—'and the center of authority will be on a spot middle-way between Sevier Tadlock's farm and Joe Pyatt's place.' " I was about to ask who Sevier Tadlock and Joe Pyatt were, but—as if reading my mind—she held up a finger to shush me. "He said, 'A railroad spur will branch off the main L&N line, run down toward Robertsville, and then branch off and turn toward Scarboro. Big engines will dig big ditches, and thousands of people will be running to and fro. They will be building things, and there will be great noise and confusion, and the earth will shake.' But here's the best part, where he talks about Bear Creek Valley, where the Y-12 Plant was built: 'Bear Creek Valley someday will be filled with great buildings and factories, and they will help toward winning the greatest war that ever will be.' " She paused just long enough to let that sink in, then read one more line: " 'I've seen it. It's coming.' "

She closed the book slowly, then looked at me over her glasses, her eyebrows rising to ask, *Well?*

To my surprise, the words had sent a bit of a shiver along my spine. By this stage of my life, I had become a bit of a skeptic when it came to matters of metaphysics. I dealt in scientific and forensic facts—grim facts, at that—and the comforting words of organized religion ignored a lot of suffering. My faith had also been pretty thoroughly undermined by the unmerited suffering and death of my wife Kathleen a few years before. Nevertheless, I had to admit that occasionally I encountered phenomena that science seemed unable to explain. This prophecy appeared to be another of those.

"He said that in 1900? Forty years before the bulldozers showed up?"

"Somewhere around there. And he died in 1915, so it's not like he saw it unfold, then stepped forward after the fact and claimed, 'Oh yeah, I had a vision about this a long time ago.' It's been pretty well documented that he came out of the woods wild-eyed, talking about factories and engines and winning a big war."

"And the bit about Tadlock and Pyatt?"

"Their farms straddled the little hill where the Manhattan Project headquarters was built," she said. "During the war, it was a huge wooden building nicknamed 'the castle on the hill.' In the 1970s, DOE—the Department of Energy—built a concrete and glass building on the same site. So it's still what Hendrix called 'the center of authority,' even today."

"And the railroad spur?"

"Goes right past his grave," she said. "Within a mile or so of the Y-12 Plant."

I nodded. "Sounds like Hendrix got it right," I said. "A lot more specific than the psychics who call up the police and say, 'I see a body in a dark, damp place.' Did he predict the Friendship Bell, too?"

She laughed—a musical laugh that reminded me of pealing bells—and I felt another tingle along my spine. "No, he didn't look that far ahead," she said, "though it seems like he should have, since he talked about great wars." Seeing my puzzled look, she explained. "There was a big controversy about the bell," she said. "The Peace Bell, most people call it. Some locals thought it was a slap in the face of everyone who'd worked on the Manhattan Project. Too much like an apology. There was even a lawsuit by some folks who claimed it was a religious shrine, and shouldn't be on public property. The controversy seems to have died down by now, though."

"Maybe because most of the people who worked on the bomb are dying down, too," I said. She gave me an odd, sharp look, and I wished I'd been more tactful.

"If you need anything, I'll be at the Reference Desk," she said, pointing to the other side of the reading room. She left me flipping through photos of bulldozers and cranes and trucks mired to their axles in mud. But the image that most occupied my mind's eye was the image of the black-haired, brown-eyed librarian reading me the prophecy of Oak Ridge and its role in winning "the greatest war that ever will be."

I hoped that the future would prove John Hendrix to be as accurate on that last point as he'd already been on the others.

12

THE MORNING AFTER THE funeral, I woke up feeling more energetic than I had in days. Maybe that was because I'd gotten a solid night's sleep, uninterrupted by needles jabbing me for blood. Or maybe it was because I'd had a nice dream about the librarian in Oak Ridge. I got to campus by seven, stopped off in the bone lab to leave some notes for Miranda, then spent a couple of hours grading the first Human Origins test of the semester.

At eleven Peggy called. "Don't forget the talk you're giving at lunchtime."

"Which talk I'm giving at lunchtime?"

Even through the receiver, her exasperated sigh carried clearly. "Rotary Club."

"Oh, the Rotary talk," I said. "Sure. I remembered. You had me worried for a second there. I was afraid maybe you'd double-booked me."

"I am *never* the one who double-books you," she said tartly.

At eleven-thirty I left campus and drove to the Marriott. The Marriott was an architectural oddity—a concrete wedge that looked like a cross between a Mayan pyramid and a misplaced hydroelectric dam—perched on a hill above the river. Townes Osborn, who had booked me for the talk, was waiting at the entrance when I arrived. Despite her questionable taste in luncheon speakers, Townes—who ran a prominent advertising agency—was the only woman ever elected president of the Knoxville Rotary Club.

After the Rotarians lunched on orange-glazed chicken breast and rice pilaf and whatever vegetable medley was the current fashion among civic groups, I showed slides from a case I'd worked near Nashville some years ago. The Williamson County Sheriff's Office had received a call expressing concern about a well-to-do middle-aged woman who lived alone in a mansion on thirty or forty acres. She hadn't made the trip down the driveway to the mailbox in more than a week, said the observant neighbor, and although her car was parked at the house, she wasn't answering the phone. A deputy was duly dispatched to check on the woman. She didn't come when he rang the bell, but the door was unlocked, so he turned the knob and opened it to call out to her. When he did, the woman's three large dogs—two German shepherds and a collie—bolted past him and into the yard.

The woman was nowhere to be seen—at least not in recognizable human form. The story, as we quite literally pieced it together, was this: The woman, who had a serious heart condition, had died, and with no other source of sustenance available, her dogs had eaten her body to stay alive. Combing the house, my students and I found only the cranial vault, the well-chewed shafts of a few long bones, and one painted toenail—just one—which the dogs had turned up their noses at for some odd reason. As the Rotarians chuckled, I thought about the shipwrecked man eating what he believed to be albatross. The dog story had a bizarre postscript: a couple of weeks later, a woman called me from a Nashville bank to ask, "Did you happen to find a seven-thousand-dollar diamond ring in that house?" I did not, I assured her. The bank, it seems, had insured the ring, and if it couldn't be found, they'd have to pay the sum to the dead woman's estate.

"There is one other place the ring might be," I said. The woman was excited to hear this. "You know she was eaten by her dogs," I said. She gasped; apparently she had not heard this minor detail. "If you could get someone to collect all the dog crap and sift through it, there's a chance they'd find that ring." She thanked me profusely and hung up. Two days later, a Williamson County deputy appeared in my classroom with a bag containing thirteen pounds of dog turds. The deputy looked quite unhappy, so I assumed he'd been the one assigned to collect the . . . evidence. His countenance brightened considerably when I told him that every single turd would have to be carefully squeezed between the fingers of my students. Misery really does love company, I concluded when I saw him grin. Once he was gone, I sent the bag of dog crap to be X-rayed. There was no ring to be seen, though I did notice a tangle of undigested panty hose in the bag—containing another toenail snagged in one stocking foot. "Next time you see your dog looking at you with love and devotion," I concluded, "remember, he might be thinking about a snack." The Rotarians laughed and clapped.

During the Q&A session at the end of the talk, Townes asked about Dr. Novak's death, since the story—including the wild speculation about the "polonium" that had supposedly killed him—had been splashed all over the media. "I can't really talk about that case," I said, "since it's still an open investigation. All I'll say is that I'm saving a lot on my light bill these days, since I now glow in the dark." The joke drew a few groans but a fair number of laughs.

As I was packing up my slide projector afterward, an elderly man who'd been sitting near the front of the room approached. "I worked in Oak Ridge during the war," he said. I was surprised; he had some years on him, but he looked strong and vigorous still.

"Didn't they have child-labor laws back then? You don't look old enough to have worked in Oak Ridge during the war."

He ignored the transparent flattery. "I was in charge of security," he said, and my head snapped up. Funny: you see a ninety-year-old at a Rotary Club luncheon, you tend to see him just as some old codger with a lot of hours to fill. You don't tend to look at him and think, *I bet this guy once helped guard atomic secrets at the world's biggest military project.* I didn't say that, of course; I just said, "That was a big job. Must have been tough."

He shook his head. "Sure beat the hell out of dying on some Jap-infested island in the Pacific," he said. "I knew I'd live to see the end of the war. And we were working on something that was supposed to help end the war, so I figured I was probably in the best-defended place on earth. I felt like a lucky guy." I nodded.

"Did you know what you were protecting?"

He shrugged. "We didn't talk about it," he said. "One of the MPs did, and a day later he was gone, just like that." He snapped his fingers. "They sent him to the Pacific. They didn't dare send him to Europe, because they didn't want to take a chance that the Germans would capture him and get some information out of him. Poor bastard was probably dead three months later." He hesitated, studying me closely, as if to determine whether I was trustworthy. "By the summer of '45, I had a pretty good idea what they were building. But I kept my mouth shut, because I wanted to stay right here."

We chatted a bit more, then he excused himself. Townes, who'd been talking to several power-suited women, came over to carry my slide carousel to the truck. I said, "Do you know that guy I was talking to? He was in charge of security in Oak Ridge back during the war."

She smiled. "You might say I know him," she said. "That's Bill Sergeant. He spent twelve years spearheading Rotary International's global campaign to eradicate polio. There's a statue of Bill downtown in Krutch Park."

On the way back to campus, I detoured through downtown and parked—briefly—in front of a fire hydrant beside Krutch Park. Seated in the southwest corner, a strong-limbed child perched on his lap, was a life-size bronze statue of a lucky, modest old codger.

13

THREE DAYS AFTER THE morgue disaster, Dr. Sorensen had data from dozens of blood samples and urine samples, which he'd gathered to track lymphocyte levels and DNA damage in our cells. That data, combined with the incident timelines we'd compiled, helped him refine his initial estimate of our exposures. He'd been surprisingly close that evening in the ER: Emert had gotten "only" 18 to 24 rads; Miranda and I, 25 to 35 rads; and Garcia, 380 to 520 rads. The lymphocyte counts for everyone but Garcia had dropped only slightly, remaining well within the range considered normal. Garcia's lymphocytes, however, had plummeted: at his first blood draw, his lymphocyte count was a robust 2,950, a number that corresponded to the nearly three billion white cells in every liter of his blood. Twenty-four hours later, it had fallen to 1100, and at the forty-eight-hour blood sample, it was hovering at 600. His bone marrow was dying, and his immune system was shutting down. According to Sorensen, Garcia was almost certain to develop acute radiation syndrome, probably a severe case. The unspoken subtext of "severe" was that he might not survive.

Garcia had been shifted to a reverse-isolation room—a "bubble" room, I'd heard it called—as even minor infections could prove fatal to him. The air was filtered and the room was pressurized so outside air couldn't seep in. Still, Miranda and I made it a point to visit the hospital once or twice a day, waving to him through the glass window and talking to him on the intercom. The second morning of his ICU stay, we entered the unit and came upon Carmen Garcia, slumped in a chair in the hallway, her face in her hands, her shoulders shaking. Miranda sat on one side of Carmen, I sat on the other, and we wrapped our arms around her as she wept. When her sobs finally stopped, she reached up and laid one hand briefly on Miranda's cheek, the other on my cheek, and then she rose and walked toward the elevators. None of us had said a word. After she was gone, Miranda and I went to Eddie's window. Switching on the intercom microphone and then kneeling down on the concrete floor, we put sock puppets on our hands and enacted a three-minute Punch-and-Judy routine, one that spoofed ourselves arguing in the bone lab about whether a mystery bone was from a human or a blowfly. Miranda's sock puppet was a caricature of me, and mine was a red-haired sock version of Miranda. She dropped her voice half an octave and did her best impression of a pompous but clueless professor, while I affected a falsetto and sang the praises of Google and Wikipedia and left-wing liberalism. After it was done, and Garcia had called "bravo!" and pretended to applaud with his bandaged hands, and told us what attentive care he was receiving, we said goodbye. In the hallway, Miranda sank into a chair—the same chair we'd found Carmen in—and wept on my shoulder.

EMERT AND THORNTON had both interviewed Novak's former wife, the woman I'd met at the funeral, and both had come away empty-handed, they reported in a three-way teleconference. Emert was of the opinion that she had Alzheimer's disease—"She kept asking me who I was," he said, "and then talking to me like I was her son, saying 'Mommy this' and 'Mommy that.' She said she'd never heard of anybody named Leonard Novak." Thornton hadn't fared much better; she'd told him she used to know someone named Lenny, but she couldn't quite remember where or when or how.

"I don't get it," I said. "That woman was sharp as a tack when I talked to her at Novak's funeral. She was lucid, she was irreverent, she was funny. She even noticed that I got spooked for a second, when I thought I saw Jess. A woman I lost."

"I think maybe the old gal's sweet on you," said Emert.

"I think maybe Emert's right," said Thornton. "And I think maybe you should see if you can get more out of her than we did. Find out what she knows about Novak, and who might have killed him, and why."

"And what 'I know your secret' meant," added Emert.

And so it was, after that conversation and a call to the phone number Beatrice had scrawled on the funeral program, that I found myself winding up Black Oak Ridge in search of her house.

I passed the house twice before I found it. It was set back off the street and down a slight slope, tucked amid hemlock trees and rhododendron bushes. It was a low, flat-roofed house with wide, overhanging eaves; judging by the clean lines, the ample windows, and the warm redwood siding, I guessed that it dated from the 1960s. It reminded me of the houses designed by Frank Lloyd Wright, who was famous for blending houses into their natural settings.

Stepping beneath them onto the flagstones bordering the front wall, I felt myself entering a zone of shelter, of sanctuary. The door—a large red slab flanked by narrow sidelights and shielded by a glass storm door—nestled within the corner of an L, and the roofline angled across the corner, creating a triangular porch at the entryway. The walkway and porch were bordered by low irregular terraces of river rock and creeping juniper. A small, artificial stream tumbled down the rocks and into a pool at the doorway. To reach the door, I crossed a huge flagstone—it must have weighed a thousand pounds or more—that bridged the pool. *Now this,* I thought, *this is an entrance.*

Beside the door, suspended from a curlicue bracket of wrought iron, hung a bell with a leather cord dangling from its clapper. I gave the cord a tentative tug, and the clapper swung gently, barely tapping the bell. I gave a stronger pull, and the clapper struck with a pure, high ring, the sort of ethereal chime you might hear wafting down from some Tibetan monastery high in the Himalayas. I waited a moment, listening for footsteps, but heard none. *She's eighty-five years old*, I reminded myself, *give her a minute.* Still no one came, so I rapped more loudly on one of the sidelights. Still no footsteps. Feeling slightly furtive, I tried the handle on the glass storm door. It was unlocked, as was the red wooden door. I eased it open just far enough to lean my head inside and called out, "Hello? Mrs. Novak?"

"Yes?" The voice had a slight quaver to it.

"It's Dr. Brockton. We spoke on the phone."

"I know we did. I might be ancient, but I'm not senile."

I smiled. Yes, she was sharp all right. "Should I come in?"

"Unless you'd rather stay outside and shout," she said, sounding simultaneously amused and exasperated, crusty and playful. "Follow my voice." I stepped inside and found myself in a low-ceilinged foyer, its walls paneled with the same warm redwood as the home's exterior. The floor was terrazzo, a glassy-smooth mosaic of marble chips set into concrete and polished to a soft lustre of green, red, black, and ivory. "I was beginning to think maybe you'd stood me up."

Her voice, together with a broad track of reflected daylight, led me to a wide doorway. When I stepped through it, the space opened up dramatically, and I blinked from both the brightness and the unexpectedness of it. "Oh my," I heard myself saying, "this is wonderful."

"Yes," she said. "I designed it to be wonderful. Back when wonderful was still a possibility."

It took me a moment to find her, just as it had taken some

effort to find her house. She was sitting in a high, wing-backed chair that nearly enveloped her; the chair was off to one side of a large living room, facing a wall of glass that looked out into the woods behind the house. The polished floor extended seamlessly beyond the glass and onto a large terrace; the terrace was partly sheltered beneath a high, wide roof overhang; the overhang was made of the same tongue-and-groove redwood as the walls and eaves of the house. Together, the architectural elements and their blurred transitions—the seamless floor, the wall of glass, and the unbroken planes of redwood—conspired to hide the boundary between indoors and out, and if not for the warmth in the sun-drenched room, I'd have been hard pressed to say whether the space was enclosed or not.

"Looks like wonderful is still possible," I said, walking to the side of her chair, "at least in here. It's Dr. Brockton, Mrs. Novak. Thank you for letting me come see you."

"Letting you? I practically twisted your arm out of the socket. Do you have any idea how seldom I have company? Almost everyone I used to know is dead or dying. It's depressing as hell. By the way, I haven't been Mrs. Novak in sixty years. Novak was three husbands ago. It's Montgomery now, and Mr. Montgomery kicked the bucket quite a while back. So call me Beatrice, unless you want to remind me I'm old and make me cranky."

"I'd hate to make you cranky, Beatrice," I said.

"It wouldn't be in your best interest," she agreed. "Sit down, and tell me what it is you want to know. The tea should still be hot—I made it about five minutes ago." A large mug sat on a table between the two chairs, and wisps of steam wafting up from it caught the slanting afternoon light. Beside the mug was a small china plate that held two round, golden cookies. "The cookies are Scottish shortbread," she said. "Butter and flour and sugar. If you don't want them, throw them out for the birds, because I'm not supposed to have them."

I headed to the rocker but stopped before sitting down. "You're not having any tea? Can I get you anything else—some water, maybe?"

"Water? Never touch the damn stuff," she said. "I'll have some vodka when it's cocktail hour."

"When's that?"

"Five," she said. "What time is it now?"

I glanced at my watch; I was about to tell her it was three forty-five when the note of teasing and hopefulness in her voice registered with me. "This watch is not worth a damn," I fibbed. "It eats a battery once a week."

She laughed. "Dear me, you are a smooth one," she said. "Too bad I'm not forty years younger. I'd make you fall desperately in love with me. You're an interesting fellow, Dr. Brockton."

"Call me Bill," I said, "unless you want to make me cranky."

She smiled, then tilted her face toward the window and closed her eyes; the low sun highlighted the wrinkles left by decades of laughter and pain, but underneath I could discern the planes of a younger woman's face. "That sun looks like a five-o'clock sun to me," she said. "Close enough, anyway. The vodka's on the bookshelf behind you. Pour me two fingers' worth, would you, Bill? There's ice in the ice bucket. Join me if you like."

"I'd better not," I said. "I can tell I need to keep my wits about me when I'm with you." I didn't see any point in telling her that I didn't drink alcohol; she might think I disapproved of drinking, and that wasn't the case. Rather, having spent years battling Menier's disease, I tended to steer clear of anything that had the remotest chance of making me dizzy.

A crystal decanter, silver ice bucket, tongs, and two tumblers sat on a silver tray on a waist-high counter running the length of the back wall. Below the counter were cabinets; above it were bookshelves containing hundreds of volumes, ranging from small paperbacks to large leatherbound volumes. I wondered if she'd read them all. I put a few ice cubes into a tumbler, then poured the vodka from the decanter, catching a whiff of orange in the liquor. Did "two fingers" mean with or without the ice, I wondered, but I hated to betray my ignorance by asking. Without, I decided, and kept pouring, since the ice alone filled at least one finger's worth of space.

One end of the counter held a cluster of framed photographs, and as I delivered the vodka, I detoured past the pictures. A half dozen or so in number, they were all in black-and-white, and I guessed by the clothing and hairstyles that they were from the 1940s. Suddenly I recognized one of the photos: I had seen it in the museum and the library the day of Novak's funeral. It showed a striking young woman perched at a console of dials and levers, and in the five seconds it took me to walk back to the chairs with Beatrice's drink, I realized that the pretty girl in the photo had the same cheekbones and jawline as the old woman facing the fading light. "That's you in the picture," I said.

"Not anymore," she said. "That was a lifetime ago. But back during the war, I was the calutron poster girl."

"What's a calutron?"

"A California University cyclotron," she said. "Invented by Ernest Lawrence, the Nobel laureate physicist from Berkeley. We used them at Y-12 to separate uranium-235 for the bomb. We weren't told that's what we were doing, of course. The foreman just told us to watch the gauges and twist the dials to keep the needles centered. So I watched and I twisted. And atom by atom, I was separating the isotopic wheat from the chaff, you might say. I was a winnower, Bill, on the threshing floor of the atomic barn."

I held out the tumbler to her, and I noticed a slight tremor in the hand that took it. The sunlight caught the ice cubes and made them glow, like golden, living things. Beatrice's skin was translucent in the sunlight; through it, I could see the spiderwork of thin purple veins, and—underneath—the withering strings of muscle and tendon. I almost thought I could see bone, too, but perhaps I was imagining it. She drew a deep breath, blew it out, and then took a sip of vodka. "I was a beauty once," she said, pointing with her glass toward the photograph. She didn't say it boastfully; it was a statement of fact, with a layer of nostalgia underneath. "As I said, that was a lifetime ago. I'm not that girl anymore. But oh, the stories I could tell you about her."

"Tell me one," I said, settling into the rocker. "Tell me the story of how she met and married Leonard Novak."

With that, she began to speak, and her words began to weave a spell.

14

ONCE UPON A TIME, *Bill, Oak Ridge blazed with brilliance and vitality, and Leonard Novak and I burned at the heart of the flame.*

It wasn't just the work; in fact, for most of us, the work was the dull, dreary part; the hours were long and the work was backbreaking or mind-numbing. It seems exciting and glamorous now, but back then, only a handful of people knew our place in the grand scheme of things. The top military leaders, like General Groves and Colonel Nichols, saw the big picture; so did the senior scientists, like Oppenheimer and Fermi and Lawrence, although those three never lived here; they just descended on Oak Ridge now and again, like visiting heads of state. Of the hundreds of scientists in Oak Ridge, Novak was one of the very few who grasped what this vast, desperate endeavor was all about.

The other eighty thousand of us were grunts; we saw only our own tiny little speck of work, and we had no idea what it meant. So I spent eight hours a day, six days a week, staring at needles and twisting knobs. Other people spent fifty or sixty hours a week pouring concrete or bulldozing mud or fitting pipe or welding. When we weren't working, we spent a lot of time standing in lines. Lines to clock in, lines to clock out. Lines to buy groceries—groceries that sometimes ran out before the line did. Lines to buy cigarettes. People would see a line and queue up, sometimes not even knowing what the line was for, because if other people were in line, there must be something worth lining up for. It was like something out of a Charlie Chaplin film, the one where Chaplin is reduced to a human cog in a huge assembly line.

You'd think we'd have been exhausted, ready to tumble into bed after so much drudgery, but we weren't. For me, staring at those two dials all day, every day created a pent-up energy, like static electricity. The tedium was exhausting, but at the end of my shift, something in me would wake up, and I'd be ready to stay up half the night. And thousands of other pent-up young people were happy to stay up with me.

The Central Rec Hall was near the middle of what was called Townsite—Jackson Square now, a couple of blocks below Chapel on the Hill. There must have been a dozen or so dormitories within a few blocks of the rec hall, and each dorm housed hundreds of young men and women, most of them single. So the rec hall was jammed every night, all night. Right around midnight, about the time the day-shift workers would start running out of steam, the people who worked evening shift would clock out and come pouring into the rec hall and stay till dawn, and just as they were staggering off to catch some sleep, the graveyard-shift workers would come in. On weekends, the dance floor would be so crowded you could barely move.

One night in the spring of 1944, my roommate Roxanne and I walked in figuring we'd do a little jitterbugging to Glenn Miller records, but instead, there was a guy singing and playing the piano. He looked sophisticated and older—twenty-five, maybe all of thirty; can you believe that? These days Oak Ridge is full of fossils like me, but back then, nearly everybody here was under thirty. Construction workers had to be young and strong to do the manual labor, and scientists had to be young and mentally agile to do the mental gymnastics. I was twenty; most of the girls I worked with had just graduated from high school.

Roxanne and I worked our way up to the front of the room, but it took a while, because we had to wiggle between scores of men to get up there, and the men didn't want to make it too easy for us to get past them. Oak Ridge in the early forties was like a Gold Rush boomtown back in the 1800s; there were fifteen or twenty men to every woman in Oak Ridge during the war, so it was always easy to get dates—some gals would double- or triple-book, starting one date at eight, another at ten, and another at midnight. But the sad truth was, what Oak Ridge had in quantity, it lacked in quality. Lots of the men were just dumb louts—fine if you wanted to dig a foundation, bulldoze a road, or tangle in a darkened doorway, but if you were looking for more, the wheat-to-chaff ratio was about as low as the ratio of U-235 to U-238.

Up close the guy at the piano looked kind of fancy. He was wearing a coat and tie, he had round, horn-rimmed glasses and wavy, combed-back hair. He looked brainy and the music he was playing went along with the look—Cole Porter. Porter's lyrics are clever and suggestive, and you could tell by the singer's inflections and eyebrow wiggles that he knew what all the double-entendres meant. But underneath the glitter, Porter was deeply cynical—like a cocktail party that sounds fun until you really listen, and then you start to hear the anger and desperation lurking beneath the laughter and clinking ice cubes. After half a dozen songs of sparkling, witty cynicism I was beginning to lose interest, but then he launched into something soft and mournful. The crowd's chatter had gotten a little louder as the set stretched on, and the first few bars of the piano were drowned out, but pretty soon everybody shut up. I'm not exaggerating, you could hear people near the back of the room shushing folks behind them so they could hear the song, a wistful number about romantic disillusionment called "Love for Sale."

I looked at Roxanne, and the look in her eyes was the same bittersweet look I felt in mine as he sang it. I looked back at the singer, and suddenly his gaze locked on me, another pair of eyes that had already seen a lifetime worth of loss. "Old love, new love, every love but true love." By the time he got to the end he was almost whispering, and he finished the song with a soft piano flourish that drifted up into the rafters like cigarette smoke. Before the notes had completely died away, he'd risen from the bench, stepped out of the circle of light, and disappeared into the mass of bodies.

The room was silent for a moment, then the crowd cheered and whistled and called for more. He did not reappear, and after several moments the PA system offered us consolation in the melodious form of the Andrews Sisters. A strapping young man in a corporal's uniform asked me to dance, and I obliged. He leered at me, to make sure I knew that he—like the Andrews Sisters—was in the mood. "Man, those gals sure can sing it," he said.

"They're fine," I said, "but that guy at the piano—he was really something. I wonder if he's on a USO tour."

"Him?" The corporal looked at me like I was an idiot. "Nah, that guy works here. He's one of the eggheads. Chemist or something."

Just then—at least, this is the way I like to remember the timing—I saw a long finger tap the corporal on the shoulder. "Mind if I cut in?" It was him: the singer; he was talking to the soldier, but he was smiling at me. The corporal looked annoyed but also embarrassed, as if he thought the guy had heard himself called an egghead, or as if the corporal had called down this punishment on himself by being an unappreciative listener.

We danced just that one dance, then he asked if he

could walk me back to my dorm. The walk was only two blocks, but that was enough to decide things for me. The corporal was right about one thing, Novak was a scientst. But he was wrong about the other—Novak wasn't an egghead; he was funny and self-deprecating, and an odd mixture of confidence and humility. He was a prodigy, with Ph.D.'s in both chemistry and physics, but he was surprisingly humble. I thought I had hit the jackpot, Bill.

We got married six weeks later, in the Chapel on the Hill. He and I exchanged vows in the very same spot where you and I saw his ashes yesterday.

I moved from the dorm to the house on the ridge that Novak was entitled to, as a senior scientist. "Snob Hill," everyone called it, even those of us lucky enough to live on it, because we knew we didn't necessarily deserve to live so much better than the people down in the valley. The difference between the ridge and the valley was amazing—down among the dormitories, trailers, and hutments, there were no trees and very little grass. During wet weather, the valley floor was a sea of mud—cars would get stuck up to their axles, and if you had to walk somewhere that didn't have a raised boardwalk, you'd sink so deep your shoes would get sucked right off your feet. During hot, dry spells, it was like living in the Dust Bowl—dust got into every nook and cranny, you'd choke if you didn't breathe through a handkerchief, and your face would be caked with red dust and streaks of sweat. Up on Snob Hill the roads were good, the yards were nice, and crime was virtually nonexistent.

Happily ever after, right?

Except that it wasn't.

But that's another story, Bill. Another story for another day.

15

BEATRICE DEFLECTED ALL MY follow-up questions about Novak. "I'm tired," she said. "It's too sad to talk about right now." And then she added, "Tell me your name again?" The sudden, vague hint of senility might just be a ploy, I realized, but if I backed her into that corner, she might never come out of it again. Given that Emert and Thornton had both struck out with her, I decided a strategic retreat was in order.

I checked my unreliable wristwatch. "I've probably overstayed my welcome," I said, "and I'd better be getting back to the university. It was so nice talking with you, Beatrice. You reckon I could come visit you again?"

She eyed me sharply, as if to size up my intentions or assess my sincerity. I smiled at her then, and it was a genuine smile—she really was a remarkable woman—and the smile seemed to tip the scales in my favor. "Of course, Bill," she said, "if you can tear yourself away from those comely UT coeds long enough to listen to an old woman rattle."

I held out my hand to shake goodbye but she ignored it, leaning a cheek toward me for a kiss. I brushed the pebbled skin lightly with my lips. She smelled of face powder and perfume and vodka, and I briefly imagined a different Beatrice, a young and beautiful Beatrice, offering her cheek or her lips to a soldier or a scientist. She would have been an irresistible force.

I was halfway back to UT when my cell phone rang. The display read THOMPSON PHOTO. It was Rodney Satterfield, and I hoped he had good news about the film from Novak's freezer. "So," I said, "what did you find on the world's oldest undeveloped film? Girlie pictures of some cute young calutron operator, circa 1944?" As soon as I heard myself make the joke, two images of Beatrice—young Beatrice and old Beatrice—popped into my head, and I felt doubly embarrassed.

"Actually," he said, "we didn't find much of anything. A clear strip of film. Looks kinda like it hasn't been exposed. Back before everything went digital, we used to get two or three unexposed rolls a week. Somebody would load the film, then put the camera away without using it. Six months later, when they got the camera out to use it, they couldn't remember whether it was a new roll or a shot roll. So they'd rewind the blank film and bring it to us to develop. And then they'd be pissed off at us because there weren't any pictures."

"Oh well," I said, "it's not like there was a note taped to the package saying, 'develop this if you want to see who killed me.' We just thought it was worth checking, since he'd gone to the trouble to wrap it up and keep it in the freezer all those years. Anyhow, thanks for trying. I'll need to take the film back to the police, just so they've got custody of it, even though it doesn't do them any good. I'm on my way to UT now; how about I swing by and pick it up on my way?"

"Actually, I said it *looked* like it hadn't been shot," Rodney corrected. "But it had. The images are just really faint. Either it's horribly underexposed, or the film's been faded by radiation."

"You mean because the guy whose freezer it was in was a walking radiographic camera?"

"Well, maybe," he said. "Or maybe just decades of background solar radiation. Over time, solar radiation can dissipate the images, even if the film is stashed in a freezer. I tried overprocessing it—letting the film soak in the chemicals about fifty percent longer, which usually helps with old film. Doesn't seem to have made much difference. But I'm not quite ready to give up on this," he said. "Mind you, the prints might not turn out black-and-white; they might turn out black-and-black. But it can't hurt to try. How far away are you?"

"I'm nearly to I-40," I said. "Ten minutes? Maybe twenty."

"You want to go in the darkroom with me? If you've got time, I'll wait till you get here."

FIFTEEN MINUTES LATER, I pulled into the parking lot of Thompson Photo Products. Rodney met me at the counter and led me to a darkroom at the back of the building. I felt privileged; although I'd brought hundreds of rolls of crime-scene photos here over the years, I'd never before been ushered into the inner sanctum, the darkroom.

The film, cut into several one-foot strips, was hanging from the photographic equivalent of a clothesline. Rodney unclipped one of the strips and held it so I could see through it. The darkroom was lit by a single red bulb, so—not surprisingly—the room was . . . *dark*. Still, despite the dimness, I could see that the cause looked hopeless.

"You weren't kidding," I said. "It's like variations on a theme of clear. Clear, clearer, clearest. How do you know where to even begin? Which one's the least bad?"

"I looked at them again on a light box after we talked," he said. "I had to put a few layers of paper over the glass to dim the light, just so it wouldn't blow everything out completely. But once I got it dimmed down, I could see a little more—not much, but enough to tell that several of them seemed to have a similar smudge of image at the center. This one right here"—he pointed to the middle of the strip—"seems about a millionth of a percent less horrible than the others."

"That good, huh?" He nodded glumly. "Well, if it takes any of the pressure off you, the bar of my expectation is about six feet under, so there's no way it can be worse than I'm expecting."

Rodney laid the film on the stage of an enlarger—a downward-pointing rig labeled BESELER that looked like a cross between an industrial lamp and an old-fashioned bellows-type camera—and slipped the film between the lamp and the lens. Then he took a sheet of 8-by-10 photo paper from a metal box and clipped it to an easel at the enlarger's base. "I'm guessing at this," he said, "but we need as little light going through this as I can get, so I've stopped the lens down all the way. Oh, and I've got a number-five contrast filter in there to pump up any trace of contrast we're lucky enough to have." He flipped a switch, and light streamed downward out of the lens and through the film, illuminating the white, empty rectangle of paper. *Let there be light,* I thought, Novak's funeral hymn echoing in my head.

The light clicked off after only a few seconds, leaving me blind for a moment—and leaving a reverse image on my retinas, a black 8-by-10-inch rectangle floating on a white background—until my eyes readjusted to the red safelight.

"Damn," I said. The paper was blank.

"Hang on," said Rodney. "You'll probably want to say that again in a minute, but we're not done yet. The image doesn't show up until we put the paper in the developer." He pointed to a shallow metal tray that contained an inch or so of clear liquid. "Faint as that image was, this'll probably develop pretty quickly, if there's anything there. Then I'll need to hustle it into the stop bath, to fix it."

Funny, I thought: a week ago—a moment before events in the morgue took their dramatic turn—Miranda had been preparing to fix Leonard's brain. Now Rodney was talking of fixing this ghostly image Novak had left behind.

Removing the paper from the base of the enlarger, he laid it gently in the tray.

I leaned close. I knew I wasn't supposed to hope for anything, but I did.

Ten seconds passed, and the paper remained blank. After another ten, an image began to materialize, like something slowly emerging from a dense fog.

By the time thirty seconds had elapsed, I could tell what that something was. A young man—a young soldier—emerged from the mists of time onto the page. He lay in a shallow, fresh depression in the earth. His head was turned slightly, and I saw a dark circle at his right temple. I had a guess what the dark circle was, although I couldn't be sure.

One thing was unmistakable, though. The open, staring eyes were those of a dead man.

PART TWO

Now I am become Death, the destroyer of worlds.

—Robert Oppenheimer,
quoting Hindu scripture after
the Trinity atomic test, July 16, 1945

Now we're all sons of bitches.

—Ken Bainbridge, Trinity test director

16

CROSSING THE SOLWAY BRIDGE over the Clinch River, I left behind the Solway community's half-mile strip of convenience marts and auto-repair shops and barren produce stands. The bridge marked a border, a boundary: once my wheels were on the other side, I had crossed over, into the land General Leslie Groves had claimed for the Manhattan Project—59,000 acres, bounded on three sides by the Clinch, on the fourth side by Black Oak Ridge, and in every direction by the peculiar sensation that World War II still lived on, somehow, in this East Tennessee wrinkle in the space-time continuum. Although the security checkpoints at Solway and the handful of other entry points to Oak Ridge had long since been dismantled, much of the site looked just as it had during the war, and it was perhaps only natural that the city and its people tended to dwell in the black-and-white importance of the past.

On a whim, I varied my route into Oak Ridge this time, taking the exit ramp marked BETHEL VALLEY ROAD, which led to Oak Ridge National Laboratory and the Y-12 Plant. Bearing right at a fork in the road, I bore right onto Scarboro Road. I crossed a low ridge, dropped down into Union Valley, and saw the vast Y-12 complex sprawling to my left behind a high chain-link fence. My eye was caught by a cluster of large, brooding buildings. Their stout concrete frames were filled in with red brick, and strips of windows had been set near the roofline to allow daylight into the cavernous interiors. From the archival photos at the library, I recognized these as the buildings where Beatrice and the other calutron girls had sifted uranium-235 from U-238 for the Hiroshima bomb.

A quarter mile later, the road cut through a gap in a low, wooded ridge, and the Y-12 Plant disappeared from view. Just beyond the gap, a blocky concrete guardhouse, its windows and gunports long since boarded up, marked what had once been one of the Secret City's gates. Passing the guardhouse, I was leaving the federal reservation and entering the town; leaving the past and rejoining the present. Yet pulling into the police department's parking lot behind the municipal building, I couldn't shake the feeling that I had one foot in the twenty-first century and one foot in World War II. And sometimes it was tough to tell which foot was on firmer ground.

DETECTIVE JIM EMERT peered at one of the prints through a magnifying glass, then laid the lens down in exasperation. "Hell," he said, "with all that grain in the image, magnifying it just makes it worse."

I'd done exactly the same thing an hour before, in my office under the stadium. Magnifying the print was like enlarging a newspaper photograph into a meaningless cloud of dots. "The prints aren't great," I said, "but it's amazing there's anything there at all." Considering how faint the images on the film had been, I wasn't sure whether to think of the guy at Thompson's as a darkroom tech or a psychic medium. After conjuring up that first startling image of the young soldier's body, Rodney had spent most of that night and all of this morning experimenting with different exposure times, contrast filters, and developer baths. He'd tried burning and dodging, which sounded like an arsonist's modus operandi, but which actually meant using masks and screens to increase or decrease the amount of light falling on different regions of the photo paper. He'd also scanned the negatives into a digital-processing computer. In short, he'd tried every trick in the book to coax every speck of image out of that ghostly film. By the time he was through, he had used a hundred sheets of photo paper . . . and produced a sequence of prints that hinted at a chilling story.

The first image showed the rear end of an antique-looking car—late 1930s, I guessed, by the black paint, bulbous fenders, and small windows. The trunk lid was raised, and a pale bundle filled the cargo space. The detail left a lot to be desired, but over the years I'd seen enough blanket-wrapped bodies in enough trunks to recognize one. The second image showed the bundle lying beside a shallow, circular hole that appeared to have been freshly dug. In the third and fourth pictures, the body—no longer wrapped in the blanket or sheet, and wearing what appeared to be dark clothes—lay in the center of the depression. It was this third exposure Rodney had printed as I'd looked over his shoulder in the darkroom. But the fifth and sixth prints were even more haunting, for they showed close-ups of the man's head and his face, the vacant eyes staring at us across the gulf of time.

Emert laid aside the last of the close-ups. "The weird thing," he said, "besides who the hell's this dead guy and what the hell's going on here, is why Novak would take the photos in the first place? And why would he go to such trouble to preserve the film all these years? And why would he leave the film undeveloped, for Christ's sake, if he wanted to keep the images?"

"That's a whole bunch of weird things," I pointed out. "You're a man of many questions."

"That's what my mom used to say when I was a kid," he said. "Since that's the way I am, might as well get some good out of it. The way I see it, you ask enough people enough questions, enough times, sooner or later you might get an answer that tells you something."

I'd been wondering about the same weird things as Emert, plus a few others. "Maybe it's not Novak the pictures incriminate," I said. I thought of the crumpled note outside Novak's front door. "Maybe it's somebody else. Somebody whose secret he knew. Maybe Novak was blackmailing whoever the pictures incriminated."

"He was a pretty lousy blackmailer if he threw away the blackmail note," Emert pointed out.

"Maybe he was still getting the hang of it," I said. "Maybe he considered sending the note, then had second thoughts."

"Come on, Doc—he'd had that film on ice for a long damn time. If he were gonna put the screws to somebody, he'd have done it decades ago, while his target was still alive, and while Novak was young enough to enjoy the money. Besides, you saw his handwriting on that legal pad. It doesn't match the note."

The detective was right. Novak's handwriting was small and precise. The lettering on the note was large and blocky. "Okay, I give," I said. "You got any theories?"

"Not really," he admitted. "All I can come up with is that maybe he wanted an insurance policy of some sort, leverage he could use if he needed to. But he wanted to reduce the risk somebody might just stumble across the pictures—the maid or the home-health nurse or whoever—so he left the film undeveloped. It's not a great theory, but it's all I've got so far."

The last three pictures in the series were different. They showed tree trunks and thickets of foliage, and—off in the distance, through a gap in the trees—a small barn. *Here's the view from the grave,* I thought, trying to think like Leonard Novak might have. *Here's how to find it again someday.*

I'd brought two sets of prints with me. I left one with Emert, and took the other with me as I left the police department, crossed the parking lot, and unlocked my truck. I slipped behind the wheel and started the engine, but then I just sat, my mind spinning faster than the motor.

A story had unspooled from that roll of film. A strange tale from beyond the grave, told by a man whose own murder was the most bizarre I had ever encountered. I didn't know what it meant yet, and maybe I never would, but I couldn't wait for the next chapter.

I switched off the key and got out of the truck.

17

I DIDN'T SEE HER at the Reference Desk, and the Oak Ridge Room was locked and empty. Disappointed, I turned to go, figuring I'd stop at the circulation desk on my way out and ask what hours Isabella, the history-minded librarian, worked. As I approached the desk, I heard a voice at my elbow, from somewhere amid rows of bookshelves. "Dr. Brockton? Is that you?"

I spun. "Oh, hi," I said. "I was just looking for you. I was afraid maybe you weren't working this afternoon."

"Till six," she said, stepping out of the shadowy stacks. "What can I do for you?"

"I was wondering if I could look through those Manhattan Project photo binders again?"

"Of course," she said. She led me back to the glass-walled room and unlocked the door. "Anything in particular you're looking for?"

"Seems like I remember there was a set of photos of houses and farms that were already here when the project started. Sort of the 'before' picture of Oak Ridge?"

She smiled. "You paid good attention," she said. Pulling a fat binder from among the dozens filling the bookcase, she handed it to me. "Anything else I can help you with?"

I almost said that she could help me with my lack of a dinner companion, but that seemed a bit forward. "Just this, for now," I said. "Thanks."

"If you think of something later, let me know," she said. She hesitated slightly before she turned and walked away. I didn't know why, but that half second of hesitation made me hope that she'd somehow read my mind, and that maybe she liked what she read there.

The binder was three inches thick, its black-and-white prints tucked into clear plastic sleeves. Flipping through the pages, I saw weathered farmhouses, ramshackle barns, tobacco sheds, haywagons, general stores, one-room churches, mule-drawn plows. I knew the photos were from the early 1940s—early 1943, most of them, because construction of Oak Ridge and its three huge installations began in earnest that spring—but many of the pictures could have passed for images from the 1920s, or even the 1890s. What inconceivable change: to go from such a rural, sleepy area—a place the transplanted scientists referred to as "Dogpatch"—to a churning, teeming enterprise, one that pushed the limits of science, engineering, and human endeavor on a gargantuan scale. What must those displaced farmers have thought? How many of them had heard of John Hendrix and the wild-eyed vision he'd shared back at the dawn of the twentieth century?

The images were fascinating without being helpful. I had opened the notebook hoping one of the photos might show a barn like the one in Leonard Novak's photos—a small barn tucked at the base of a wooded ridge, a silo at one end. Although the binder contained pictures of barns and silos and woods, none of those pictures combined all three elements: here was a photo of a barn with no silo; there was a photo of a silo with no barn; a few pages farther, a barn and silo but no hillside or woods.

I closed the binder and sighed.

Just then I heard a slight tap on the glass. Looking over my shoulder, I saw Isabella, and I stood up. She opened the door. "I'm sorry to interrupt you," she said. "I was just about to take a break, and thought I'd ask if you need anything before I disappear."

"Thanks for asking, but I think I've hit a dead end here," I said.

"Oh, I'm sorry. Is there anything other than a photograph that might tell you what you need to know?"

I smiled. "What I need to know? There's no end to the things I need to know; just ask my colleagues or my secretary or my graduate assistant. But the thing I was hoping to find out just now? I'm not sure anything but a photograph would work." She looked confused, and I didn't blame her. "Here, I'll show you, if you don't mind," I said. "But if you want to take your break instead, don't let me keep you."

"Show me," she said.

I opened the manila envelope I'd brought with me, the prints of the Novak film. Reaching to the back of the sheaf of photos so as to keep the photos of the dead man tucked inside the envelope, I slid out the last few. "These are old, crummy pictures, taken somewhere near here—I *think*—in the 1940s. Maybe. Somewhere in the woods, apparently"—I used the end of a pen to point to the trees, and she nodded—"but with a view of what appears to be a barn and a silo." She bit her lip and bent low over the photo, her black hair hanging down and curtaining off her face. "Hard to tell much from these pictures, but I didn't see any pictures in the notebook that looked like they could possibly be this barn."

"And you're trying to identify this particular barn?"

"Yes," I said. "Well, not exactly. What I'm really trying to do, if you want to split hairs, is find the spot from which this photograph of this barn was taken."

She puzzled over that a moment. "In other words, if you knew where this barn was, you could figure out where this photographer was standing when he or she took this picture?"

"Exactly," I said. "Is there any hope?"

"Absolutely none," she said. Seeing my face fall, she laughed. "I'm kidding. I'm not making any promises, but if you'll let me scan a copy of this, I'll do some research. This is a lot more interesting than most of the questions I get."

"Scan away," I said. "That would be a big help."

"If I find it, then what?"

"Then maybe I could buy you dinner," I said, "to say thank you."

"Oh," she said, looking flustered and turning red. There was an awkward pause before she added, "I meant, then should I call or email you?"

"Ah," I said, taking my turn to blush. "Calling is better. I'm not big on email." I handed her one of my cards, which contained my office number and my home number.

She glanced at the card, then up at me. She paused again. "When I call to say I've found it, do you want the details over the phone? Or over dinner?"

I felt myself smile. "To tell you the truth," I said, "I'm not all that keen on the telephone, either. How about over dinner?"

She did that half-second pause again, then nodded, and I left the library—walking or floating, I couldn't have said which. This time, when I cranked the truck's ignition key, the engine sounded not like aimless spinning, but like power and energy, awaiting my direction. I shifted out of park, pointed the wheels toward the east end of Oak Ridge, and gunned the gas. The vehicle surged forward, and I thought, *Now we're getting somewhere.*

Then I thought, *In your dreams,* and laughed at myself.

18

FROM THE LIBRARY, I headed east on Oak Ridge Turnpike, then meandered up the winding street to Beatrice's house. I had set up another visit with her—Miranda and Thornton called it a date—in hopes of learning more about Leonard Novak, her not-so-happily-ever-after marriage to him, and the secret that had gotten him killed in such bizarre fashion.

I called her on my cell phone to make sure she was still expecting me. "Of course I'm still expecting you," she said. "My dance card's not exactly full these days. I'll leave the door open for you. Just let yourself in and pour me a vodka."

"Yes ma'am," I laughed.

She must have made the tea and filled the ice bucket after she hung up the phone, because the tea was still steaming and the ice had not yet melted when I made her drink and sat down in what I had begun to think of as "my" chair.

"I drove past the Y-12 Plant on my way into town today," I said. "I thought about you in there at the controls of your calutron."

"What a tedious thing to think of," she said. "My calutron is only interesting thanks to the hindsight of history. It helped make the bomb, so we've decided it was important and fascinating. But it was bloody boring to operate, I can tell you that. Like working on a Detroit assembly line, but without the satisfaction of seeing the car take shape. Without even seeing the conveyor belt move. We weren't making a goddamn thing, as far as we could see. So even though we were cheered on every day by patriotic billboards and PA announcements, the inspiration wore pretty thin after a few hours of staring at those damn dials and needles. Only time things were interesting was when they went wrong." Her lips twitched upward slightly at a memory.

"What sort of things went wrong?"

"Well," she said, looking arch, "one evening in late 1943, when I was working the 3-to-11 shift, there was a bit of a commotion, and I glanced around and saw General Groves and Colonel Nichols and two civilian men, fairly well dressed. The officers were being very deferential to the civilians, especially the good-looking one in the expensive suit. He looked around, then came over to my cubicle—I was the best-looking girl working that evening—and asked my name. When I told him, he said, 'Beatrice, would you mind if I borrow your calutron for a moment?' I looked at my supervisor, who practically fell over himself to pull me away from the controls. 'This is far too low,' the man said. 'You'll never produce enough at those settings.' He fiddled with the controls till the needles were practically off the scale. 'There,' he said, 'you'll get a lot more . . . *product* . . . at those settings.' They turned and left. I said to my boss, 'So who was that fancy guy?' My boss, looking all starstruck, said, 'That was Ernest Lawrence, the inventor of this machine.' Five minutes later, we heard a boom. My calutron had exploded."

I laughed. "That's a great story," I said. "Is it really true?"

"Mostly true," she said. "Ninety-nine percent of the time it was mind-numbing work. You shouldn't think of me running a calutron. You should think of me singing or painting or playing Beethoven or writing poetry instead."

"You can do all those things? I'm impressed."

"I didn't say I can do them, Bill. I just said you should *think* of me doing them. Where's your imagination, man?" I laughed. "Now Leonard, he could do all those things. And brilliantly."

"But he couldn't be a brilliant husband to you."

Her head snapped up at that. "Is that why you're here? To grill me about Leonard's failings?"

"Beatrice, we're trying to figure out how he ended up with a pellet of iridium-192 in his gut," I said, "and whether other people might be in danger, too. Not his failings. His vulnerabilities, maybe."

She looked out the window for a long time. "All right," she said finally, still looking outside. "I don't suppose there's any virtue in guarding his secret any longer." She turned to face me. "Leonard was a fairy. 'Gay,' it's called these days. Queer as a three-dollar bill." I wasn't sure which I found more surprising, the fact that he was gay, or the fact that she expressed it so coarsely. She must have seen the startled look on my face. "Today, nobody cares, but things were different then," she said. "It was considered a perversion. He'd never have been able to keep his security clearance if they'd known."

She was probably right about that. "I don't mean to be indelicate," I said, "but how could you not have realized that before you got married?"

"I told myself that he was being a perfect gentleman," she said. "That he had set me on a pedestal and didn't want to risk sullying my reputation." She looked down. "Or maybe I was so thrilled to have caught a big fish, I chose to ignore the warning signs."

"If he was gay, why did he ask you to marry him?"

"Maybe to protect his secret," she said. "Or maybe he actually hoped he could overcome it. People thought that back then, you know. But he couldn't overcome it, of course. On our wedding night, he kissed me on the lips, but it was the sort of kiss you might give a sister or an old friend—a quick peck with pursed lips. Then he pulled away and looked at me, and his eyes were full of shame and sadness. 'Oh, Beatrice,' he said. 'What have I done to you?' Then he turned his back to me and cried. My bridegroom—the brilliant, sparkling wonderboy of the Manhattan Project—wept because he did not want me, and he never would. We didn't talk about it. You just didn't, in those days, unless you were Oscar Wilde. We entered into a pact of silence, without even speaking about the pact. Even the pact was a secret. He carried his burdens alone; I carried mine alone. After the war, after the bomb, I asked him for a divorce." She fell silent, and I let her sit with her thoughts awhile.

When she finally turned and looked at me, I said, "I'm sorry. That must have been painful for you both. I'm not sure it sheds any light on his death, but I appreciate your trusting me enough to share that with me."

She shook her head. "What difference could it make now? He's dead, and I will be soon. Who on earth could possibly care?" She drew a deep breath. "There was one other burden Leonard carried." From the end table beside her chair she lifted a creased, yellowed piece of paper. "This was an entry in his laboratory journal from November of 1943," she said. "He wrote it right after the Graphite Reactor went critical. Then he started to worry that if the military snoops read it, he'd be considered unpatriotic, so he cut it out." She handed me the paper. As I unfolded it, I worried that the creases would tear completely through the fragile paper. The ink was fading, yet the words, written in small, precise script, seemed to leap off the page as I read them.

November 4, 1943

It is thrilling. And it is horrifying.

We have built the world's first plutonium production reactor, and it works. It is a huge leap, technologically, beyond the Chicago pile. It is far bigger in scale and far more complex than Fermi's simple, can-we-do-it? experiment. It has been built to operate not for a few experiments, but for many years.

And it has been built with the dreadfully single-minded purpose of making implements of wholesale death.

Fermi's makeshift reactor had the rationalization of research attached to it. It was a scientific gamble, and no one knew whether it could sustain a fission reaction. We all had the luxury of being eager and excited when it succeeded.

Now we know, beyond doubt, that controlled fission works, and we know that we can scale it up, bigger and deadlier. We know we can start it, stop it, speed it up, slow it down, exactly as we wish. We now know we can harness it to create slow heat or instantaneous explosions or exotic new elements. Including plutonium, which careful calculations indicate will make just as good a bomb as uranium.

"Just as good a bomb": what an ironic, oxymoronic, and nihilistic phrase. One might as well speak of "a beautiful murder" or "excellent torture."

Groves and his armies of construction are already building the mammoth next stage—gargantuan versions of this reactor in the Columbia River Valley, in some godforsaken part of eastern Washington. They'll send me out to make sure it works, and it will. And within months after they start up, those reactors will produce enough plutonium to obliterate entire cities in Japan.

When I look at the face of the reactor we've built here—a twenty-foot-high wall of concrete, pierced by hundreds of neatly placed holes where slugs will be irradiated to create plutonium—the technician in me feels pride. A tight, tidy gridwork of tubes burrows through the heart of the reactor in a pattern dictated by meticulous science. But the human being in me screams "no!" at what we've done, and why, and especially at what we're racing to do. I have no God to pray to, but if I did, I would pray for an end to this terrible endeavor, and to the war that makes such madness seem like sanity. And to my own conflicted complicity.—LN

19

JIM EMERT CALLED JUST as I was about to swing by the hospital and visit Garcia; he wondered if I could sit in on a Novak meeting in an hour. "Thornton says the Bureau has some leads on the radiation source."

"I'll be there," I said. I figured Garcia would rather I attend the meeting than hover outside his window. Miranda was planning to visit him at lunchtime; by then she'd need a break from the skull she was reconstructing. A contractor's crew in North Knoxville, demolishing a block of old houses to make way for another strip mall, had unearthed a human skeleton. The bones, which were old and fragile, had been no match for the bulldozer that had churned them up. An adult human skeleton normally contained 206 bones; from the construction site, we'd sifted somewhere between 800 and 1,000 pieces. Miranda had weeks of tedious reassembly work ahead.

WE MET IN a conference room in the Oak Ridge Municipal Building. When I told Emert and Thornton what I'd learned from Beatrice about Novak's homosexuality, the FBI agent looked intrigued; when I described his crisis of conscience over his role in producing plutonium for the bomb, he looked troubled. He scribbled some notes, and when he finished, he shook his head doubtfully. "A ninety-three-year-old," he said. "Seems harmless and grandfatherly, right? Then you start poking around in his past and you find pictures of a murdered guy, and a secret sexual life, and misgivings about helping his country win the war. Funny what a good disguise old age can be." He shook his head again, this time as if to shake off his concerns about Novak and to refocus on what he'd come to tell us. "Okay, so here's the latest from our forensic rad lab in Savannah River," he said. "It is indeed iridium-192, as Duane Johnson determined the day of the incident," he said. "It's a sealed, metallic point source; you guys saw it in the morgue, so you already knew that. Tiny, but hotter than hell. It was roughly ninety-eight curies at the time of the autopsy. By now, it's down in the mid-eighties, maybe high seventies. Eight weeks from now, it'll be at fifty curies. You still wouldn't want to swallow it, though."

"Or pick it up with your fingers," I said. "Or hold it in the palm of your hand." I was surprised at the angry edge I heard in my voice.

"No, you wouldn't," he said, looking at me with concern.

"So how the hell did it wind up in Novak's gut?" said Emert. "Unless somebody jammed it down his throat, he picked it up and put it in his mouth and swallowed it. Any chance he might have done it on purpose? Did bomb-guilt finally get to him? Or maybe fear of spending years as an invalid with no family to take care of him?"

"The Behavioral Sciences folks don't think so," Thornton said. "They've talked to a lot of Novak's neighbors. He was energetic and positive. The guy walked a mile or two every day; hell, he was playing tennis until a couple years ago. Only reason nobody was worried about not seeing him lately was because of the cold weather. They figured he'd come back out once it warmed up. You saw all those espionage books on his desk. I think he was on the trail of a spy, and I think that's why somebody fed him a pellet of iridium-192."

"I can't figure out how they did it," I said. "It must not have been hidden in a hunk of meat or cheese. He'd have broken a tooth or at least spit the thing out."

"I've been thinking about that," Thornton said. "If you're a health-conscious old guy, what do you swallow a lot of every day?"

"Ex-Lax," said Emert, drawing a laugh from everyone.

"Pills," I said. "Vitamins."

"Exactly," said Thornton. He turned to Emert. "Remember the medicine cabinet?"

"Looked like a damn pharmacy," said Emert. "Mostly nonprescription stuff, though. Super-omega-this and antioxidant-that and mega-ultra-prostate formula. Flaxseed and glucosamine and St. John's wort and I don't know what-all else. The old dude was scarfing down twenty, thirty horse pills a day."

"The iridium source," I said. "How big was it?"

"Not very," said Thornton. "About an eighth of an inch in diameter. Plenty small enough to slip inside one of those capsules. I bet if we go back and look at all those bottles, we'll find a pill bottle that doesn't have as many fingerprints as the rest."

"Because somebody wiped it clean after hiding the pellet inside the capsule," said Emert.

Thornton nodded, then shifted back to the rad lab's findings. "The half-life of iridium-192 is only seventy-four days," he said. "So seventy-four days before the incident in the morgue, the pellet—assuming it was irradiated and fabricated that long ago—was twice that hot: nearly two hundred curies."

"I'm assuming this thing wasn't pried out of a household smoke detector," said Emert.

"Not a chance," said Thornton. "Smoke detectors use a different isotope, americium-241, and they use tiny, tiny amounts. Like a microcurie."

"A microcurie," the detective said. "That's, what, a thousandth of a curie?"

Thornton shook his head. "A millionth," he said. "A smoke detector contains one-millionth of a curie of radioactivity, and it's mostly alpha radiation, the kind that can't penetrate your skin or even a piece of paper. This iridium source in Novak's gut was a hundred million times hotter, and it was spewing gamma, which can shoot through several inches of steel and come out the other side still feeling frisky."

"What about a TheraSeed," said Emert, "those little radioactive pellets they put in the prostates of old farts like me to shrink tumors?"

"Those are tiny," Thornton said. "Small enough to be injected through a syringe. And they're generally palladium-103 or iodine-125. They're also very, very weak compared to this. You wouldn't want your prostate to get cooked like Novak's gut, would you?" Emert shuddered. "Speaking of medical isotopes, though," Thornton went on, holding up an index finger to indicate that he found this an interesting sidelight, "one of the uses of iridium-192 is to create medical isotopes like palladium and iodine." I was losing track of all the isotopes, but Thornton seemed to have no trouble keeping them straight.

"One isotope creating another," I said. "The atomic ripple effect?"

"More like billiard balls," Thornton said. "All those protons and neutrons and electrons and photons ricocheting around on the pool table of the universe. I'm amazed everything hangs together as well as it does. One of these days, seems like, the cosmic cue stick will strike, all the balls will scatter, and then they'll drop, one after another, into the corner pockets and side pockets of oblivion."

"Why, Agent Thornton," I said, "you're a poet."

He laughed. "Nah, it's just smoke and mirrors. I'm

desperately trying to distract you from the realization that I don't really understand this stuff."

Smart, poetic, and self-deprecating, to boot—no wonder Miranda seemed to be taking a shine to him. "So this iridium-192," I said. "UT Hospital has a pretty big nuclear-medicine department. Is there any chance this iridium-192 might have come from there?"

"Yes they are, but no it couldn't," he said. "They do create radioisotopes there. They've got a cyclotron right above the morgue that Ernest Lawrence would've given his left nut for. But UT doesn't use iridium-192 sources."

"Then who does?" Emert and I asked the question at the same time.

"I'm so glad you asked," he smiled. He tapped the cursor pad on his computer, and a washed-out blue slide appeared on the white wall behind him. Thornton pointed at the fluorescents overhead, and Emert killed the lights. When he did, the FBI logo blazed from a deep blue background.

The intro slide faded to black, and then another image faded up. It was a nuclear power plant, its iconic cooling towers sending billows of steam skyward. "The pressure vessel and the cooling-water pipes in a reactor like this are about six inches thick," he said. "Those components have to be strong as hell, and so do the welds that hold them together." He flashed through a series of ghostly images, X-ray-like pictures of fissures and streaks and bubbles in metal tubes; cracks and voids in seams. "These are radiographs of pipes and welds in a nuclear plant," he said. "And this is the camera that took them."

The next slide showed a four-wheel dolly loaded with an instrument the size and shape of a footlocker. "This is an industrial radiography camera," Thornton said. "Think of it as a turbocharged big brother to a medical X-ray machine. It uses gamma radiation rather than X-rays, because gamma has higher energy and can penetrate steel much better." He flashed to a close-up view of the box on the cart; enlarged, it looked like a footlocker with dials and cables in one end. "This particular camera uses cobalt-60, not iridium, as the gamma source; this is three hundred curies, which is a good bit hotter than what we're dealing with."

I recalled a tour I'd taken once of TVA's Watts Bar Nuclear Plant, located downstream from Knoxville. "Nuclear plants have pretty tight security," I said. "Wouldn't it be pretty tough for Bubba to wheel that cart out the gate and wrestle it into the bed of his pickup?"

"You're right. So who else uses radiographic cameras?" He flashed up a series of slides showing mammoth industrial complexes—sprawling, three-dimensional mazes of pipes and girders and steel exhaust stacks filled the wall. "Petroleum refineries. Chemical plants. Just like nuclear plants, they're pumping nasty stuff at high temperatures and pressures, through heavy-gauge pipe. So are these guys." He flashed rapidly through several slides showing pipelines—the Alaskan oil pipeline, a water pipeline in the West, a natural-gas pipeline. "Every pipeline company in the world worries about weld failure," he said. "Right now, as we sit here, there are dozens of technicians—maybe hundreds—scurrying around the country taking radiographs of power plants and refineries and chemical plants and pipelines." He paused to let that sink in. "And a lot of them aren't using the big rig on the cart. A lot of them are using gadgets like this." He tapped the cursor again.

I found myself looking at the legs and waist and dangling left arm of a man photographed in mid-stride. Clutched in his hand was a bright yellow gizmo whose size and shape reminded me of a construction worker's lunch box—the black, barn-shaped kind, with a rectangular base to hold the sandwich and apple and chips and cookies, and a cylindrical top to hold the thermos. A heavy, pipe-fitting-looking extension jutted from one end of the yellow box, though, and the universal warning sign for radiation was emblazoned prominently on the side. "This camera is handheld, obviously," said Thornton. "Very compact; very portable. The case is rugged enough, with enough shielding, to allow a two-hundred-curie iridium source to be legally transported in any vehicle."

He flashed to another picture, this one showing a boxier gadget topped by a tubular handle. This picture showed considerably more detail. "Another handheld radiography camera," said Thornton, "the RadioGraph Elite, made by Field Imaging Equipment Company, in Shreveport, Louisiana." He pulled a laser pointer from his shirt pocket and traced the instrument's rectangular outline with the dot of light. "This is fourteen inches long by five inches square—the size and shape of those newspaper boxes people out in the country put underneath their mailbox. The case is stainless steel; inside the case is a shielding block of depleted uranium. It's small, and you can carry it by that handle, but you wouldn't want to carry it far, because that sucker weighs fifty pounds. The manufacturer calls it portable; I'd call it luggable."

He replaced the photograph with a cutaway drawing of the camera. Most of the interior consisted of the block of depleted uranium. A hollow tube or tunnel traced a shallow S-curve through the center of the block, and Thornton ran the laser dot back and forth along a wire nestled within that S. "This cable is called the pigtail," he said, "and here at the end of the pigtail"—the laser dot jiggled on a small, rounded bead—"is the gamma source: not much bigger than a grain of rice, but it's two hundred curies of iridium-192." The bead looked chillingly familiar.

"How does it work?" Emert asked. "There's a lead shutter at one end? It opens and sends a beam of gamma rays out the tube?"

"This is the strange part, to my way of thinking," said Thornton. "To take a radiograph, you put the film behind the pipe, you hide behind a shield, and you turn a crank that pushes the pigtail out the end of the box. That lets the gamma rays from the source go through the pipe—and pretty much anything else nearby—and hit the film."

"Seems kinda primitive," said Emert.

"Kinda dangerous, too," I added.

"Yes, it does," said Thornton. "And yes, it is. Anytime somebody's using one of these, it's important to get everybody else out of the area. The people who use these things tend to get the highest annual radiation exposures of any workers in the nation—ten times what somebody at a nuclear power plant gets. And that's if the thing's working right. If something goes wrong, it can get real bad, real fast." He showed a picture of a pigtail—just the wire cable and the bead of the source, detached from the camera. "Occasionally the pigtail comes loose," he said. "The operator thinks he's reeled it back into the camera, but instead, it's lying on the ground, sending out all this gamma at anybody unlucky enough to come close."

"Or pick it up," I said bitterly.

"Or pick it up," he echoed. He proceeded to tell us, and to show us, the story of a pipeline welder in the mountains of Peru who—late in the afternoon of February 20, 1999—found a short length of wire cable lying on the ground. Thinking he might be able to use the cable or sell it for scrap, the man picked it up and put it in his pocket. It remained there until he took off his pants that night and draped them over the back of a chair. The man's wife sat briefly in the chair.

Then, at 1 A.M., came a knock at the door. During the evening, the radiographer had tried to take an image of a weld. When he developed the film, he found that it was blank; unexposed. Backtracking, he checked the camera and discovered that the pigtail was gone. A frantic search began, which led to the welder's house, where the source was recovered. The iridium had nestled against the man's thigh for six hours; it had hovered at the base of his wife's back for a few minutes. But in those hours and minutes, everything changed.

Twenty hours after pocketing the source, the welder entered a hospital in Lima. A red oval had appeared on the back of his right thigh, and he was vomiting. By the following day, the oval was an open ulcer, surrounded by a halo of inflammation. Within a month the crater extended almost to the bone, and infections and tissue damage were rampant. Six months after the man's exposure, surgeons in Paris amputated his right leg and removed the right half of his pelvis—skeletal trauma that exceeded almost anything even I had ever witnessed—along with much of his intestinal and urinary tract. The man's wife was luckier; she developed a burn at the base of her back, but it healed.

The wall went dark, but the images hung in my mind, and no one said anything for a while. Finally Emert did. "That guy *lived*?"

"He lived. He's alive still," said Thornton. "If you call that living."

My thoughts flew from hospitals in Peru and Paris to one in Knoxville. I prayed that I had not just witnessed a preview of what lay in store for Eddie Garcia's hands or Miranda's fingers.

"So you guys think the gamma source in Novak's gut was from one of these industrial radiography cameras?"

"We're virtually sure. Field Imaging Equipment is sending somebody from Shreveport up to Savannah River to verify that."

"And they can tell us whose camera the source came from?"

He shook his head. "I wish it were that simple. There are thousands of these cameras out there—all over the Texas oil patch and the Gulf Coast, for instance—and they're not as tightly regulated or closely tracked as you might think. When a refinery or a pipeline-inspection contractor buys one, they're required to register it with the NRC, the Nuclear

Regulatory Commission. But after that?" He shrugged. "They can chuck it in a jeep and drive from one coast to the other with it. If it gets lost or stolen, the owner has to report that to the NRC. But what if nobody knows for a while? They might use the hell out of it for a week or two, then lock it away in a tool closet for six months or a year. Hell, hundreds of these cameras went missing in the chaos caused by Hurricane Katrina. Lost, mostly, but probably some were stolen."

"Hundreds?" The number astonished me.

"Several hundred. Nearly all of them recovered since."

"Nearly?"

"A few are still unaccounted for," he acknowledged.

"So one of those missing Katrina cameras could have supplied the source that killed Novak?"

"Hang on," he said, "I'll get to that in a second. Another complication is that there's no serial number on the source we found in Novak."

"Garcia," I said. "Garcia found it in Novak."

"Sorry," he said. "Yes, the source Dr. Garcia found in Novak. There would be a serial number on the camera, but there's no room on the source. Which is too bad, since the source is what we have." He shrugged again, and for some reason, I found the shrug—the even-keeled, accepting shrug—intolerable.

"Damm it!" I halfway shouted. "Isn't there anything we can do to find out where this came from? Isn't anybody in the government worried about these things? Isn't anybody *anywhere* worried besides me?" Thornton and Emert stared at me, astonished at the outburst, and I realized that my anger stemmed not so much from the perils of portable radiography sources—peril could be found in any technology if you looked for it—but from my helplessness to do anything for Miranda or Garcia. "I'm sorry," I said. "That was out of line."

"I understand," he said. "You've got people whose health

and safety have been compromised. On the bright side, we do have a couple of things that might help us narrow the search."

"Tell me," I said. "I could use some good news."

"Remember, the half-life is just seventy-four days. So if you put a fresh two-hundred-curie source in your Radio-Graph Elite, seventy-four days later it's down to a hundred curies, and by a hundred and forty-eight days it's down to fifty curies. At the end of a year, that stuff has decayed through five half-lives, so it's down to six curies. Knowing the source in Novak was still around a hundred curies tells us something very useful."

"It tells you the source was fresh," I said. "And it tells you it wasn't from one of those cameras that went missing in Katrina."

"Bingo," he said.

"So who actually makes the sources?" I said. "And how, and where, and when? Does this outfit in Shreveport have a reactor or a cyclotron or whatever is used to make iridium-192? Do they make big batches of these things—hundreds of things at once?—or just a few at a time? How hard can it be to track down everybody who got one sometime in the past three months?"

He smiled at the burst of questions. "It's harder than I wish it were," he said. "That's why we've got a hundred people working on it. You know the old saying about the tip of the iceberg?" I nodded. "Well, I'm just the guy standing on top of the tip of the iceberg. Everything below is shrouded in fog."

Just then his cell phone rang—an odd, warbling tone I'd never heard from a cell phone before. He looked startled, then murmured, "Excuse me." He turned his back on us and spoke softly, but I could make out a few words, mostly "yes sir" and "no sir" and "thank you, sir." He ended the call with a promise to phone with an update before the end of the day. He turned back to us, looking somewhere between embarrassed and shell-shocked. “I’m sorry,” he said, “I had to take that. The man calls, you answer.”

“Which man?” I asked. “Your boss? The head of the WMD Directorate?”

“His boss’s boss’s boss,” said Thornton. “The director. Of the FBI. He wants progress reports three times a day. This case is a big target on his radar screen.”

I felt a sudden tightening in my throat, and a sudden surge of hope that we’d find out who had killed Novak—and who might be slowly killing Garcia.

20

THE NEXT MORNING MIRANDA and I had a short but cheerful visit at the hospital with Garcia. Garcia still looked weak, his burned hands were quite tender, and his lymphocyte count remained dangerously low, yet his spirits were surprisingly high. He was six chapters into a sterilized copy of *The Making of the Atomic Bomb*, one of the books I'd seen on Leonard Novak's desk. The book was propped on a reading stand, and Garcia was turning the pages with the eraser of a pencil, which he managed to grip with his bandaged right fist. "Great book," he said. "Those Manhattan Project scientists were big thinkers. Complicated human beings, though." I was surprised at his choice of reading material, but delighted to see him in good spirits.

After leaving the hospital, we returned to the bone lab. We'd just started reconstructing the cranium of the North Knoxville skeleton when Chip Thornton came knocking on the door. "Wow," he said. "Skeleton in a kit. Looks like fun."

Miranda made a face at him. "You came to help?"

"Yes," he said. "Okay, no, that's a lie. I was in the neighborhood and figured it was just as easy to relay this in person as on the phone." *That's a lie, too,* I thought. *You figured you'd stop and flirt with Miranda.* "We've had some people digging out old security files," he said, "and they found an interesting note in Dr. Novak's. Apparently there was some suspicion at the time that Novak was a homosexual. Army intelligence recommended that he be removed from the project as a security risk, but General Groves himself nixed it—he wrote that Novak could consort with farm animals as long as he produced sufficient plutonium in the reactors in Oak Ridge and Hanford." Miranda looked appalled. My guess was that her disgust had less to do with the notion of interspecies love than with Groves's readiness to ridicule the scientist at the same time he was depending on him.

"Poor Novak," she said, confirming my thinking. "What on earth was he doing in the boonies of Tennessee?"

"It's where the project was," said Thornton. For such a smart guy, he had an unfortunate tendency to take things too literally at times. "Groves picked Oak Ridge as the main site for the Manhattan Project for a bunch of reasons," he said. "Far enough inland that the Germans and Japanese couldn't possibly attack it. Isolated enough to stay below the radar screen. Good access to rail lines and cooling water and hydroelectric power and a civilian workforce." I nodded; I'd read this in several of the history books I'd hauled back from the Oak Ridge library in the past week. "I don't know if this was another factor in the selection," he went on, "or just something that Groves came to appreciate as the project progressed, but folks in Appalachia tend to be pretty tight-lipped."

Miranda pursed her lips, then said, "Yup." Thornton and I laughed.

"Conservative, too," he said. "Oak Ridge was practically the polar opposite of Los Alamos. Los Alamos was filled with loose-lipped liberals, from the top down. Hell, up until Groves put him in charge of Los Alamos, Robert Oppenheimer gave money to Communist causes. Oppenheimer's wife, Kitty, was a member of the Communist Party. So was his younger brother, Frank. So was Oppenheimer's girlfriend, until she committed suicide."

"Wait, wait," said Miranda. "Girlfriend as in 'before he married Kitty'? Or girlfriend as in 'running around on Kitty'?"

"Maybe both," said Thornton. "He was engaged to a woman named Jean Tatlock before he married Kitty, and he stayed in touch with her occasionally afterward. One of the creepier things in Oppenheimer's file is a report by an army intelligence agent, Boris Pash, who followed Oppenheimer from Los Alamos to Berkeley in June of 1943. Pash watched Oppy go inside Tatlock's apartment, wrote down what time the lights went out, and then wrote down what time they came out of the building the next morning."

"Yuck," said Miranda.

"It might seem intrusive," conceded Thornton, "but these guys were working on a life-and-death, fate-of-the-nation project. Oppenheimer was in the most sensitive position of all the scientists. And Berkeley, where he and a bunch of other Los Alamos scientists came from, was a hotbed of communism. You think Berkeley was leftist in the 1960s and 1970s, you should've seen it in the thirties and early forties."

"If the choice is between peeping Toms and left-wing liberals," said Miranda, "I'll take the Berkeley crowd any day."

"Swell place," said Thornton, "if you like Marx and Lenin." I heard a faint warning bell begin to ring in the back of my mind, but I shrugged it off. "Oppenheimer and the people he brought to Los Alamos were brilliant, no doubt about it," the agent continued. "They were the ones who put the pieces of the bomb together. But Los Alamos leaked like a sieve. Oppenheimer ran Los Alamos sort of like a university physics department. He held seminars where people talked openly about the bomb. He gave folks a mimeographed handout—*The Los Alamos Primer,* it was called—that summed up everything they knew about how to build an atomic bomb."

"Probably helped speed things along," said Miranda. "Synergy, cross-fertilization of ideas, intellectual critical mass—all that stuff we liberal ivory-tower types believe in, you know?"

Thornton frowned at her slightly; he didn't seem to approve of the handout, and he didn't seem to like the edgy comment, either. "It might have helped speed the Manhattan Project, but it also helped speed the Soviets," he said. "One of the Los Alamos physicists, Klaus Fuchs, gave a copy of the primer, or the key details from it, to a Soviet intelligence agent in June of 1945. It was like handing over a set of blueprints for the bomb. The guy betrayed us for five hundred bucks."

I wasn't sure I'd heard correctly. "Five hundred dollars? The Soviets got America's atomic secrets for five hundred dollars?"

He nodded. "I like Oak Ridge," he said. "Oak Ridge was way bigger than Los Alamos, but a lot tighter-lipped. A lot more compartmentalized, too. Most people didn't know what they were working on. They tended not to talk about it or speculate about it. And if they did, they got escorted out the gate, because anybody they talked to could have been a snitch."

"A snitch?" Miranda sounded offended by the word. "What makes you say snitch?"

"Only word for it," he said. "Security was a huge priority in Oak Ridge. There were hundreds of military intelligence officers in Oak Ridge. Some in uniform, some not. Some had cover jobs—they went around testing batteries and changing lightbulbs, menial work that let them watch and listen to workers all over the place. But the serious snitching was the Acme Credit Corporation."

Miranda snorted. "Acme? How corny is that? Sounds like something from a Road Runner cartoon."

Thornton smiled slightly. "It does sound corny these days, doesn't it? It might not have sounded so corny back then—back before Road Runner. Back in the middle of a struggle for world domination."

Miranda flushed slightly. "Sorry," she said. "I didn't mean to get all cynical and ironic on you. What was the Acme Credit Corporation?"

"A bogus name and a post-office box in Knoxville," said Thornton. "If the military intelligence people decided you were trustworthy—from your background check or their eavesdropping or whatever—they'd ask you to keep your eyes and ears open, and report anything that seemed suspicious. If you agreed, they'd give you these preaddressed ACME CREDIT CORPORATION envelopes and blank cards, and if you thought something or somebody seemed fishy, all you had to do was jot down their name and what they said or did on the card, then drop it in the mail. If you *didn't* see anything, you sent in a blank card. Every tip got investigated."

Miranda leaned back in her chair and bit her lower lip slightly. In my experience, anytime she did that, an argument was about to ensue. "What kind of fishiness? 'So-and-so is making bombs in his basement' fishiness? Or 'so-and-so likes to wear his wife's underwear' fishiness?"

"Probably some of each," he said. "One episode I heard about involved a fellow who was spouting off at lunch one day about the Soviet system of government being better than the American system. A day or two later, Acme got a note, and the guy was gone—given his walking papers and told not to come back."

"Whatever happened to freedom of speech?" Miranda was shaking her head. "Sounds a lot like East Berlin during the Cold War, the way people ratted out their friends and neighbors to the Stasi."

"Oh, come on," said Thornton. "We were in the midst of a horrific war. Global, apocalyptic war. Secret codes, spies, sabotage—those were real things, legitimate concerns. A slight erosion of civil liberties in a top secret military installation seems pretty far down on the list of World War II evils, if you ask me."

"Children, childen," I said. "Let's not bicker." I heard Miranda draw a deep breath, and saw her relax, which meant Thornton and I could relax, too. "Does the army have a card that could tell us why Leonard Novak was reading books on espionage when he was killed?"

"That's what I'm hoping," he said. "We've got people combing the Venona transcripts to see if they can find anything that might connect with Novak."

Miranda looked puzzled. "Venona was the code name for a massive counterespionage operation," Thornton explained. "Between 1944 and 1948, the agency that's now called the NSA—the National Security Agency—intercepted and decoded thousands of telegram cables sent to Moscow from Soviet consulates around the world. Most of them were boring, bureaucratic stuff. But some, especially the ones from New York to Moscow, were spy reports. They used code names for people and places—the messages were in code, so the names were codes within codes—but the code-breakers eventually managed to decipher most of them. Amazing feat, really, because the Soviets were using complicated codes that changed every day. Cryptanalysists have extra gears in their minds—like physicists—that help them grasp things we mere mortals can't make sense of. Anyhow, one of the interesting intercepts was telegram 940—"

"Telegram 940? I like it," Miranda interrupted. "It even *sounds* like something from a spy thriller." She was leaning forward on the table, rapt with attention now. Thornton smiled, pleased to have won her over, or relieved that she was off her civil-liberties high horse.

"Telegram 940 was sent in December 1944," he said. "It listed seventeen scientists who were working on what it called 'the problem.' The names included Enrico Fermi, Hans Bethe, Nils Bohr, George Kistiakowsky, Ernest

Lawrence, Edward Teller, John von Neumann, and Arthur Compton—some of the top brains of the Manhattan Project."

I held up a hand, which I practically had to wave directly between Thornton and Miranda to catch his attention. "I know some of those names," I said, "but not all. Fermi was the guy who cobbled together the little reactor under the stadium in Chicago. But Bethe and Bohr—remind me. Physicists?"

"Right," he said. "They were in the Theoretical Division at Los Alamos. Bohr was a Nobel laureate—so were Lawrence and Fermi, of course. Bohr escaped from Denmark under the noses of the Nazis, who were hoping to recruit him. He made it to London, then he and his son were flown to the States in an army transport plane."

"Edward Teller," said Miranda. "I'm not a fan of his."

"No, I wouldn't expect you to be," he said. "Teller's big claim to fame came in the late forties and fifties, of course, when he pushed for the hydrogen bomb—the 'super,' he called it—over the objections of Oppenheimer. Back during the Manhattan Project, Teller and von Neumann helped develop the implosion trigger for the plutonium bomb, the one used on Nagasaki." I saw Miranda's eyes cloud at the mention of Nagasaki; I'd noticed that anytime a discussion turned from the herculean labors of the Manhattan Project to the explosive fruits of those labors, it troubled her.

I tossed in another question, hoping to lead us away from Nagasaki. "How about Kistiakowsky? I never heard of him."

"Interesting guy," said Thornton. "Explosives expert. He cleared the first ski slope in Los Alamos by using rings of explosives to cut down trees."

"Cool dude," said Miranda. "See, that's a use of explosives I can really get behind." I was just congratulating myself on asking about Kistiakowsky when Thornton dropped the other, unfortunate shoe.

"Kistiakowsky was one of the unsung heroes of the project, if you ask me," he said. "He was the bridge between the pie-in-the-sky theoretical physics and the nuts-and-bolts realities of building the bomb—the 'Gadget,' they called it in Los Alamos—and making it actually explode. Kistiakowsky came up with what's called the implosion lenses for the plutonium."

"Lenses?" I hadn't known the atomic bomb involved optics.

"Not really lenses," he said. "That was the term they used for wedges they formed out of conventional high explosives. The lenses surrounded the spherical core of plutonium. The theory was, when the lenses exploded, they'd create a very focused shock wave, which would compress the plutonium enough to cause critical mass."

"And kablooey?" The edge on Miranda's question was so fine as to be nearly invisible. I noticed it, but Thornton didn't.

"Kablooey," he said, with unfortunate cheerfulness. "But the wedges, the lenses, had to be machined with incredible precision—like, accurate to zillionths of an inch. Nobody thought Kistiakowsky could do it, including Oppenheimer. In fact," he went on, warming to the story, "one reason they did the Trinity test with a plutonium bomb was because they were confident the uranium bomb would work but afraid the plutonium bomb would be a dud. Poor Kistiakowsky was already being set up as the scapegoat for failure. He finally got so fed up with the skepticism that he bet Oppenheimer a whole month's pay—against just ten bucks from Oppenheimer—that it would work. And of course it did."

"So Kistiakowsky got his ten bucks," said Miranda, "and Nagasaki got vaporized." Her voice dripped sarcasm. "A real win-win."

"Could've been worse," said Thornton, finally punching back. "Fermi could've won his bet."

Oh hell, I thought, *here we go.*

"And what was Fermi betting," she snapped, "that maybe we'd come to our senses and not use the damn thing on innocent civilians?"

"Guys, guys," I said, trying to de-escalate the conflict, but the chain reaction had gotten out of hand.

"No," shot back Thornton. "Fermi was betting the bomb would ignite the atmosphere. He was taking side bets, too: Would it incinerate the whole world, or just New Mexico?"

"Jesus," said Miranda. "That is sickening."

"You. Weren't. *There.*" Thornton's voice was quiet but hard as steel. "How dare you judge them? How dare you? You and I are part of the most sheltered, pampered generation ever to walk the face of this earth. These scientists, a lot of them, were refugees, Jewish refugees, from Europe—the land of Hitler, the land of the Holocaust, remember? Six million Jews murdered, just for being Jews. Tens of millions of other civilians killed just for living in the wrong place, the wrong time, the wrong politics. If those scientists felt the need for a little gallows humor, who can blame them? The gallows was casting a shadow over the whole damn world at the time. How dare you sit there in your privileged, liberal smugness and pass moral judgment on them?"

Miranda drew back as if he'd slapped her. "Excuse me," she whispered. She stood up, and before I knew what was happening, she was gone, the steel door of the bone lab banging shut behind her.

Thornton and I sat staring at each other. "Well, shit," he finally said. "I just scorched the earth, didn't I?"

"I should've stopped you somehow," I said. "Kicked you under the table. Clobbered you with a femur."

He rubbed his face with his hands. "The hell of it is, I really like her," he said. "I thought maybe she liked me, too."

"She did," I said. "And she's notoriously picky."

"Crap."

"Oh well," I said. "You'll always have Paris. Or Verona. Or Venona. Was there anything else about Venona or Novak or—I don't know, about *anything*—you'd planned to tell us, before you went stomping across the minefield of Miranda's opinions?"

He sighed. "A little," he said. "Nothing concrete yet; just some tantalizing possibilities. There are lots of code names in the Venona transcripts that have never been deciphered—hundreds of Soviet spies in the United States back in the forties that have never been identified. We're hoping, if we sift back through the transcripts again, maybe we'll get lucky; maybe find something that ties to Novak."

"Not to be too negative," I said, "but if they threw thousands of people and millions of dollars at this back when it really mattered, isn't it likely to be a dead end by now?"

"Not necessarily," he said. "New things still bubble up. Just a couple years ago, we got some new insight on one of the few spies who infiltrated Oak Ridge. A health physicist, guy named Koval, who worked at Oak Ridge and Los Alamos and Hanford during the war. His job was checking radiation levels, so he got a look at all the crucial process equipment for creating weapons-grade uranium and plutonium, and nobody suspected him at the time, even though he'd lived and studied in Russia."

"I thought you said security in Oak Ridge was tight. They turned a Russian loose with a Geiger counter?"

"His parents were Russian immigrants, but Koval was an American, actually—born in Iowa, and christened George. Millions of European and Russian immigrants came to the U.S. in the early part of the twentieth century—the 'huddled masses yearning to breathe free,' remember? Koval's parents were among them."

One of the notations on Leonard Novak's yellow notepad popped into my head. "George Koval?" Thornton nodded. "Novak wrote the initials 'GK' shortly before he died, and he was reading books about Venona at the time. Maybe he knew about Koval. Maybe they collaborated. Can you guys interrogate George, see if our guy Novak was one of his comrades?"

"George is outside our jurisdiction," Thornton said dryly. "Moved to Moscow in 1948, died in 2006. After he died, Vladimir Putin awarded him Russia's highest medal."

"Damn," I said. "Well, between the Acme Credit Corporation and the Venona transcripts, maybe something will turn up."

He gave a rueful smile. "Unlike Kistiakowsky, I wouldn't bet a month's pay on it," he said. "Hell, I wouldn't bet ten bucks. But we'll keep digging." He thought of something. "You still in the good graces of the woman in Oak Ridge?"

I blushed. "The librarian? Isabella?"

He shook his head. "No, the old lady. Beatrice. The one that married Novak without having done due diligence about his sexual orientation."

"Ah. No, I haven't talked to Beatrice since she outed Novak as gay, but it's not like she and I have had a spat."

"Lucky you," he said. "Listen, since you seem to bring out the gift of gab in Madame Beatrice, how about chatting her up some more, see if she thinks Novak was giving secrets to the Soviets?"

"If she snitches on him, should I send a note to the Acme Credit Corporation?"

"Sure," he said. "We check the P.O. box twice a day." He pushed back from the table. "I reckon I'll slink back to my office now," he said. "I've done enough damage here for one day."

"You mean Miranda?" He nodded. "Surely you're not throwing in the towel so soon," I said. "I thought you G-men never gave up. 'We always get our man'—wasn't that an early FBI slogan?"

"Nah, that was the Canadian Mounties," he said. "They had a better sloganeer than we did. Besides, this thing with

Miranda, it's outside my field of expertise. The bad guys, they're pretty easy to figure out, Doc. It's the great women that are truly mysterious."

"I know, Chip," I said. I walked him to the door of the lab. "That's what makes them great."

21

FOUR HOURS AFTER THE blowup in the bone lab, as I was about to head to Oak Ridge for another stroll through the past with Beatrice, I heard a light tap on my door. Looking up, I was surprised to see Miranda; normally she just barged right in, her arrival accompanied by a wisecrack—usually one at my expense. Her eyes were red and she looked off-balance. I pointed to an empty chair that was shoved against the radiator under the window.

"No offense," I said, "but you don't look so hot."

"I look a lot better than I feel," she said. I was alarmed—was she developing symptoms of radiation sicknesss?—but she read my expression and swiftly waved a hand to let me know her problem wasn't medical.

"You want to talk about it?" It seemed a safe question, since she'd shown up at my door, but as fragile as she seemed, I wanted to go easy.

"Some of it," she said. "The ideas part. Not the boy-girl part."

I wasn't sure what she meant. "The ideas?"

"The ideas. The *ideals*. The people. Patriots and traitors. Hard choices and hellish compromises."

"Maybe we should send out for pizza," I said. "And a six-pack of philosophers."

She plunked down into the chair with a sigh. "In a way, the problem all boils down to the difference between

Groves and Oppenheimer," she said. "And it's all written in their eyes." I furrowed my brow at her. "Groves was like the ultimate can-do guy," she said. "The steamroller of the Manhattan Project. Get it done, get it done, get it done. No matter what. He and his secret project had *so much power.* Groves had the authority to take whatever he wanted, build whatever was necessary. Not enough copper to make the Y-12 calutrons? No problem; we'll just take fifteen thousand tons of silver from the U.S. Treasury. Not sure the calutrons can make enough uranium? We'll build a gaseous-diffusion plant, too, the biggest factory in the world. Not sure uranium's the ticket? Let's make plutonium, too. He hedged all his bets, but in the end, all his bets paid off." I nodded; to lessen the risk of failure, Groves had indeed pursued multiple paths to the bomb, and all of them succeeded. "But look at him, Dr. B."

She pulled a photo of General Groves from a folder she'd brought with her and laid it on the desk. It was a famous photo, one I'd seen countless times since cutting Novak from the ice. The picture showed Groves studying a map of Japan. No, not studying it, exactly; more like burning a hole in it with his eyes. The general's belly was doughy and his jowls were flabby, but his eyes were like lasers locked on a target. "That man's horizon didn't extend one inch beyond Japan," she said. "Build the bomb; drop the bomb."

"He was a good fit for the job," I said.

"Now look at Oppenheimer," she said, slipping another photo from the folder. The physicist was wearing the porkpie hat that had been his trademark, much like the battered fedora of Indiana Jones. A cigarette hung from Oppenheimer's lips, and a wisp of smoke wafted up the left side of his face. A skinny tie was cinched around a scrawny neck—no flabby jowls on Oppenheimer—and the nubby collar of a tweed jacket gapped open above bony shoulders. At the center of the image was a pair of haunted, haunting eyes. They were staring straight into the lens, but they seemed to be focused on something far beyond it. "Do you see? Those are the eyes of a man who's been chained to a rock; a man staring at eternity," she said. "Where's the border between America and Japan, or America and Russia, when you're staring at eternity?"

"Are you sure he can see that far, Miranda? And are you sure you can see into his soul?"

"Come on, Dr. B. When the Trinity test worked, this guy didn't say 'yee haw' or 'hot damn' or even 'oh shit.' This guy said, 'I am become Death, the destroyer of worlds.' He agonized. He tried to rein in nuclear weapons after the war, and he was painted as a traitor for that."

"He did try," I said. "But not until after the war."

She frowned. "I know," she said, "and that's part of what's tragic about him. He built the bomb, and then he hated what it did, and hated the arms race it triggered. And then he was destroyed for opposing the arms race. Meanwhile, look at Werner von Braun. Von Braun was the brains behind the V-2 rockets that rained down on London during the war, but he became an American hero because he started building rockets for us instead of Hitler. Which brings me back to Klaus Fuchs, sort of. Was he a patriot or a traitor?"

"Traitor," I said. "No question. He sold atomic secrets to our enemies."

"But he was Jewish," she said. "To him, the ultimate enemy was Hitler. And if the enemy of your enemy is your friend, that makes Russia your friend. Besides, they were our ally. In theory, at least."

"Big difference between theory and practice," I said. "Stalin was a tyrant and a butcher—before the war as well as afterward."

"He was. But what's the only nation on earth to have ever used weapons of mass destruction in an act of war? The United States. Twice."

"We did it to save lives, Miranda," I said. "Not just U.S.

lives; Japanese lives, too. We fire-bombed Tokyo one night in March 1945. The firestorms destroyed fifteen square miles of the city and killed a hundred thousand civilians. Fire-bombing Tokyo didn't move Japan to surrender. It took the symbolic power of the atomic bomb to end the war."

"Highly debatable," she said. "The Japanese sent out surrender overtures in late July, before Hiroshima. But we brushed them aside, because by that point we'd tested the bomb. We knew it worked, and we wanted to drop it. Not just to cinch the victory over Japan, but to intimidate the Russians, because we could already tell they were going to be our next big problem."

"But they weren't all that intimidated," I pointed out. "Because by then they had blueprints of the bomb from Fuchs in Los Alamos. And descriptions of uranium-enrichment equipment from George Koval. Who knows, maybe they even had plutonium reactor blueprints from Leonard Novak."

Miranda groaned. "Dammit," she said. "Is. A. *Puzzlement.*" It was a line she often quoted from an old Broadway musical—*The King and I*—and it made me smile. If she was up to quoting show tunes, her angst had eased. "Okay," she sighed, "I know it breaks your heart to hear this, but I need to go home and feed Immanuel Kat now."

"Does this mean we're not sending out for pizza and philosophers?"

"Not tonight," she said. "Maybe tomorrow, when we take up the problems of genocide and starvation in Africa."

"I can hardly wait," I said, as she disappeared through the doorway.

She leaned her head back around the frame. "So, um . . ." She trailed off.

"Ye-e-s-s-s?"

"Thornton," she said. "A shame. I was kinda liking him."

I suppressed a smile. "I think he was kinda liking you, too. And I hear he's notoriously picky."

"Crap," she said, and disappeared into the hallway again.

Then she reappeared once more. "The fundamental moral and ethical problem," she said, "is this. I suspect Thornton's a Republican. I could never sleep with a Republican."

"Heavens no," I said. "That would be a hellish compromise."

22

AS I PARKED AT Beatrice's curb and headed toward her door, I noticed that I felt eager, almost as eager as if I were heading to a death scene to recover a skeleton. I told myself that this was natural; I was returning, after all, at the request of Emert and Thornton, who hoped I might extract more information from her than they had. But that wasn't it, or wasn't entirely it; her stories had shed a few glimmers on Novak, but mostly it was Beatrice herself who occupied the limelight of her stories. I knew better than to push her too hard about Novak; the one time I'd tried it, she'd all but played the senility card, just as she'd done with the law enforcement officers. But there was another reason I let her ramble on about herself, rather than demanding answers about Novak. The truth of the matter, I realized as I entered her house and poured her vodka, was that I'd fallen under the spell of the old woman and her stories, just as I'd fallen under the spell of the black-and-white photos and films in the museum and the library. The images gave me vivid glimpses of another time, when men and women toiled desperately in secret cities, and when science attained tragic greatness. Beatrice's stories gave those images a human face and a human voice.

It was that reflective mood, I suppose, that prompted me to say, "It's odd, isn't it, that I'm sitting here again, back for another story?"

"No, not at all," she said. "It couldn't be any other way. Each moment of your life is the sum total of all the prior moments. There's not a single thing that happens to you that doesn't leave its mark; doesn't redirect your course somehow; doesn't make you more fully who you are. It took every single step—even the steps you took as life dragged you by the hair of your head—to put you exactly where you are. When I was a girl, life dragged me from Tennessee to New York and then back to Tennessee."

"Tell me about that," I said. "Tell me the story."

23

MY FATHER DIED WHEN *I was ten. My mother was a night auditor for a hotel in Chattanooga, so I got used to being alone at night at an early age. Getting used to it's not the same as liking it, though. My father was gone for good; sometimes it seemed like my mother was, too.*

The Christmas I was thirteen, Mother took me to New York on the train. My Aunt Rachel and Uncle Isaac lived there—Aunt Rachel was my father's sister—and Mother said she wanted to visit them and show me the sights of New York for Christmas. We changed trains in Raleigh about lunchtime on a Friday, and we rode all night to get to New York. We shared a bunk in a sleeper car, and I remember falling asleep with my mother's arms wrapped around me, which was something that hadn't happened in years.

We got to Penn Station—this was Old Penn Station, mind you, which was spectacular, a lot grander than Grand Central—late in the afternoon on Christmas Day. From there we took a cab across town to Rockefeller Center. The outdoor ice-skating rink there had just opened, that very day. It was December 25, 1936. It was so beautiful it made my heart ache—all those Christmas decorations and lights, and everybody dressed up in their best winter clothes.

The country had just begun to crawl up out of the Great

Depression, and that Christmas night in Rockefeller Square, I think people weren't just celebrating the birth of Jesus, they were celebrating the rebirth of America. Mother and I waited in line for hours to skate, dragging our battered little suitcases with us. I didn't mind the wait; I was giddy with the sights and sounds and glamour of it all. Finally, when we got up to the front of the line, Mother told me that she wasn't going to skate; she would stay with our suitcases and just watch me. She asked a boy in line behind us if he'd help me get the hang of it. He was about my age, maybe a year or two older. Old enough to be interesting to me; not so old as to be scary. He held my hand and pulled me along, wobbling and shrieking and laughing. Every time we made a lap past the place where Mother was standing beside the rail, she'd wave and yell something encouraging.

And then the boy let go of my hand, and I was skating by myself. It was terrifying and thrilling—I'm sure I was just inching along, but it felt so daring and grown-up, and I couldn't wait to circle back around and see Mother's face when she realized I was doing it without any help. But her face wasn't there. The fat man in the red scarf, who had been standing right beside her, was still there; so was the nun who had been on the other side. But she was gone, and the space where she had been standing was already closing up behind her.

I slid past the fat man and the nun—I was confused, and I also didn't know how to stop—and went around the rink once more. The second time I came around, I ran into the rail to stop. I was still a few feet away from the two faces I recognized, so I pulled myself along the rail, my feet sliding out from under me again and again. I remember people laughing and pointing every time I caught myself on the rail and then hauled myself back up. By the time I got to the fat man and the nun, my heart had turned to ice, and I could feel tears running down my face—not because people were laughing at me, but because I knew something was wrong.

Our suitcases were both still there, wedged up against the railing right where she'd been standing. The nun told me my mother had needed to run to the restroom, and would be back in a few minutes. But somehow I knew she wouldn't be.

After I'd stood at the railing crying for half an hour, the nun helped me change out of the skates and back into my shoes, then she took me over to a policeman who was standing near the entrance to the rink. I told him what had happened, and I could see him sizing me up—a scrawny girl from the sticks, with a tear-streaked face and a dripping nose and a cheap cardboard suitcase. He got this sad, weary look on his face, and that's when I knew I'd never see my mother again.

On the cab ride up from Penn Station, Mother had tucked a big envelope into my coat pocket. She'd made a big production about how Aunt Rachel's address and phone number were in the envelope, along with a five-dollar bill and a Christmas card for Rachel and Uncle Isaac. "You hang on to this for me," she'd said. "You're such a big girl now, and you know how I lose things. This way, when we get in the taxi for Brooklyn, the address and the cab fare will be right there, safe in your pocket." As she said it, she patted the pocket.

When I told the policeman about Aunt Rachel and the envelope, he had me take it out and open it up. The Christmas card contained two letters. One was to Aunt Rachel, explaining how Mother had met a man she loved and wanted to be with, but the man—she didn't even say what his name was—just couldn't take on a thirteen-year-old. She was going away with him to South America, she said, where he would be working on a big construction project. She apologized for the unexpected Christmas present—me—and asked Rachel to please be kind to me.

The other letter was to me. She told me she loved me, and always would, and she hoped I could understand and forgive her someday. I never could, and I never did.

I don't know how Mother afforded the train tickets, but two possibilities occurred to me years later. Maybe she embezzled the money from the hotel where she worked. Or maybe the man she abandoned me for gave her the money.

I don't know whether she actually went to South America with the man. She might have just said that to throw us off the scent. Maybe she and her man settled down in Schenectady or Cincinnati. For that matter, I don't even know if there really was a man; maybe she made that up, too, as a plausible reason for turning her back on a child. All I know is that I never saw or heard from her again.

Aunt Rachel helped me get an after-school job in a Woolworth's five-and-dime in Brooklyn. It didn't pay much, but my little paychecks helped me feel like I was less of a burden to them. The summer after I graduated from high school, I got a job at the Grumman aircraft factory on Long Island. Grumman built fighter planes for the navy—the Wildcat and the Hellcat, which became famous for their toughness against the Japanese—and I helped build the instrument panels for them.

Aunt Rachel never said so, but I could tell I'd long since worn out my welcome, so as the summer went on, I mentioned that it might be time for me to get out on my own. New York was expensive, though, so I worried about how I'd manage. She mentioned her other brother—my father's brother, the one my mother had never liked. This uncle, Uncle Jake, lived in Knoxville, and he'd written Rachel to say that every girl in Tennessee was being hired for war work near Knoxville.

I stepped off the train in Knoxville in September of 1943, and a week later I started helping build the bomb, atom by atom.

24

I WALKED INTO THE bone lab and saw Miranda bent low over a lab table in concentration. It was a posture I'd seen her in so many times, for so many hours on end, that it sometimes surprised me to see that she was capable of standing, or even sitting up straight, rather than bending over bone fragments.

"Crap," she said. "I'm too stupid and klutzy for this."

"What are you working on?" I leaned around, expecting to see tiny bone fragments and a bottle of Duco cement. The skull of the North Knoxville skeleton had been crushed into dozens of pieces, some the size of rock salt. Instead of the drabness of bone, though, I saw a splash of vivid color: a small piece of fuchsia paper, creased into a bristling profusion of small triangles. "Is that origami?"

"It's supposed to be, but it's not. *Dammit!*" In frustration, she crumpled the paper and tossed it at a waste can beside the table. It missed, landing on the floor atop a heap of other wads of fuchsia.

"This might be a dumb question—" I began.

"Wouldn't be the first," she said.

"But if this is so frustrating, why are you doing it?"

"Because of a girl named Sadako," she said. "And a friend named Eddie."

"Sadako," I said. "Neighbor? Daughter of a neighbor?"

"No. Sadako was a two-year-old living in Hiroshima in

August of 1945. She was a mile and a half from the epicenter of the bomb blast. Sadako survived, but when she was twelve, she was diagnosed with leukemia." Miranda slid another square of paper from the package on the table and folded it into a triangle. "Someone who came to visit her in the hospital told her that if she folded a thousand paper cranes and made a wish, her wish would come true. She made it to six hundred and forty-four, and then she died."

Miranda folded the triangle in half again and again, into smaller triangles, and then gave the paper an angry yank that almost created wings, but not quite. I was formulating a logical response to her story about the girl—I thought of the dead in Pearl Harbor, the hundreds of thousands raped and slaughtered in China, the million projected to die in the assault on the Japanese home islands—when I noticed the misshapen wings begin to flutter. Miranda's hands were shaking, and as I looked at them, I noticed that three of her fingertips, the three that had touched the iridium pellet in the morgue, were red and blistered. "Jesus, Miranda, we need to get you to the ER and get your fingers examined."

She shook her head. "I went early this morning," she said. "Dr. Davies met me there, and he talked to Dr. Sorensen on the phone. If the pain gets bad and the tissue gets necrotic, they'll give me painkillers and ointments and antibiotics. But for now, there's nothing to be done except 'watchful waiting.' Watching and waiting to see if my fingertips die or heal. Watching and waiting to see if Eddie heals or dies." She studied her fingertips. "The necrosis has started in his hands." She said it calmly, but then the shaking got worse. The tremor traveled up her arms to her shoulders, which began to quake. She said "dammit" again, very softly, and I knew she was not cursing the complexities of origami now. "Why," she said, "God in heaven, why?"

"I don't know, Miranda. I can't think of anybody who deserves this less than you and Eddie."

"Oh, Dr. B.," she cried, "I'm not asking 'why' about Eddie and me. I'm asking 'why' about everything else. Everybody else. All the horror we've inflicted on one another."

I'd known Miranda for years now; she could be as tough as cheap steak about her own hurts, but her heart bled freely for others. By "everybody else," I figured she meant the dead of Hiroshima and Nagasaki, and maybe even more than those: maybe also Dresden and Auschwitz, Gettysburg and Shiloh, Rwanda and Darfur and Baghdad. I laid one hand on her shoulder; with the other, I reached behind me and retrieved a Kleenex box from the desk. The paper bird fell from her hand, fluttered to the floor, and lay still. "Fucking war," she whispered through clenched teeth. "God damn it to hell."

"Yes," I said. "God damn it to hell."

I set the Kleenex box on the table, gave her shoulder a squeeze, and eased out of the bone lab. I hung the DO NOT DISTURB sign on the knob, locked the door behind me, and retreated to my office at the far end of the stadium. There, I locked my own door and unplugged the phone. I did a quick search of the Internet and clicked on a link that filled my computer screen with purple squares and triangles, crisscrossed with dotted lines. "Best Origami Crane Folding Instructions," the caption read. I took a sheet of paper from the printer tray and folded it diagonally. I creased it between my fingertips until the edges were sharp as a blade.

THAT NIGHT I had a dream. In my dream, Garcia and Miranda reached out to me for help, but their outstretched hands crumbled before my eyes, leaving bloody stumps at the ends of their wrists. Then the dream shifted, and I was speaking to a large crowd in an auditorium in Oak Ridge. I realized I was talking to them about the atomic genie their city had helped loose from the bottle, and I realized I was distraught. I heard myself say to them, "Was anyone ever helped by it?" There was a stunned silence when I said it; even I, who dreamed the words, was shocked by them. Then, near the back of the room, I glimpsed movement. A woman rose slowly to her feet and stood. Her head was wrapped tightly in a scarf, in the manner favored by women who have lost their hair to radiation or chemotherapy. The woman didn't speak; she didn't move; she simply stood, holding that space, a calm answer to the bitter question I had posed.

Heads had swiveled in her direction when she stood, and the atmosphere in the dream-room suddenly felt alive and electric, the way the Tennessee air prickles just before a summer thunderstorm. Then a second person stood, and soon a dozen other people were on their feet, all bearing silent witness to cures effected, diseases diagnosed, homes heated, pipelines and airliners made safe.

The last person to stand was directly in front of me. He rose slowly, as if it cost him some pain to stand, and his head was bowed. He raised his head slowly, and I found myself staring into eyes that were both haunted and hopeful. I found myself staring into the eyes of Robert Oppenheimer.

When I awoke—or dreamed I awoke—I seemed to see the world through such eyes myself.

25

THORNTON HAD SENT A peace offering to Miranda—a dozen stems of iris, not yet unfurled, looking like green artists' brushes dipped in indigo paint. Seven small sunflowers were tucked amid the blue tips, blazing like a week of summer days. Miranda wasn't in the lab when I saw them; I knew they were from Thornton by the business card lying beside the vase, bearing his name, the FBI logo, and the word "Peace?" The man had flair, and he seemed smart and spunky, so maybe he was still in the game.

But he wasn't ready to risk a personal appearance just yet, so I agreed to pick him up at the Federal Building, in downtown Knoxville, for our trip to Oak Ridge National Laboratory. I'd come up with an idea about how we might search for the dead man shown on Novak's film, and Thornton wanted to talk with someone in the Lab's radioisotopes program, so we decided to ride-share.

Once we crossed the Solway Bridge, we headed west on Bethel Valley Road, a long, straight, prairie-flat ribbon of two-lane leading to the research complex. Five miles out Bethel Valley we stopped at a security checkpoint, where an armed guard consulted a clipboard and my driver's license, then nodded slightly at me. He practically genuflected at Thornton's FBI shield. Not that I was jealous or anything.

The road beelined along another two miles of valley

floor, lined on either side by pines and hardwood. It grazed the end of a frozen cove on Melton Hill Lake, then entered the sprawling laboratory. Oak Ridge National Laboratory—known as "the Lab" to most of the scientists who worked there, as "ORNL" to the acronym-inclined, and as "X-10" to the blue-collared hourly workers—was the only research facility created in Oak Ridge during the Manhattan Project. The Y-12 and K-25 plants had been huge production facilities staffed by hourly workers like Beatrice. The wartime Lab, though, had a higher ratio of physicists, chemists, and engineers. The Lab had been built around the Graphite Reactor—a much bigger version of Fermi's makeshift Chicago reactor—so that Leonard Novak and his colleagues could devise the means to create and purify weapons-grade plutonium.

As Thornton and I turned off Bethel Valley Road and entered the research complex, we found ourselves surrounded by gleaming new buildings of glass and steel. Although the Lab was owned by the federal government—the Department of Energy—it was jointly operated these days by UT and Battelle, a research institute with billions of dollars in government contracts. Clearly the partnership had been a fruitful one, at least architecturally speaking.

After parking, Thornton and I threaded our way past the new buildings, and I began to recognize the massive Cold War buildings I remembered from a prior visit, years before. The old buildings hadn't been replaced by the new buildings; they'd simply been supplemented and screened from initial view. We walked down a one-lane alley between two looming buildings, labeled 4500 NORTH and 4500 SOUTH, and then entered a metal doorway set in the vast brick wall of 4500 South. Just inside, a staircase led down into a basement and upward to two additional floors of offices and labs. We climbed one flight, then entered a hallway labeled H CORRIDOR. I knocked on the open doorway of the first office—the office was dark, which made me worry that I'd somehow gone astray—but a voice called, "Come in."

Arpad Vass emerged from the dimness to shake my hand and turn on the light; the fluorescents were bright enough to hurt my eyes at first, and I could understand why Arpad might prefer the dark, at least for computer work.

Arpad was one of the most innovative graduate students I'd ever had. Rather than focusing on physical anthropology—bones, essentially—Arpad's Ph.D. research had focused on chemicals. Specifically, he developed a way to interpret the chemicals of decomposition like a clock, one that told the time since death.

For the past five years, Arpad had been collecting and analyzing the gases given off by bodies as they decomposed. In one corner of the Body Farm, he'd buried four bodies in graves of varying depths. He threaded the graves with a grid of perforated pipes leading to the surface of the ground. Every two weeks since burying the bodies, he had collected air samples from within and above the graves, and had run the samples through a gas chromatograph—mass spectrometer, a sophisticated analytical instrument that isolated individual compounds from the smelly samples. Over the course of the experiment, Arpad had identified nearly five hundred separate compounds given off by bodies as they decay. Many of the compounds were common, found virtually everywhere in nature; however, he'd found about thirty key compounds that—collectively—could be read as the fingerprint of a buried body. More specifically, as the fingerprint of a buried *human* body, rather than as the rotting remains of, say, a deer or dog or pig.

But Arpad wasn't just analyzing the chemical fingerprint of a buried body; he was also developing a gizmo that could detect that fingerprint out in the field. The gizmo, which he called "the sniffer," was a mechanical version of a cadaver dog's nose, and it was designed to find clandestine graves. The last time I'd seen him, Arpad was testing a prototype of the sniffer.

After shaking hands with Arpad, Thornton closed the door to the office. Arpad—a dark-haired, brown-eyed man of Hungarian descent—raised his eyebrows in an unspoken question. At Thornton's request, I hadn't told Arpad what we wanted to see him about; only that an FBI agent and I wanted to consult him about a forensic case.

"This is fairly sensitive," said Thornton. "We have evidence that a murder occurred in the vicinity of the Laboratory back during the Manhattan Project. We also suspect that espionage—spying for the Soviets—may have played some part in the murder."

"Interesting," said Arpad. "What's the evidence?"

Thornton nodded at me. I opened the manila envelope I'd brought with me and slid out the photographs, laying them on Arpad's desk. As he studied the images of the body and the shallow grave, he smiled. "That looks like pretty good evidence," he said. "This evidence has just come to light?" I nodded. "This body was never found?" I nodded again.

Arpad smiled again. "*Very* interesting," he said.

"Tell me about this sniffer you're working on," Thornton said. "How does it work—and how *well* does it work?"

If I hadn't known Arpad well, I probably wouldn't have noticed the flicker of impatience in his eyes. It lasted only a split second, and then—almost like flipping a switch—he was in presentation mode, pitching himself and his work to the agent. "The research is funded by the Department of Justice," he said. "We've been exploring two technologies for detecting clandestine graves. One is a simple off-the-shelf technology; the other is something more sophisticated, which we're creating from scratch for DOJ." He walked around the desk and picked up a pistol-shaped device from a bookshelf that lined the long wall of the office. In the place of a metal barrel, though, was an eighteen-inch black rubber tube, with a metal tip on the end. "This is a TopGun

H10X commercial Freon detector," Arpad said, "just like air-conditioning technicians use to check your central air for leaks." Thornton looked puzzled, and I was pretty sure I did, too, as I hadn't heard this part of Arpad's pitch before. "It turns out," Arpad went on, "that among the thirty key compounds a decaying body gives off, three are Freon compounds. So this is an easy way to do a crude search with existing, cheap technology. Here, I'll show you." Arpad opened up a file cabinet and removed a small glass vial sealed with a rubber stopper. Inside was about a teaspoonful of something that looked like garden-variety dirt.

"This is a soil sample from the surface of a shallow grave at the Body Farm," he said. He pried out the stopper; I sniffed, but I didn't smell decomp. "If the body had been on top of this, this would really stink," he said, and I nodded in agreement. "But since it was above the body, the volatile fatty acids weren't soaking into the dirt. Instead, as the bodies underneath off-gased, the gases slowly migrated up through the soil. Much, much fainter." He dug around in the file drawer and found a plastic bag, then laid the vial in the bottom of the bag. Next he flipped a switch on the detector. It growled to life, with a noise somewhere between a squeal and electronic static. Arpad dialed a switch and the noise subsided to an occasional chirp. Inserting the end of the Freon detector's wand in the bag, he clutched the bag tightly around the tube to seal it. After a few seconds, the detector began to chirp faster and faster, until soon it was almost back to a continuous squeal.

Thornton nodded, but there was a grudging quality to the nod. "So as long as somebody bags the body for you and you stick that wand in the bag, you can find the body?" This time anyone could have detected the impatience in Arpad's expression.

"That's about thirty grams of soil," Arpad said. "An ounce. There's probably a few picograms—a few billionths of an ounce—of decomp chemicals in that sample. This isn't infallible, but it's not bad for starters, considering that you can buy it on eBay for eighty bucks."

"So that's not the sniffer you're creating for DOJ, right?"

"Right. *This* is the sniffer we're creating for DOJ." Arpad opened a cabinet and removed an instrument that appeared to be a cross between a metal detector and a weed whacker. On closer inspection, I noticed that instead of a loop or a cutting head, the lower end of the device held a small cylindrical probe. Arpad flipped a switch at the upper end of the device, and it clicked slowly, much like a Geiger counter. "Depending on which sensors we put in the probe," he said, "we can search for a fresh body, a decaying body, or a really old one." He inserted the probe into the bag, and after a few seconds the clicks ran together into a machine-gun-fire buzz.

Thornton leaned forward and studied the sniffer. "So how long would it take to search an area with that rig?"

"Depends on how big the area is," said Arpad. "These photos seem to indicate the general location, but we could still be talking about an area a hundred yards square. If you tried to put the probe into the ground every square foot, you'd be taking eight hundred thousand samples. You got months to spend poking the tip of this into the ground?"

Thornton shrugged. "If that's what it takes. We've spent years looking for Jimmy Hoffa."

"Well, I don't have years," said Arpad. "I don't even have a week, because my DOJ sponsors are breathing down my neck to lock the design of this thing so they can start getting it into the hands of police departments all around the country."

"Any suggestions," I intervened, "on how we might harness this as efficiently as possible?"

"I suggest we bring in a cadaver dog to prescreen the search area, see if there are places he's interested in. Dogs cover ground faster than we can; a good dog could save us days or weeks of gridwork."

"I thought the idea behind this was to replace the dog," said Thornton.

"More like 'supplement' the dog," Arpad said. "Dogs have spent millions of years evolving great noses. They can be trained to pick up tiny, tiny traces of specific scents—bombs, drugs, truffles, tumors, human bones. Not only can they detect it, they can track it, swim upstream—figuratively speaking—to the source of it. Scent isn't a static, stationary thing; it's almost got a life of its own, like moving water: it flows, it pools, it sinks, it creeps along underground layers of rock. A good cadaver dog can work his way up that current of scent—a few molecules at a time—till he gets closer and closer to the source. If we bring in a good cadaver dog, we could narrow the search area by ninety percent or more."

"Sounds like a good idea," I said. "You know any good cadaver dogs?"

"Actually, yes," said Arpad. "A German shepherd named Cherokee. He found some bare human bones in a creek bed up near Bristol, which isn't particularly amazing; he found a freshly drowned man in twenty feet of water in the Big South Fork River, which *is* rather amazing. I actually worked with Cherokee to help calibrate the sniffer. I ran different decomp samples past him to see if he'd alert on them—to make sure he'd recognize them as human remains. Then I repeated the process with synthetic, laboratory mixtures of a few of the key chemicals in decomp. Cherokee alerted on them; so did the sniffer. All that was indoors. Then we went out into the woods, where we did all that again with buried samples. The dog found them all; so did the sniffer."

Thornton settled back in his chair and drummed his fingers together. "So, no offense intended," he said, "but what's the sniffer got that the dog doesn't have?"

"It's got stamina," said Arpad. "A dog's nose gives out pretty quickly—the neurons that send signals to the brain just get tired and quit sending. A cadaver dog can work intensely for maybe half an hour, tops, then he's got to rest. The only thing that gives out in the sniffer is the battery, and that takes sixty seconds to replace."

Thornton nodded, satisfied. "You reckon we could get Cherokee out here anytime soon to scout around, help us narrow down the search area?"

"I'll call and see," he said. "Where's the search area?" He reached back to a credenza tucked beneath the window and grabbed a cylinder of rolled paper. Unfurling a topographic map of the Oak Ridge Reservation, he spread it on his desk and weighted the corners with books.

Thornton and I looked at each other. "There's the rub," I said. "We're not exactly sure." Arpad's gaze swiveled from me to Thornton and back again. I laid one of the hillside pictures on the map. "We think it's buried here, where this picture of this barn was taken."

"And where's the barn?"

"That's the thing," I said. "We don't know where it is. Or was."

He looked stunned. "You're saying it could be—or could have been—anywhere on the reservation?" I nodded glumly. "And you don't even know if it still exists?" I nodded again. "This is a chemical probe, guys, not a magic wand," he said. "You're talking about a search area that's, what, fifty thousand acres? It would take a lifetime to probe this whole place. Several lifetimes. I don't mind looking for a needle in a haystack, but this is fifty thousand haystacks. Call me when you can narrow it down to just one."

AS WE DROVE away from the research complex, I said to Thornton, "Arpad's a little low-key, but he's really excited about this."

Thornton guffawed. "Yeah," he said. "And Miranda's voting Republican in the next election."

Now it was my turn to laugh. "Okay, he's not so excited," I admitted. "I was trying to be upbeat. Sorry we wasted the trip."

"Wasn't wasted," he said. "I can call up Arpad's sponsor at DOJ and tell him the gadget works. Long as you already know where the body is." I must have looked alarmed, because he quickly added, "Kidding. I'm kidding."

We headed east, back toward Oak Ridge and Knoxville, for about a mile, then Thornton pointed to a sign on the left. "There it is—SPALLATION NEUTRON SOURCE," he said. "That's my stop." The road wound uphill in a series of gentle S-curves; at the top of the ridge sprawled an immense new building, five curving stories of green glass and brushed aluminum.

"Wow," I said. "Arpad needs to make friends with these guys. They've got better digs." I parked near the entrance in a spot marked VISITOR, though we could have taken our pick of dozens of other convenient spots. "More parking, too."

"I think they're still putting the finishing touches on this," he said. "I don't believe the neutrons are spallating fully just yet."

"Remind me what spallation means," I said, as we walked toward the glass doors.

"Comes from the same root word as *spa-lat*," he said, then he laughed. "Nah, kidding again. It's from *spalling*—chipping—like concrete does. Spallation's a subatomic version of concrete chipping. This thing fires zillions of neutrons out a huge linear accelerator—see that long, straight dike of dirt there, running from the main building over to that smaller building way over there? I think the accelerator's under there. Anyhow, it shoots neutrons at experimental targets or materials, and then people who are a lot smarter than I am figure out all sorts of important things about those materials, based on what happens when the neutrons bash into them."

"Bash?"

"Bash. Splat. Wham. Take your pick. They're all scientifically rigorous and precise."

"Rigorous," I said.

"And precise."

"So they make radioisotopes here with some of the bashing?"

"Huh? I don't think so," he said. "Where'd you hear that?"

"Well, you have a meeting with an isotopes-production guy," I said, "and we're here."

"Ah," he said. "A reasonable inference, but wrong. They make the isotopes at a research reactor, the High-Flux Isotope Reactor. But the security's tighter there, and the digs are better here. And the isotopes guy is apparently better connected than Arpad."

Thornton's "isotopes guy"—the program's director, it turned out, named Barry Vandergriff—met us in the atrium and motioned us toward a cluster of overstuffed armchairs in an alcove of the lobby. I excused myself from their meeting and wandered among a series of displays that showed cutaway drawings of the facility's accelerator and neutron-beam guides and experimental capabilities. Some of it was over my head, but I did grasp the notion that neutrons—and how they got deflected or scattered as they bounced off materials, or passed through them—could shed a lot of light on the molecular structure of metals, plastics, even the proteins that make up living organisms.

I had just begun to study a large, mercury-filled metal tank—the mercury served as an immense catcher's mitt, apparently, to stop the neutron beam after it had passed through its experimental target—when Thornton tapped me on the shoulder. "I'm done," he said. "You ready, or did you want to study up some more?"

"I'm ready," I said. "I'm up to my eyeballs in neutrons."

As we walked out of the building, Thornton said, "I wanted to talk to this guy to get more background on the iridium sources for radiographic cameras—who makes those sources, and how, and where."

"And could he? Did he?"

"He could," he said. "He did."

"And?"

"For years, the only U.S. source of iridium-192 was the High-Flux Isotope Reactor, right here in Oak Ridge."

"But now there are other U.S. sources?"

"No. Now not even HFIR's making it. Too expensive. Now it's imported from reactors in Belgium and the Netherlands and South Africa."

"It's cheaper to make it overseas and ship it in?"

"I guess so," he said. "Maybe those governments subsidize the isotope reactors better, or maybe safety standards are lower or labor's cheaper. Anyhow, that complicates our efforts to pin down where this came from."

"Damn," I said. "If this stuff has a half-life of only seventy-four days, how's there time to ship it halfway around the world?"

He shrugged. "They ship sushi from Tokyo to New York, and sushi has a lot shorter half-life than this stuff. It's just a matter of figuring out a fast, reliable delivery system. Hell, iridium-192 can be air-expressed on DHL or FedEx if the shipment's not huge and the container's approved."

I almost wished he hadn't told me that. I wasn't sure I'd look at those delivery trucks in quite the same way ever again.

26

"WHERE DO YOU WANT to have dinner?"

The question caught me by surprise. "Excuse me?" I pulled the cell phone slightly away from my ear and glanced at the display, hoping for quick enlightenment. I didn't recognize the number, but I did recognize the 482 as an Oak Ridge number. *"Oh,"* I said, a smile breaking across my face. "I think you should be the one to choose. Since I gather you've hit the jackpot. Or found the barn."

"Maybe," said Isabella, the librarian. "If I'm wrong, I'll pay you back. But I don't think I'm wrong."

"Then pick a good restaurant," I said. "The best in Oak Ridge."

"The best in Oak Ridge? That's easy."

Ninety minutes later, I parked my truck in the lot beside Wildcat Stadium, the high school football field in Oak Ridge, and one of the city's earliest landmarks. Although the original high school had long since been demolished—replaced by a sprawling, modern complex two miles away, right across the Turnpike from Isabella's library—the stadium had never been replaced. Tucked into a natural hollow in the side of Black Oak Ridge, the stadium—home to quite a few championship football teams over the years—felt like small-town Americana. From where I parked, I could see the stadium, Chapel on the Hill, and the Alexander Inn. Clustered so close together, they seemed an architectural trinity of sorts, embodying human play, spiritual sanctuary, a scientific crossroads. Such a small town; such a big legacy.

Crossing Broadway, the two-block street that separated the football field from Jackson Square, I strolled beneath a sidewalk awning and stepped into the finest restaurant in Oak Ridge, and one of the finest in East Tennessee: Big Ed's Pizza.

Big Ed's was the creation of Ed Neusel, and the nickname was actually an understatement. Big Ed was a mountain of a man, as anyone who'd seen him perched on the bar stool at the back of the pizzeria could attest. Big Ed had long since gone to that great pizza kitchen in the sky, but his legacy and his likeness lived on. The restaurant's glass front window featured a larger-than-life caricature of Big Ed's face. T-shirts featuring the same likeness—and the quote I MAKE MY OWN DOUGH—were considered must-have souvenirs by tourists savvy enough to appreciate Oak Ridge's contributions to history and cuisine.

The kitchen was open, and ran most of the length of the deep, narrow restaurant. Behind the counter that separated the kitchen from the dining area, eight or ten high school kids—all wearing Big Ed's T-shirts—hustled beneath fluorescent lights, twirling disks of dough, dealing out toppings, shuttling pies in and out of a wallful of ovens. During his lifetime, Ed Neusel had always been quick to give a kid a job, and I was pleased to see that his policy, like his pizza, had survived his passing.

The dining area was dark as a cave—black ceiling, dark hardwood floor, dingy walls, dim lights. That was probably for the best. I felt my foot slip slightly, on grease or tomato sauce or a mix of the two, until its skid was halted by a sticky patch of drying beer or soda. There was probably a health inspector's rating posted on a wall somewhere in here, but I didn't want to see it.

I scanned the dim interior for Isabella. I didn't see her.

For that matter, although the place was full, I didn't see much of anybody—not well enough to discern identifying facial features, at least. The place could have been packed with Anthropology Department faculty and graduate students, and I wouldn't have been able to recognize any of them.

At my back, I felt a blast of cold air as the door to the street opened. "Hi." I heard her voice at my elbow again. She had a way of sneaking up on me that I was starting to like. "We had an after-hours staff meeting that ran long. Somebody's been cutting the racy paintings out of the art books, and we're trying to figure out how to catch them."

"Art thieves in the Oak Ridge library," I said. "Who'd've guessed? Is nothing sacred anymore?"

"Maybe theft; maybe censorship," she said. "Hard to tell. Either way, it's bad for the books. Shall we sit?" She nodded at a booth tucked into a narrow alcove just inside the door, and we slid onto facing benches. Some of the fluorescent light from the kitchen spilled into the booth—not so good for the appetite, but better for watching as she talked. She handed me a menu—a simple card listing sizes and toppings, the paper translucent with grease. "What do you like?"

"Just about everything except olives," I said. "Pepperoni, sausage, ham—any of those. What about you?"

"I'm a vegetarian," she said. "How about we order two? One for you, one for me?"

One of the high schoolers, a lanky redhead sporting torn jeans and red Converse high-tops with his T-shirt, came to take our order. Isabella pointed him to me, so I ordered a Coke and a small Hawaiian pizza, with ham and pineapple and onion. She made a face, then ordered a beer and a veggie special for herself. The kid jotted it down and turned to go, then turned back. "The veggie—also small?"

"Actually, no," she said. "Make mine a large."

I laughed. "Aren't you a dainty thing?"

"Hey, you're buying. And I want leftovers."

I called our server back a second time and changed my order to large as well.

"So," I said to her, "you got something for me that's worth a large veggie special and a beer?"

"If you don't think so," she said, "we'll split the tab."

She tugged a handful of napkins from the dispenser huddled against the wall—they were small, flimsy napkins, better suited to dabbing a crumb of crumpet off a powdered cheek than to soaking up grease and sauce—and swabbed the table with them. Then she reached into a shoulder bag and pulled out a magazine whose cover proclaimed it to be the *ORNL Review*. I'd seen an issue or two of it; it was published by Oak Ridge National Laboratory, and it contained a mix of articles—some breezy, others way over my head, technically—that summed up what a billion dollars a year would buy these days, in the science-and-energy department. *Your tax dollars at work,* I always thought when I ran across the magazine. Better in Oak Ridge, and better in the cause of science, than in a lot of other places and ways I could think of.

She opened the magazine, and I saw a print of the Novak photo tucked into the pages. She rotated the magazine and the photo toward me, keeping the photo positioned over the one page of the spread—keeping me in suspense, I guessed. That was okay with me; I was enjoying this. It felt like a dance—the closest thing to dancing I'd done since Jess, whom I'd loved and lost less than a year before.

"So this, obviously, is your picture," she was saying. "Not a lot to go on. Woods and a hillside and a barn. Doesn't narrow things down a lot here in East Tennessee." I shook my head sorrowfully, signaling that I knew the cause was hopeless—that it would take a miracle or a genius, or both, to solve this enigmatic puzzle. "I'll pretend not to notice that you're mocking me," she said. I laughed, and so did she. "Anyway. I kept looking at this after you left, and thinking I'd seen that barn before. Of course, anytime you stare at something long enough, your mind plays tricks on you, right?" I nodded, not teasing this time, because I realized I'd been staring at her, and my mind was playing some tricks on me at this very moment. "So. I have some regulars—patrons who like to hang out in the Oak Ridge Room. Old-timers, mostly, people who lived through the stuff that's archived on the shelves. It's an easy trip down Memory Lane."

"Sure," I said. "I'm fascinated, and it's not even my history."

"Right," she said. "Well, one of my regulars—oh, *stop,*" she scolded, kicking me slightly under the table for wiggling my eyebrows—"one of my regulars used to be Ed Westcott, the photographer who took all the pictures in those notebooks. His job was to document it, capture the Manhattan Project on film, for posterity. Unlike anybody except maybe General Groves or Colonel Nichols, Westcott could go wherever he wanted, see whatever he wanted, and photograph whatever he wanted. Pretty amazing, when you think about it. He had a stroke a couple of years ago, and he has trouble speaking, so he doesn't get to the library much anymore. But he's lucid, and he emails. So I emailed your picture to him. I also sent it to Ray Smith, who writes history columns about Oak Ridge history for two newspapers. I figured if anybody might recognize that barn, it'd be either Ray or Ed." She paused and leaned back so she could study my reaction to what she'd said so far.

Or maybe she was just leaning back so the high school kid could set our drinks on the table. My Coke came in a paper cup; her beer arrived in a frosted-glass mug. Evidently Big Ed or his successors had considered beer to be higher than Coke on the beverage chain. She hoisted the mug in my direction, so I raised my cup to toast. "To historical detective work," I said, and we tapped the glasses together. The paper cup did not produce a particularly satisfying sound or feel, but the gesture still felt celebratory. "And was either of these regulars of yours able to shed light on the mystery of the barn?"

She reached down, and without taking her eyes off my face, she slid the blurry photo off the magazine. I looked down and there it was, printed on the page. Set against a hillside was a simple, windowless wooden barn with a tall, thin silo at one end. I was not looking at a photograph; I was looking at an illustration, something like an architectural rendering. As I read the accompanying story, I heard myself saying "hmm" and *"hmm"* repeatedly. The "barn," I read, was not a barn at all, though it was carefully designed and built to look like one. It was the camouflaged entrance to an underground storage bunker for bomb-grade uranium-235, the precious product Beatrice had helped sift from tons of uranium-238. The entire quantity of U-235 Oak Ridge produced during World War II would have fit easily—lethally, but easily—into a couple of shoe boxes. But producing that U-235 had required hundreds of scientists, tens of thousands of laborers, and hundreds of millions of scarce wartime dollars. The nation—though only a handful of people knew it—had bet hugely on this roll of the scientific dice. Small wonder, then, that General Groves wanted to hide it well.

The silo beside the barn was actually a guard tower of reinforced concrete, the article explained. Looking closely at the illustration, I saw windows—bulletproof glass, the text noted—tucked beneath the silo's overhanging metal roof. Beneath the windows were small slits in panels of thick steel: firing ports for machine guns.

I picked up the scan of Novak's photo. The quality was terrible, but not so terrible as to keep me from seeing that the proportions of the building and the silo were the same as those of the uranium bunker. The perspective was different, to be sure—the illustration had been drawn from a ground-level perspective, while Novak's photo had been shot from somewhere above, looking down through a gap in the trees. But the similarity was unmistakable. Even the silo's roof—an odd, octagonal hat of a roof, rather than the round dome found atop most silos—was a dead-on match.

Our food arrived, so I scooped up the magazine and the print. The two aluminum platters filled the tabletop. The sauce was steaming, the cheese was molten, and the wedges of pizza were immense. After he'd set down the trays, our server handed us two plastic forks, flimsier than I'd ever seen before, and two tiny paper plates—saucers, really—for the massive, messy slices of pizza. *Big Ed,* I thought, *is up there somewhere, and he's laughing at us.*

And that, too, was okay with me.

WE DEPARTED LADEN with leftovers, the boxes heavy and already beginning to sag from the grease as we crossed the street and walked into the parking lot adjoining the football field. I had rolled up the photo and the magazine, which she told me to keep, and tucked them in a hip pocket. I didn't feel authorized to tell her details, but I said there might be someone buried near the spot where the photo was taken.

"I knew it," she said.

"How?"

"Dead people are your thing," she said. "They're what you do. They're what you care about. If you're going to this much trouble, it's for a dead person." On their face, the words might have seemed like an insult or an accusation, but there was nothing in her tone to suggest she'd meant them that way. They were simply how she saw me, and the assessment was accurate, if unsentimental.

"And what's your thing? Books?"

She shook her head. "Not exactly. I have a master's in history, actually; I did my thesis on the Manhattan Project and Oak Ridge."

"Did you grow up in Oak Ridge?"

She shook her head. "Louisiana," she said.

"What got you interested in Oak Ridge history?"

"A family connection," she said. "My father. And my grandmother."

"Was she one of the calutron girls separating uranium at Y-12?"

"No," she said. She hesitated. "She was involved with the plutonium part of the Manhattan Project. The work they did at the Graphite Reactor."

"Physicist? Chemist?"

She shook her head. "Nothing that fancy," she said. "Listen, I should go. Thanks for the pizza and the company."

"My pleasure," I said. "On both counts. Where are you parked?"

"I'm not," she said. "I live just up the hill. I'm walking."

"Let me drive you," I offered. She shook her head.

"There's a shortcut through the football field," she said. "It's close, and I like the walk."

"Then I'll walk you home. I'll carry your pizza, since you don't have any books."

"Thanks, but I'm fine," she said. "Oak Ridge is very safe. Well, except for the occasional bizarre murder."

I laughed. "At least let me walk you partway. Till we get past the dark place where the monsters lurk." I tugged gently at the pizza box.

She relented, and we ambled up a paved ramp to the level of the football field. At the far end of the field she angled upward onto a footpath that led to another large, grassy field. Like the football field, this one was also nestled in a natural bowl, but this bowl was surrounded by trees rather than grandstands. The lights of 1940s-vintage houses shone through the barren trees. "This is a practice field," she said. "The football team does workouts here; soccer leagues use it, too." At the far end of the practice field, the woods closed in tightly. "Watch your step," she said. "There's a deep hole there. A big storm sewer starts there. Runs under the fields and all the way down the hill to the Turnpike. You fall in there, we might not find you till the spring rains washed you out near the Federal Building."

I peered down into the darkness but I couldn't see much. "You been spelunking in there? Sounds like you know your way around."

"Only on paper," she said. "I have maps. Well, the Oak Ridge Room has maps—the old Manhattan Project drawings from when they first laid out the roads and sewers. I'm probably the only person alive who thinks a 1945 map of the storm-sewer system is interesting."

"Some of us like dead people, some of us like sewer maps," I said. "It takes all kinds. I find it interesting that you find those interesting."

She pointed to an opening in the treeline. "There's the sidewalk up to my street," she said. "Thanks again. It was lovely."

Before I knew it was happening, she made a quick move toward me and kissed my cheek. Then she darted away, through the gap in the trees, into the darkness.

"Wait," I called. "Your pizza."

I listened for footsteps, but all I heard was the winter wind soughing through the empty arms of the branches. The wind was chilly, but my cheek felt warm.

27

THE VEHICLES BEGAN GATHERING just inside the security checkpoint on Bethel Valley Road at 10 A.M., which was late enough to let the morning ORNL traffic die down and—mercifully—allow the sun to knock the frost off the morning. I'd called Thornton and Emert the night before, and—at their insistence—had phoned Arpad as well to see how quickly we could orchestrate a search near the old uranium bunker.

An ORNL security vehicle was already waiting, idling on the shoulder of the road, when Miranda and I cleared the checkpoint. I tucked in behind the white SUV and shut off the engine. Miranda fished a sheaf of folded pages from her pocket. "Here, read this," she said.

I unfolded the page. It appeared to be a printout off the Internet—a biography of George Kistiakowsky, the Los Alamos explosives expert who had triggered the blowup between Miranda and Thornton. A small photo of Kistiakowsky, at the top of the article, showed a balding man with deep-set eyes and a slightly sour expression, or maybe just a serious one. The photo was Kistiakowsky's ID badge photo from Los Alamos. I scanned the beginning of the article. "Hmm," I said. "Another Russian."

"What, you thought 'Kistiakowsky' sounded Irish?"

"I dunno; maybe Polish," I said. "I'm just saying, there sure were a lot of comrades running around Los Alamos."

"No way this guy was a Commie," she said. "He was an anti-Commie, see?" She pointed to a paragraph describing how Kistiakowsky had fought in the White Army against the Reds before escaping to the West. "But skip ahead, to page two," she directed. During the Cold War, page two informed me, President Eisenhower had asked Kistiakowsky to improve America's planning for nuclear war. Despite resistance from the Joint Chiefs of Staff and the Strategic Air Command, Kistiakowsky had overhauled the war plans and created the National Nuclear Target List—a coordinated list that assigned specific Soviet and Chinese targets to specific U.S. bomber wings and nuclear-armed submarines.

I was puzzled by Miranda's excitement. "I don't get it," I said. "This guy's career seems to embody everything you're opposed to. The National Nuclear Target List? I'd think you would consider that a doomsday to-do list."

"It is," she said, "but look." She pointed triumphantly to the last paragraph of the bio. Kistiakowsky ended his career, the article said, by leading a group called the Council for a Livable World, opposing nuclear testing and campaigning to ban nuclear weapons. She'd highlighted the paragraph in pink—a fitting color, I thought—and added a note in the margin reading, "Great minds think alike!"

"Congratulations," I said. "That's some major ideological ammo you've got there—ten megatons, at least. You gonna drop that on Thornton today?"

She shook her head. "No need to," she said, smiling slightly. "It came in the mail the day after the flowers. He highlighted that part. He wrote that in the margin."

The age of miracles was not over after all, it seemed. Then, somewhere underneath my initial surprise and delight, I felt the stirrings of something unpleasant. Was it jealousy? Surely not. I shook it off.

Just then Arpad's Subaru wagon arrived from the opposite direction, making a tight U-turn to pull in behind the security SUV and my UT truck. A couple of minutes later Emert's Oak Ridge police car arrived, followed shortly by a white Ford F-150 pickup. The Ford had an extended cab, a shell over the bed, and an abundance of decals and bumper stickers reading K-9 and SEARCH & RESCUE.

Arpad got out of the Subaru and came to my window. "That's Cherokee, the cadaver dog, in the white truck," he said.

"No kidding," I said. "He's a good driver."

"You want to come meet him?"

"Sure," I said. "Miranda? Want to meet the famous Cherokee?" We walked back toward the truck; as we passed the Oak Ridge police car, Emert and his boss, Lieutenant Dewar, opened the front doors and fell in behind us. The ORNL guard leapt out and joined the procession.

The driver's window on the Ford whisked down. "Uh-oh," said a folksy voice from inside. "Looks like I'm in big trouble." The door opened and a man stepped out and raised his hands in the air, then laughed and shook hands all around. Cherokee's chauffeur—his trainer and handler, Roy Ferguson—stood a little over six feet tall. He looked about sixty; he wore bifocals and a scholarly look—not surprising, since he had a Ph.D. in education—but he talked and joked like a country boy. Roy and his wife Suzie owned a business, 20/20 Optical, in Sevierville, but it was hard to imagine how their volunteer activities left time to fit eyeglasses. They raised guide dogs—"leader dogs"—for the blind, Arpad said, and held Lion's Club fund-raisers to save eyesight in developing countries. They also worked with a search-and-rescue team to find missing people, dead or alive. Normally Roy would have been accompanied by five or ten other team members, but in this case Arpad and Thornton and Emert preferred to keep the search as low-profile as possible.

Thornton's unmarked FBI sedan showed up ten minutes after everyone else. The agent pulled alongside the group chatting by the road and rolled down his passenger window. "Hey, guys," he called out. "Sorry I'm late. There was a wreck on I-40, and it took me a while to get past."

"You should ask Uncle Sam to give you a blue light," I said, though I was pretty sure he had one in the glove box, or a pair built into the grille of the car.

"Nah," he said, "that would just give me an exaggerated sense of self-importance." He flashed a crooked, self-deprecating grin that could have been lifted straight from the face of Indiana Jones, and I started to forgive him for keeping us all waiting. Then I noticed him reach down toward the console and hoist a big Starbucks cup to his lips. He tipped the cup only slightly, which meant that it was still nearly full. *A wreck on I-40—yeah, right*, I suddenly thought. *That coffee's probably still piping hot. And he probably practices that grin in front of the mirror.*

The rest of us returned to our vehicles, and with the Lab's security guard in the lead, our caravan headed west on Bethel Valley Road toward the main complex. Well before we got there, though, the white SUV turned right, up a gravel road marked WALKER BRANCH WATERSHED. The single lane of gravel meandered beside a small stream—Walker Branch, I guessed it to be. A few hundred yards later, we reached a small clearing tucked into the base of the ridge. Parked along a gravel pad were a handful of vehicles, including two government-green pickup trucks labeled TENNESSEE WILDLIFE RESOURCES AGENCY. Across the road from the miniature parking lot was a blue corrugated-metal building which could have passed for a machine shop or farm building, except for the state seal and TWRA logo beside the windowless steel door. The security guard parked in front of the door, turned on his flashers—maybe out of habit, or maybe to tell the rest of us that he'd only be a moment—and ducked into the building. He emerged a minute or so later, accompanied by a uniformed TWRA officer, who glanced at our convoy, waved us on casually, and then disappeared back into the metal building.

As Miranda and I reached the end of the structure, I saw something that caused me to slam on the brakes. The truck slithered to a quick stop, and close behind me I heard another set of tires—Arpad's tires—rasping across the gravel as he, too, locked his wheels. "Look," I said to Miranda, pointing up and to our right. Just beyond the end of the shedlike building rose a tall, cylindrical structure—a concrete silo—capped with an octagonal metal roof. Tucked beneath the roof's overhang were grimy horizontal windows and rusting steel gunports. The state wildlife officers were housed in what had once been a top-secret uranium storage bunker, although the charming wooden barn that had once disguised the bunker's entrance had been replaced with a boring blue box.

My adrenaline surged. In the blink of an eye, history had jumped off the page and become alive to me. This tiny speck of East Tennessee woods had once been a top-secret installation, heavily guarded and cleverly camouflaged. Oak Ridge's eighty thousand wartime workers—and the Manhattan Project's hundreds of millions of scarce dollars—had funneled into a small bunker tucked beneath this isolated hillside. I suddenly thought of an immense magnifying glass, focusing the rays of the sun into one tiny, intense point of light and heat and energy. The uranium-235 stored under the watchful eyes in this concrete tower had been such a focal point. It was here that the genie of atomic energy was squeezed into the smallest of bottles, so it could be unleashed later with devastating force.

I looked at Miranda; I wanted to express everything that had just raced through my mind—the sense of awe and humility and excitement that had gripped me in an instant—but I wasn't sure I was capable of it. She studied my face for a moment, then looked again at the stained concrete with the filthy windows and rusting gunports. "Yeah," she said. "Pretty damn amazing, huh?"

"Pretty damn amazing," I agreed. Behind us, a car horn tooted briefly. I took my foot off the brake and made my way back to the present, back to the caravan of vehicles, and back to the task at hand: searching for an unknown and unreckoned casualty of the Manhattan Project.

28

THE GRAVEL ROAD CONTINUED along the streambed for another hundred yards or so, then crossed a steel culvert and began snaking up the opposite hillside. As it climbed, the road narrowed; the gravel gradually gave way to dirt, and the dirt soon disappeared beneath a layer of leaves and branches. It appeared that the road had not been used in years.

We had negotiated several switchbacks and climbed well above the silo when the procession stopped. I heard a brief whoop from a siren, which I guessed might be a signal that we had reached our destination. I put the truck in park, set the brake, and got out to look. Up ahead a huge, mossy tree trunk blocked the rutted track.

Off to the right side, the hillside fell away sharply, almost vertically; looking down, I saw the roof of the TWRA building and, beside it, the octagonal roof of the fortified silo. From this angle, I could not see the windows at the top of the tower—and that meant the guards in the tower could not have seen anyone who was standing in this spot back in 1945. I felt another surge of adrenaline as I realized that I was standing near the place where a body had been hidden some sixty years before. Near the place where human bones might still lie hidden, awaiting discovery.

I walked back to my truck and opened the door. "We might be right where we need to be," I said. "Can you hand me the photograph?" Miranda reached into a manila folder tucked down beside the console. Without the barn as a visual reference, it was hard to be certain, but the angle of the silo—seen from above, from what appeared to be a ledge or shelf—looked remarkably similar to what I'd just glimpsed.

Emert and Dewar got out of the Oak Ridge police cruiser, each clutching a copy of the photo as well. Roy emerged from the F-150, eyeing the pictures with obvious interest, so I handed him the print I'd brought. His eyes widened as he took in the body, then his head swiveled and he scanned the valley down below. A broad smile spread across his face. "This is getting interesting," he said. "A lot more fun than asking, 'What's the smallest line you can read?' or 'Which is clearer, 1 or 2?' "

"Beats grading papers, too," I said.

Thornton was the last to join the group. Instead of the photograph, he was clutching the Starbucks cup in one hand. He tapped Miranda on the shoulder and, without a word, took her copy. "Make yourself at home," she said.

"Thanks," he said. He looked briefly at the silo, then at the photo, before handing it back to her. Then he looked back at the group. "Now what?"

I looked at Arpad. Arpad looked at Roy. "I was thinking maybe Roy and Cherokee could do a sweep through the area, see if the dog indicates any interest, to narrow down where we need to probe."

"Sure," said Roy. "He feels cheated if he doesn't get to hop out and sniff around." Roy bent down and picked up a dry leaf. Then, raising his arm to shoulder height and extending his hand, he crushed the leaf and sifted the fragments through his fingers, watching them drift in a breeze almost too slight to feel. "Looks like the air's moving downhill and downstream," he said. "Which means that the scent—if there is any—would be moving in that direction, too. Scent is like water—it tends to flow downhill, and tends to pool in low spots. Cool spots, too." He glanced at the steep hillside and the line of vehicles, frowning slightly. "I hate to be a bother," he said, "but could we maybe all back up a couple of hundred yards? I'd like to work him along the road, but the gas and oil fumes will pretty much overpower anything else that's here."

Roy ambled back to his truck, and the rest of us headed for our vehicles. After a few moments of tense, hesitant backing down the narrow pair of ruts, we all parked again. Roy opened the hatch of his camper shell and dropped the tailgate. I heard him talking in a low, soothing voice, and then a large German shepherd on a stout leather leash jumped down from the truck. Roy stood at least six feet tall and probably weighed somewhere around 200 pounds, but the dog was pulling him as if he were a child. "As you can see, he really gets into this," Roy said. As they pulled alongside the group, Roy gave a quick tug on the leash. "Cherokee, sit," he said firmly. The dog sat, but even sitting, he strained at the leash.

Miranda leaned slightly toward the dog. "Is he friendly? Can I pet him?"

"He's a sweetheart," said Roy, "but he's more interested in work than love."

Emert laughed. "Reminds me of my ex," he said.

"Reminds me that dogs are more useful than men," said Miranda. The rest of us—the six men she had just skewered—laughed briefly and changed the subject quickly.

Roy led the dog upslope to pee, then had him sit again, slightly apart from the group this time. "Okay, the smell from the vehicles has probably dispersed enough now," he said. "I'll start by letting him off leash for what's called a hasty search—pretty much what the name implies—and see if he picks up anything. If he doesn't, I'll work him through the area again on a grid pattern."

Thornton raised his hand, like a kid in elementary school. "Yes sir?" said Roy.

"The dog doesn't work on commission, does he?"

Roy looked puzzled, and so did everyone else. Everyone except Miranda, who snorted. "Like, ten percent of the bones?"

"Ten percent seems a little steep," the agent said with a grin. "Anything over five seems greedy."

"I wish you were running the IRS," Miranda said.

Just then Thornton's cell phone jangled loudly. "Sorry," he said, snatching it from the holder clipped to his belt. He frowned at the display but answered anyway. "Hello? Who?" His frown deepened. "Yes," he said. "Listen, I'm in the middle of something right now. Can I call you back?" He slumped—a dramatic gesture meant to telegraph his frustration to those of us watching him. It was the sort of gesture a man would make if his wife or girlfriend or teenager called him at an inopportune time. "You know, it really wasn't that big a deal," he said. "Anybody else would have done the same thing." He paused, listening, shaking his head. "You'd have done the same thing, too," he said, "in a heartbeat. Look, I really, really can't talk right now. Gotta go. Sorry. Bye." He snapped the phone shut with a wince, then looked apologetically at the group. "I am *so* sorry," he said, and flashed us that damn Indiana Jones grin again.

"Okay," said Roy, "if y'all are ready, I'll go ahead and let Cherokee work the area." He looked around, and everyone nodded. "If everybody would just stay down in this area, that'll minimize the scents and the distractions for him."

"Would it be okay if I took a few pictures," I asked, "long as I stay back here?"

"Absolutely," Roy said. "Long as you promise to shoot only my good side." With that, he bent over and wiggled his butt.

"You Ph.D.s," Emert grumbled. "Always showing off your brains."

Roy reached into a pocket of his coat and pulled out a plastic water bottle. When he did, the dog's demeanor changed instantly: his ears and tail stood up, and he began trotting back and forth almost like a Tennessee walking horse. "Cherokee, sit," said Roy, and the dog sat, almost quivering with eagerness. Roy gave the bottle a squeeze, and a small stream of water shot out, which Cherokee lapped noisily from midair. Capping the bottle and putting it back in his coat, Roy made eye contact with the shepherd. "Zook mort," he said, or at least that's what it sounded like. It didn't take a rocket scientist to figure out that "mort"—related to "mortal" and "mortality"—was a dog-handler term for "dead guy." I remembered enough of my foreign-language studies to realize that "zook" was probably based on the German word for "seek." I smiled at the thought that Roy was speaking German so that the dog—a German shepherd—could understand him.

Roy set off up the narrow dirt road, walking slowly. The dog ranged slightly ahead, ambling back and forth across the ruts, pausing occasionally to sniff at a tree or patch of moss. He reached the mammoth fallen trunk and stopped, looked back at Roy, and whined once. As Roy drew close to the trunk, he turned to his left, walking parallel to the trunk, and said quietly, "Get back to work." The dog snuffled along the trunk toward the tree's ragged base.

There, as Roy rounded the end and made to rejoin the dirt road, Cherokee did an abrupt U-turn, doubling back to the place where the tree's roots had been ripped from the ground. Novak's photos showed a raw crater torn in the ground, but in the intervening decades a fair-sized tulip poplar had taken root in the hollow. The dog circled the area slowly, his nose low to the ground, then sniffed his way toward the tree at the center. Once there, he simply sat, staring at the base of the tulip poplar. I waited for the dog to bark or whine or lie down, as I'd seen other cadaver dogs do to show they'd found something, but Cherokee simply sat and stared.

"Well, this is gripping," muttered Emert. "I can't stand the suspense. Will he pee, or won't he?"

"Shh," said Miranda.

Roy sidled closer and studied the dog for a moment. "Cherokee, show mort," he said. The dog stood up, slowly sniffed his way around the tulip poplar, and then sat again, in almost the same spot as before. This time, he bent down and touched his nose to the ground at the base of the tree. "Good boy! What a good boy!" The dog leapt to his feet and whirled, just in time to catch a knotted-up towel Roy had pulled from a pocket and tossed in his direction. With the force of a bear trap snapping, the dog's jaws closed around the fabric, and he began biting and thrashing his head, as if he were trying to dismember a rat. With one paw, he held the end of the bundled fabric on the ground and shredded it with meticulous savagery.

"Glad that's not my throat he's got ahold of," commented Dewar.

After the towel was reduced to bits, Roy led the dog back to our waiting group. "It looks like maybe there's something near the base of that tulip poplar," he said.

"No kidding," said Arpad. "I guess it's my turn."

He opened the back door of the Subaru and brought out the TopGun Freon detector. It squealed when he switched it on, then the noise died down to an occasional chirp as Arpad walked toward the base of the fallen oak. We followed, since the gadget—unlike the dog—wasn't prone to distraction by people or extraneous smells.

Stopping midway between the dead tree and the live one, Arpad bent down and eased the tip of the wand through the leaves and into the soil. The detector continued to chirp at the same slow rate. Stepping closer to the tulip poplar, he repeated the maneuver, with no discernible change. Next he positioned himself right where the dog had indicated and took another reading. The chirping might have sped up slightly, or I might simply have imagined that it did. Arpad frowned, looking puzzled and slightly embarrassed. "As cold as it's been, it could be that the Freon compounds just aren't volatilizing," he said. "Or maybe they're long gone, if we're looking for something sixty years old."

"Or maybe the dog's just smarter," said Emert, earning a scowl from Arpad.

He took the Freon detector back to his car, swapping it for his prototype sniffer. As the gizmo fired up, I noticed how much I preferred its understated clicking to the Freon detector's electronic squeal. As before, Arpad stopped short of the target area, gently working the instrument's probe into the top of the soil. It continued to click quietly, almost like a clock ticking. Despite the chill of the day, I thought I saw glimmers of sweat on Arpad's brow, and I realized that he had a lot riding on this field test. If the dog gave a positive alert but Arpad's sophisticated instrument did not, should we excavate anyway? I thought we definitely should; after all, the dog had an impressive track record in other searches, and he seemed to show no hesitation or doubt once he started zeroing in on the tulip poplar. There was no guarantee we'd dig up anything, but it seemed only fair to give the dog the benefit of the doubt—after all, if we didn't trust the dog, we shouldn't have enlisted him in the search.

But would Arpad—a former student and now a valued colleague—take offense if we seemed to trust the dog more than the gizmo? I hoped not, but I knew scientists could be sensitive if it appeared their work was being questioned.

As I was turning over the alternatives in my mind, trying to settle on the most diplomatic way of handling the dilemma, I became aware of a quietly insistent sound. Arpad now stood at the center of the circle with the gizmo's probe in the ground, and the slow, steady ticking had given way to a sound almost like muted machine-gun fire. A smile spread across Arpad's face. "Eureka!"

"Cool," said Miranda.

Thornton reached into his pocket and pulled out a folded handkerchief, which he knotted into a ball. I was puzzled, until he said "Good boy" and tossed the handkerchief onto the ground in the direction of the gadget's probe. Suddenly I glimpsed a streak of movement at the edge of my vision. Moving at lightning speed, Cherokee swooped in, grabbed the handkerchief, and began ripping it to bits.

Miranda burst out laughing. "Holy *crap,* that was fast," she said. "Serves you right for being a smart-ass." Thornton just flashed her that grin again, bigger and more sheepish than ever. Miranda turned to me; it might have just been the effect of the chilly breeze, but her cheeks looked pink. "Does this mean it's our turn to look now?"

"I think it does," I said. I tapped the two Oak Ridge detectives on the shoulder as Miranda and I started toward the truck. "You guys mind giving us a hand?"

They followed us to the back of the truck and I handed a rake and galvanized-metal bucket to each of them. Miranda grabbed the two shovels, and I carried a large plastic bin containing smaller items: evidence bags, trowels, rubber gloves, a tape measure, a compass, a handheld GPS unit, a topographical map, my digital camera, a clipboard, pens and Sharpie markers, and a blue plastic tarp. I spread the tarp near the area we were about to excavate, and we laid the rest of the gear on it.

I began, as always, by taking pictures—several wide shots at first, showing the entire area, the vehicles, and the group of people. Then an inspiration hit me, and I took several shots of the fallen tree, the small valley, and the concrete silo, reproducing Novak's perspective as closely as possible. The comparison photos would be an interesting addition to the file, I thought. An interesting footnote to Oak Ridge history. An interesting thing to show Isabella over pizza. Next I took tighter shots of the fallen tree, the area near the base of its trunk, and the orange survey flag Arpad had stuck in the ground. Miranda switched on the GPS unit, held it over the flag, and pressed a button to save the latitude and longitude coordinates. I found it amazing that a three-hundred-dollar gadget, about the size and shape of a calculator, could home in on satellites hovering thousands of miles overhead, pinpointing and remembering this precise location on an isolated hilltop: an electronic x marking a tiny spot on a big planet. I marveled at the technology, though I still didn't entirely trust it. That's why we had the compass and tape measure: in addition to marking the site on the topo map, Miranda would draw a more detailed sketch of the search area, showing the dirt road, the fallen tree, and the excavation, with compass directions and measurements—the diameter of the excavation, for instance, and how many feet west of the trunk the dog and the sniffer had alerted.

I had tried to talk Miranda into letting me bring one of the other graduate students in her place—I worried that the burns on her fingers hurt, and I feared she might damage them—but she insisted on coming. "I'll wear an extra pair of gloves," she said, "and it'll be fine." I hoped she was right.

After I'd taken a dozen or so photos and Miranda had sketched the key landmarks of the site, we began to rake the leaf litter off the soil. When the big tree had been ripped from the earth, long ago, its roots had torn a crater in the ground, six or eight feet in diameter and several feet deep. Gradually, though, the crater had filled as dirt fell from the edges, rainwater trickled down the sides, and decades of leaves swirled into the hole and crumbled into dust. By now all that remained was a slight, subtle hollow—with a sixty-foot tulip poplar growing from it. If not for the massive oak trunk touching one edge of the rim, the low spot would have seemed simply a slight, random variation in the surface of the ground. By excavating carefully, I hoped Miranda and I could work our way back to the original, deeper contour of the hole, as a starting point in our quest for whatever might lie at its center. It wouldn't be easy, though.

"So," said Miranda, "that *tree* sure is in the way. Wonder what we could do about that pesky *tree*?"

"Just a thought," said Emert, picking up on the sly tone and the elbow-in-the-ribs emphasis, "but I'm thinking *chainsaw*. If only we had a chainsaw right about now."

They laughed; Roy and Arpad and the ORNL guard looked puzzled, so Emert told the chainsaw story. "Go ahead," I said. "Rub it in. But next time your heart is breaking, don't expect sympathy from me."

Roy spoke up. "I feel your pain, Doc. I'm pretty attached to my Husquevarna. Matter of fact, it's in the back of the truck. If you promise not to steal it, I might be willing to share the love."

The Husquevarna wasn't as nice as the Stihl—it didn't feel quite as solid, somehow—but it sliced through the eight-inch trunk in a couple of minutes. I cut the tree at about waist level, first, then—once it was down—cut the stump almost flush with the ground. I thanked Roy for the saw, handed it back, and then picked up the three-foot length of trunk and carried it to my truck. Emert asked, "You running low on firewood?"

"Souvenir," I said.

The edge of what had once been the crater in the ground—the border between "hole" and "not hole"—wasn't at the surface, so I used a shovel to remove a thin layer of topsoil, beginning within the slight depression and skimming outward, beyond the rim. The shovel slid easily at first, which told me that the soil here was loose; after about a foot, though, I encountered more resistance: the resistance of packed, undisturbed earth. I lifted the shovel and looked at the swath I'd just sliced. Sure enough, closer to me, the soil appeared lighter, fluffier, and more crumbly; then—across a faint and irregular but unmistakable line—the soil was denser and darker, infused with rocks and clay that appeared to have lain undisturbed since the dawn of time.

"Okay," I said to Miranda, "here's the rim. How about we excavate about halfway around the circumference, then work in from the edge?"

"Whatever you say, Kemo Sabe," she said.

"Excuse me, Dr. Kemo Sabe," said Thornton. "Can I ask a dumb question?"

"No such thing as a dumb question," I said.

"That's not what the instructors at the Academy used to tell me," he said. "Why start excavating at the edge? Why not just aim right for the bull's-eye, which seems to be somewhere around that stump you just made?"

"If we dig straight down and there is something there, we'll keep knocking dirt down onto it," I said. "The sides of the hole will keep collapsing. Plus we'd be on top of the bones; we might end up breaking some of them. Coming in from the side means a little more digging—but a lot more control."

"Ah," he said. "Anything we can do to help you?"

"Sure," I said. "If you don't mind lifting buckets of dirt, you guys could haul out dirt as we excavate."

"Sounds like something we might be able to handle," he said.

"Arpad," I said, "how long since you've used a trowel?"

"To dig up bones, or to plant tulips?"

"To dig up bones."

"Not so long ago that I've forgotten the backaches," he said. "Ten, twelve years, maybe."

"About time you brushed up," I said, handing him a trowel.

I was about two feet in from the rim of the crater, and about eighteen inches below the level of the leaves and twigs Miranda and I had raked off the surface, when my trowel hit something hard. Using its triangular tip, I flicked at the soil underneath what I'd hit, and as the dirt fell away from the object, I gradually made out the distal end—the elbow end—of a humerus, an upper arm bone. "Eureka!" I said, echoing Arpad's earlier exclamation. Burrowing a bit farther, I unearthed the medial ends of the radius and ulna, the bones of the forearm. From the angle at the elbow, I could tell the arm was slightly flexed, with the hand probably somewhere in the vicinity of the hip. "This is the right arm," I said. "He's lying facedown. Assuming it's a male." I troweled away more soil, exposing the distal end of the forearm, the loose, pebbly bones of the wrist, and the carpals and metacarpals of the hand.

Emert leaned in and squinted at the stained bones. "You're sure it's human," he said, "not a bear? I saw the bones of a bear's paw once, and I'd have sworn it was a hand or a foot."

"Well, unless these Oak Ridge bears are smart enough to tell time, I'm pretty sure it's human," I said, "because it's wearing a man's wristwatch." With the tip of my trowel, I pointed to a disk of corroded metal hidden beneath the wrist.

"Eureka indeed," said Thornton.

Before I even had a chance to ask her, Miranda left the spot where she'd been working and came to kneel beside me. We'd done this so many times, our teamwork was seamless, wordless, and almost telepathic. I shifted to the upper arm and began excavating toward the shoulder and head; Miranda began working her way along the hand and then down the right leg.

As I troweled my way along the shoulder and toward the area of the head, the dirt began to drop away, revealing the rounded surface of a skull. Working with only the tip of the trowel, I started teasing the soil free. Occasionally I was forced to trade the trowel for small gardening shears, so I could snip away roots that clutched at the bones.

As the back of the skull came into view, I saw a prominent bump at its base. The bump—the external occipital protuberance—had once served as an attachment point for muscles at the back of the neck. The bump's presence and prominence told me that the skeleton was definitely male, and a robust male, at that. I'd been fairly certain of the sex just from the size and muscle markings on the humerus, not to mention the wristwatch, but the external occipital protuberance confirmed it.

The head was rotated, so that instead of facing straight down, it was turned toward the left shoulder; it was tilted slightly backward at an odd angle as well. For a moment I wondered if the neck had been broken—hard to tell, with all the soft tissue gone—but I quickly rejected that theory in favor of another, simpler explanation: the body had simply been rolled down into the hole, and had come to rest slightly askew.

With three of us excavating, the work moved fairly quickly, but even so, it was midafternoon before we had worked our way around the entire skeleton. Rather than removing bones one at a time, we left the skeleton in place until we had exposed it completely, digging down on all sides so that the bones lay on a raised platform of earth—a technique called "pedestaling." The soft tissue had decayed completely, as had all the clothing, except for thin, crumbling remnants of the leather soles of the shoes.

One by one, Miranda and I snipped the tulip poplar's remaining roots, freeing the bones from their grasp. By the time the roots were cut and the stump pulled from above the torso, the stump itself looked skeletal and dismembered.

The torso posed a challenge. Normally a body in a shallow grave would gradually collapse, the vaulted rib cage flattening as the cartilage decayed and the ribs detached from the spine and sternum. In this case, though, a latticework of tree roots supported the ribs.

By this point I'd been on my hands and knees for the better part of four hours, so I groaned my way to my feet and clambered out of the hole we'd dug. Excusing myself from the group, I wandered into the woods, ducked behind a large tree, and took a much-needed bathroom break. Arpad and Miranda headed off in other directions to do likewise. In years past, I'd had female graduate students for whom the lack of bathroom facilities in the field posed problems, ranging from minor inconvenience to full-blown crisis, but Miranda had long since jettisoned most of her modesty about such matters. "Oh, good *grief*," I'd once heard her chide a squirming female colleague, "we're out here scooping up some dead guy's rotten guts, and you're too refined to tinkle in the bushes? Get *over* it already." From the direction of a pine thicket about fifty yards away, I heard a yelp. *"Jeepers,"* Miranda shouted, "you guys have no idea how cold it is out here."

"Next time I'll bring a propane bun-warmer just for you," called Arpad.

Once we regrouped, I photographed the skeleton from every angle, including wide shots and close-ups, and then prepared to remove the bones from the pedestaled grave. I asked Miranda to record the inventory of the skeletal elements—the listing of every bone—and Arpad to bag them in evidence bags.

I began with the skull. As I eased it from the ground, lifting and rotating it, I got my first glimpse of the right temporal bone, the oval bone just above the ear. A small, neat hole pierced the bone. The location coincided exactly with the dark circle on the head of the dead man in Leonard Novak's photographs. "It's you," I said to the skull. "It really is you."

The hole was about a quarter inch in diameter at the outer surface, but it flared wider as it bored through the bone. The beveling was the unmistakable signature of a bullet blasting its way through the skull. Any kid who's ever shot a BB gun through a plate-glass window has seen the same physics, on a smaller and less lethal scale: as the BB enters the glass, it creates a shock wave that fans out like a cone, fracturing a steadily wider cross-section until it emerges on the other side of the window amid a shower of tiny shards.

The entry wound was about an inch above the opening

for the right ear, and judging by its perfect roundness, the bullet had been fired directly toward the center of the cranial vault, since an angled trajectory would have caused an oval hole. There was no exit wound on the left side of the skull. I gave the skull a vigorous shake and was rewarded with a clattering inside. "I think we've still got the bullet," I said. "Probably a .22. The entry wound's small, and the bullet didn't have enough oomph to punch out the other side."

"Had enough oomph to do the job, though," said one of the detectives.

"Funny thing about a .22," I said. "Seems like a sissy gun, but the bullets tend to ricochet around inside the skull and really chew up the brain. Sometimes a .22 does more damage than a larger-caliber bullet that just blasts right through."

"Reckon what he was doing," said Emert, "when that bullet hit him?"

"Trying to steal atomic secrets," said Thornton. "Or trying to keep them from being stolen."

"Or making a pass at the wrong guy's wife or girlfriend," I said.

"Pleading for his life," said Miranda.

We had not unearthed any artifacts besides the watch in the process of pedastaling the skeleton. Now, though, as we removed and bagged the bones, I came across seven small objects embedded in the soil. Six were metal buttons—one in the region of the chest, where a left shirt pocket would have been; three along the midline of the body, spaced between the chest and the pelvis; and one at each ankle. The seventh object, at the waist, was a rectangular plastic buckle, olive green, with a rotting bit of canvas webbing still threaded through it. As I handed each object to Arpad, as carefully as if it were a precious gem recovered from a pharaoh's tomb, the law enforcement officers crowded around to inspect them. At the sight of the buckle, Emert voiced what I'd been thinking. "This guy was wearing army coveralls," he said. "I've still got my dad's in a chest in the attic." There were no coins or keys in the grave, which led me to believe that the pockets had been emptied. I was therefore not surprised, though I was disappointed, that the grave contained no dog tags.

"So we've got a dead G.I. from World War II here," said Emert. "Swell. There were only, what, ten thousand of those here in Oak Ridge?"

I thought we were finished—through the bones, down to the dirt—when the tip of my trowel snagged on a clump of clay. But it wasn't clay. A chunk of it broke off, and when it did, it revealed odd striations within the soil. Looking closer, I began to discern a lump, a shape, about a foot long and slightly narrower, somewhat paler than the rest of the red clay lining the grave. I probed gently at the edge I had exposed. The striations were quite thin—paper-thin, I realized, as the proportions of the rectangle registered in my brain. "I don't know what this guy was doing when he died," I said, "but it seems to have involved a mighty thick stack of papers."

29

I HOPED THE BONES might tell us more than the papers did about the dead soldier. Officially he was case 09-02, the second forensic case of 2009, but a number was a poor substitute for a name.

One of my UT colleagues in the College of Agriculture—a scientist in the Forest Products Laboratory—had confirmed that the rectangular lump we dug from the grave was indeed a stack of paper. From the thickness, he estimated it to be somewhere between 400 and 500 pages, and he said it appeared to be a low grade of typing paper—long on wood pulp, short on linen fibers. Because it was cheap and pulpy, it tended to crumble into chunks, rather than peeling apart into individual sheets. "I managed to pry apart a few fragments," he told me, "but I'm afraid there's not much there. Ink smears and mold. Whatever's written on those pages, it hasn't stood the test of time."

The bones, on the other hand, had held up well. After a day of simmering in hot water, Biz, and Downy fabric softener, followed by some gentle scrubbing with a toothbrush, Miranda had laid the clean, caramel-colored bones of G.I. Doe—that's what she'd dubbed 09-02—in anatomical order on a table in the osteology lab. She had also taken skeletal measurements with a 3D digitizing probe. After entering the measurements in the Forensic Data Bank, she plugged them into ForDisc, the software developed by one of my computer-savvy colleagues at UT. According to ForDisc's analysis of the data—the size of the skull, spacing of the eye orbits, width of the nasal opening, and the length and diameter of various bones, among others—G.I. Doe was a white male of about 180 centimeters, or five feet eleven inches, in stature. None of that surprised me; after all, ForDisc had been programmed to make, quickly and automatically, the kinds of calculations and analyses physical anthropologists had spent years learning how to make with calipers, and slide rules and calculators.

ForDisc was not, on the other hand, programmed to estimate age. Estimates of age required looking at multiple features of the skeleton and making judgments, sometimes complicated or subjective ones, about the degree of development or maturity in the bones. Those weren't the kinds of automatic calculations a computer program could perform.

It was my custom, when doing a forensic examination of a skeleton, to keep quiet until my students had examined the bones and offered their opinions. Miranda was used to this, and she required no prompting, beyond a tilt of my head and an inquiring lift of my eyebrows. She began by setting the skull upside down in a doughnut-shaped cushion, exposing the upper teeth and the roof of the mouth. Then she picked up the lower jaw in her left hand, pointing with the little finger of her right hand at the teeth. "So. Both third molars in the mandible are fully erupted," she said, "which would indicate an adult." Still holding the mandible in her left hand, she touched her pinkie to the wisdom teeth in the upper jaw, which were small and well below the level of the second molars. "The third molars haven't erupted in the maxilla," she said, "but these appear to be impacted, unlikely ever to erupt through the gums. So, his teeth say that he was probably at least eighteen years of age."

She laid the mandible down and lifted the skull from the cushion that cradled it. Cupping it in her left hand, she used the tip of a probe to trace the pattern of the four sutures, or seams, in the roof of the mouth. One of these, the palatomaxillary suture, ran from one side of the palate to the other, like a line drawn between the second molars. Another, the incisive suture, also ran sideways, just behind the four incisors at the front of the jaw. Two of the sutures ran along the midline of the roof of the mouth: the intermaxillary suture extended from the front of the mouth to its intersection with the palatomaxillary suture, and the interpalatine suture ran from that intersection to the back of the palate. In most subadults—people under eighteen—these four sutures were not fully closed; the joints were still in the process of being filled with new, growing bone. By eighteen, though, they tended to be fused, and during the decades of adulthood, the suture lines gradually smoothed and faded, or obliterated, sometimes disappearing altogether. In 09-02, the maxillary sutures were fully fused, but their lines remained vividly drawn. "The maxillary sutures are fully fused, so we know he was an adult," Miranda said, "but probably a young adult. Not a geezer, for sure." I smiled at the way Miranda bounced back and forth between scientific formality and slang.

"I'm gonna save us both some time here," I said. "I know you know the basics. You've probably got the whole osteology handbook memorized by now, right?"

"I'm a little fuzzy on some of the specifics on page two," she said.

"What's on page two?"

"All that Library of Congress copyright stuff," she said.

"I'd be worried if you were wasting brain cells on that. Okay, let's skip ahead. Instead of talking me through the whole skeleton, show me what you think can pin down his age more precisely."

"Three things," she said. "First, the anterior iliac crest." She pointed to the large, curving edge of the hipbone and used her finger to trace a line near the edge. A faint seam there marked a joint in the broad bone, as if the Creator had decided the hips were a touch too narrow and had gone back and tacked another sliver of bone along the outer edge. It wasn't actually an afterthought, of course, but an epiphysis, a joint that had remained open while the bones were still growing, then closed when the final growth of adolescence was done. "The epiphysis is completely united, so that suggests he was in his early twenties, at least, and maybe mid-twenties or later. The prime of life, in other words." She wiggled her eyebrows, and I smiled; Miranda was poised between her mid- and late twenties.

"I'm following you so far," I said, "even though my brain is well past its prime. Second?"

"Second, the pubic symphysis." She picked up the two halves of the pubic bone and showed me the face where they met at the midline of the body. "The symphyseal face shows a lot of beveling in the ventral area," she said, pointing to the rear portion of the joint. "That suggests late twenties or beyond."

"Are you basing that on the work of Todd, or McKern and Stewart, or Suchey?"

"All of the above," she said.

I smiled. "Good answer. Third?"

"Third is always most important," she said. "Third, the clavicle." She picked up the left collarbone, which was nearer the edge of the table, and indicated a faint, smooth seam near the end that joined the shoulder. "The lateral epiphysis is fully fused, which you'd expect, since the dude's a grown-up. But the medial epiphysis"—she pointed at a ragged, incomplete seam near the bone's other end—"isn't completely united yet; it's still undergoing terminal union."

"Leading you," I said, "to conclude what?"

"To conclude that G.I. Doe was thirty. Plus or minus a year or two."

"Bravo," I said. "I agree. Now let's look at trauma. Did

you see any skeletal trauma other than the wound to the head?"

"Nothing," she said. "There's a small amount of osteoarthritic lipping on some of the vertebrae, but that's just the beginning of age-related wear-and-tear, not trauma. Nope, I think one shot to the head did it."

I picked up the skull and, using a pair of calipers, measured the diameter of the entry wound in the right side of the cranium. The hole was almost perfectly circular, but not quite. At its widest, it measured nearly a third of an inch—about the size of a .32-caliber bullet. At its narrowest, though, which was the crucial dimension, the hole measured less than a quarter of an inch. That made it too small to be caused by anything larger than a .22. Short of cutting off the top of the skull, there was no way to get the calipers inside the cranium to measure the hole's diameter as it broke through the bone and entered the brain, but by shining my key chain flashlight into the hole, I guessed the inner diameter to be nearly half an inch, because of the conical beveling gunshots always produced. The force of the bullet had also caused three small fractures, each about an inch long, to radiate outward from the hole.

A small, ragged blob of metal lay on a tray beside the skull. I laid the skull down and picked up the blob. Although it was small, it felt heavy and soft. "You got the bullet out," I said.

"I did," she said. "I managed to shake it out the foramen magnum," the opening at the base of the skull through which the spinal cord exited. "Took me back to my childhood days, when I shook coins out of my piggy bank."

As I studied the deformed bullet, I was struck by its shape. "Does this remind you of anything?"

"Reminds me not to get shot in the head," she said.

"No, I mean the shape."

She plucked it from my hand and held it in her fingertips, and the gesture clutched at my heart: It was the same way

Garcia had held and studied the iridium in the morgue. It was the same way Miranda had plucked the deadly pellet from his grasp with these very fingertips. Now, though, they were tipped with white gauze.

"Well, I'll be," Miranda said. "This bullet is a dead ringer for a mushroom cloud."

30

I DIALED THE OAK Ridge Public Library at five minutes to eight and asked for Isabella. "Sir, the library's closing now," said the young woman who'd answered the phone. "I don't think she's still taking questions."

"It's not a question," I said, "it's an answer. It'll just take a second, and she'll be glad to hear what it is."

There was a pause, and then the woman said, with more curtness than I thought necessary, "Just a moment, sir, I'll see if I can catch her."

Another pause, then a click. "Library Reference; how can I help you?"

"You already did," I said. "We found him."

She laughed. "I don't even need to ask what you're talking about. Congratulations! You found him somewhere near that barn?"

"I'll show you a picture," I said. "The trees are taller and the barn's turned to metal, but the view of the silo is dead-on."

"Do you know who he was? Who killed him? Why?"

"No," I said. I thought of what Thornton said. "Maybe he was stealing atomic secrets. Maybe he was saving atomic secrets. Maybe he just made a pass at some hothead's wife." I wanted to keep talking. I imagined the lights in the library going dark, Isabella sitting at the Reference Desk in the empty building, connected to me, sitting in my dark living room. "The bullet in his skull? It was shaped like a mushroom cloud," I said. "Like a tiny atomic bomb going off in his head." I laughed. "Oak Ridge is a strange place," I said. "I think it's making me a little strange, too."

She was silent for a moment. "What do you think of strange love?"

"Huh?" I was baffled by the sudden shift in topic. "Well, let's see," I hedged, stalling for time, trying to think of something to say that might be clever and maybe even slightly naughty—was that what she wanted, sitting alone in the darkened library?—but not offensive. "I think strange love is a matter of personal . . . you know. . . ."

"No, silly. Not 'strange love,' as in kinky sex. 'Strangelove,' as in *Dr. Strangelove*. The movie."

I was still at a loss. "*Dr. Strangelove?* Sounds like something from the adult section of the video store."

"You don't mean to tell me you've never seen it—*Dr. Strangelove, or: How I Learned to Stop Worrying and Love the Bomb*? It's a classic. You grew up during the Cold War; how could you have missed the greatest Cold War satire ever made?"

"I lived the Cold War," I said. "Duck and cover. Hiding under the desk at school. Running to the basement at home. I didn't need to see it on the screen."

"But your Cold War experience isn't complete until you've seen this film," she insisted. "What are you doing right now?"

"Huh?"

"You keep saying that," she said. "It makes you sound far less intelligent than you are. What are you doing right now?"

"I'm looking at chainsaw brochures," I said.

"Oh, good grief," she said. "Your cinematic education has a hole in it the size of Lake Michigan, and you're squandering your precious time on power-tool porn?"

I laughed again. "I am not going to touch that line."

"Yeah, I know: with a ten-foot pole," she said. "Stay right there. I'll be there in an hour."

"You're coming here? To my house?"

"Yes. The wonders of MapQuest. And I'm bringing *Dr. Strangelove* with me. Unless you'd rather I didn't."

"No," I said.

"No, which?"

"No, I wouldn't rather you didn't. Yes, I'd rather you did. I mean, please do."

She hung up without another word, and I found myself staring stupidly at the receiver. Isabella was coming to my house? At nine o'clock at night? To bring me a movie?

I wasn't sure what else, if anything, to make of it. I'd put on a pair of scrubs after I ate dinner—for some reason I'd always felt silly in pajamas, but scrubs gave me the comfort of PJs without the self-consciousness. Now I changed into a pair of jeans and a sweatshirt.

Forty-five minutes later, I saw headlights in the driveway, and then the doorbell rang. When I opened the door, I saw that Isabella had a canvas book bag hooked over one shoulder.

"You're nuts," I said. "Why didn't you just hand it to me next time I came to the library to flirt with you?"

"Because I know you'd never get around to watching it if I just handed it to you," she said. "You'd set it aside and look at bones. Or chainsaw brochures."

"So you're not just handing it to me now?"

"Not a chance. We are going to sit down and watch this together."

"What—now? You're making me watch this right now?"

"You'll thank me later," she said. "Your moral and intellectual development hangs in the balance. Besides, it's funny as hell. Also scary as hell, because things haven't changed as much as they should've." She reached into the bag and pulled out a DVD case, which she handed to me. "Okay, you start the movie while I start the microwave."

"Why are you starting the microwave?"

"To pop the popcorn, of course." She reached into the

bag again and pulled out a pack of Pop Secret. The name made me smile. Or maybe it was the way she wiggled her eyebrows as she wiggled the package. "I brought Diet Coke for you, Original Sin for me."

I was almost afraid to ask. "Original Sin?"

"Hard cider," she said brightly. "Apple juice for grown-ups. You should try it sometime."

"I've got Menier's disease," I told her. "Occasional vertigo. The last thing I need is something else that makes me dizzy."

"One bottle of cider would not make you dizzy," she said. "But no peer pressure. I would never dream of telling you what to do. Now go start the movie."

"Yes, ma'am," I said. I pointed her toward the kitchen, and a moment later I heard the microwave beep as she keyed in numbers and hit START. Then, as the FBI copyright warning on the television screen gave way to the film's opening credits, I heard the staccato fire of corn kernels exploding. Over the noise in both rooms, I called, "Do you want me to pause this?"

"No," she yelled. "I've seen it fifty-seven times. Sit. Watch."

I sat. I watched the credits roll. "I didn't know Peter Sellers was in this. I love the Pink Panther movies."

"He plays three roles in this," she said from the doorway. "He was originally supposed to play four, but he sprained his ankle and couldn't do the fourth."

The film appeared to be in black and white, which seemed odd. "When was this made? I thought color film was invented in the 1930s."

"In 1964. It's in black and white to look like the Cold War and civil defense films and whatnot. Now *shush*! Watch. And marvel."

I shushed. I watched. And I marveled. Starting with the notion of "mutual assured destruction"—the Cold War strategy that created nuclear arsenals capable of incinerating the planet many times over—the film took the arms race to its logical conclusion, if "logical" can be used to describe a scenario in which one superpower booby-traps the entire planet and the other superpower springs the trap.

As I sat there on the sofa, it was almost as if there were two of me. One "me" was intent on the film. The other was acutely conscious of the woman sitting beside me, a bowl of popcorn nestled between us. Every time she took a handful of popcorn, I felt the bowl press slightly against my thigh. I wondered if she felt the same sensation when I reached into the bowl, and if she found it as electrifying.

The film ended badly for the human race—mushroom clouds blossoming everywhere, synchronized to the lilting melody and chirpy lyrics of "We'll Meet Again Some Sunny Day." Despite the incineration of the planet, though, the film managed to walk the tightrope between horror and hilarity. Generals and heads of state bickered like kindergartners. Doomsday dawned because an unhinged Air Force colonel became convinced that fluoridated drinking water was a Communist plot. And Peter Sellers—playing a gentlemanly British officer, a wimpy U.S. president, and a deranged ex-Nazi guiding U.S. weapons policy—turned in three brilliant performances.

"Okay," I said as I got to my feet and switched off the TV, "you were right. I had a shameful gap in my cultural education. Thank you for filling it."

"I seen my duty and I done it," she said. She set the greasy bowl on the coffee table and stood, stretching. "I wouldn't have slept a wink tonight if I'd left you in ignorance. Not knowing *Dr. Strangelove* is like not knowing *Casablanca* or *Citizen Kane*."

"Citizen who?"

"*Citizen Kane*," she said. "Please tell me you're not serious?"

"Oh, Citizen *Kane*," I said. "Right. Of course. That's that movie about . . . you know . . . that . . . *citizen*."

"That *citizen*? Oh my *God*," she groaned, "you have a *Citizen Kane* gap, too. You're hopeless." She swatted me on the chest with an open palm. Once. Twice. The third time, she let her hand rest there on my chest. I reached up and laid one of my hands atop hers.

"Hopeless? Really?" A lopsided, sheepish grin seemed to be twitching at my mouth. Was I imitating Thornton, who seemed to have the gift of charm? Or was this just the way guys grinned when they were falling for someone pretty and smart? Would my version of the grin charm Isabella as thoroughly as Thornton's seemed to charm Miranda?

"Really," she said. "What am I going to do with you?"

"Well," I said, "you could kiss me, if you had a mind to. I have a kissing deficit, too, which I personally think is a lot more worrisome than my *Citizen Kane* deficit."

"A kissing deficit?"

I nodded gravely. "I've practically forgotten how."

She took a small step forward, which brought her to within about an inch of me. She left her hand on my chest. I put both of mine on her shoulders. The air around us changed; the hairs on my arm and the back of my neck tingled, as if lightning were about to strike, and then it did: tilting her head slightly back and to the side, she raised her mouth to mine. Her lips were softer than I would have imagined; softer than I could have imagined any lips to be. I reached a hand up and stroked her hair—that thick, wavy black hair—and when I did, she trembled.

She pulled away from the kiss and laid the other hand on my chest, dropping her head onto my shoulder. Her breathing was quick and shallow, and she was still shaking. "Oh my," she murmured. "I wonder how it'd be if you were in practice."

"I don't know," I said. "But it'd be nice to find out."

I bent to kiss her again, but she turned her face and pushed me away slightly. "Wait," she said, and I feared I had overstepped, crossed some boundary in my eagerness.

Her hands fumbled at the back of her neck. She unfastened a black cord and removed a necklace that had been hanging inside her sweater. The pendant, which was silver, looked striking—an abstract rendering of something real; a figure that was angular and curving and ancient and modern at the same time. She slipped the pendant in the pocket of her jeans. Then she kissed me again, and my interest in the necklace evaporated. I reached for her hair again, and ran my fingers through it like a comb—a comb that twisted and tugged gently as it wove through the strands—and when I did, she made a small soft sound. Half sigh, half whimper, it was the most thrilling sound I had ever heard. I drew in my breath and felt my fingers tighten, and felt her body begin to shake again.

She slipped out sometime after I fell asleep; I don't know when. All I know is that I awoke at dawn to a sunrise the color of a blood orange.

31

PEGGY DID A DOUBLE-TAKE when I stopped by her office to retrieve my mail and ask if there were any meetings on my calendar. "What happened to you?" she asked.

"What do you mean?"

"You're smiling like you just got named 'Professor of the Year' or something," she said. "What's wrong?"

"It's a beautiful day, I love my work, and I'm surrounded by bright, interesting people," I said.

She shot back, "It's cold as hell, the budget cuts are wreaking havoc with our equipment needs, and two of your junior faculty just sent a memo to the dean complaining about you."

"Complaining about me? Why on earth would any of the Anthropology faculty complain about me?"

"It's those two new culturalists you hired last year," she said. "They told the dean, in no uncertain terms, that 'race' is a social construct, not a physical trait. They demand that you cease all references to 'the three races of man'—which is sexist, too, they say—in your classes."

I laughed. "See," I said, "very interesting people. Boring guys like me, we study an Asian, an African, and a Scandinavian skull, and we come to the simplistic conclusion that the differences in the cheekbones and the slope of the jaws and the width of the nasal opening are structural—that they reflect millennia of evolution and adaptation by those three populations. Interesting folks, on the other hand, they look at those same cheekbones and jaws and noses, and they see social constructs."

"Go ahead, make light," she said, "but this is going to cause you headaches." She eyed me more closely. "I know that smile," she said. "This is about that librarian, isn't it? Miranda told me about her. *That's* why you're making all these trips to Oak Ridge." She grinned triumphantly.

"I can't imagine what you're talking about," I said innocently.

As I turned to go, she summoned me back. "This came through the fax machine for you," she said. "From somebody over in the tree lab."

I practically ripped the page from her hand. "I'll be down in the osteo lab," I called over my shoulder. "See if you can get Detective Emert and Agent Thornton on a three-way call."

"What should I tell them it's about?"

"Tell them it's about the forensic power of the chainsaw," I said.

"SO THE TREE rings," came Emert's voice from the speakerphone, "can tell us whether he died in 1948 or 1984 or whatever?"

"They can," I said. "In fact, they already have."

I'd taken the three-foot section of tulip-poplar trunk to one of my colleagues in the forestry lab. He had recut the end with a fine-toothed table saw—he'd also bored out a core sample—and had counted the growth rings. According to both counts, the tulip poplar was sixty-three years old. "That means it started growing in the spring of 1946," I said.

"Meaning it was sometime before that," said Miranda, "that G.I. Doe was planted."

. . .

EDDIE GARCIA LOOKED weak and scared. It had been only two days since I'd seen him, but in those forty-eight hours he'd worsened dramatically. They'd begun giving him blood transfusions of packed red blood cells, because his bone marrow had virtually ceased to function. Ironically, the transfused cells were irradiated to kill germs. As an extra precaution against infection, every nurse or doctor who entered his room had to scrub up and suit up in full surgical garb. Looking through the window, as a pair of masked figures checked his monitors and changed his IV bag, I was struck by the discrepancy between appearance and reality: it looked as if they were protecting themselves from Garcia, when in fact it was Garcia they were taking extreme precautions to safeguard. The most distressing sight, though, was his hands, swathed in thick layers of gauze. Unlike Miranda's—so far, at least—Garcia's localized burns had gone necrotic. His hands were dying.

I brought Garcia up to date on the Oak Ridge case, and he seemed intrigued, although maybe he was merely grateful for a distraction from his battle against acute radiation syndrome. But the drip must have contained something to ease his pain, because as I was telling him how the tree rings allowed us to estimate G.I. Doe's time since death, his eyes lost their focus and he fell asleep. It shamed me to realize it, but I was relieved for the chance to ease away.

LATE THAT AFTERNOON I heard a dull thud outside my office door—the sound of something heavy hitting the floor—followed by the clatter of the stairwell door banging shut.

"Whoo," gasped a voice I recognized as Thornton's—a recognition confirmed by the appearance of his head in the entrance of my office as he tapped on the doorframe.

"You all right? Sounds like you're hauling furniture up those stairs," I said.

"Feels like it," he said. "I thought you might like to see this." His head disappeared and I heard a labored grunt. He reappeared, lugging a brushed-aluminum case, the sort generally filled with expensive electronics or video gear. I cleared off the center of my desk, and he set it down with a gentler thud than he had out in the hallway. Then he laid it on its side, flipped four latches on the edge, and swung the lid up.

When I realized what it was, I jumped back. "What are you doing? Get that thing out of here."

"It's safe," he said. "We've checked it up one side and down the other. There's no source in it—nothing radioactive. Only way this thing can hurt you is if you get a hernia trying to lift it. Which I think maybe I've done. Or if it falls on your foot, which would cripple you for life."

Inside the case was an instrument I recognized as an industrial radiography camera—one of the two models Thornton had shown us, in fact, in his PowerPoint briefing about sources of iridium-192. "I thought the manufacturer was sending somebody to Savannah River to look at the source," I said. "They decided to send a camera here instead?"

He shook his head. "We got lucky," he said. "This is the very camera somebody raided for the iridium that killed Novak. Has to be."

"My God," I said. "Where'd you find it? How?"

"One of the things we assigned agents to do right away was to canvas scrap-metal recycling yards," he said. "They started in Oak Ridge and fanned out from there. Our thinking was, the safest way to transport the iridium would be to leave it in the camera till you were ready to use it, since there's all that built-in shielding. We hoped maybe the camera would get dumped after the pigtail was removed. Sure enough, it turned up at a salvage yard on Sutherland Avenue in Knoxville."

My mind was racing. "Who brought it in? Did you get prints? Did you make an arrest?"

"We're looking for the guy," he said, "but it's not our killer. Couldn't be. Selling the camera would be a stupid risk to take for five bucks, which is all the scrapyard paid for it. The guy that brought it in was Hispanic, spoke almost no English, looked to be a day-laborer sort. That's about all the fellow at the scrapyard remembers about him. A couple sets of prints, but the only hit is a match with the guy at the scrapyard, who stole a car years ago."

The find was exciting, but frustrating, too, since it might be a dead end. "Now what? How do you figure out who took the pigtail out of the camera?"

Thornton unfurled a slow smile. "We send a planeload of agents down to New Iberia, Louisiana, to track down who stole it from Pipeline Services, Inc. And to find out why Pipeline Services never reported the theft to the NRC."

32

IT HAD BEEN THREE days since I'd watched Dr. *Strangelove* with Isabella; two and a half days since I'd awakened at dawn, alone but content. My first impulse had been to send her flowers that morning, but something told me to give her some breathing room. She had bolted the night we'd shared pizza at Big Ed's, and that skittishness was probably ratcheted up considerably higher now. And so I'd waited as long as I could stand to, then called and invited her to lunch. "I hear the Soup Kitchen's good," I said, "and it's the right weather for hot soup and crusty bread."

She hesitated, and I began to panic, but then she relented. "I only have half an hour for lunch," she said, "one to one-thirty, so I'll need to eat and run."

"That's okay," I said, grateful she hadn't turned me down. "Any longer than that and you'd find all sorts of other woeful gaps in my cultural education. You want me to pick you up at the library?"

This time she didn't hesitate. "I'll meet you there," she said. "I need to swing by a cash machine on my way."

Don't push your luck, I told myself. "Okay, see you there at, what, ten after one?"

"That sounds about right. Thanks. Bye." She clearly wasn't the sort for long goodbyes.

I half expected her not to show up, but three hours later, as I lingered outside a low, whitesided building distinguished by its savory smells and steamed-up windows, she rounded the corner briskly and nearly bumped into me. "Oh!" she said.

"Fancy meeting you here," I said. I felt a goofy smile spreading across my face.

She looked down and slightly away from me, and once again her hair made curtains that hid her face from view. "I'm actually a lot shyer than you think," she said. I thought I glimpsed a smile, and I reached a hand beneath her chin to tip her face toward me. She flushed, and ducked her head again, but as she did, there was no doubt about the smile.

"I'll try not to make any sudden moves," I said, opening the door amid billows of steam. As we made our way to the counter, I could feel my stomach rumbling and my salivary glands awakening.

The Soup Kitchen served soups and salads and bread cafeteria-style. The day's soups—seven, usually, though by the time we got there they were down to five—were written in marker on a dry-erase board behind the serving counter. I ordered chili topped with a mound of Fritos and shredded cheddar; Isabella chose a creamy spinach soup that looked thick enough to clog arteries with a single serving. She got a small, round loaf of brown bread to go with hers; I figured the Fritos counted as my bread.

The chili was tangy but not spicy, with just the right balance of tomato, ground beef, onion, and toppings. I nodded my approval. "You were so smart to suggest this place," I said.

"I didn't. You did."

"Well then," I said, "I was so smart to suggest this place."

"You were. It's the second-best restaurant in Oak Ridge."

Just then my cell phone rang. I frowned at the interruption, but when I saw the number, I murmured an apology to Isabella and answered the call. "I am about to make you a happy man," said Jim Emert. "A very happy man."

"Don't get me wrong, Detective, I'm flattered," I said, "but I just don't feel attracted to you in that way. I have a strong preference for women." I winked at Isabella across the table, but she was too busy slicing and buttering her bread to notice.

"Very funny," he said. "Just for that, never mind."

"Never mind what?"

"Never mind the great news I was about to share with you."

"You caught the guy who killed Novak?"

"You might think this is better," he said.

"You figured out who killed Novak *and* who killed G.I. Doe?"

"Better," he said.

"The secret to world peace?"

"Better, better, better," he said.

Suddenly it hit me. "No kidding? You're serious?"

"I am," he said.

"This is huge."

"I knew you'd appreciate the significance," Emert said. "We should have it safely in hand in another ten minutes."

"I'll be right there."

He laughed. "This is worth dashing over from Knoxville at two hundred miles an hour?"

"It is," I said, "but I don't have to; I'm already in Oak Ridge. In fact, I'm only a couple of blocks downhill. Isabella and I are having lunch at the Soup Kitchen."

"Very handy," he said. "Just mosey on up when you get done."

I snapped the phone shut. "Big break in the Novak case," I said. Her eyes widened. "They're finally draining the swimming pool. I'm about to get my chainsaw back."

She looked deeply confused for a moment, then gave her head a brisk little shake, as if trying to shake off a deep fog or a hard knock. Then she laughed in disbelief. "Greater love hath no man," she said.

"Don't be jealous," I teased. "I'd hate to have to choose. I would miss you."

She rolled her eyes, then pinched off a piece of bread and flicked it at me across the table.

A STONE'S THROW from the Soup Kitchen, a staircase led upward through a small garden—or what would have been a garden in any other season of the year—and brought me out on Jackson Square, the original heart of wartime Oak Ridge. Since the city's earliest days, the Jackson Square pharmacy had been dispensing medications, and the community theater had been dispensing tragedy and comedy. Slightly higher up the hill stood the Chapel on the Hill and the Alexander Inn, dramatic reminders of how the past of a place could thrive or could be allowed to die.

Crossing the street and stepping onto the sidewalk leading up to the inn, I noticed that the gutter alongside the curb ran dark with brackish water. A fire hose had been hooked to a drain notched into the embankment beneath the pool, and the hose was now dumping the pool's contents down the gutter. With a gurgle and a swirl, the foul water plunged through a cast-iron grate and into a storm sewer. I heard a distant splashing sound—either the sewer pipe was huge or this drain emptied into a deep shaft—and I remembered Isabella talking about the elaborate network of tunnels the Army had built beneath Oak Ridge at the time of the city's creation.

A small utility truck marked OAK RIDGE FIRE DEPARTMENT was parked alongside the pool, as was Emert's car. Emert, wearing a red parka, stood at one end of the pool chatting with a firefighter. The detective hoisted a hand to wave as I approached. "Good timing," he said. "We're getting close to the bottom of the pool now. Unless it's the deepest motel swimming pool ever dug."

My eye was caught by a water-filled container standing between Emert and the firefighter. It was the trash can I'd given Emert on the loading dock of the hospital the day he fished Leonard Novak's wallet and driver's license from his pants pocket. Only ten days had passed, but it seemed like a lot of time—and a lot of innocence—had flowed beneath the bridge. Two people who mattered profoundly to me—a physician I respected deeply, and a student I felt closer to than anyone else on earth—hung in limbo, waiting to find out if they would lose fingertips or hands or even life itself. If Garcia's bone marrow and immune system did not recover, a minor infection could quickly escalate and kill him. Even if he survived, he might well be disfigured for life; his injuries could end his career, and deal a crushing blow to his spirit and his family life.

I pushed the thoughts from my mind. There was nothing I could do to change the outcome for Garcia or Miranda, and there was no reason to burden Emert with my worries. "Okay," I said, "so let's talk strategy here. How do we get the saw out of the pool and into the trash can really quick?" I pointed to the swimming pool's ladder. "That only goes halfway down the side of the pool, and you know that the concrete's got to be slick as glass."

"We're way ahead of you, Doc," he said. He pointed to the fence behind him. A long aluminum pole lay there, a lifeguard's version of a shepherd's crook. "We'll just hook that through the guard bar," he said, "and hoist it up. Rescue complete."

A moment later, I nudged him. The curving, tubular guard bar of the saw came into view as the water receded. It was followed by the top of the saw's orange casing, its brightness dulled considerably by a layer of slime.

The firefighter picked up the pole and threaded the crook through the guard bar. Spreading his feet wide for balance, he raised the pole with a hand-over-hand motion, almost as if he were reeling in a fish. As the saw cleared the edge of the pool, I took hold of it—slime and all—and unhooked it from the pole, then lowered it, engine first, into the clear water in the trash can. "The gods be praised," I said.

"I'll be damned," Emert said.

I looked at him, puzzled, but he wasn't addressing me. He was addressing the bottom of the pool, where the water, as it continued to recede, was revealing the unmistakable outline of another corpse. Protruding from its chest was the handle of a knife.

PART THREE

I feel we have blood on our hands.

—Robert Oppenheimer to President Harry S. Truman, October, 1945

Never mind. It'll all come out in the wash.

—Truman's response to Oppenheimer

33

EMERT, THE FIREFIGHTER, AND I stared down at the body in the pool, the knife jutting from the chest. The first thing Emert did—after letting a few more cusswords fly—was call Hank Strickland at REAC/TS and say, "You got that Geiger counter handy?" Evidently Hank did. "Could you come check out another body for us? I don't want to turn another medical examiner into a human gamma detector." Emert had his phone in one hand and his personal radiation monitor in the other. The chirper remained reassuringly quiet, even when Emert stretched it out over the pool.

Hank arrived fifteen minutes later. By then the parking lot was filling with police cars and fire trucks. "Have gadget, will travel," Hank said.

"Your office is only two blocks away," I said, pointing down the hill to the hospital. "You call that traveling?" Hank shrugged. "How come it took you fifteen minutes to travel two blocks?"

"I was in the middle of a very important email," he said. "A chain letter, only it's email. Break the chain, you're in for seven years of bad luck." He looked at the body in the pool. "Maybe this guy broke the chain."

"I'd say a knife in the chest is more like seven seconds of bad luck," I said.

"I'd say it's more like bad karma," Emert said. "Somebody catches a stray bullet in a drive-by shooting, that's bad luck. Somebody catches a dagger in the left ventricle, that's probably not so random."

"So answer me this," said Hank. "How come Novak's body was frozen in the ice, but this guy sank to the bottom? And don't tell me it's because he had a chainsaw for an anchor. The chainsaw was a postmortem decorative accent, if the story I heard is true." He grinned at me.

"True," said Emert, "every word. Doc, you got a scientific explanation?"

"Maybe he's got rocks in his pockets," I said. "Or just denser bones. Novak was ninety-three, after all. His bones were probably pretty porous. But some people are floaters, and some are sinkers. I've got a friend who bobs like a cork, but I'm like a shark—if I don't keep swimming, I sink to the bottom."

Hank stretched the Geiger counter's wand out over the edge of the pool; he set the detector for gamma radiation first, then beta, then alpha. The instrument emitted only the slow, comforting ticking I'd come to recognize as the sign of background radiation. Armed with that reassurance, he ventured down into the pool, with the help of a ladder off one of the fire trucks, and surveyed the body at close range. Satisfied that it posed no hazard, he climbed out.

Next to descend the ladder was Emert, who donned his coroner's hat long enough to confirm that the man who'd been submerged for days or weeks with a knife in his heart was indeed dead. I couldn't help thinking of the scene in *The Wizard of Oz* where the coroner in Munchkinland pronounces the witch crushed by Dorothy's house to be "not only merely dead," but "really most sincerely dead."

Emert had called Art Bohanan and asked if Art would mind looking for prints on one more piece of evidence, and Art had agreed. Using a set of tongs he'd taken from an evidence kit, Emert worked the knife from the man's chest, taking care not to touch the handle. He sealed the knife in an evidence bag, labeled it, and handed it up to me. Even through the bag's plastic, even through the smear of body fluids and water on the blade, I thought I discerned the distinctive swirls of Damascus steel. "Looks like the missing knife from Novak's display case," I said.

"It is," he said. "I'd bet a month's salary on it."

A CLOUD OF mist shrouded the knife handle. Art squeezed the spray bottle twice more. Mopping a few stray droplets from my face, I said, "And why is it you're wetting it?"

"The moisture helps the superglue latch onto the oils from the print," he said.

"I knew that," I said.

He laid the knife in the transparent chamber of a boxy glass and metal apparatus—"the Bohanan Apparatus" was its official name, and it was patented—and switched on the device's heating element. As the element vaporized the glue, white fumes swirled into the chamber hiding the knife from view. After several minutes Art switched on a fan, which sucked the fumes out of the glass chamber, up through an exhaust hood, and away from the KPD crime lab.

Holding the knife by the blade, Art lifted it from the fuming chamber and held it under a magnifying desk lamp. After studying it for a moment, he leaned back. "Take a look at the tang," he said.

"Okay. Where do I look to see the tang?"

He laughed. "The tang is the part of the blade the handle is riveted to," he said. "This knife has a thick blade, so the tang's thick, too—an eighth of an inch, maybe three-sixteenths. That handle is horn, which is hard to print, but the metal tang can actually be etched by the oil in a fingerprint. Look right there," he said, pointing to a spot near the guard that separated the tang from the sharpened edge of the blade. Dozens of closely spaced lines crossed the tang, with one tiny swirl at the center. "That's a pretty good print," he said.

"But it's less than a quarter-inch wide," I said. "Is that enough to match to anything?"

Art picked up a printout that showed a complete set of prints. "Look at the right thumb," he said. I took the page and held it under the magnifying glass. "What do you think?"

"That loop in the center has the same little break as the one on the knife," I said. "I think it's the same print."

"I think so, too," he said, "and I'm pretty good at this stuff."

I glanced at the words on the paper. The prints had been reproduced from a U.S. government security clearance file. "Damn," I said. "He didn't go gentle into that good night, did he?"

In his final moments, Leonard Novak—a ninety-three-year-old walking ghost—had stabbed to death a man roughly half his age.

34

THE AUTOPSY OF THE third Oak Ridge victim—case 09-03—was almost redundant, since the cause of death had been sticking out of the man's chest. According to the Nashville medical examiner, the lungs contained a small amount of water, which suggested (but did not prove) that the victim had drawn a partial breath as his heart shuddered and stopped. Beyond that, the autopsy report contained nothing extraordinary, though it did shed some light on the guy's life: a middle-aged white male, he stood five feet eleven inches tall, with blue eyes, thinning blond hair, and a gray beard. Thin, whitish scars indicated prior surgeries on the right ankle and left shoulder. A series of whole-body X-rays revealed numerous healed fractures—four ribs on the right side of the chest had been broken, as well as six ribs on the left—two of them in more than one place. The right femur bore evidence of a childhood fracture, the report noted, and was a quarter-inch shorter than the left. The spine, particularly the cervical spine, showed osteoarthritic lipping—ragged fringes of bone rimming the vertebrae in the neck—that was surprisingly severe for a man his age. My first thought, from the variety of skeletal trauma, was *too many bar fights*. But the victim had well-developed leg muscles and—until the knife blade made its entrance—a robust circulatory system. *Maybe not bar fights after all,* I thought. *Maybe bicycle wrecks.* Regardless, the guy seemed to have been rode hard and put away wet.

Miranda, Emert, Thornton, and I were huddled around a table of stale cookies and stale coffee at the ORPD. I had come straight from the KPD lab, so Miranda had caught a ride with Thornton. Strictly speaking, there was no compelling reason for her to be here, but it had become important to find things to occupy Miranda's time and energy. Her three burned fingertips were getting worse—they'd progressed from blisters to open, oozing wounds, wrapped in gauze, and she couldn't do the delicate reconstruction the North Knoxville skeleton required.

She also couldn't shake her fear for Garcia. Somehow, despite the best precautions of the ICU staff, he'd picked up an infection, and his condition seemed more perilous than ever. He was unable to eat or drink anything, and his GI tract was racked with cramps and bloody diarrhea as the lining of his gut sloughed off. In the weeks or months to come, the lining might slowly regenerate, but it might not. His bone marrow was virtually destroyed, and the search was on for a matching marrow donor, but the prospects weren't good. Even if a donor could be found, Garcia might not be robust enough to survive the transplant.

"The pool guy was carrying no identification," said Emert. "No wallet, no credit card, no car keys, nothing. Some loose change in his right hip pocket, a pack of chewing gum in his left pocket." He paused. "But he had *this* in his shirt pocket." The detective slid a ziplock bag toward the center of the table. It contained a small, rectangular piece of white paper, stained with dirty water and smeared ink. Emert flipped it over to reveal the other side. Thornton, Miranda, and I leaned in to see. There, despite the smearing, four words remained legible: "I know your secret."

"Damn," I said.

"Interesting," said Thornton.

"Creepy," said Miranda. "These notes are like a modern-day version of those snitch reports Oak Ridgers sent back during the Manhattan Project. Only now, instead of sending them to Acme Whatchamacallit—"

"Credit," Thornton supplied. "Acme Credit Corporation."

"Right. Whatever," she said. "Only instead of going to Acme, these are going straight to the people being spied on." She frowned. "You know what else this makes me think of? Y'all know those REPORT SUSPICIOUS ACTIVITY signs on the interstate? The ones with the 800 number you're supposed to call—800-something-TIPS—if you spy something fishy?"

"800-492-TIPS," said Thornton.

"It worries me that you know that," she said. "My point is, imagine you're driving along I-40 and suddenly your cell phone rings and a voice whispers in your ear, 'I see what you're doing.' That's what these notes make me think of. This whole spying and snitching thing is creeping me out."

"Spoken like a woman with a guilty conscience," I said. I was only teasing, so I was surprised when she turned red. A thought occurred to me, and I glanced at Thornton to see if he was blushing, too, but the FBI agent's face was a study in nonchalance. Or was he feigning nonchalance, so as not to embarrass Miranda further? I couldn't tell, and I realized it wasn't any of my business if they had kissed and made up, ideologically or otherwise. I turned again to Emert. "So how do you figure out who our modern John Doe is?"

"Well, yet again, we've come up empty-handed on missing-person reports in Oak Ridge," he said. "Nothing remotely similar in Knoxville or surrounding counties, either. We're checking NCIC"—the National Crime Information Center—"to see if there's anybody elsewhere in the country who fits the description. But NCIC has its shortcomings." He looked at Thornton. "No offense."

"None taken," said Thornton. "NCIC is the Bureau's creation, not mine. We know it's not perfect—if a missing-person report lists someone's age as thirty-seven, and a cop plugs in thirty-to-thirty-five in the age range, the system won't connect those two dots. But if the cop follows up with a second search, for ages thirty-six-to-forty, he'll get the report he needs to see. Nothing's perfect, but it's a help."

"Sure," said Emert. "Anyhow. We're running the guy's fingerprints through the state's automated fingerprint identification system, and the Bureau's AFIS, too. So if he's been arrested and printed, we might get lucky enough to ID him that way. Other thing we're doing is running a picture of him in the *Oak Ridger* this afternoon."

I was surprised to hear that. The dead man's face—openmouthed and glassy-eyed, the skin beginning to soften and slough off—was strong stuff for a small-town newspaper. "I'm guessing subscribers will be calling for the editor's head when they see that photo," I said.

"Not a photo," he said. "We had an artist do a sketch. Not a perfect likeness, but maybe more recognizable—and less gruesome—than the photos. Surely somebody will be able to tell us who this guy was."

In the Novak case, Thornton had disappointing news to relate about the radiography camera. Pipeline Services, the Louisiana company that owned the camera, had filed for Chapter 11 bankruptcy protection two weeks before—probably within days or weeks after the fresh iridium-192 source had been shipped to New Iberia and loaded into the camera. The pipeline contractor's doors had been padlocked, and no one seemed to know the camera had gone missing. "We found a window that was unlocked," he said, "and the door to the lab where the camera was kept had been pried open."

"Damn," I said. "A town that small, lots of folks would've known the company had gone belly-up. Almost anybody could've stolen it, right?"

"Theoretically," he said, "but I doubt it. Think about it: somebody who just happens to live in Podunk, Louisiana, suddenly sees their chance to make off with a radiography camera they've always wanted? I don't believe in coincidences that big. We're combing through the personnel records, and we'll interview all the employees. And their neighbors and friends. And all the folks who aren't their friends. I'm flying down there this afternoon. We're getting close," he said. "I can smell it."

Then it was my turn to talk about G.I. Doe. "If we're lucky, we might be able to ID him from his teeth," I said. Three of the soldier's lower molars had fillings, I explained, including one of the third molars, or wisdom teeth. My hope was that the cavity in the third molar—a tooth that erupted around age eighteen—had been filled by an Army dentist. If that was the case, maybe there was a dental chart. The trick, I pointed out, would be to find it among the millions of army dental charts.

"First we found the film," said Emert, "then we found the bones. Things come in threes. You'll find it. G.I. Doe wants to be identified."

When the meeting ended, Miranda, Thornton, and I headed outside. Thornton had parked in front of the building; I'd parked out back. The three of us stood together on the front steps of the municipal building. I said to Miranda, "You mind if I wander down to the library for a few minutes?"

"Why would I mind?"

"Well, you might be in a hurry to get back to campus."

"But I rode with Thornton," she said, "so it doesn't matter."

"But I thought you were riding back with me," I said. "I thought Thornton had to catch a plane to Louisiana." I looked at Thornton; he looked at Miranda.

"But . . . I dropped off my car at the Jiffy Lube on Bearden Hill on the way over here," she said. "He . . . we were planning to swing by there on the way back."

"But Bearden Hill's just five minutes from my house," I said. "Why don't I just run you by there on my way home at the end of the day? That way you know they're done. We don't want Thornton to miss his plane."

"It's all right," he said, a little quicker than necessary. "It's practically on my way to the airport. And I've got time."

"Okay, great," I said, a little more cheerfully than I meant. Bearden was far out of his way, but there was no future in pointing that out. Clearly they wanted to be together, but didn't want to say so. "I might just work in the library for the rest of the afternoon. Miranda, could you see about tracking something down for me later? A master's thesis on Oak Ridge by Isabella Morgan?"

"Anthropology?"

"No, history," I said.

"UT?"

"Yes," I said. "Wait. Maybe not. Maybe Tulane or LSU."

"Could you be any vaguer?"

"Sorry," I said. "Never mind."

"No, it's okay," she said. "I'll see what I can find."

"Thanks," I said. "I'll see you tomorrow."

"Okay," she said. "Tomorrow. Goodbye."

"Goodbye," I said. It might have been the first time we'd ever said something as formal as "Goodbye" to each other. Awkward as it felt, I hoped it would be the last.

I WAS STILL slightly off-balance as I walked into the library and back toward the Reference Desk. The chair was empty, but the telephone receiver was out of its cradle and the HOLD light was blinking, so I hoped Isabella had just stepped away to look up the answer to a caller's question. "I'll be right with you," said a voice behind me, and a gray-haired woman I didn't know stepped behind the desk, lifted the phone, and pressed the blinking light. "He was born November 13, 1955," she said. "In St. Joseph, Missouri. Yes, I believe that *was* the eastern end of the Pony Express route.

You're quite welcome. Glad I could find that for you." She smiled as she hung up the phone. "Can I help you?"

"I was actually looking for Isabella," I said.

"She's not in today. Is there something I can help you with?"

"It's not a reference question," I said. "I'm . . . I'm a friend of Isabella's. I was just going to say hi."

I saw recognition register in her eyes. "Oh, of course," she said. "Yes. Well, she was in earlier, but then she had to leave rather suddenly. Apparently her father has fallen quite ill." After she said it, she looked uneasy, as if she wasn't sure she should have divulged this information to me; if I didn't already know, was I authorized to know? *Report Suspicious Activity,* I thought, and imagined the librarian phoning the TIPS number.

"That's too bad," I said. "Thank you. Sorry to bother you." As I left the library and climbed the hill to my truck, part of my mind was feeling concern for Isabella; another part was spinning in surprise and confusion. I knew so little about her. She'd said something about her grandmother and the Graphite Reactor, but it was a passing mention we'd never circled back to. It had never occurred to me to ask about her parents. Or maybe I simply hadn't had a chance yet. We'd flirted over photos and food; we'd shared the excitement of the search for the uranium bunker; we'd shared a night of passion. But what I knew about her was slight compared with what I didn't know. Isabella was a bright, beautiful enigma.

35

DESPITE WHAT I'D SAID to Miranda about heading straight home from Oak Ridge, I drove to campus instead. I parallel-parked between a pair of concrete pillars under the stadium, then wandered upstairs to the departmental office to check my mail and messages. "Well, I'll be," said Peggy. "You *are* alive. I'd just about decided you were dead."

"Just missing in action," I said. "Speaking of MIA, could you call up Joe Cusick at CILHI for me?" Joe was a former student of mine; after earning his Ph.D., he'd gone to work for the U.S. Army's Central Identification Laboratory in Hawaii. The lab's official name had changed recently—to J.PAC, which stood for something I couldn't remember—but I still thought of it by the old acronym, CILHI, pronounced "SILL-high." I'd served on CILHI's scientific advisory board for several years early in Joe's tenure there, and I was always glad for an excuse to call or, better yet, pay a visit.

"You think he'd be at work already? It's six hours earlier in Honolulu, you know."

I checked my watch; it was 1:45 P.M. in Knoxville; 7:45 A.M. there. "He gets up with the chickens," I said. "He'll be there."

I ducked into my seldom-used administrative office, through the doorway that adjoined Peggy's office, and dumped the mountain of mail on the conference table that butted up against the front of the desk. "It's ringing," said Peggy. "Do you want me to go ahead and switch it to you?"

"Please," I said.

"Uh," grunted a voice two rings later. "Yeah. . . . Hello. . . . This is Joe Cusick." It was not the voice of a man who'd gotten up with the chickens—not unless it had been a long, rough night in the coop.

"Good morning, Joe," I said sunnily. "It's Bill Brockton. Did I catch you before your coffee kicked in?"

"Woof. Give me just a second here," he said. "Bill. Hey there. Haven't had coffee yet. I'm in Cambodia. It's, I dunno, two in the morning here."

"Oh hell, Joe, I'm sorry," I said. I'd forgotten that the number we had on file for him was a satellite phone. "Go back to sleep. I'll call you eight hours from now."

"No, no, it's okay," he said, sounding more alert now. "I'm used to this. Happens all the time. I'll be snoring again five minutes after we hang up. I can fall asleep on a dime; I'm famous for it. Go ahead."

"Okay," I said, "if you insist. But what are you doing in Cambodia?"

"Looking at some bones in the hills near the Vietnamese border," he said. "Supposedly an American pilot who crashed here in '68 or '69. If we can identify him, that'd leave only another seventeen hundred and fifty MIAs in Southeast Asia. What's up? What can I do for you?"

"I'm hoping CILHI might be able to help us ID a World War II soldier," I said. "His skeleton just surfaced in Oak Ridge. He was shot in the head and buried in a shallow grave out on the DOE reservation."

Even though he was half a world away, our conversation bouncing off a satellite orbiting thousands of miles high, Joe's whistle came across clearly. "So this was murder, not KIA," he said.

"Probably not killed in action," I agreed. "Not a lot of enemy combatants in Tennessee."

"Did you find his dog tags?"

"That's the problem," I said. "No dog tags, no driver's license. A wristwatch and the buttons off a pair of army-issue coveralls. Oh, and a really thick stack of papers. We're wondering if he might've been spying."

"If somebody caught him spying, wouldn't they have turned him in, either before or after they shot him?"

"Maybe," I conceded. "The picture in Oak Ridge is a little murky." I told him about Novak's bizarre death, and the film in the freezer, the additional body we'd found when the pool was drained.

"And I thought Southeast Asia was complicated," he said. "Well, if this soldier was shot and buried on the sly, he'd have been reported AWOL pretty quick. And if he didn't turn up in a month, he'd have been flagged as a deserter. We've got a database at CILHI that lists deserters. Let me call the office and have somebody take a look. So this was in Oak Ridge, sometime in the 1940s or 1950s?"

"Actually," I said, "we think he was killed in 1945 or early 1946. He was buried sometime after a uranium bunker was built—that was in '44—but before a tree started growing in '46."

Joe laughed. "Well, that should narrow down the list of potential deserters," he said. "I'll ask somebody to take a look and give you a call. Let me know how it all turns out."

"Thanks, Joe. 'Preciate you. Sorry I woke you. Safe travels. Sleep fast."

Two hours later, Peggy forwarded a call from Pete Rossi, an investigator at CILHI. "Our database turned up two deserters in East Tennessee in the summer of 1945," Rossi said. "One was a guard from Camp Crossville, a prisoner-of-war camp up on the Cumberland Plateau where German and Italian officers were held. The guy from Camp Crossville was caught in Kentucky three months later and court-martialed. He claimed he was AWOL, not a deserter, and said he was gonna report back once his mama got well. He must have been convincing at the court-martial, because he got off with a two-year sentence and a dishonorable discharge."

"And the other deserter?"

"The other was a corporal named Jonah Jamison," said Rossi. "He was assigned to the Special Engineer Detachment—the military unit associated with the Manhattan Project—and posted to the Clinton Engineer Works. Never caught; vanished without a trace."

"Clinton Engineer Works," I said. "That was the army's name for the Oak Ridge complex. That's got to be our man."

"Sounds like it," Rossi agreed.

"How soon you reckon we can get his army dental records?" As soon as I said it, I remembered. "Oh crap. That might be a problem, huh?"

"Might be," said Rossi. "Like the Pope might be Catholic."

What I'd suddenly remembered was the fire. The National Archives stored tens of millions of military service records in a huge repository in St. Louis, Missouri. In 1973, a fire broke out on the sixth floor of the building, which contained two-thirds of the military files. By the time the blaze was extinguished, the files of seventeen million soldiers had been destroyed, singed, or soaked. To keep the waterlogged files from molding, archivists had put them all in refrigerated storage. Some of the damaged records were being reconstructed, by scanning their soggy pages to create duplicate files; however, progress was excruciatingly slow, and many records had been lost altogether. On two previous occasions, I had sought military dental records from the St. Louis facility. In one case, the records I needed had survived; in the other, they hadn't. Eighty percent of the records from the 1940s had been destroyed, Rossi said, so he wasn't optimistic about finding a dental record that would tell us whether or not it was Jonah Jamison's skeleton laid out on a table in my bone lab.

"But I'm actually in St. Louis right now," Rossi added, "looking through some Vietnam era records for Cusick. I'll see if Jamison's personnel file survived the fire."

Statistically, the odds weren't good—just one in five. But then I remembered Emert's words. "Things come in threes. You'll find it."

Bless him: Emert was right. Jonah Jamison did want to be identified.

"JAMISON MUST HAVE been a scientist or technician of some sort," I said to Thornton. "Isn't that the kind of folks who were in the Special Engineer Detachment?"

"Most of them were," said Thornton. The agent was on a three-way call from New Iberia with Emert and me. "Jamison was different, though. He was a writer."

"A writer? What the hell was a writer doing in a scientific and technical outfit?"

"Immortalizing the great endeavor," he said. "General Groves had one eye on Japan and the other eye on history. Or fame." I thought back to the photograph Miranda had shown me, and her comments on how narrowly the general's horizon was drawn compared to Oppenheimer's. "Groves had still photographers and cinematographers scurrying around all over the place, capturing everything on film," Thornton was saying, "but apparently he wanted the story set down on paper too, and in style."

The more I thought about it, the more sense it made. If the Manhattan Project succeeded, it would clearly play a pivotal role in human history. If it didn't succeed, well, having the costly failure detailed on film and in print would likely be the least of the general's worries. "So Jamison wrote for the Knoxville paper before the war?"

Thornton laughed. "Not exactly. Groves was aiming for greater glory," he said. "Jamison was a *New York Times* reporter before the war. After he was drafted, he was assigned to write scripts for training films—how to clean your rifle, how not to get VD, that sort of thing—when Groves reached down and plucked him from the basement of the Pentagon."

"How do you know all this stuff," I asked, "when we didn't even know who he was until twelve hours ago?"

"Because the FBI has files, too," he said, "and ours weren't stored in a firetrap in St. Louis. And because Jonah Jamison was considered a potential security risk."

"A security risk?" That made no sense to me. "If they didn't trust him, why didn't they get somebody else to write about the project? Why take the chance?"

"Well, he looked like a red-blooded American risk," said Thornton. "His Achilles' heels were booze and women. And Groves really wanted him. Jamison had written some flattering pieces about Groves in 1942, when Groves spearheaded the construction of the Pentagon. That was the Army's biggest project before the Manhattan Project, and apparently the stories made Groves look brilliant. Jamison was drafted at the end of '42, and Groves had him posted to Oak Ridge in early '43. He was reported AWOL on August 4, 1945—two days before Hiroshima."

"And he disappeared without a trace?"

"Until you dug him up," Thornton said. "Him and that thick stack of pages."

"I sure wish we could read what was on those pages that were in the grave," said Emert.

"I sure wish we knew who killed him for writing it," I said. "Anything in his security file shed light on that?"

"Unfortunately, no," Thornton said. "But speaking of security files, your storytelling gal pal turned up in two of the snitch reports to Acme Credit."

"Beatrice?"

"Yup. One came from a neighbor, anonymous, who wrote, 'That woman has the morals of an alley cat.' "

I couldn't help it; I laughed at that. It was impossible to

imagine Beatrice, her silver hair and wrinkled face, behaving scandalously. "The bad girl of AARP," I said.

"Maybe not now," he said. "But maybe back then. The other report came several months after that first one. An army doc at the Oak Ridge field hospital wrote that she came in bleeding and running a fever. She claimed she'd had a miscarriage. But the doctor suspected she'd had an abortion."

36

***WE WORE BADGES EVERYWHERE** in those days—not just to work, but to the grocery store, the post office, even church. Heaven forbid you should try to gain access to Jesus when your clearance was only for Yahweh. MPs ranged everywhere checking badges. The black section of town, Colored Town, was practically fenced off. If the face on your badge wasn't black, a guard or MP sitting in a jeep beside the road into Colored Town might wave you over and ask what business you had in there.*

The business I had in there was an abortion.

A year after I married Novak, I realized I was pregnant. This was not happy news. For one thing, I was working with radioactive materials.

We know a lot more now than we knew then about radioactivity and birth defects. I was working with equipment that flung atoms of U-235 and U-238 all over the place. In theory, the calutrons were collecting all the uranium, but in practice, it wasn't so neat and tidy. It was probably like one of those big movie-theater popcorn poppers, the kind with the pot suspended up high inside a glass box. It's designed to contain the popcorn, but if you look at the floor back there behind the concession stand, you'll always see stray kernels that have ricocheted out through a gap in the gizmo. The calutrons were like that. At the end of every shift, they would run Geiger counters over us as we were leaving, and sometimes they'd find a stray particle or two of U-235 on somebody's coveralls, which they'd remove with a magnifying glass and tweezers. It wasn't that they were concerned about our health; it was that the uranium was so precious, they couldn't afford to let a speck of it slip out the gate.

Today, they won't let you have an X-ray in the doctor's office if you're pregnant. Back then, though, there were thousands of young women of childbearing age working in areas filled with radiation sources. It amazes me there wasn't a whole herd of babies with birth defects born in Oak Ridge in 1944 and 1945.

But the reason I needed an abortion wasn't because I was worried about birth defects. The reason I needed an abortion was because the baby wasn't Novak's. After twelve months of marriage, we'd still never consummated it. Leonard Novak was many things—smart, funny, a brilliant scientist, a great jazz pianist—but heterosexual wasn't one of them. At least not with me.

I had done my best to seduce my husband. At bedtime, I would undress in front of him. Sometimes I'd brush my hair out, a hundred strokes, sitting in my slip in front of the mirror. I'd get him drunk, hoping that would lower his inhibitions. Once the lights were out and we were under the covers, I would press myself against him. None of it worked, ever.

Do you have any idea what it's like to be a woman whose husband shows absolutely no desire for her? Never makes any move to touch her? I knew enough by this point to know that I liked sex. Needed it, too. Maybe it was because my father died and my mother abandoned me when I was still young. Whatever the reason, I craved affection. Or maybe I just wanted sex because I was a healthy, fertile young woman surrounded by healthy, virile young soldiers and construction workers.

Within a week of marrying Novak, I knew I'd made a

mistake, and within six months, I was getting restless and flirting with other men. Around noon every day, while Novak was off making plutonium at the Graphite Reactor, I'd walk down the hill to the recreation hall and strike up a conversation with some guy at the soda fountain. Sometimes we'd just talk for a while and then I'd catch the bus out to Y-12 for my evening shift at the calutron; sometimes the guy, whoever he was, would take me to a dorm room or a car or a trailer. It felt furtive and dirty, but it took away some of the loneliness. It gave me something to look forward to—and something to remember—during those long afternoon hours in a factory filled with vacuum pumps and invisible atoms and magnetic fields that pulled the bobby pins out of my hair. And it gave me something to cling to in the long, empty hours at night, when my husband gave me a peck on the cheek and rolled to the far side of the mattress.

Novak had to know I was being unfaithful to him. He was a smart man, after all; how could he not notice that the woman who's been throwing herself at him, night after night, suddenly isn't anymore? Did his relief that I was letting him off the hook make it easy for him to keep quiet about whatever he was noticing or wondering or suspecting? I can only guess that it must have. And I chose to interpret his silence as tacit approval, in some way.

But a baby: I knew a baby would change everything. A baby would have forced us to confront the issue, if you'll pardon the pun. I couldn't do it. And so it was I found myself one Saturday night—a night when I was pregnant and Novak was away—on the bus into Colored Town.

I wasn't alone. I was riding with a young black woman from Y-12. Mary Alice was a cleaning woman in my building. That was the only sort of job they gave black people during the war—manual labor or janitorial work. I'd gotten to know her during smoke breaks and I liked her. Her mother, she said, was a sort of midwife, nurse, and healer.

And an abortionist. When I found out I was pregnant, it hadn't been hard for me to come up with a pretext for catching a bus with Mary Alice to Colored Town. I would sneak in by posing for the cameras.

When I became the calutron poster girl, I'd gotten chummy with the photographer, Ed Westcott. Nothing improper, not with him, but anytime he was taking pictures in my building, he'd stop by and chat for a minute. And when I found out that Mary Alice and her mother could help me out of my dilemma, I came up with an idea. Westcott was always looking for human-interest pictures—kids playing in a swimming hole, Cub Scouts learning to build campfires, cars stuck in the mud. Once he shot Santa Claus being frisked by security guards. Christ, we thought, if even Santa's getting checked for contraband, who are we mere mortals to complain?

Westcott was famous, in a way. As the project's photographer, he was free to come and go pretty much wherever he pleased, and he'd been ranging all over the townsite and the plants since the very beginning. Most of the guards would motion him right through checkpoints, smiling and waving; some of them would stop him just long enough to strike a pose and ask him when he was going to take their picture. Occasionally he did, which earned him all sorts of goodwill.

Anyway, what I suggested to Westcott was a picture showing me giving reading lessons to Mary Alice and some of the other girls in Colored Town. "I think it could be a good civic project," I said. "Maybe if you did a picture and the paper ran it, we'd drum up some interest and some volunteers." He liked the idea, and he agreed to meet me at the colored recreation hall. So when the bus driver asked me why a white woman was heading into Colored Town on a Saturday night, I told him Mr. Westcott was coming to take a picture of me teaching colored girls to read. That seemed to be a good enough reason.

Colored Town was officially called the "colored hutment area" on the map. Hutments were shabby, prefab plywood shacks, sixteen feet square. They were trucked in by the thousands and shoehorned together, about ten feet apart. There was a hutment area for whites, too, but the white hutments were better. The colored hutments didn't even have real windows, just screened-in openings covered with hinged panels of plywood. If the people inside wanted daylight, they'd swing up some of the hinged panels and prop them open. That might have been okay in decent weather, but when it was cold, the choice was between warmth and light, and even the warmth wasn't all that warm—every hutment had a cast-iron coal stove in the middle of the room, but as drafty as the buildings were, and as scarce as coal rations were, people in the hutments were miserably cold in the winter. The other thing about the colored hutments was that there were men's hutments and women's hutments, four people per hutment. Black couples who were married got split up so the army could cram four people into every one of those dreadful little shacks.

Colored Town had its own rec center, too, and the story there was the same—it was cheaper and crummier than the white people's version. No Ping-Pong tables or pool tables or piano; just a few tables and chairs. Even so, when Mary Alice and I walked in that night, the place was crowded and lively. Couples sat at some of the tables playing bridge; groups of men with poker chips at others. At one end of the room, somebody had a radio, and couples were jitterbugging to the music. The instant I walked in the door, the noise died down and every head turned in our direction. Thousands of black people crammed in a shabby ghetto, and in walks a lily-white woman.

"You in the wrong place, white girl," said a man just inside the door, but then Mary Alice called him by name and told him to mind his business. "She's all right," Mary

Alice said. "She's with me." She led us to a distant corner of the room where a middle-aged man and woman sat in straight-backed chairs angled toward each other. "Mama, this here is Beatrice, that I told you about." Her mother looked me up and down. The man looked away, as if to give us a measure of privacy, and I was grateful.

"You sure this is what you got to do?" I nodded. "You got the money?"

"Yes ma'am," I said, and took two ten-dollar bills out of my skirt pocket. She smoothed and folded them, then tucked them into her blouse.

"Mary Alice," she said, "you come with me and this white girl."

She led us through a doorway into the women's restroom. The restroom held one sink and three toilet stalls, none of them with a door. It smelled like it hadn't been cleaned lately. She must have seen the look of revulsion on my face, because she said, "You want a nice doctor's office, you come to the wrong place, white girl. You want to change your mind about this?"

"No ma'am," I said. "I'm just scared."

"Ought to be," she said. "This is scary business. Sad, too. How come you not want to have this child?"

"I can't," I said. "I just can't."

"Course you can, baby," she told me. "You just won't. 'Can't' not the same thing as 'won't.'" She pointed at the third stall. "You need to pull off your panties and raise up your skirt. Sit on that toilet and scootch up to the front of the seat. You got to spread your knees wide and hang your bottom off the front edge so I can get in there. But you ought to pee first, if you can."

I stared from her to Mary Alice and back again. "It's all right," said Mary Alice. "She's done this a hundred times. She knows what she's doing. I'll be right there beside you. You go on and use the bathroom, and I'll come in when you flush."

I sat down on the toilet and bent over to hide my face while I peed, then reached back and flushed the toilet. Then I pulled off my underpants, and Mary Alice squeezed into the narrow space between the toilet and the wall.

"Now scoot on up here and open up your legs," said Mary Alice's mother. "I know you know how to do that."

"Mama!" Mary Alice sounded shocked.

"Mary Alice, don't you start with me," she said. "I know you've been opening yours for a while now, too. Women been gettin' told to open their legs since the fall of man. That's one part of the Lord's curse. This here's another part."

She pulled a small bottle from her apron pocket, uncorked it, and handed it to me. "Here, drink this down. Absinthe. Help you relax." The liquid in the bottle smelled like licorice, but it burned like whiskey going down. Within seconds I felt the heat in my stomach, then felt it spread through my belly and out into my arms and legs, and my head began to hum. Next she took a handkerchief from her apron and tied it into a fat knot. "Open your mouth," she said, and when I did, she jammed the knot between my teeth. "Now you bite down hard. This gonna hurt some." I clenched my jaws, and felt the knot begin to flatten under the pressure. "Mary Alice, you get ready."

Somehow, despite the narrowness of the toilet stall, Mary Alice managed to turn and swing one leg over me, so she was straddling me—one leg on either side of the toilet—facing me, her chest in my face. She reached down and took my hands in hers, lacing her fingers through mine. I felt her mother kneel between my knees. "All right, easy does it," she said. "If you can relax, that'd be good. If you can't, you hold real still. This be over before you know it."

I felt something cold and sharp pierce me to the core, and I heard a scream burrowing its way out of my throat and through the knot of fabric. My knees jerked up and my shoulders strained forward as my body fought to curl itself into a ball. "By God, white girl, you hold still. If you want to stay alive, you hold still," she said. "Mary Alice, you got to hold her good."

My nose closed from my tears, and the handkerchief filled my mouth. I could not breathe, and I began to gasp and gag. Everything started going black—everything except for the white-hot flame of pain. Then, just when I was sure I was dying, I felt the fabric yanked from my mouth, and I could breathe again and see again. "Done," I heard Mary Alice's mother say. "Done. Lord forgive us, it's done." I felt my belly cramping, and every spasm felt as if I were clenching shards of glass or slivers of metal deep within me. "I got to put these rags inside you," she said. "Catch the blood. You wait till tomorrow evening to take 'em out." I gasped when she prodded at me again, but it was a duller pain this time.

Mary Alice let go of one hand and swung her leg back across me, so she was beside me again. She gave my shoulder a squeeze. "You done just fine," she said. "You'll be all right now." I shook my head and cried.

I heard water running in the sink, and a moment later Mary Alice's mother stepped into the stall again, holding two damp cloths. She handed one to Mary Alice, who mopped my face; with the other, she bent down and swabbed my blood-smeared thighs and bottom.

Suddenly there was a series of raps on the door. I nearly cried out with fear; the two black women exchanged swift, worried looks. More knocking, louder now. "Mary Alice? Miss Beatrice?"

"Yes, what is it?" Mary Alice said.

"Y'all about done in there? Y'all just about ready to get your picture took?"

I started to call out—I have no idea what I would have said—but luckily Mary Alice laid a hand over my mouth. "Just about," she said. "One more minute." She hauled me to my feet. "You splash some water on your face and comb your hair and put on this lipstick," she said. "Then we got to get out there and act like everything is fine."

In a daze—the cramps searing and my head buzzing—I rinsed my face and dabbed on lipstick. Then Mary Alice took my hand and led me out the restroom door. It was as if I had walked onstage in a play: a card table in front of us glowed in a pool of light, and as Mary Alice and I stepped forward dozens of faces watched. Most of the faces were black, but several were white, and I recognized the uniforms and black armbands of MPs.

A few books were stacked on the table, and one lay open, its spine broken. It was the Bible, and it was open to the story of Adam and Eve. Westcott stepped toward us and ushered us into two chairs, which were angled at one corner of the table. "Ladies, you look lovely," he said, though he looked at me closely, with what appeared to be concern. "Lean forward over the book a little, Beatrice. You, too, Mary Alice, and point to a word, like you're asking Beatrice what the word is."

Mary Alice's index finger—blue-black skin, with a pink, pearly nail—traced a wavering line down one page, then came to rest beneath a verse. "What this Bible verse say right here, Miss Beatrice?" Her voice was a singsong caricature—like a darky in a Hollywood film—and I wondered if it was me she was mocking, or Westcott, or the segregated city and nation in which we lived and worked.

I looked, and I read the verse aloud: "The tree of the knowledge of good and evil, thou shalt not eat of it: for in the day that thou eatest thereof thou shalt surely die."

"Amen," said Mary Alice as the flash blinded me.

The MPs—sent by the bus driver, apparently, to make sure the white woman wasn't set upon by sex-crazed black men—stayed while Westcott packed up his camera and lights and loaded them back into his jeep. Mary Alice and I had remained seated while the gear was packed. When everything was loaded, I stood up to go, and when I did, I felt my dress sticking to the metal folding chair. I looked down, and the seat was sticky with blood. Mary Alice glanced at the chair, then quickly stood beside me, an arm around my waist. With her free hand, she signaled to her mother, who came and stood close behind me. We walked that way, the two black women and I, out of the building and into the night. Mary Alice helped me onto the bus, and as I stepped up into the enveloping darkness of the bus, I heard one of the MPs say something to the other.

What he said was, "Nigger lover."

37

BEATRICE TURNED TO LOOK at me. It had cost her some pain to tell me the story, I could tell.

"I'm sorry," I said. "You must have been desperate to have risked so much. You could have died. Or gone to prison."

"Prison comes in all shapes and sizes," she said. "So does death." She turned and looked out the windows. "How did you know to ask me about that?"

I probably wasn't supposed to say, but I felt I owed her a disclosure in return for what she'd just told me. "The FBI is looking at old files," I said, "trying to figure out why Novak was killed. A doctor at the hospital reported that he suspected you'd had an abortion."

"That son of a bitch," she said. "I knew him for forty years, and I never could stand him."

I realized I had no right to ask, but I asked anyhow. "Whose baby was it, Beatrice?"

"I don't know," she said. "That's another reason I had the abortion." She sighed. "Novak was traveling out to Hanford a lot in the spring and summer of 1945," she said. "The big plutonium production reactors out there were coming on line, and there were technical problems to solve. It turned out that trace amounts of boron were absorbing neutrons and slowing down the chain reaction. 'Poisoning' it, that's the term they used. Novak had to solve the mystery of the boron poisoning. He'd be gone for a week or ten days at a time, and I got into the habit of going down to the Rec Hall at night, to pass the time."

"You were lonely when he was gone," I said.

"I was lonely when he was here," she said. "Maybe lonelier. I think I was the loneliest when he was sleeping in the same bed with me, twelve inches away but beyond reach. When he was gone, at least I could do something about the loneliness. Sometimes I even brought a man home with me. I'm sure I was indiscreet; I'm sure the neighbors talked."

Or snitched, I thought. "I should go," I said.

"Where? Home? Do you have a good woman waiting for you, Bill? Or a good man?"

"No. I have work waiting for me," I said. I stood to go. Something on the end table beside her chair caught my eye. Resting atop a stack of opened mail was a small, rectangular piece of white paper with blue lettering.

"Good God," I said.

"What?" She followed my eyes. "Oh, *that,*" she said. "What a jerk."

The lettering read, "I know your secret."

"AMAZING," I SAID to Emert. I had called him when I left Beatrice's house to share what she'd told me about the note. Thirty minutes later, as I sat in his office, he had already gathered a remarkable amount of information. "So this guy was just on a random fishing expedition? Trying to trick Oak Ridge geezers into spilling whatever beans they had to spill from the bomb project or the Cold War?"

"Espionage-flavored beans," said Emert. "He was pitching a documentary to the History Channel. *Atomic Secrets,* he called it." Emert waved a one-page printout—a bad photocopy of a fax, or a really good photocopy of a really bad fax. "This is a one-page treatment he'd faxed to the History Channel. He didn't have a deal for it yet, though—it was just a proposal."

I read the subtitle. “No wonder he didn’t have a deal,” I said. “Get a load of that subtitle. *How Soviet Spies Pierced the Heart of the Manhattan Project*. How clunky is *that*?”

“Yeah, well, Ken Burns he wasn’t,” said Emert. “But you gotta love the irony of ‘pierced the heart,’ considering how he died. Apparently he was hoping to dig up something juicy in Oak Ridge, something that would hook the History Channel.”

“How’d you get this so fast?”

“I’ll never tell,” he said, holding a finger to his lips, like the World War II billboards that reminded Oak Ridgers to keep quiet.

“Okay,” I said.

“Oh, all right, I’ll tell,” he said. “Right after you called from Beatrice’s driveway, I got a call from a desk clerk at the Doubletree, who saw the sketch in the newspaper. The secret-sniffing guy—Willard Clarkson was his name—checked into the hotel seventeen days ago, on January ninth. On the tenth, he faxed this to New York. He also asked for extra chocolate-chip cookies.”

“The Doubletree makes a damn good cookie,” I said.

“Yeah, but you’re only entitled to one cookie, and only at check-in,” Emert said. “This guy went back for seconds. He thought the regular rules didn’t apply to him.”

“What are you, the cookie police? You’re saying he deserved to die because he went back to the desk clerk and said, ‘Please, sir, could I have more?’? Hell, I’ve done that.”

“Never do it again,” he said. “Look where you could end up.”

“Clearly the desk clerk had sufficient motive,” I said. “So, this bush-league documentary guy—”

“Sapling,” said Emert.

“Sapling?”

“Bush-league’s a little harsh,” he said. “Clarkson had already done some other History Channel shows. Things about World War II aircraft carriers and fighter planes and bombers. Not bad. Some glitzy stuff for A&E, too. But as I was saying—"

"Before you were so rudely interrupted?"

"Before I was so rudely interrupted," he echoed. "The afternoon of January tenth, he sends the fax and asks for illegal seconds on the cookies. And then nobody at the Doubletree ever sees him again."

"They thought he'd skipped out?"

"They just thought he was weird, or reclusive. He'd said he'd be staying for several weeks. They had his credit card on file, and the DO NOT DISTURB sign was hanging on the door. They were leaving him alone."

"January tenth," I said. "That was right before East Tennessee turned into Antarctica, if I remember right."

"It was," he said. "It was also one day after Leonard Novak checked out those library books about the Venona Project."

EMERT HEADED TO the Doubletree, to lead the search of Willard Clarkson's room. I headed down the hill once more, to the library. I was hoping that perhaps Isabella was back by now, her father's health improving, but the substitute at the Reference Desk dashed my hopes. She dashed my fallback hope as well: no, she didn't have any further details about how he was doing, or where I might send a get-well card, or when Isabella might be back. I tried to mask the frustration and embarrassment I felt; I must look like either a stalker or a fool, I realized, to be pursuing a woman who didn't consider me worth turning to in a crisis.

"I was hoping to do a bit of history research today," I said. It wasn't true—it was a flimsy excuse for my presence here—but she unlocked the Oak Ridge Room for me, and I found it soothing, somehow, to be there. I looked through the notebook of photos from ORNL, and saw the Graphite Reactor take shape on a hillside, against the backdrop of a wooded ridge. I saw the immense U-shaped structure of the K-25 plant, which separated a gaseous form of uranium. The K-25 plant was the last to be completed but the largest in capacity, like some lumbering uranium freight train finally gathering momentum. I saw the oval racetracks of Y-12, their D-shaped calutrons linked by thousands of tons of silver borrowed from the U.S. Treasury. And I saw Beatrice, perched on her stool, one hand forever poised on the controls, altering the trajectory of uranium atoms and human history.

Looking through a binder labeled "Life in Oak Ridge," I saw men and women lined up for cigarettes, boys and girls decked out in Cub Scout and Brownie uniforms, football players in helmets and pads, baseball teams in caps. I saw two pretty young women—one white, one black—looking at a book together, the black woman pointing a finger at the page as the white woman read aloud. The white woman's eyes looked glassy.

I saw musicians playing and couples dancing. And among the dancing couples, I spotted Beatrice yet again. She was a photogenic young woman; if I were a photographer in wartime Oak Ridge, I'd have taken her picture every chance I got, too. In this photo, she was dancing with a handsome, smiling young man—a man who was not Leonard Novak. I checked the date on the photo: August 1, 1945. The Trinity test had shaken New Mexico two weeks before; in five more days, the city of Hiroshima would be decimated, and in eight days Nagasaki would share its fate. And at some point in the days or weeks after the photo was taken, the smiling young man would be shot at point-blank range and buried in a shallow grave, along with hundreds of pages of typescript. Were the pages a manuscript for posterity, or secrets for the Soviets? Or were they both?

I dialed Emert's number and the call rolled immediately to his voice mail. "I'm at the library," I said, "and I'm looking at a picture of Beatrice dancing with Jonah Jamison on August 1, 1945."

When I ended the call, my phone beeped to tell me I'd received a voice mail. While I'd been leaving the message for Emert, the detective had been leaving one for me. "Maybe our dead documentary guy was after a big fish after all," his message said. "We're in his hotel room, and he's got a fat file of transcripts from the Venona Project."

As soon as I hung up, my phone rang. It was Emert again, live and in person this time. "Clarkson made some interesting notes in the margins of these Venona cables," Emert said. On July 22, 1945, someone whose code name was "Chekhov" had traveled from Oak Ridge to Hanford; the cable added that "Pavlov" had found the way to "Chekhov" and would soon submit a detailed account of the project. Clarkson had highlighted "Chekhov" and written "Novak?" in the margin. He'd also highlighted "Pavlov" and scrawled a pair of question marks.

"I think we should go see your friend Beatrice together," he said, "and ask her some more questions about her husband and her boyfriend."

38

BEATRICE STUDIED THE COPY of the photograph I'd duplicated at the library. She looked from my face to Emert's and back again.

"Jonah was a handsome man, wasn't he? Yes," she said, "I had an affair with him." She turned to me. "That's why I had to have the abortion. How could I have a baby whose father had shot himself because of me?"

The casual way she said it stunned me, but Emert just shook his head. "I don't believe you," he said. "Why would he shoot himself over you? Why didn't you call the MPs when it happened? How'd you get the body way the hell out by that uranium bunker?" The man did like to fire off multiple questions.

Now it was Beatrice shaking her head. "Don't you see, if I'd reported it, the scandal would have ruined Leonard's career, and that would have destroyed Leonard. Leonard buried the body. To protect us both."

I felt ten steps behind, struggling to catch up. "But Leonard was deeply conflicted about working on the atomic bomb anyhow," I said. "It might have been a relief to be forced off the project."

"No, you're wrong," she said. "Leonard's moral pangs about the bomb were his own private pain. Public humiliation would have been intolerable to a sensitive man like Leonard."

"So let me see if I understand this," said Emert. "You're saying he was too sensitive to face embarrassment, but not too sensitive to bury a body in the woods?"

"Absolutely," she said. "Leonard was used to keeping secrets, and he was used to self-recrimination. He had a streak of martyrdom in him—but he wanted to be the one to nail himself to the cross, rather than be nailed there by anyone else. There was an edge of arrogance on his finely honed sense of guilt."

Something was nagging at me. Something written in four words on a small piece of paper. "Beatrice, did you talk to Novak after you heard from the man making the documentary about atomic secrets?" She looked startled.

"I . . . I don't think so," she said. "I really can't remember."

"The phone company's computer can tell us if you two talked by telephone recently," said Emert.

"I might have," she said. "Wait, yes, I did. Briefly. Leonard called and asked if I had said anything to that dreadful television man about . . . anything. I told him no. I told him not to worry—that the man was just a TV muckraker. But Leonard was very upset. He said the man had all but accused him of giving the Russians information about the bomb during World War II."

Emert leaned forward. "And *did* Leonard give the Russians information about the bomb?"

"Leonard? Heavens no," she said. "But it wouldn't surprise me if Jonah did. I wasn't his only girlfriend, you know. He spent far too much money on women and whiskey. I don't see how he could afford his vices on a corporal's salary."

Emert stared at her stonily. "Lady, I think you're lying to me. I want you to come down to the police station tomorrow afternoon and give me a statement. I'll be asking you to take a polygraph test, too, unless you're afraid it will incriminate you."

What she did next startled both Emert and me. Beatrice

laughed. "Afraid? Detective, I believe every word I've said. Why on earth would I be afraid of a lie detector." Suddenly her head nodded forward, then jerked upright again. "Oh my, this has all been quite exhausting," she said. Her voice quavered a bit. "Would you gentlemen mind if an old woman goes to bed now? It sounds like I have a grueling afternoon in store for me tomorrow."

Emert scowled, but he rose from the chair, so I stood up as well. "One o'clock," he said. "Bring an attorney if you need one."

"What I need is a time machine, detective," she said, struggling to her feet and shuffling to the door with us.

39

THE PHONE RANG A dozen times or more before she answered. "Hello?" She sounded old and tired. Not quavery, like last night; I was pretty sure the quaver had been for effect, to hurry Emert and me on our way. This sounded like the real deal. It was the same exhausted, defeated tone I'd heard an hour before in Eddie Garcia's voice, when he'd told me that the national registry contained no matching bone-marrow donor, and that Carmen's mother was coming up from Bogotá to help take care of the baby for a while.

"Beatrice, it's Bill Brockton," I said. "I'm sorry to call so early. I'm wondering if I could come see you this morning?"

"You and that hateful policeman?"

"No," I said, "just me. I'm hoping you can tell me another story."

"I see," she said. "You're keeping me around for the entertainment value. Like that Persian king What's-his-name."

"Which king?"

"King What's-his-name. I don't remember his name. Nobody remembers his name. It's the storyteller we remember. Scheherazade."

"Oh right," I said. "The *Thousand and One Nights.* She kept herself from becoming a one-night stand by spinning stories that never ended."

"It wasn't just that they never ended," she said. "They wove together to make a tapestry, stories threaded within other stories. Like life, Bill, but without the boring parts. She was the queen of the cliffhanger, Scheherazade. Every dawn, just as he was about to lop her head off, she'd leave him in suspense."

"I'm feeling some pretty strong suspense about something myself," I said.

She was silent. "I could probably dredge up another chapter," she finally said. "How soon should I expect you?"

"I could be there in thirty minutes, but I'll wait a while, if you'd rather."

"No need to wait. *Tempus fugit,* Bill. *Sic transit gloria mundi.*"

"What?"

"Time flies; so passes the glory of this world. I'll have the door open and my vodka in hand."

"Beatrice, it's only nine A.M."

"It's five P.M. somewhere. It's a big world, Bill. Don't draw your boundaries small."

THIS EARLY IN the day, the walkway to her front door was deeply shadowed by the roof overhang and the evergreens. Through the windows, though, the redwood paneling glowed warmly in morning sun that streamed through windows. I rang the bell, mostly to hear the high, clear tone that pealed forth when I tugged the clapper. Then I let myself in as usual, calling out, "Beatrice? It's Bill."

She didn't answer, so I headed for the living room. She was sitting in her wingback chair, and as I entered the room, she raised a tumbler of vodka to me in a toast.

She waved me toward my chair, and I sat down and began to rock. A steaming cup of tea sat on the end table; I took the mug and cradled it in my hands, glad of its warmth, for I felt cold inside.

She studied me through watery eyes. "What sort of story would you like to hear today?"

"I'd like to hear a true one," I said, meeting her gaze. "A true one about the death of Jonah Jamison."

"How do you mean?"

"I realized something today," I said. "Or heard something. It was as if Jonah's bones whispered a secret to me; as if he, too, had a story to tell."

"And what was the story? What did he whisper?"

"He whispered that he didn't shoot himself."

She leaned forward and cocked her head slightly—probably the very same posture she'd seen me assume for hours over the past two weeks. Then she frowned and shook her head. "Back up," she commanded. "You've jumped straight to the ending. Begin at the beginning."

I was confused. "Which beginning?"

"The beginning of the story Jonah's bones told you. 'It was a dark and stormy night in the anthropology lab . . .' or whatever. Set the scene; let it unfold. Have I taught you nothing?"

"Ah," I said. "Now who's being kept around just for the entertainment value? I'm not as good a storyteller as you."

"No one's as good as I am." She smiled. "But you have to keep trying. It's the only way to get any better."

I thought for a moment, then drew a breath and began again. "The neighbor's dog woke me up before dawn today," I said. "Not because he was barking loudly—it was only one little yip—but because I was half awake already. Sleeping badly. Fretting about something. I didn't even know what it was, but I knew where it was. It was on my desk under the stadium. Down in that labyrinth whose windows look like they haven't been washed since the Manhattan Project."

She gave me a nod of approval. "Much better," she said. "Go on."

"Whenever I think I'm overlooking something in a case, what I do is put the bones on my desk where I can see them. Every now and then I'll stop whatever I'm doing—grading papers or reading a journal article or eating a sandwich—and look at the bones. I try to keep my mind as empty as I can make it, and just *look,* hoping something new will catch me by surprise. Present itself to me. Speak to me. It's like I'm trying to sneak up on something I already know, somewhere deep down, but can't quite get ahold of."

"That's a good skill to cultivate," she said. "You'll need it more and more as you get older and start to lose track of things—names and faces and where you left your reading glasses and why you walked into the living room."

I had the feeling she was trying to stretch my story out, and I couldn't blame her. "I've been looking at Jonah Jamison's skull that way for a week now," I resumed, "but it hasn't been working. Nothing new. Today, having dragged myself to work at six A.M., I found myself getting mad whenever I glanced at that damn skull. Almost as if he were being deliberately uncooperative. Too watchful for me to sneak up on, or something."

"Well, he died during wartime in a top-secret city," she said. "You can't really blame him for being vigilant, can you?"

"But I did," I said. "I finally got so irritated I picked up the skull and put it in the box and closed the lid."

"I guess you showed him," she said.

"And that's when I saw it," I said.

"Saw what?"

"His left arm."

"His left arm? What about it?"

"It was strong."

She frowned, studying on this. "He was young. He was a soldier. Of course he was strong."

"What I mean," I said, "is that his left arm was stronger than his right arm."

"But how can you possibly know which arm was stronger? The muscle was long gone, wasn't it?"

"Yes. But the muscle left its story behind on the bone."

She looked puzzled, so I tapped on the surface of the small pine table between us. "You see these two knots in this wood?" She nodded. "Two branches grew out of the tree trunk in those places, right?" She nodded. "Which of those two branches was bigger and stronger?" She tapped the knot closer to her, which was as big as the face on my watch—twice the diameter of the other knot. "The places where muscles fasten to bones are called muscle attachments; not a very imaginative name, but it's easy for students to remember." I flexed my left arm and made my bicep as big as I could, which wasn't all that big. Then I pressed the tip of my right index finger against the inside of my elbow and wiggled the finger. "The tendon from the bicep muscle attaches to the bones of the forearm right here, so that when you tighten your bicep, it pulls your forearm up." She set her glass down and copied what I was doing.

"Feels like twigs and thread," she said. "Nobody would ever mistake this for a strong arm."

"Well, maybe not," I conceded. "But you're right-handed, so the twigs and thread are a little thicker and stronger in your right arm than in your left. So the muscle attachments in your right arm are a little sturdier than in your left. Now, UT football players—or Arnold Schwarzennegger, or anybody else with really big biceps—will have big, sturdy muscle attachment points, like knobs or ridges, where the bone is reinforced to carry the load."

"So just like a nation or a generation," she said, "bone is tested and strengthened if you challenge it."

"Exactly," I said. "And what I realized today is that Jonah Jamison consistently—day in, day out, thirty years—challenged his left arm more than his right. That tells he was left-handed. So does the wristwatch, which he wore on his right wrist. His handedness: that's how I can tell he was murdered."

She dropped both hands in her lap and looked down at

them. "Handedness," she said. "What a small detail for a story to turn on."

"Yes," I said. "Crucial, but small. So small a man wouldn't give it an instant's thought if he were about to blow his brains out. He'd be preoccupied with bigger things—wondering how it came to this, wondering if he'll feel the bullet, wondering if he really has enough courage or enough despair to pull the trigger. It would never occur to him to wonder which hand to hold the gun in. He'd automatically, instinctively pick it up in his preferred hand. If he were Jonah Jamison, he'd pick it up with his left hand and press it to his left temple. Not his right temple."

"Yes, that has the ring of truth to it," she said.

"So the story I'm asking for," I said, "is the story of Jonah Jamison's murder. And don't circle back and claim that Novak shot him, because Jonah was already listed as AWOL by the time Novak got back from Hanford."

She sat perfectly still for a long time. The only sound in the room was the hollow ticking of a wall clock. The slow, steady ticking of background time. "All right," she finally said. "One last story."

40

***I CAME TO TENNESSEE** on a train from New York in the fall of 1943; that much of what I told you before was true. But I wasn't just coming home to Tennessee. I was sent here.*

I told you my father died before my mother abandoned me in New York; that's also true. What I didn't tell you is that he was a union organizer, and he was beaten to death for helping organize a strike at a Chattanooga steel mill in 1933. He worked for the Industrial Workers of the World, a union that tended to attract socialists and communist-leaning workers.

I was only ten when he was killed, but I remember hearing him say that if Jesus had been born in our lifetime, he'd have preached the gospel of communism. He loved the Bible story where Jesus fed the multitude by passing around communal baskets of loaves and fishes, and every time he told that story, he'd finish by saying, "Clearly Jesus was a Fellow Traveler." Not the sort of thing that's likely to win friends in the Deep South.

Most people today think the notion of an atomic bomb was completely unknown during World War II, except to a handful of brilliant physicists, but that's not true. The lid of secrecy clamped down after the Manhattan Project began, but beforehand, any physics graduate student who was paying attention knew it might be possible. In the spring of

1939, the American Physical Society had an open meeting in Washington, D.C., where nuclear fission and atomic bombs were hot topics of discussion. The meeting was written up in the New York Times, *which reported, among other things, that it might be fairly easy to create an atomic explosion that could destroy Manhattan completely. Even decades before that—all the way back in 1914—H. G. Wells predicted that whole cities would be destroyed by atomic bombs. Oddly enough, Wells was a major influence on Leo Szilard, the physicist who persuaded Albert Einstein to write FDR that famous letter. So Szilard actually helped bring the prophecy of H. G. Wells to pass. And the prophecy of John Hendrix, for that matter.*

A few years after my mother abandoned me, I started looking for my father—not literally, but spiritually and intellectually—and I seemed to find him when I started spending time with labor organizers and socialists and communists. The summer I worked in the airplane factory, one of my socialist friends introduced me to a Russian man named Alexander, who seemed very interested in my work. That was in 1939, when it was becoming clear that the Soviet Union would bear the brunt of the war against Germany. Alexander talked about how hopeless the air battle would be with the Soviets' primitive aircraft. By the middle of the summer, I was filching parts for him. By the end of the summer, he gave me a little camera, and I took pictures of engineering drawings. Alexander made me feel important and clever and brave—things I'd never felt before. "You are a citizen of the world," he told me, and I believed it. Or I pretended to, at least, because I liked how special I felt when I did things for Alexander.

In the summer of 1943, Alexander introduced me to two physicists who were going to Los Alamos. They told me that a lot of work on uranium separation was being done in Tennessee. The three of them encouraged me to go to Knoxville, get a job, and learn whatever I could about the processes. I agreed, and Alexander arranged a contact for me in Knoxville.

When I got off the train in Knoxville I asked around for work, saying I'd heard there were defense plants in the area that needed help. I was practically snatched off the sidewalk and put on a bus for Oak Ridge. I had a ten-minute job interview, which was just about long enough to tell how I'd been orphaned in New York and how my uncle in Tennessee said I might find a job here. I figured they'd be too busy to check on me closely, and I was right.

It was my wits that got me a job operating a calutron in the heart of the Y-12 Plant. But it was luck that steered me to Leonard Novak the night he played and sang. You asked how I could not have known Leonard was gay. I did know. I also knew Leonard was marrying me to deflect suspicions about his homosexuality. But Leonard never knew I was marrying him to get information about his work. I didn't get much; maybe his lips were looser with whatever lovers he took.

But I hit the mother lode with Jonah, who was tagging along with the photographer, Westcott, the day I became the calutron poster girl. If not for Jonah, I might have had nothing to show for two years of work but dial readings and the story about Lawrence blowing up the calutron. As luck would have it, though, while Westcott was setting up the camera and lights for the calutron shoot, Jonah was flirting and bragging about how he had a bird's-eye view of the bustle and brilliance. That's when I realized he could be my eyes all over Oak Ridge. That's when I realized I had to make Jonah fall in love with me.

Once he did, it wasn't hard to plant the idea in his head that we'd have more time together if he'd dictate his history of the project and let me type it up.

I didn't dare make carbon copies; instead I took photos of Jonah's manuscript pages, just as I'd done with the engineering drawings at the aircraft plant. My film drop was in the cemetery of First Presbyterian Church in downtown Knoxville, a block behind the bars on Gay Street. I could get a ride into Knoxville just about any weekend—Leonard was working eighty hours a week, and as long as I didn't get into trouble, he felt guilty enough to let me do as I pleased. Everybody makes a big deal about how Oak Ridge was the city behind a fence, but the security guards were mainly searching guys for guns or hooch. Carloads of cute young women, out for a night on the town? The guards eyed us pretty closely, but they weren't looking for film.

By the summer of 1945, the gaseous-diffusion cascades at K-25 were finally turning out significant amounts of slightly enriched uranium, and the calutrons at Y-12 were doing a good job of turning that into bomb-grade material. Leonard's chemists at the Graphite Reactor had worked out how to create and extract plutonium, and the giant reactors out at Hanford were starting to crank that out steadily. In the two years since I'd gotten off the train, everything had come together. Groves pulled together all these theory-minded physicists and chemists, created immense factories around their ideas, and damned if it all didn't work just like they said it would.

And Jonah Jamison wrote it all down, the epic saga of Oak Ridge. He was a good storyteller; much better than I've ever been. I read every word he wrote, and took pictures of them all.

Until the day he caught me, just as we were nearing the end of the story.

Leonard was on a trip to Hanford—as you know—so Jonah and I had gotten careless. He'd brought the typewriter over to the house, because his metal trailer was like a solar oven. He'd told me he'd be gone all morning, so I'd laid out some pages of typescript on the kitchen table, where the light was good, and I was shooting copies with my little Minox camera. I guess I'd forgotten to lock the door, because all of a sudden it opened, and there stood

Jonah, the light pouring in around him, staring at me, staring at the pages on the table, staring at the tiny camera in my hands. We stood like that for what seemed like several minutes, just looking at each other, then he stepped inside, closed the door, and grabbed my wrist with his left hand. By the way, Bill, you're right—his left arm and his grip were very strong. He bent my wrist back until I thought it would snap, and with his other hand he took the camera from me.

It was a hot day—early August, in a house with no air-conditioning. I wasn't wearing much—just a short-sleeved shirt of Leonard's, and it wasn't even buttoned. When Jonah twisted my wrist back, the shirt came open, and Jonah looked down at my body. And even though he knew I was betraying him—knew I was betraying everything he was writing about—I saw that he still desired me, at least in that moment. When I saw the hunger, that's when I knew I had a chance. Maybe he saw hunger in my eyes, too, mixed with my fear and desperation.

So we're standing there, my wrist still bent back in his left hand, my shirt wide open, and Jonah takes the camera from me and sets it on the table, then he slides his hand down my throat and down my body. I'm trembling, and I can see that he likes that. He's got his teeth clenched, and his nostrils are flaring, and his breath is getting ragged, and he's starting to tremble, too, and then he starts fumbling with the buttons of the army coveralls he wore all the time.

"The bed," I say. "Please. The bed."

He picks me up and carries me into the bedroom and drops me onto the bed. He yanks down his coveralls, and he's on top of me and pushing into me, biting my neck, clutching my hair. I can tell it isn't going to take him long, so I arch my back and put my arms over my head and reach under the pillow for the pistol that I know Leonard keeps there. And just as Jonah groans, the gun fires, and then everything falls silent.

Leonard got home the next day. I met him at the door with a drink and told him something terrible had happened. Then I told him I'd been unfaithful—that wasn't a surprise—and that Jonah had begged me to get a divorce so I could marry him. When I turned him down, Jonah had threatened me, I said. I pulled out the gun for protection, but Jonah grabbed it from me and shot himself.

I begged Leonard not to tell the MPs; it would ruin us both, I said, and that was true. "He's probably already been reported AWOL," I said. "What if he just stays AWOL?" He thought about it and agreed that might be best. That evening he wrapped up Jonah's body and Jonah's manuscript in an Army blanket and put the bundle in the trunk of his car.

He never told me where he went that night. He never came right out and challenged my story. But I knew, by the way he looked at me, that whatever odd affection we'd had was gone. Poisoned, the way the reactors at Hanford had been poisoned by boron. The difference was, there was no way to fix this.

A week later I realized I was pregnant. A month after that I had the abortion, and six months later I asked for a divorce. I didn't need to say why, and he didn't need to ask. We knew too many secrets about each other now, he and I. Enough to ruin each other. Our own domestic version of Mutual Assured Destruction. And like the superpowers, we somehow managed to tiptoe past Armageddon.

So, there you have it, Bill. No more cliffhangers; no happy ending, either. Just an old woman reaching the last chapter in her story.

41

"AND WHAT DID YOU think of that story?" Her voice sounded far away. I looked around, halfway surprised to find myself sitting in a sunny living room on a bright winter morning with a silver-haired woman. In my mind, the gunshot was still echoing, the whispers of conspiracy still hanging in the heat of a long-ago August.

"I think it still has a few loose ends," I said. "Did you kill Novak, too?"

"Christ, of course not. What makes you think I would?"

"Because he was about to spill your secret to the documentary guy?"

"I could spill his, too," she said. "And I told him I would, if he breathed a word of mine. Mutual Assured Destruction, right up to the end. Leonard and I were good Oak Ridgers, in our different ways. He kept his secrets, I kept mine. Besides, where would an old bat like me get a lethal source of radiation?"

She had a point there. "Did you give the film of Jonah's manuscript to the Soviets?" She nodded. "Why didn't you go to Russia after the war? Surely you could have found a way to get there."

"Russia? Why on earth would I want to live in Russia? I was a spy, not an idiot." I had to laugh at that. "So what happens now?"

"We wait for Detective Emert or Agent Thornton to show up. I called them from the car when I got here to say I thought you'd killed Jamison. As soon as I told Emert, he said, 'Then she was the spy, too.' I didn't believe it. I guess he's smarter than I am."

"Not smarter," she said. "Less trusting." She raised her glass to her lips—she'd left the drink untouched during her story—and drank deeply. She gave a slight shudder, then drew a long breath and let it out slowly. "You're a good man, Bill. I'm going to miss you."

"Oh, I'll still come see you," I said.

"Ah, but you can't," she said. She raised her glass in my direction, then drained it. "Not where I'm going."

"Beatrice? What have you done?"

"I said there were many forms of prison, and many forms of death. Leonard died a hard death. I'll die an easy one. Vodka and Nembutal, which I bought from an obliging veterinarian last time I was in Mexico. I hear the combination's quick and painless."

Nembutal was a barbiturate, I knew—a powerful sedative, used mainly to euthanize suffering animals. I groped in my pocket for my cell phone.

"Too late," she murmured. "Far too late."

Just as I flipped it open to dial 911, the glass slipped from her hand and shattered on the terrazzo floor. In a voice that sounded sleepy and peaceful and somehow young, she murmured "Hold my hand, would you, dear? I do so hate to sleep alone."

I knelt beside her and took her hand in both of mine. She clutched my hand with both of hers, and her grip tightened. Then it slackened, and she was gone. I felt for a pulse, and there was none. Still I knelt there, her fingers laced through mine, her head leaning against one wing of the chair back. Thornton found us that way when he arrived.

"She's dead," I said.

He looked at her closely, then studied me. "What'd you do, interrogate her to death? Squeeze her hand really, really hard?"

I hesitated, unsure whether to tell him about the Nembutal. Would there be any harm in not telling him? It wasn't as if Beatrice had given away any secrets in the past half century. True, she'd murdered Jonah Jamison, but she had just executed herself. Why not leave her a bit of privacy and a shred of dignity?

Because, I realized. Because I remembered something Art Bohanan had said to me a year or so before, when he and I went to confront a man who had murdered a serial pedophile: If you cross the line once, it's easier to cross a second time, and it gets steadily easier, until finally you lose sight of the line altogether. "She killed herself," I said. "She drank vodka and Nembutal, and I had no clue until it was too late." I caught his gaze and held it. "I thought about not telling you," I said. "Seemed almost like a sleeping dog. But I couldn't let it lie."

"That's good," he said. "Otherwise it would've been awkward when I heard the recording."

"Recording?"

"We got a warrant for audio surveillance before your first visit," he said. I must have looked startled. "Leonard Novak was once a high-level atomic scientist," he explained, "and somebody killed him with an intense radioactive source. The director considered this case a high priority. He'd be very disappointed if I didn't investigate every angle thoroughly. And I'd be very disappointed if you held back the truth." He hesitated. "But I guess I'd also be disappointed if you hadn't given some thought to an elderly woman's reputation. Even if the old gal was an underhanded, soulless Commie spy."

I laughed and sighed and shook my head all at the same time. "How'd you end up as a cop instead of a diplomat?"

"Didn't want to end up huddled in an embassy compound in some plague-infested, two-bit, Third World shit-hole," he said.

"Too bad," I said. "With that silver tongue, you'd have made one hell of an ambassador."

"Damn skippy," he said. "By the way, I wouldn't be surprised if we wanted this kept fairly quiet. The Bureau and the NSA are still trying to track down quite a few Cold War spies. We might not want to let on that we're wise to Beatrice."

The logic seemed flimsy, but then I had another thought. "Agent Thornton, is it possible? Is there a bleeding heart somewhere behind that FBI badge?"

"Not a chance," he said. But I thought I saw a hint of a smile as he called for an ambulance to ferry Beatrice to the afterworld.

42

I SPENT ALL THE next morning and most of the afternoon at the hospital with Miranda and Carmen. A hand surgeon cut three fingers from Garcia's right hand and amputated the left hand entirely, because everything below the wrist had died. There was a good chance, the surgeon assured Carmen, that Garcia could resume his work someday, with the help of sophisticated prosthetics and extensive rehabilitation. What the surgeon didn't say was that there was also a chance Garcia might yet die from a runaway infection or internal bleeding.

Miranda's fingertips, thank god, had begun to show signs of healing. She'd lost some tissue from the tips of her thumb and first two fingers, but Sorensen predicted she'd be left with little or no permanent scarring. She was getting off far more easily than she might have. Miranda had driven Carmen to the hospital, and once Garcia was back in his isolation room, still sedated, Miranda drove her home.

The light was fading and a cold, pitiless rain had begun to fall as I parked at the library in Oak Ridge. Thornton had left a message on voice mail while I was out of signal range inside the hospital. They'd identified a suspect in the radiography-camera theft—a Japanese-American immigrant named Arakawa—but he had died just as the agents were about to question him. He died, said the message, of radiation poisoning.

Opening my briefcase, I removed the large, padded envelope Miranda had handed me just before my drive to Oak Ridge and stared at it again. A yellow Post-it note on the outside, in Miranda's handwriting, said, "Only grad student named Isabella who's done a thesis on Oak Ridge." The envelope itself was from UT's Interlibrary Loan service; inside was a bound copy of a master's-degree thesis, sent from the History Department at Tulane University. "The Role of National Myth in Legitimizing Mass Murder," read the title. "From Oak Ridge to Nagasaki," the subtitle added. The author of the thesis was listed as Isabella Arakawa, M.A.

My mind was careening and ricocheting in directions I didn't want it to go. One by one, the billiard balls of fate seemed to be dropping into corner pockets and side pockets that were dark and bottomless. But I saw Isabella's Prius tucked into the far corner of the parking lot, and that gave me a shred of hope as I pulled in beside it and parked.

I ducked, dripping, beneath the protective overhang of the library entrance just as one of the staff was locking the door. It was the gray-haired woman who'd seemed suspicious of me the other day. "You must have heard the news," she said, with a sympathetic smile. "She's very sad. I gather she and her father were very close." The woman held the door for me and patted my shoulder as I went in. The library's interior, usually filled with light and people, was silent and dim, lit only by a few of the fluorescent fixtures.

She wasn't at her desk. I turned to the left and checked the Oak Ridge Room, but it was dark. Water dripped from my coat and pants onto the blue carpet as I tried to make the pieces of the puzzle fit together some other way, any other way.

A slight movement caught my eye. Something—someone—was within the darkened glass of the history room. It was Isabella; she was fumbling with a bag on the table. "Isabella," I called. I ran to the door and pulled, but it was locked. She whirled and faced me, and even in the dimness of the unlit room I could see the wildness in her eyes.

"Isabella, open the door," I said, rapping on the glass with a knuckle, then beating on it with the heel of my fist. She was looking at me, but also looking through me, beyond me. I'd seen versions of that distant look before. I'd seen one version in the haunted eyes of Robert Oppenheimer; I'd seen another in the vacant stare of Jonah Jamison. Without taking her eyes off me, she reached into her bag and pulled out a gun. She raised it, the barrel pointing at me, and then she turned it toward herself. "No!" I tore at the door handle with both hands. The glass door rattled and strained against the lock, and then the handle broke off in my hands, sending me staggering backward. She closed her eyes and pressed the barrel against her temple.

"No!" I shouted again. I had fallen against a table, one hand clutching at the back of a square-cornered wooden chair. I seized the chair, lifted it over my head, and hurled it at the glass. The air itself seemed to explode as the glass curtain shattered and sheeted down. I heard a scream; I didn't know if it came from her or from me or from both of us. When the cascade of glass subsided, I expected to find her down and shattered, too—bloody fragments on the floor, a bullet in her head—but still she stood, frozen, dazed. Her arms were crossed in front of her face; shards of glass glinted in her dark hair.

I sprang forward, through a wall that no longer existed. I grabbed the gun with one hand, her wrist with the other. She cried out when I pried her fingers open and wrested the gun from her. There was dismay in the cry, but there was pain, too—physical, primal, wounded-animal pain. I looked at her hand, and it was as if I were seeing a far worse version of Miranda's hand. Her fingertips were raw, oozing sores. "Oh dear God, Isabella," I groaned, staring at her hands and all the terrible things they confirmed. "What have you done?"

Tears began to roll down her face, as if shards of shattered glass and shattered lives were pouring out of her. "I never meant to hurt so many," she said. "Not Dr. Garcia. Not Miranda. Least of all you. Please believe that. Only Novak: his life for my grandmother's life. My grandmother and all the other grandmothers and grandfathers and parents and children of Nagasaki. He was the only one I meant. I thought I could keep it pure."

"Pure? What on earth does that word mean to you?" I tried to reconcile what she'd just said with what she'd done. How could grief for an unknown grandmother move her to murder an old man who had once been a cog—a crucial cog, but a cog nonetheless—in the machinery of the Manhattan Project? How could the loss of an ancestor so unhinge this bright, sensitive woman?

"It was too big for me, it got away from me," she said. "I should have known it would. I should have learned more from all this history." She reached up to the back of her neck. "Here," she said. "I want you to have this." She flinched as she fumbled with the clasp, and whimpered, and this whimper—unlike the whimper of desire I'd once heard from her—was excruciating. She lifted the silver pendant from within her shirt and held it out, suspended between us. "It's the Japanese symbol for 'remembrance,'" she said. "I had it made ten years ago," she said, "when I decided to kill Leonard Novak for my grandmother's sake. In ten years, I've never taken it off except for the night I was with you. I take it off forever now." Her tears were falling faster now, and I felt answering tears on my own face, too. "My mother died long ago. My father is dead now, too. And I am a walking ghost."

She stretched her arm toward me, offering the pendant. I reached to take it, but just before my fingers closed around it, it fell. I lunged to catch it, and in that instant she darted past me, over the ridge of crumbled glass, out into the main reading room. I turned in time to see her duck into the darkened stacks of books. I followed, racing from stack to stack, aisle after aisle, without a glimpse of her. Then I heard footsteps racing through the lobby, and the thud of a distant door banging. I sprinted after her, out into the twilight, splashing through the puddles and pools accumulating on the sidewalk and the parking lot.

By the time she reached the Prius I was gaining on her. Fifty yards, now forty, now thirty. She struggled with her keys; I thought I heard another cry of pain, and I saw the keys splash at her feet. She hesitated, then spun and began running again—out of the parking lot and across the wet grass of the park behind the library. Half scurrying, half sliding, she flung herself down an embankment and into the small stream that bisected the park.

As I watched in astonishment Isabella disappeared, leaving only a black, empty circle and rushing water where she had been. She had scrambled into the end of an immense pipe, which could only have been the outlet of the city's storm-sewer system.

Isabella had vanished into a subterranean maze—a labyrinth constructed beneath the very foundations of the Secret City in the year 1943.

43

I SLID DOWN THE bank and into the icy water of the creek, which swirled around my thighs. The tunnel was a tube of concrete six or eight feet in diameter. The water pouring from it looked to be knee-deep; the blackness appeared infinitely deep.

I flipped open my cell phone and hit the call button; the phone automatically dialed the last number in its memory, which was Thornton's. The call went immediately to his voice mail, which meant he was on another call. "It's Brockton," I said. "Isabella killed Novak. She knows we know. She's in the storm sewers under Oak Ridge. Between the library and the police station. I'm going after her. Tell Emert."

I snapped the phone shut and stepped up into the pipe. The water was shallower than in the creek, but it was moving more swiftly. I dug into my pocket and fished out my key ring, which had a tiny flashlight on it—one miniature bulb, about the size of the iridium pellet that had killed Leonard Novak. I squeezed the switch on the side of the case and the bulb glowed blue-white against the darkness. It wasn't much light, but then again I didn't need much light: the sides and top of the tunnel were only a foot or two away, and the bottom was hidden by the swirling water. I could see, faintly, twenty or thirty feet before the gray-white tube faded into darkness. I hoped that would be enough.

I started slogging up the pipe, upstream against the current, which resisted every step I took, shoving each foot backward as I lifted it. It was like running into the surf at the beach, except the wave never broke and every step was work. I found myself lifting my knees higher and higher, and eventually I settled into an awkward high-stepping jog, which I knew I wouldn't be able to maintain for long.

I hadn't gone far—a hundred yards? two hundred? There was no way to tell how far I'd struggled against the blackness and the current—when I came to a side tunnel angling off to the right. This one was smaller, perhaps four feet in diameter, but still large enough for a person—large enough for Isabella, and large enough for me—though it would require stooping. Which would she have taken?

I kept to the main tunnel—if I were fleeing, I'd want as much distance and as much room as I could get, and the main tunnel seemed to offer more of those. Here and there, I passed small pipes, ranging from six inches to eighteen or twenty inches in diameter. I was grateful I didn't have to decide whether she might have taken one of those, but they posed a different sort of problem: water shot from them into the main tunnel with enough force to strike the opposite wall. I had to force my way through them, and each one battered at me icily, sapping my strength and my body heat. Desperate though she was, I was amazed Isabella could force her way through this. Was she moving in utter darkness and blind panic, or did she have some small glimmer of light, too?

I came to another side tunnel; again I chose the main line. The current was running faster now, or maybe I was just giving out. I could no longer lift my knees clear of the water; it was getting deeper and flowing faster, and I was exhausted. My teeth began to chatter. My tiny light seemed to be dimming as well, though perhaps it was an optical illusion, a trick played by the darker concrete in this section of pipe, or played by my own fatigue and despair.

And then I came to a harder choice: a Y-shaped intersection, two four-foot tunnels angling to the right and left. No main line to make the decision easy for me anymore; two choices, with no way to know what I'd find in the one I chose—and no way to know what I'd miss in the one I didn't.

As I reached the intersection, the concrete walls around me gave way to a wider chamber made of brick. Iron bars jutted from the bricks—the rungs of a ladder set into the wall. Overhead was a large black disk; water poured down on me through a dozen or more holes spaced evenly inside its circumference. I was directly beneath a manhole, and I was confronted by not two alternatives but three.

I shone my faint light on each. I didn't much like the tunnel branching to the right; it seemed to be carrying more water than the one to the left, so between the current and the stooping, the going would be extremely difficult. Of the two, I'd be inclined to take the left fork.

But there was also the manhole. A world of freedom, an infinite number of paths to freedom, lay just beyond that barrier of iron. I made my choice. I grasped a rung and began to climb.

As I neared the top, some ten rungs up, doubts and questions set in. Would she have seen the manhole, if she didn't have a light? Would she be able to raise the heavy disk? Would *I* be able to raise it? *Well, if you can't, she probably didn't,* I realized. *Might as well try it.*

Gripping the topmost rung with my left hand, I leaned back slightly into the vertical shaft and pushed upward at one edge of the manhole cover. It did not move. I tightened my grip and pushed harder, and the disk lifted slightly. I shifted my feet on the iron rung and put more force behind the push. The cover tilted upward—six inches, a foot, more—and then the iron rung in my right hand tore from the mortar between the bricks, and I was falling. When I hit the water, the shock of the fall and the chill of the water nearly claimed my consciousness. I struggled to regain my footing but the current was too swift, the walls were too smooth, and I was too weak. I felt myself swept along, down the dark passage, down toward icy oblivion. And then, just as I felt myself slipping into inner darkness, I shot out into a deeper pool of water, into a world lit by strobing blue lights, and unseen hands were bearing me up to safety.

44

"OKAY, HERE'S WHAT WE'VE been able to piece together so far," said Thornton. "Alvin and Theresa Morgan were young American missionaries who went to Japan in 1935, right after their marriage. By virtue of some incredibly bad luck, they settled in Nagasaki. In August 1945, Theresa was eight months pregnant. She was badly injured by the bomb. The doctors couldn't save her, but they did manage to save the baby. Newspaper stories in Japan called him 'the Nagasaki miracle.' That baby was Isabella's father, Jacob Morgan."

"That's a hell of a beginning," I said. "What next?"

"He was adopted by another missionary couple. Raised in Japan. Married another Nagasaki survivor—a young woman who was the daughter of a Japanese nurse and an Italian physician. He took his wife's family name, which was Arakawa."

"So Isabella was only one-quarter Asian," I said. That was why, despite her dark, exotic beauty, she didn't look Japanese. "But why turn killer? Lots of people lost parents or grandparents in the bombings without becoming murderous."

"Isabella's mother died of bone cancer when Isabella was ten. Her father was treated for prostate cancer in his fifties. I'm sure she blamed the bomb for their cancer as well as her grandmother's death. I suppose, for someone looking to avenge a Nagasaki family's suffering, the guy responsible for the success of the plutonium reactors seemed a logical target."

Miranda shook her head sadly. "Three generations of fallout from Nagasaki," she said. "Gives a sad twist to the term 'radioactive daughter product,' doesn't it?" Nobody smiled at the grim pun. "But if Isabella's Japanese heritage mattered so much, why'd she change her name from Arakawa—that was the name on her master's-degree thesis—to Morgan?"

"Two reasons, I suspect," said Thornton. "First, in memory of her grandmother, the one who was killed by the Nagasaki bomb. Second, to make her connection to her father and to Japan harder to trace, once she set the wheels in motion."

"Say some more about her father's part in all this," I said.

Thornton nodded. "Remember, Jacob Arakawa lost his mother and his wife and maybe his prostate to the bomb," he said. "So it's possible he raised his daughter on hatred. But that's just speculation. What we do know is this. Four weeks ago, he retired from Pipeline Services, Inc., on the eve of the company's financial collapse. Three weeks ago, according to credit-card transactions at gas stations, he drove from New Iberia to Oak Ridge. The very next day, he turned around and drove home again."

"So he made the trip just to bring the radiography camera he'd stolen," said Emert.

"Looks that way," said Thornton. "Shortly after he got back to Louisiana, he showed up at a hospital ER in New Orleans. Two days ago, just as we were closing in on him, he died of acute radiation sickness."

"From removing and handling the iridium source," I said.

"Exactly," said Thornton. "We'll probably never know which one of them put it into the vitamin capsule Novak swallowed, or how they got the capsule into Novak's pill bottle. From the burn you saw on Isabella's hand, she must have handled it at some point—probably longer than Miranda did, but not as long as Dr. Garcia." Miranda shot me a look of pain, and I knew she was grieving for Garcia's hands.

"So," I said to Emert, "where's Isabella now?"

"Don't know," he said. "It's like she's evaporated. She never showed up at her house, never came back for her car. Every officer in Oak Ridge has her picture committed to memory. If she surfaces here, we'll nab her. But I think she's gone. She knew we were onto her, Doc. She was about to skip out when you showed up at the library."

I turned to Thornton. "What about you guys? What are y'all doing?"

"We've frozen her bank account," he said, "we've tagged her credit cards, and her picture's at every international airport and border crossing in the country. We're also talking to everybody she worked with here and down at Tulane during graduate school. So far, we've got nothing. An elusive woman and her dead father. If she could find a way to get there," he went on, "she might try for Japan. Her whole sense of identity seems to revolve around Nagasaki. Turns out she's been there five times in the past ten years. But I don't see how she'd get out of the country now."

The memory of her hands, and how she'd cried out when I'd pried her fingers from the gun, stabbed at me.

Miranda shifted in her chair. "I hate to be the one to bring this up," she said, "but is there a chance she's still underground? Still somewhere in the sewer system?"

"Come on," said Emert. "It's been a week. Surely you don't think she's been hiding out down there in the dark for a week?"

"No," she said quietly. "That's not exactly what I was thinking." She glanced in my direction, saw the pain in my eyes, and looked away.

"Ah," said Emert awkwardly. "Well, we haven't been able to search all the tunnels yet. Some of the pipes are fairly small, and the folks who work on the sewers all seem to be fairly stocky guys." He seemed to have something more to say, but he stopped. Nobody else seemed to want to say it, either.

"You might want to call Roy Ferguson," I finally said. "And Cherokee." The room was silent except for the faint buzz of the fluorescent lights. I stared at the table, and at my hands, which rested on it, the fingers spread slightly. "If there's scent from . . . human remains . . . in one of the tunnels . . ." I had to pause; I took a breath, and then another. "The scent would spool downstream with the water. The dog should be able to detect it at the outfall near the library." I focused on the right index finger on the table and willed it to move. The finger lifted slightly, yet still it seemed not quite my own. "Excuse me," I whispered.

I left the room and turned down a dim inner hallway, heading for a rectangle of light—a glass door to the outside world. Just as I reached it, I heard a voice behind me. "Dr. B.?" I turned, and saw Miranda running toward me. She stopped a foot away. In the light pouring through the glass, her eyes shone with such kindness and compassion, I wondered what I could possibly have done to deserve them. Maybe nothing; maybe—like grace or mercy—they were unearned yet freely given, dropping as the gentle rain from heaven. I started to speak, but she held up a hand to stop me. "I need to say something to you," she began, "and it's really hard for me to say, because I know it will be hard for you to hear. I'm sorry about Isabella—that's the truth, but that's not what's hard, because the fact is, you barely knew Isabella. But you did know Jess, and you did love Jess, and deep down, I think you're still not over Jess's murder. Not by a long shot. I think you're lost in a maze of love and grief—more lost than you know—and you're having a tough time finding your way out. It's not just my fingertips or Eddie's hands or some old scientist's guts that are in tatters, Dr. B.; it's your heart. And it's not the storm sewers of Oak Ridge that are the labyrinth; it's your life." Miranda's words shocked me—shocked me with the force of pure, blindsiding truth. "If you can work your way out of the maze, fine," she went on. "Work as if your life depends on it, because it does. But if work isn't the way out, then find another way instead. Talk to a therapist, take a sabbatical, get a dog, go on a pilgrimage. Whatever it takes to heal, do it. Do it for those of us who love you. Do it for Jess. Do it for yourself."

With that she laid a hand on one of my cheeks, kissed me softly on the other, and then retraced the hallway and disappeared around a corner. I turned toward the light again, pushed open the door, and stepped into the cold February sunshine.

A slight breeze was sighing through the pines on the hill behind the police department. To my left, I saw a bright-yellow school bus stop at the entrance of the American Museum of Science and Energy. Dozens of youngsters, the age of my two grandsons, poured out of the bus and into the museum, with its displays and stories about the Secret City and the Manhattan Project. Below and to my right—just across the small stream emerging from a seven-foot circle of pipe—lay the blocky buildings of the Oak Ridge Civic Center and Public Library.

Straight ahead, through the trees and farther away, was a third destination, the one I chose. Approaching it from above, all I could see was a wooden, pagoda-like roof. Only as I descended the slope through the woods did the long, cylindrical shape of the Peace Bell come into view beneath the sheltering overhang.

The breeze kicked up slightly, and some of last fall's dead leaves swirled around my feet. Most were brown, but some still bore traces of red and gold.

And fuchsia.

As I drew nearer the bell, a stream of fuchsia leaves flowed toward me from its base. But they were not leaves. Angular and sharply creased, they were paper cranes. Origami cranes. Hundreds of them; perhaps even a thousand.

I reached into my pocket, and my fingers closed around the hardness of silver and the softness of a silken cord.

I took the symbol of remembrance from my pocket and laid it at the base of the bell, amid a swirling flock of cranes.

Acknowledgments

Many people, past and present, contributed to this story. Chief among them are the legions of scientists, engineers, soldiers, construction laborers, calutron operators, and other workers who brought the Manhattan Project to such swift, spectacular, and sobering fruition.

A number of physicians generously contributed their time and knowledge. Dr. Doran Christensen, of REAC/TS, answered countless questions about radioactive materials and acute radiation syndrome, as did REAC/TS health physicist Steve Sugarman, Department of Energy expert Steve Johnson, and State of Tennessee rad-health official Billy Freeman. Numerous other insights into emergency-room procedures, autopsies, and other medical matters came from Drs. Laura Westbrook, Shannon Tierney, Court Robinson, and Coleen Baird. University of Tennessee medical physicist Wayne Thompson provided remarkable and reassuring insight into how UT Medical Center could respond to a radiation emergency such as the one described in these pages. Special Agent Gary Kidder and Special Agent Chris Gay—both of the FBI's Knoxville Field Office—offered valuable information about the Bureau and its WMD Directorate. Ron Walli, of ORNL's Communications & External Relations Office, got us inside the fence and made us welcome, as did Al Ekkebus of the Spallation Neutron Source.

Bob Mann and Tom Holland—anthropologists and also fellow authors—provided helpful details about the Joint POW/MIA Accounting Command (formerly known as the Central Identification Laboratory—Hawaii) and about World War II-era military records. Bob also graciously forgave a phone call that unintentionally awakened him at 3 A.M. in Cambodia.

Oak Ridge historians Ray Smith and Bill Wilcox shared their knowledge generously and enthusiastically, as did Bill Sergeant, security guardian turned polio crusader; Barbara Lyon, founding editor of the *ORNL Review*; and Helen Jernigan, who grew up near a Tennessee POW camp that housed German and Italian prisoners. Ray Smith's newspaper columns on Oak Ridge history made for fascinating reading and provided splendid anecdotes, and his help in reviewing the manuscript, securing photos, and accessing historic structures on the Oak Ridge Reservation went above and beyond the historian's call of duty. So did the staff of the Oak Ridge Public Library, whose reference librarians are remarkably resourceful and helpful. Three other employees of the City of Oak Ridge offered extraordinary assistance: Cindi Gordon, ORPD Lt. Mike Uher, and public-works director Gary Cinder (the keeper of the storm-sewer tunnels). We're also indebted to William Westcott (Ed's son) for a guided tour of the labyrinth, and to Nicky Reynolds of the Oak Ridge Convention and Visitors Center for her swift, gracious photo help.

Several people appear in these pages under their own names, with gracious permission. Ray Smith is one of those. Others are fingerprint guru Art Bohanan (whom our returning readers will remember from our prior books); legendary Manhattan Project photographer Ed Westcott, whose cameras brilliantly captured an amazing slice of history; K-9 handlers (and dear friends) Roy and Suzy Ferguson, and their amazing dog Cherokee, whose recent death was a deep loss; ORNL research scientist Arpad Vass, who really has developed a "sniffer" for the Department of Justice; darkroom wizard Rodney Satterfield; and Darcy Bonnett, James Emert, and Townes Osborn.

Putting a story into the hands of readers requires a surprising amount of work by a large number of people. We're fortunate to have many bright and gracious people helping bring that to pass. Our agent, Giles Anderson, has been a wise and enthusiastic partner with us for six books now. Our first editor at William Morrow, Sarah Durand, was a wonderful colleague for five books, and we shall miss her. Our new editor, Lyssa Keusch, promises to be equally splendid. Assistant editors Emily Krump and Wendy Lee never cease to amaze us with their capable efficiency, and production editor Andrea Molitor remains a miracle worker. Our publisher, Lisa Gallagher, has been consistently, blessedly supportive; Morrow's associate publisher, Lynn Grady, is also an enthusiastic and creative champion. Morrow's sales and marketing staff have worked tirelessly and successfully to put our books in bookstores and readers' hands; so has our hardworking and cheerful publicist, Buzzy Porter.

Other colleagues and friends have also played key roles in supporting our work. Heather McPeters offered crucial encouragement, a keen critical eye, and countless suggestions for turning fragmented drafts into a cohesive, compelling story. Sylvia Wehr once again provided a beautiful, peaceful writing haven along the banks of the Potomac River at crucial moments. JJ Rochelle offered Oak Ridge hospitality, friendship, encouragement, insights, and miles of running company along the gravel roads of Black Oak Ridge. Carol Bass is unfailingly supportive and loving; so are the many other members of the Bass and Jefferson clans. We love and appreciate you all.

On Fact and Fiction

It's with no small amount of trepidation that we've dared to spin a fictional tale of murder and espionage against the epic backdrop of World War II, the Manhattan Project, and Oak Ridge. We've mentioned many historical characters, including General Leslie Groves and physicists Enrico Fermi and Robert Oppenheimer, because no story about the Manhattan Project would seem credible without those famous, larger-than-life figures. However, our plot and our main Oak Ridge characters—Beatrice, the storyteller; Novak, the murdered scientist; and Isabella, the librarian—are creations of pure fiction.

We've tried to follow the chronology of Oak Ridge and the Manhattan Project faithfully, with one notable, willful departure: the uranium storage bunker that figures prominently in the story was not built until 1947. But the camouflage scheme chosen for it by General Groves—a rustic Tennessee barn and silo—was simply too good to pass up.

THE SKULL

BONES OF | PARTS OF

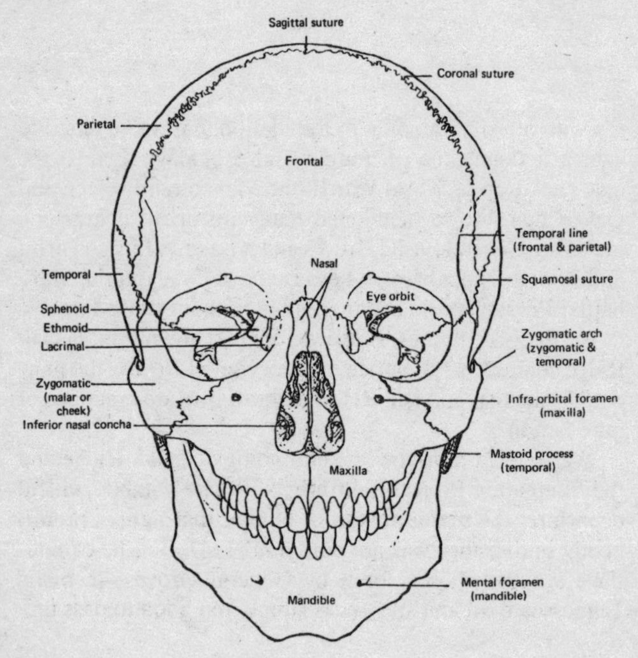

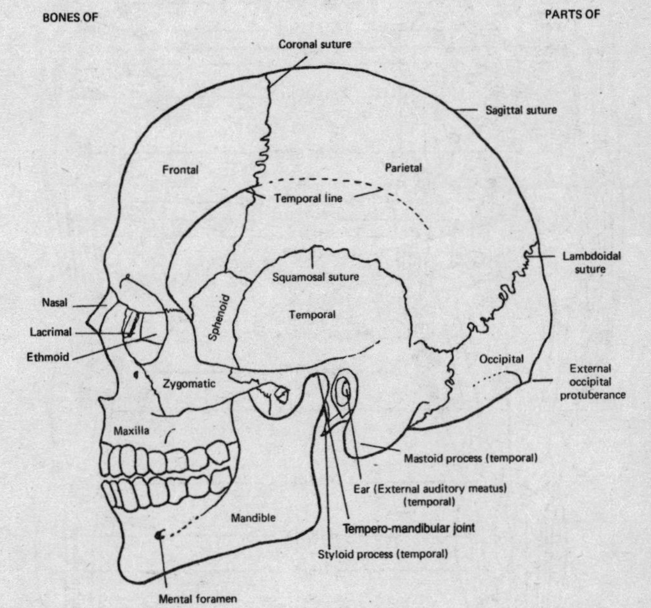
THE SKULL
BONES OF
PARTS OF
Coronal suture
Sagittal suture
Frontal
Parietal
Temporal line
Lambdoidal suture
Squamosal suture
Sphenoid
Temporal
Nasal
Lacrimal
Ethmoid
Zygomatic
Occipital
External occipital protuberance
Maxilla
Mastoid process (temporal)
Ear (External auditory meatus) (temporal)
Mandible
Tempero-mandibular joint
Styloid process (temporal)
Mental foramen

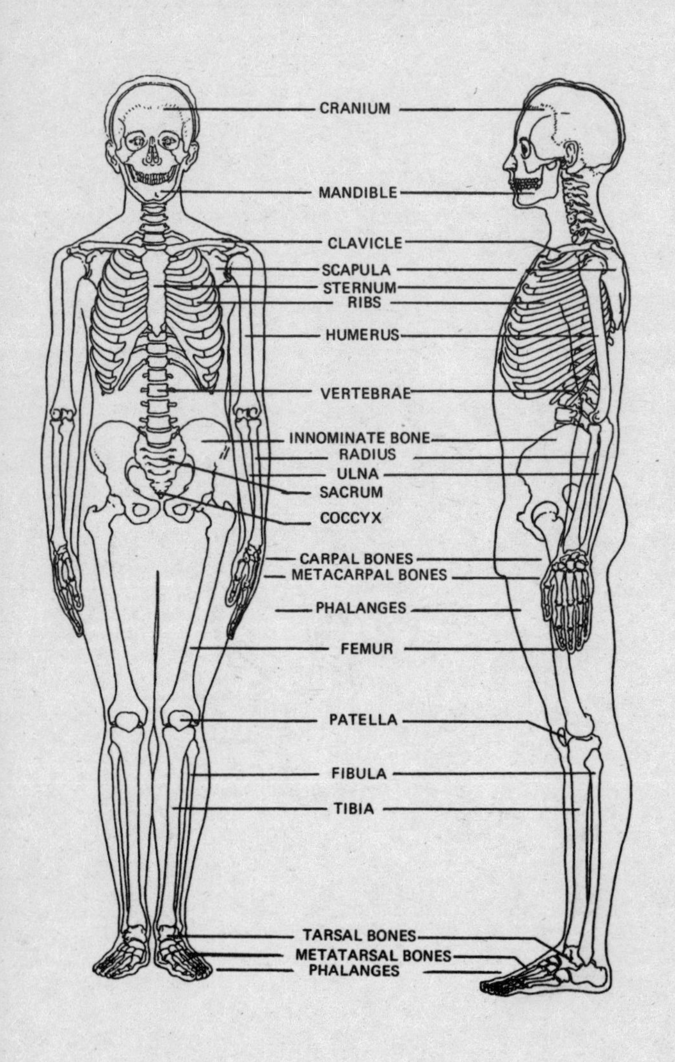
CRANIUM
MANDIBLE
CLAVICLE
SCAPULA
STERNUM
RIBS
HUMERUS
VERTEBRAE
INNOMINATE BONE
RADIUS
ULNA
SACRUM
COCCYX
CARPAL BONES
METACARPAL BONES
PHALANGES
FEMUR
PATELLA
FIBULA
TIBIA
TARSAL BONES
METATARSAL BONES
PHALANGES

It was a seemingly routine case . . . until Dr. Bill Brockton discovered that the corpse was missing its arms and legs. Now the FBI has recruited him in their search for the operator of a postmortem chop shop, but Brockton's realized another use for the grisly black market items—one that could save a friend . . . .

Join the hunt for

THE BONE THIEF

Coming soon in hardcover from William Morrow

THE WOMAN'S FACE BLURRED and smeared as I pivoted the camera on the tripod. Then her familiar, photogenic features—features I'd seen a thousand times on my television screen—whirred into auto-focused crispness: thick, wavy black hair; indigo eyes; a model's cheekbones; perfect teeth outlined by Angelina Jolie lips. Knoxville News anchor Maureen Gershwin was forty-two—middle-aged, technically speaking—but she was a low-mileage, high-dollar version of forty-two: beautiful and vibrant and healthy, except for one minor detail. Maureen Gershwin was dead.

"Pardon my cynicism," said Miranda, "but I can't help noticing that out of dozens of corpses to choose from, you've picked one worthy of Victoria's Secret for your little photo shoot."

Miranda Lovelady was both my graduate assistant and my social conscience. A smart, seasoned Ph.D. candidate, Miranda was a young woman of liberal opinions, liberally dispensed. We didn't always see eye to eye, but we viewed each other with respect: we had six years of collegiality and friendship to temper our occasional personal differences. As my graduate assistant—a term essentially synonymous with "indentured servant"—Miranda ran the bone lab, the Anthropology Department's osteology laboratory, which inventoried more than a hundred donated skeletons and twenty or thirty murder victims a year. Running the bone lab also meant keeping track of the donated skeletons before they were reduced to skeletons: keeping tabs on the burgeoning population of corpses at the Anthropology Research Facility, better known as "the Body Farm."

Despite the name and the abundance of vegetation, my

"farm" was beginning to resemble the suburbs, or even the city, at least in population density. Initially a sixteen-foot-square chain-link fence enclosure, the Body Farm currently encompassed three acres of wooded hillside behind the University of Tennessee Medical Center. As the research facility had grown, the woods surrounding it had shrunk, and my postmortem lab was now bordered on three of its four sides by parking lots for hospital employees. We were rapidly running out of elbow room—and ribcage room, and skull room. Lately, Miranda had taken to mapping the location of each body with GPS coordinates. With a few keystrokes, she could print out an up-to-the-minute map of our postmortem subdivision; the technology helped us keep track of where we'd already put people, but it also helped us pinpoint patches of unclaimed ground in which to house new residents: beneath the low branches of this maple sapling, perhaps, or behind that tangle of honeysuckle vines.

We'd tucked Maureen Gershwin—known to television viewers throughout East Tennessee as Maurie, or sometimes by her nickname, "The Face"—in the most distant corner of the fenced-in area, to minimize the gawking. Gershwin had risen through the television ranks, from weather girl to reporter to anchorwoman, and recently had added occasional commentaries she called "Maurie's Minutes," which tended to take a philosophical or spiritual tone. Those had made her more popular than ever, so I wanted to give her some measure of privacy at the Body Farm, even as I was photographically invading it.

It wasn't as if the facility was accessible to the general public, but between the anthropology grad students, the UT police force, the instructors and students of the National Forensic Academy, FBI trainings, and the occasional, strong-stomached VIP visitor from the University's Board of Trustees, our grisly research facility had a surprising amount of traffic. Like all our donated corpses, Maurie Gershwin was officially known only by a number—her metal armband and legband identified her only as "21-10," the twenty-first donated body of the year 2010—but she was so well-known to Knoxville television viewers that there was no hope of keeping her anonymous, at least not until the bacteria and bugs had rendered her famous face unrecognizable.

As I tinkered with the camera's zoom control, Miranda took the opportunity to chide me further. "The T-shirt and sweatpants ensemble she's wearing—you sure you don't want to swap those out for something flashier? Maybe a little black dress that shows some thigh and some cleavage?"

"Come on, Miranda, you saw the donor form," I snapped. "She *asked* to have her decomposition documented. And I'm only photographing her face, not her body."

"But you can see my point," she persisted, "can't you? Don't you think it's a tad creepy that you're aiming this camera at this particular corpse, the most beautiful corpse in the history of the Body Farm? Crap, Dr. B., she looks better dead than I do alive."

I glanced from the newswoman's face to Miranda's: peaches-and-cream skin and green eyes framed by a cascade of chestnut hair. I actually preferred Miranda's looks, but I knew she wouldn't believe me if I told her so. "Not for long," I said. "Day by day—hell, hour by hour—she'll get a lot less gorgeous. We'll end up with one glamour shot and hundreds of pictures where she goes from bad to worse, and from worse to worser."

"I don't understand why she asked for this."

"Doesn't matter," I said. "I understand, and more to the point, she understood. She talked to me about it a year or so ago, back when she produced that three-part series about the Body Farm for Channel 10. You remember the end of the series, when she added a 'Maurie's Minute' about the importance of body donations? I thought that was a great touch, ending the commentary by signing a donation form on camera."

"I hated it," Miranda said. "Too much. Playing to the camera."

I stepped away from the camera, caught Miranda's eye, and pointed to the corpse. "Excuse me," I said, "but I beg to differ. She meant it, clearly. 'Wouldn't it be interesting,' she told me later, 'if we could hang around awhile after death and watch ourselves rot?' She even talked about letting her colleagues do a story someday about her decay. An extreme form of participatory journalism, I guess you could say; one last story from beyond the grave." I snapped a picture, then checked it in the display on the back of the camera. The framing was slightly off, but I had to agree that Miranda had a point: even dead, Maurie Gershwin was a beauty, at least for a few more hours. "Her looks did have a lot to do with her success," I conceded, "but I don't think they defined her, at least not to herself. In fact, I think she had a healthy sense of irony about the fleeting nature of physical beauty."

"Too bad her cardiovascular system wasn't as healthy as her sense of irony," said Miranda. "Stroking out at forty-two, and right there on camera, no less."

"Aneurysm," I said. "Not stroke." Gershwin had died of an aortic aneurysm that ruptured catastrophically, and in the middle of a newscast, no less. In hindsight, a diagnostic clue had gone undetected. "Did you see the news any of the last few nights before she died?"

Miranda nodded.

"Did you notice her voice was a little hoarse?"

She looked at me sharply, her eyebrows shooting up in a question.

"One of the laryngeal nerves—the recurrent vagus nerve, which controls the voice box—wraps around the aortic arch. A fast-growing aneurysm on the aorta can stretch that nerve, causing hoarseness. Maurie thought she'd just strained her voice last week during a charity telethon—that's what she said on the air two nights ago, just before she died—when in fact, her body was trying to warn her."

Miranda shook her head. "Sad. Ironic. Here's another irony for you: her death made her a lot more famous than all those years of reporting the news. Somebody posted a YouTube video of that clip from the newscast where she collapses in mid-sentence. They called it 'Film at 11: Hot News Babe Dies on Camera.' As of this morning, thirty million people had watched her die."

"Thirteen million people have seen that footage?"

"*Thirty* million."

The figure stunned me. "That's probably twenty-nine-and-a-half million more than ever watched her live."

"YouTube fame's an odd viral thing," she shrugged. "You remember Susan Boyle?"

I shook my head.

"Sure you do; you just don't realize you do. That dumpy, middle-aged Brit who belted out a song on the limey version of 'American Idol'?"

That did ring a bell, I realized.

"Her clip's been watched fifty or sixty million times. She became this overnight mega-celebrity. Of course, that was a year or so ago. She's old news by now." Miranda studied the newswoman's face, reaching down to shoo away a cloud of blowflies. It was absurd, of course, since the whole point of putting Gershwin out here was to allow nature to have their way with her, but the fly-shooing was a reflexive gesture of respect, so I kept my mouth shut. "What do you plan to do with all these pictures of the Face of Channel 10?"

"Couple things, probably," I said. "I need to do a funding proposal for the dean's office—apparently they've got some deep-pocket donor they think might be interested in adopting us—and I could see using a few of these photos to illustrate our decomposition research. I'll probably also do a slide presentation at the national forensic science conference next February. 'Decomposition Day by Day' or some such. Thirty slides, thirty days; talk for a minute about each slide."

Miranda closed her eyes and let her head slump forward, then feigned a loud snore. "A slide presentation? That's lame, totally twentieth century," she said. "How about a podcast—a real-time video camera, streaming continuous images to the web? That would actually fit the spirit of our gal's life and work and last request."

"Broadcast this on the web?" I shook my head. "No way. I don't have nearly enough fingers and toes to count the ways that could get us in hot water."

"Well, at least make a movie," she said. "That would be cool."

"But this is a still camera," I pointed out. "Besides, neither one of us has the time to hang around and film a documentary."

"Neither one of us needs to," she said. "You're setting the timer to take a picture, what, every few minutes, or every few hours, or some such?" I nodded. "So once she's through skeletonizing, in a month or two, string all the pictures together into a video, and it'll fast-forward through the entire decomp sequence in a minute or two. That would be fascinating to students in the intro forensic class. It might even be a hit on YouTube. The next Susan Boyle."

"A movie," I mused. "I like it. We could call it *Face Off.* Or *Gone in 60 Seconds.* You like?"

She shook her head. "Those are already taken," she said. "How about *Shuffle Off This Mortal Coil* or—ooh, ooh, I've got it!—*Memento Maurie*?"

She was punning, I knew, on the Latin phrase *memento mori*, "reminder of death." In old *memento mori* paintings, some token of death—a skull or some shriveled flowers or a bloody pheasant—might show up somewhere in a portrait of a healthy, wealthy patron as a reminder of mortality.

"Or maybe *Economento Maurie*," I said, "since we're hoping to reel in some funding."

Miranda cringed. "Your puns are getting worse by the day, Dr. B."

"That's worse than *Memento Maurie*? I don't think so."

"Oh, much worse," she said. "*Memento Maurie* had *so* much going for it. Didn't you admire the way it echoed 'Maurie's Minutes'? But what I'm wondering is why the fundraising folks think seeing this woman's face decay will inspire some rich guy to fork over big bucks for body bags and bone boxes and such?"

"For your assistantship, I'm hoping," I said. Miranda's head snapped around, and I wished I hadn't said it, even though I was mostly kidding. "Sorry. Bad joke. You're covered." She shot me an interrogatory look, hard enough to make me flinch. Miranda would make a terrific prosecutor or detective, I thought, if she ever got tired of forensic anthropology. "At least, I *think* you're covered."

"You're the chairman of the Anthropology Department," she shot back. "If anybody should know, it's you."

"I do know you're not affected by the cuts I proposed," I said. "But the dean has to approve the budget before it goes to the chancellor and the president. The football scholarships are safe and the coaching salaries are safe, but nothing else is guaranteed."

I zoomed in a bit more, filling the viewfinder with the face, then snapped another test picture. Taking care not to jostle the tripod, I removed the camera from the mount and called up the image. The photo showed a lovely woman, but clearly there was no light or life left in her eyes, and her face was slack. I used the cursor to enlarge the center of the image and saw that the camera had caught one blowfly in midair, just above her face. Another was already emerging from the slightly opened mouth. Looking from the camera's display to the body on the ground, I saw that those two flies had been joined already by dozens of others, swiftly drawn to the odor of death, even though I could detect no trace of it yet. Within minutes, small smears of grainy white paste—clumps of blowfly eggs—would begin to fill her mouth and nose and eyes and ears; by this time tomorrow, her face would be covered with blowfly larvae, a writhing mass of maggots.

I fiddled with the camera's digital menu, calling up the control screen for the built-in timer. Initially, I'd planned to set it to take a photo every twelve hours, but as I glanced down and saw more and more flies swarming, I realized that I'd miss too many details of her decomposition that way. The funding people might not be interested in the subtle shifts of her decay, but I certainly was. What about a photo every half hour or even every ten minutes? For that matter, why not just camp out here in person and watch it all in real time? Finally I compromised: one picture every fifty minutes, the length of a typical classroom lecture. I did the math: a picture every fifty minutes would yield thirty pictures a day; at the end of two months, I'd have 1,800 images, and at thirty frames a second, 1,800 images would make a video sixty seconds long, exactly the running time of "Maurie's Minutes."

Swapping out the camera's small digital memory card for a larger one—a two-gigabyte chip, large enough to hold hundreds of images—I latched the camera back onto the tripod, and Miranda and I left the Body Farm, chaining the wooden gate shut and latching the chain-link fence behind us. As I snapped the outer padlock shut on the Body Farm's newest and most famous resident, I found myself thinking of the words she'd used at the end of every newscast for years. "Good night," I murmured as I snapped the outer padlock shut. "We'll see you tomorrow."

THE BACKHOE LURCHED and bucked as its claw tore into the wet, rocky clay of Old Gray Cemetery, Knoxville's most ornate burial ground. The name felt apt; the day was gray, and the air was as cold as the mound of chilly soil piling up beside the monument. Astronomically speaking, spring had arrived; the planet had tilted on its axis, tipping the northern hemisphere halfway toward the sun, but the earth itself still felt as devoid of warmth and life as a corpse.

The diesel engine labored against some sudden resistance, and as the machine strained, it wheezed out a cloud of black smoke. The soot drifted on a whisper of breeze for ten feet or so—just far enough to engulf Miranda and me—and then hovered.

Miranda fanned a hand dramatically across her face. "Remind me why we're here?" She punctuated the question with a delicate little stage-cough.

I was still a bit vague on our mission as well—not the task itself, but the late-night, last-minute nature of the phone call I'd received barely ten hours before, asking for my help. "We're here to help figure out if Trey Willoughby fathered a child by Amanda Burchfield," I said.

Miranda nodded toward the inscription chiseled into the grave marker, a towering obelisk of glossy pink granite. "Trey Willoughby, beloved and faithful husband?"

"Trey Willoughby, at least," I said. "Not sure about the 'beloved' and 'faithful' bits. 'Beloved' is in the eye of the beholder, I suppose, but the bone sample we're about to take could cast a serious shadow on the 'faithful' part."

"Or the *unfaithful* part," she said.

"So to speak," I granted.

"What if the DNA's too degraded for a paternity test? And what's the story on Amanda Burchfield, who might be the mama? I take it she's not Trey's loving wife and grieving widow?"

I shook my head. "Amanda might have been someone's loving wife and grieving widow," I said, "once upon a time, but she wasn't Willoughby's. When I moved to Knoxville twenty years ago, Amanda Burchfield was Knoxville's most famous madam."

Miranda laughed. "Well, she was well named, I'll give

her that. Doesn't Amanda mean something like 'she who must be loved'?"

"Been awhile since I took Latin," I said, "but that sounds plausible and certainly consistent with her history. Amanda was arrested a bunch of times for prostitution-related crimes—pandering, soliciting, I don't know what-all—but she never actually came to trial. Perhaps the pen really is mightier than the sword."

"The pen?"

"The pen that wrote in Amanda's little black book," I said. "Apparently she was a meticulous record-keeper, and rumor had it that her client list included half the judges, prosecutors, and defense attorneys in Knoxville. Funny thing, when she died, which was maybe ten years ago, her little black book was never found. I wouldn't be surprised if some enterprising associate of hers got hold of it and has been collecting hush money for a decade now."

The backhoe's bucket screeched—a harsh, grating sound, like immense steel fingernails on a monumental blackboard—as the claw raked mud from the top of Trey Willoughby's metal burial vault. Miranda grimaced, then shook violently, like a wet dog flinging water from its fur. "Argh," she shuddered. "Glad I don't have any fillings—my head would be exploding right about now. So what's the scoop on this love-child Amanda might or might not have had with our man Willoughby? You say she died ten years ago; unless she died in childbirth, I assume the child is older than that."

"Considerably," I said. "Somewhere in his thirties. I'm not sure why he's just now getting around to tracking down his paternity."

"Maybe he just found Amanda's black book in a shoebox of memorabilia," Miranda said, "with the words 'Big Daddy' down in the W section, beside Willoughby's name."

"Maybe," I said. "All I know is that Judge Yates signed

the exhumation order last night, and here we are this morning, at the request of the man behind the wheel of that car." I pointed to the cemetery's entrance, where a gleaming black sedan—the sort of vehicular offspring you'd get by mating a Mercedes with a Rolls-Royce—was gliding through the wrought-iron gates.

Miranda groaned. "Oh, God, you didn't tell me we'd be working for Satan on this case."

"Now, now," I soothed. "Grease isn't really the Prince of Darkness; he just puts on the horns and the hooves when he goes to court."

"Grease" was Burton DeVriess, Esquire, Knoxville's most colorful and aggressive attorney. Over the years, DeVriess and I had sparred often, in murder cases where I'd testified for the prosecution and he'd defended accused killers. A masterfully manipulative cross-examiner, Grease had always managed to get my goat, or at least infuriate my goat, on the witness stand—not by successfully refuting my forensic findings, but by maneuvering me into losing my temper. After years of antagonism, though, Grease and I had turned an unexpected corner a couple of years back. Confronted with an unusual situation—namely, a client who was actually innocent—Grease had hired me to help prove that the so-called murder victim had not, in fact, been stabbed to death but had died of injuries sustained in a bar brawl. During that case, I'd grown to respect the attorney's intelligence and commitment to his client. My respect had later turned to deep gratitude, when DeVriess helped me clear my own name. Framed for the murder of a woman with whom I'd just begun a love affair—Chattanooga medical examiner Jess Carter—I'd swallowed my pride and turned to DeVriess for legal help . . . and he'd responded by saving my reputation, my career, and my skin. In the process, he lightened my bank account by fifty thousand dollars, but he'd also revealed more human decency than I'd suspected he possessed. Grease wasn't a saint—not unless the ranks of the saints included materialistic, cunning extortionists—but he was a far better guy than most of Knoxville gave him credit for being.

Miranda's eyes tracked the sedan—it was a Bentley, one of several in DeVriess's capacious garage—as it eased toward us, curve by curve. She frowned, probably out of habit, then laughed at herself. "Much as it pains me to admit it, he does seem to have a warm-blooded mammalian heart beating somewhere in that chest, beneath the reptilian scales," she said. "But I think maybe I see a pitchfork in the backseat of the car." She paused. "And get a load of that tag." The vanity plate on the front bumper read "$2BURN." I assumed it was a reference to a multimillion-dollar settlement Burt had won recently in a class-action suit against a crematorium that was caught dumping bodies in the Georgia woods rather than incinerating them. The tag's combination of cleverness and boastfulness was classic DeVriess. But as I read the plate again, I realized it also sounded like an offer: a taunting Faustian bargain rendered in stamped metal on a luxury sedan bumper. And that, too—the in-your-face frankness of the crass equation—also smacked of pure Grease.

The sedan eased off the pavement and hushed to a stop on the brown grass, its mirrorlike finish reflecting the leaden sky and my bronze pickup truck. The driver's door swung open and DeVriess slid off the glove-leather seat. His car was worth more than my house; his outfit—a suit of pale gray wool, probably handmade in Italy, the trousers draping onto lustrous black shoes—was probably worth more than my car. Walking toward us, he stepped into a stray clod of clay, which oozed up the side of his shoe and clung to the hem of his trousers. He stopped, glanced down, and then laughed. "Morning, Doc," he called over the din of the backhoe. "And the lovely Miranda," he added, bowing slightly and smiling broadly. Miranda—possibly in spite of herself—gave a tiny mock-curtsy and smiled back.

DeVriess walked to the edge of the grave—more mud coating his shoes and hems—and peered in. The backhoe was now chewing through waterlogged clay at the base of the vault and water oozed from the surrounding walls and poured back into the grave each time the operator lifted another bucketful of soil from the opening. The man had evidently foreseen this complication, for he paused, easing the machine's giant mechanical arm toward the ground, resting its weight on the curved underside of the bucket, creating the odd image in my mind of some fallen athlete or skateboarder, frozen at the moment of impact, the hand flexed into an acute, wrist-breaking angle. Clambering down from the backhoe, he bent forward, lifted a torpedo-shaped pump, and lowered it into the watery grave. A muddy, flattened firehose connected to one end of the pump slithered down the slight slope behind the backhoe and into a swale at the edge of the cemetery. The man clambered back onto the machine and flipped a switch and the rumble of the diesel engine was joined by a higher-pitched whine as the impeller of the pump spun up and began sending water up from the grave. The hose swelled slightly, pulsing occasionally as the pump's intake slurped and gasped. Judging by the granite obelisk that towered above the grave and above our heads, Trey Willoughby's burial had been quite an affair. His unburial, though less posh, was something of a production as well.

Thirty minutes later—a half-hour marked by three repositionings of the sump pump and two wrestling bouts with a sling of steel cable and a bracelet of heavy chain rattling from the wrist of the backhoe—the steel vault emerged from the grave, trailing muddy water and watery mud. The operator swung it expertly to one side and set it gently on the ground. Then, after opening a pair of latches at the base of the vault, he hoisted the domed top off the vault, exposing the coffin underneath.

"Kinda like Chinese boxes," said DeVriess, "one inside the other."

"Or Russian matryoshkas," said Miranda. DeVriess looked puzzled, so she added, "Those nesting wooden dolls."

"Of course," he said. "I was thinking that, too. Russian matryoshkas."

"Or Egyptian sarcophagi," I said. "Be interesting if the vault and the coffin were painted with Willoughby's likeness."

The coffin was gunmetal blue, its glossy finish dulled by years of dampness and postmortem vapors. A few patches of superficial rust marred the lid, but considering that it had been in the ground for years—seven, according to Willoughby's death date—it looked to be in remarkably good condition. Miranda glanced from the coffin to my truck. "You should park in the underground garage on campus instead of the outdoor lot," she said. "That coffin's paint job is holding up a lot better than your truck's."

"Yeah, but I bet the interior of my truck smells sweeter."

"We'll see," she said. "Sweet is in the nose of the beholder, and on the way over here this morning I think my nose was beholding some not-so-sweet aroma from that body we hauled back from Nashville in your truck last week." She was probably right; Miranda had a keener nose than I did, and the Nashville body—a floater fished from the Cumberland River—had been particularly ripe.

"Speaking of the truck," I said, "would you go get the Stryker saw, the scissors, and the pliers while I open up the coffin?"

"I live to serve," she said, and although it was a joke—one of her favorite ways of simultaneously acknowledging and mocking the professor-assistant disparity—she said it with genuine goodwill.

"So, the pliers," DeVriess said. "I'm thinking those aren't for opening the coffin."

"Right," I said. "I'm an anthropologist, but what I really want to do is postmortem dentistry. Enamel's the hardest substance in the body, so the DNA in the pulp of the teeth has a decent chance of being undamaged. I'll pull a couple of molars, but I'll also cut cross-sections from the humerus in the upper arm and the femur in the thigh. The cortical bone—the outer structural layer—is pretty thick there, so the inner layer might also have some intact DNA."

Burt nodded, and I thought I saw a flicker of impatience in his eyes. Was I droning on in too much detail? Had I already explained, in last night's phone call, why I needed to go to such lengths to get samples for a simple paternity test? Or had he done enough research on his own before calling me to know that DNA could be destroyed by the formalin in embalming fluid, and that the teeth and long bones were the body's most protective vaults for archiving genetic material?

"It looks like there's not a lot of research data out there yet on DNA degradation," he said, as if reading the question in my mind. "Nobody seems to have a good handle on how long nuclear DNA hangs around after death and what factors affect the rate of decay."

"Not much," I agreed. "Forensic DNA analysis is still a brave new world. Remember, it wasn't until the early 1990s that DNA testing became readily available."

"I remember," he said. "I was at the beach when the O.J. Simpson case began. I vividly remember sitting in the living room of that beach house, watching him inch along the freeway in that white Ford Bronco, with dozens of cop cars trailing him like some huge police funeral procession. That, the World Trade Center collapse, and the first moon landing, back when I was a ten-year-old kid. Those are the three most powerful television events I can remember, the only three where I can tell you exactly where I was and what I was doing when the story unfolded on the screen."

"The moon landing, O.J.'s circus trial, and 9/11," said Miranda, back with us, tools in hand. "From the sublime to the ridiculous to the sublimely sad."

I knelt at the head of the coffin and groped the underside

until I found what I was looking for: a hinged metal crank that I unfolded and began turning counter-clockwise. Slowly, almost as if it were levitating of its own accord, the upper one-third of the lid swung upward, revealing the face of Trey Willoughby. The skin was ashen, with a slight mottling of dark gray mold—just as the coffin was slightly mottled with rust—but otherwise, the face in the coffin was a surprisingly good likeness of the face I'd seen in an old photo I'd found on the Internet a few hours before. In life, he'd been a handsome man—not as beautiful as Maureen Gershwin had been, but almost—and even now, even seven years post-mortem, he was still looking pretty good. Miranda gave a low, appreciative whistle and DeVriess murmured, "wow."

"It's a good embalming job," I agreed. "Maybe the best I've seen. You don't always get what you pay for, but in this case, the funeral home seems to have done first-class work."

I shifted to the foot of the coffin and cranked up the lower portion of the lid to expose the arms, torso, and legs. Judging by both the embalming and Willoughby's burial clothes, he must have had an open-casket service. His suit, I noticed, rivaled DeVriess's in elegance, though it was silk rather than wool. That made sense: according to the obelisk and the newspaper archives, he'd died in August. Heaven forbid that the corpse should swelter in wool in the heat of summer. The thin, finely woven fabric hung damply on the arms and the legs.

I reached out a hand and Miranda wordlessly placed a pair of scissors in them. Reluctantly—for this was a far better suit than I'd ever owned or ever would—I snipped open the right leg of the pants. The V of the scissor blades tore effortlessly through the silk, the tip of the lower blade gliding up the flesh of the leg. The smoothness surprised me; I'd expected the point to snag in crumbling flesh or bang against a jutting kneecap.

But the smooth motion had nothing to do with the quality of the embalming job or the firm flesh of the leg, I saw as the fabric parted. I stared, then sliced open the left trouser leg, revealing the same startling sight. I reached for the corpse's hands—gray, clammy flippers extending from the silken sleeves of the jacket—and both hands slid free and dangled in mid-air. They had been severed at the wrists. "Holy crap," said Miranda, as I swiftly slit the right sleeve, then the left. "Holy *crap*."

The reason the scissors had slid so smoothly up the legs was solved, but another mystery now loomed larger: Who had replaced Trey Willoughby's limbs with plastic pipe? And why steal the arms and legs of a dead man?

ELECTRIFYING SUSPENSE FROM
NEW YORK TIMES BESTSELLING AUTHOR

JEFFERSON BASS

CARVED IN BONE

978-0-06-075982-7

Renowned anthropologist Dr. Bill Brockton has spent his career surrounded by death at the Body Farm—the research facility where human remains lie exposed to be studied for their secrets. Now he's diving into a baffling investigation involving the mummified corpse of a young woman who's been dead for thirty years.

FLESH AND BONE

978-0-06-075984-1

Dr. Bill Brockton is called upon to help unravel a murderous puzzle in nearby Chattanooga. But after re-creating the death scene at the Body Farm, Brockton's career and life are put in jeopardy when a second, unexplained corpse appears in the grisly setting.

THE DEVIL'S BONES

978-0-06-075990-2

A burned car sits on a Tennessee hilltop, a woman's charred, lifeless body seated inside. Bill Brockton must discover the truth hidden in the fire-desecrated corpse. Was it an accident . . . or was she incinerated to cover up her murder?

Visit www.AuthorTracker.com for exclusive information on your favorite HarperCollins authors.

Available wherever books are sold or please call 1-800-331-3761 to order.

BAS 1108

THE NEW LUXURY IN READING

Introducing a Clearer Perspective on Larger Print

With a 14-point type size for comfort reading and published exclusively in paperback format, HarperLuxe is light to carry and easy to read.

SEEING IS BELIEVING!

To view our great selection of titles in a comfortable print and to sign up for the HarperLuxe newsletter please visit:
www.harperluxe.com

*This ad has been set in the 14-point font for comfortable reading.

HRL 0307

BECAUSE THERE ARE TIMES WHEN BIGGER IS BETTER